COMING HOME TO SEASHELL COTTAGE

WELCOME TO WHITSBOROUGH BAY BOOK 4

JESSICA REDLAND

Boldwood

First published in Great Britain in 2020 by Boldwood Books Ltd.

A CIP catalogue record for this book is available from the British Library.

Paperback ISBN 978-1-83889-122-0

Ebook ISBN 978-1-83889-123-7

Kindle ISBN 978-1-83889-124-4

Audio CD ISBN 978-1-83889-232-6

MP3 CD ISBN 978-1-83889-817-5

Digital audio download ISBN 978-1-83889-121-3

Boldwood Books Ltd
23 Bowerdean Street
London SW6 3TN
www.boldwoodbooks.com

Some friends come and go. Others stick around. To Susan who's been in it for the long-haul xx

1

Late September

'What the hell is that in the fruit bowl?' I cautiously leaned forward on Ben's sofa to get a closer look, hoping it wasn't an enormous spider about to scuttle over me.

'Apples, pears, kiwis and bananas,' Ben said. 'Don't tell me that you've reached the grand old age of thirty-three and you still can't identify your basic fruits.'

I raised my eyebrows at him. 'Ha ha! You're hilarious. You should be on stage, so you should.' I reached my hand out towards the object.

'Argh!' yelled Ben as I was about to touch it.

I snatched back my hand, screaming.

'Sorry. Couldn't resist.' He rolled around on the sofa, laughing hysterically.

'You eejit!' I whacked him with a cushion. 'You scared the life out of me! Is this what it's going to be like living with you? Because if it is, I can check into a hotel for the next few months instead. Are you ready to say goodbye to that new kitchen?'

I worked for a company called Prime PR, managing public relations campaigns for large corporates. Having recently been promoted, I needed to relocate from London to Leeds. Ben – or

Saint Ben, as I called him – was the brother of my best friend, Sarah, and he lived in Leeds so I'd adopted him as my meal buddy for the past few years every time I visited on business. Meeting up with a friend for some good craic was far more appealing than dining in a hotel restaurant surrounded by suits staring into space, eating meals for one. On my last trip, I'd moaned about the prospect of living in a hotel for a month or two while I found somewhere to rent and, being the saint he was, Ben immediately offered me his spare room. Grand idea. It meant I could pay Ben rent using my allowance for not staying in a hotel, giving him the funds to refit his prehistoric kitchen. Win-win. Of course, he refused to accept payment, but I wore him down eventually.

Ben put his hands up in surrender as I lifted the cushion to whack him again. 'Sorry. But you'd have done the same if it had been the other way round. You know you would.'

'Perhaps.'

'Definitely.'

I smiled. He was right. 'So, what is it, then?'

Ben reached into the fruit bowl, then held out the black object in the palm of his hand.

'It's a chess piece,' I said, looking at the black king. 'Why's there a chess piece in your fruit bowl?'

He shrugged. 'I came home from work last Tuesday and, quite randomly, it was on the front doorstep.'

'With a note?'

'No note. Just the king on his own.'

'And it's yours?'

'Nope. I don't play chess.'

'Oh. Very random. But do you know what's even more random? Why the hell it's in your fruit bowl instead of the bin.'

'It seemed like a good place for it.'

'But you don't know where it's been. It could have been peed on by a dog. Or worse.'

Ben looked at the king thoughtfully. 'Good point. Just as well it was between the bananas and kiwis, then, wasn't it? They've got skins.' He leaned forward and put it back.

'Ben! Put it in the bin.'

'No.'

'*Ben!*'

I reached forward but he grabbed me and started tickling me, which he knew was a pet peeve of mine. I squealed, leapt to my feet and darted past him into his kitchen. Thankfully, I was saved from another attack by the arrival of our Indian takeaway.

'Get your hands washed before you touch that food,' I ordered Ben.

He winked at me. 'I love it when you're bossy.'

I dug out some plates and we busied ourselves dishing up the food.

'Shall we watch a film while we eat?' Ben asked. '*The Count of Monte Cristo*'s on TV and I've never seen it. My mate Pete said it's really good.'

'Is that the one with Jim Caviezel in it?'

'I think so. And Guy Pearce.'

'Ooh, two hotties. Grand. Count me in.'

* * *

'Your friend Pete was right,' I said, when the closing credits started rolling. 'Cracking film. What did you think?'

'I agree. The king thing was a spooky coincidence, don't you think?'

In the film, best friends Edmond and Fernand exchange a chess king when one of them overcomes a challenge, to symbolise who is 'king of the moment'.

I nodded towards the king nestled in his fruit bowl. 'Did you plant it there knowing it was in the film?'

Ben shook his head. 'Honestly, I've never seen the film or read the book so I didn't know about the chess piece. I genuinely found that bad boy sitting on my doorstep, just like I told you.'

'Are you sure?'

'Have you ever known me to lie?'

He made a good point. He was one of the most honest people I knew, although, unlike me, he was tactful with his honesty. Generous to a fault, ridiculously considerate of others and gifted in spades with patience, Ben definitely deserved his nickname of 'Saint Ben'. By contrast, I could be pretty blunt and to the point, not particularly patient and quite selfish. I was lucky he only called me 'Irish' because I probably deserved something a little less affectionate.

'Tell you what we can do.' He grinned at me, wrinkled his nose in a clear act of mischief, then lifted the king out of the fruit bowl. Picking up a chilli pepper discarded from his curry in his other hand he said, 'If you eat the whole chilli, you win the king.'

I was about to refuse his stupid challenge, but then he added, 'I bet you can't do it.'

Defiantly, I picked up the chilli and shoved it in my mouth. Tears streamed down my face, my nose ran like a tap and my head felt as if it were about to explode. But that king was going to be mine. Nobody told me what I could and couldn't do and I would come out on top whenever challenged. Always.

'Oh my God! I can't believe you just did that.' Ben handed me a box of tissues. 'Serious respect to you, Irish.'

I gasped for breath and rasped, 'Wait till I tell your sister what a mean boy you are.'

He laughed. 'You're king of the moment, Irish. He's all yours.'

And so it began.

2

Three Months Later

'I now declare you husband and wife. You may kiss your bride.'

Sarah radiated happiness as Nick gently kissed her before they turned to face the congregation. I put my fingers in my mouth and released a piercing whistle that echoed around the church. The vicar's eyes widened and he looked as if he were about to protest at my crassness in a place of worship. Bollocks to that. I whistled again, then started a round of applause, which everyone joined in with. I gave the vicar a hard stare, challenging him to stop me, but he surprised me by smiling and joining in instead.

Sarah and Nick signed the register and posed for some photos.

'Nice whistling,' Ben whispered to me, as we shuffled out of the pew. He was an usher and I was a bridesmaid alongside Sarah's bestie since primary school, Elise, and Nick's sister, Callie. 'I thought the vicar was going to tell you off, though.'

'So did I. But he didn't scare me.'

'I don't imagine anyone or anything scares you, Irish.'

I laughed, but my stomach did a somersault. There were two people who still scared me. I wasn't going to let *them* ruin my day, though. Time for a change of subject.

'I'm liking the morning suit on you,' I said, taking in the navy three-piece Ben was wearing. 'I don't think I've ever seen you in a suit.'

'That's probably because I don't own one.'

'It's just as well Lemony isn't here. She'd probably get ideas of dragging you up the aisle herself after seeing you dressed like this.'

He raised his eyebrows at me. 'It's Lebony, and you know it.'

'Either way, it's not a real name. So, what's *Lebony's* excuse for missing your sister's wedding?'

Ben didn't get to answer the question, as the photographer shuffled us towards opposite sides of the line-up. After several photos at the church, we moved onto the reception at Sherrington Hall. An ivy-covered Georgian manor house perched on a clifftop about twelve miles south of Sarah's North Yorkshire coastal hometown of Whitsborough Bay, it was pretty impressive as a venue. It was four days before Christmas and Sarah, a florist, had certainly pulled out all the stops to decorate it beautifully and achieve a balance between Christmas and nuptials. Swathes of ivy, bunches of mistletoe, and church candles everywhere was pretty special. Champagne-coloured roses and teal flowers – no idea what type; not my specialist subject – matched the colours of our dresses and the men's waistcoats.

As Sarah and Nick cut the cake and giggled together after the meal, I smiled and had what Sarah would describe as a 'warm and fuzzy moment'. They were a good match. I liked Nick a lot. Despite my cynicism about relationships and marriage, it warmed my heart to see my best friend and her new husband looking so happy together.

Elise leaned towards me. 'Are those tears in your eyes, Clare?' she teased.

I cleared my throat. 'Tears? You talk bollocks. As if I'd cry at a wedding. Unless it was in sympathy for the poor buggers for ruining their lives and blowing their savings on what's effectively a big piss-up.'

'You can deny it all you want, but I know that's *not* how you really feel.' She nudged me gently. 'It'll be you one day, you know.'

I turned round to face her, confident that any tell-tale tears had retreated. 'Me? Married? Are you for real? Aside from the fact that I think marriage is a pile of shite, you have to be in a relationship to get married and, as you well know, I don't do relationships.'

'That's because you've never met the right person. I reckon your Nick's out there somewhere and you just have to open your heart up to finding him.'

I stared at her, wondering for a moment if she was just winding me up, but something told me she wholeheartedly believed what she was saying. 'Do weddings turn you a bit loopy? Never met the right person? Open my heart and I'll find him? Seriously?'

Elise smiled. 'Yes. Seriously. We're ten days from New Year and I reckon you should make a New Year's resolution to actually let someone in, for once.'

I shook my head as I topped up my glass of wine and took a sip. 'This sort of bollocks is one of the many reasons you and I haven't always been friends.'

Elise twiddled one of the auburn ringlets dangling from her up-do. 'Does that mean we're friends now?'

I'd walked into that one. I had to admit that, despite battling with her for a decade or so, I now really enjoyed Elise's company. It had taken a huge bust-up while planning Sarah's hen do, where we'd both said some nasty things – particularly me – for us to get over it and start behaving like adults. We'd probably have plodded along tolerating each other if I hadn't discovered Elise's secret and been there to support her as she came to terms with it.

I grinned back at her, a feeling of genuine affection flowing through me. 'Maybe,' I said. 'But I can easily scrub you off my *very* short and *very* exclusive friends list if you keep spouting bollocks like that. Anyway, why aren't you jaded and cynical like me, after what you've been through this year?'

'Because I still believe in love.'

'More fool you.' Elise had discovered that her husband, Gary, was gay when she walked in on him in the shower with our friend Stevie's best mate, Rob. During twelve years of marriage, Gary had managed to kid himself that their friendship was enough to make their marriage work. Eejit. To help her get through her divorce, Elise started seeing Daniel who also turned out to be a liar and a cheat. Then she discovered she was pregnant. With her sister giving birth to twins and Sarah's wedding approaching, Elise was adamant that she didn't want to steal anyone's thunder by announcing her own news so only a select few people knew and Sarah wasn't one of them.

I really felt for Elise. She'd been desperate for a baby but having one as a result of a brief fling with a tosser like Daniel wasn't quite the way she'd planned it. But when did life ever go to plan?

The meal was delicious and everyone on our table had a great craic. It was good to catch up with Ben who I hadn't seen so regularly since moving into my rented apartment in Leeds city centre.

While we ate, I couldn't fail to notice Elise and Stevie chatting animatedly. If ever there was another perfect match, it was those two, but neither of them was ever going to make a move. Just as well I'd never been one for pussyfooting around things. When Stevie excused himself, I turned to her and challenged her on making her move that evening but she indicated her stomach.

I shook my head. 'I think he fancies the arse off you too and the baby should make sod all difference to you getting together.'

She wasn't buying it, insisting he'd made it clear that all he wanted was friendship since finding out she was pregnant. Bollocks. Friends do not look at each other the way Stevie had been looking at her all night.

When I spotted him returning, I suggested she give him some sort of sign that she was interested because I was certain he'd respond. I hoped she'd be brave enough to give it a go.

When the coffees had been served, the conversation turned to what everyone was planning for Christmas and New Year. Arse. Worst subject in the world, ever. Sarah's Auntie Kay told us her plans, then her partner, Philip, looked towards me. *Oh no! Here goes...*

'What will you do, Clare?' he asked.

I gritted my teeth. *Must try to sound light and friendly.* 'Absolutely nothing.' He stared at me, frowning, and I realised I wasn't going to get away without explaining it. I took a deep breath. 'Christmas is family time. As far as I'm concerned, I have no family. Therefore, I don't do Christmas and I've always hated New Year.' There. I'd said it! I hoped nobody had noticed the shake in my voice.

'What about you, Elise?' Philip asked, quickly averting his gaze from me.

'I'm going to my sister's for Christmas...'

Everyone continued to chat about their plans while I shrank back into my chair, hoping nobody would try to bring me into the conversation. Surely my response to Philip had given the very clear message that Christmas and New Year were taboo subjects.

Ben turned to me and said quietly, 'If you've got no plans for Christmas, why don't you join me at Mum and Dad's? It'll be strange with no Sarah.'

I was very aware of Elise listening and could almost hear her willing me to say yes. No doubt, she couldn't bear the thought of anyone being on their own on Christmas Day. 'Thank you, but no thank you,' I said. 'I'm fine on my own.'

'New Year, then?'

'No, again.'

'Please.'

'Why? Why would anyone subject themselves to hot, smelly pubs packed with obnoxious, drunk eejits, then pay five times the normal taxi fare to get back home? Assuming someone hasn't already nicked their pre-booked taxi, that is. I can't think of a more hideous way to spend an evening.'

'And that's not how we'd be spending it,' Ben countered. 'I'm going to a party at Pete's house and it's walking distance from mine so you can crash in your old room.'

'No thanks.'

'Why?'

'Because it's New Year's Eve. I don't care whether it's spent in a pub, at a house party or at home in front of the TV. I still hate it.'

'But—'

'Ben! I suggest you drop the subject. Right now!'

Desperate for some space away from the questions and judgemental looks, I grabbed my empty wine glass and a part-finished bottle. 'I'll be going to freshen up,' I muttered to nobody in particular. 'See you later.'

Without waiting for a response, I stormed across the room,

through reception, then took the stairs two at a time until I reached my bedroom.

Empty wine glass and bottle still in my hands, I pulled open the doors to the Juliet balcony and gulped in the cool night air, waiting for my heartbeat to return to normal and the butterflies in my stomach to settle. Every year. Every single year. *They'd* done this to me. *They'd* turned me into this. I hated this time of year, thanks to *them*. Hated it.

But I hated *them* more.

3

My twenty-minute time-out – and half a bottle of wine – calmed me down considerably. I returned to the bar feeling a bit childish for having stormed out earlier. It wasn't Ben's fault that I hated Christmas and New Year.

'Ah! Here she is,' Stevie announced, as I joined him, Ben, Elise, Sarah and a few others. 'Your ears must have been burning, Clare. We were just talking about you.'

Anger flashed through me again. How dare they discuss me behind my back? 'Can't you just accept that some people don't like this time of year?' I snapped.

Ben flung his arm around me. 'Relax, Irish! That's not what we were talking about. I was just telling everyone that you can't resist a dare and how our last challenge nearly got me arrested.'

I relaxed against him. 'Will that be the challenge where you did a lap of the Indian with only a rapidly disintegrating poppadom to protect your dignity?'

'That would be the one.' Ben hung his head in mock shame. 'The worst part was that I ran outside straight into a passing PCSO.'

Gasps of horror came from the group. 'Oh my God! How do I not know about this, Ben?' Sarah demanded.

'It's a tad embarrassing.'

'Fortunately, the PCSO was female and clearly a huge Ben fan,' I said.

'*Huge* Ben? I didn't think you'd noticed.'

I grimaced and elbowed him. 'Gross! And not something you should be discussing in front of your sister, either!'

Ben laughed. 'Fortunately, she let me off as long as I re-dressed immediately and disposed of what was left of the poppadom in the nearest bin.'

'So, what possessed you to strip off and streak in the first place?' Stevie asked.

'This.' Ben withdrew the king from his pocket.

'It's a chess piece,' Elise said.

'That's right. The black king.'

She shrugged. 'And that made you strip off and streak because...?'

'Have you seen the film *The Count of Monte Cristo*?' Ben asked her.

As Head of English and Drama at a local comprehensive, this was bound to be Elise's specialist subject. 'The 1975 version, the 2002 one and I've read the book,' she said. 'Oh! I get it.'

'The king's gone back and forth several times,' I said after quickly explaining the relevance to those not familiar with the story, 'but Ben's had him too long this time. I need to win him back.'

'And I know how.' Ben dangled the king in front of my eyes. 'It doesn't involve stripping off, eating anything gross or doing anything embarrassing. I'd say it's the easiest challenge you'll ever have to face.'

'Doesn't sound like much of a challenge,' Stevie said.

'It is, because it's something she's already said no to.'

My heartbeat quickened. I knew where this was going.

'If you want to win the king back, you'll join me at that New Year's Eve party at Pete's and you'll stay until midnight.'

I felt all eyes on me.

'Ben! You know I hate New Year.'

'Do you think I liked stripping off and streaking round The Taj Mahal?'

'No.'

'Exactly. The point of the challenges is to face your fears or do things you hate. You'll hate this. It's therefore a challenge.'

I planted my hands on my hips. 'Why are you so keen for me to join you at this stupid party?'

He shrugged. 'No reason, other than I hate the thought of you being alone. Besides, it might be fun. And if it isn't, we can get drunk and pretend we're somewhere else on a different day of the year, if that makes you happy.'

'Why can't you take Lebony?'

'Because she's not coming home for Christmas or New Year. She's in Vietnam at the moment and cash is tight. Please say you'll come.'

I sighed. 'If I agree to come – and it's a big if – you promise we can leave at midnight?'

'As soon as the clock's strikes twelve, I'll declare you king of the moment and we're out of there.'

I sighed again and stared at the king standing on his outstretched palm. Arse! I might have started off thinking of it as a scabby item that belonged in the bin, but my competitive streak had taken over after the chilli challenge and winning had become an obsession. I needed it. I needed to prove that nothing scared me. Well, almost nothing. 'I might live to regret this, but you're on. King's mine, Saint Ben. King's mine.'

4

'I can't believe it's three days till Christmas and you haven't bought any presents,' I said to Ben as I drove into the multi-storey car park in Whitsborough Bay the morning after the wedding. 'You've normally bought and wrapped everything before the summer holidays.'

Ben laughed. 'I'm not quite *that* bad but I honestly don't know where this year's gone. I kept thinking I had plenty of time but clearly not. Thanks for agreeing to stay.'

'It's grand. I've nothing to rush back to Leeds for and the promise of lunch in The Chocolate Pot is far too good to turn down.'

We headed down in the lift and through the town's small shopping centre.

'I can probably get most of the gifts on Castle Street,' Ben said as we made our way down the pedestrianised precinct. 'I promise it won't take long.'

Being the last Sunday before Christmas, the town was unsurprisingly busy. A brass band played Christmas carols while fraught-looking shoppers struggled through shop doorways with armfuls of bags. I felt a little sad watching them. What must it be like having stacks of presents to buy, or rather lots of friends and family to buy for? I only ever bought two presents each year – one for Sarah and one for the Secret Santa at work – although I'd also bought Ben something this year to say thanks for his hospitality.

I was happy to explore the shops in Castle Street. There weren't any chain stores among them and Ben picked out some really nice gifts. He didn't take long either. He knew exactly what he wanted and, within an hour, we were pondering over the lunch menu in The Chocolate Pot, shopping complete.

We'd just placed our orders when his phone rang. 'It's Auntie Kay,' he said, answering it.

I tuned out of his conversation and gazed round the café. I'd been in there several times with Sarah and loved the food and the décor. None of the tables and chairs matched yet they looked great together. The walls were covered in vintage metal signs depicting seaside images, food and drink. We'd managed to secure a table near the back of the café with two high-backed leather armchairs. Warm white and red fairy lights and a slim tree near the window covered in wooden decorations made the place really festive.

'Sorry about that,' Ben said, hanging up. 'Would you mind if we do another detour after lunch? I left my washbag in my room at Sherrington Hall. Auntie Kay's got it.'

* * *

Ben and Sarah's Auntie Kay lived in the Old Town, roughly ten minutes' walk from the town centre. It would probably take longer to drive there than it would to walk so we dumped Ben's bags in my car and set off on foot.

'I love the Old Town,' Ben said as we walked along the cobbled lanes between the houses. 'It's like stepping back in time. I think the newest house is about one hundred and twenty years old and most were built two or three hundred years ago.'

Cute cottages nestled among four- and five-storey townhouses. Some were made from brick, some from stone, and others were painted.

'And this is my favourite one,' he said, stopping in front of a white-washed double-fronted cottage with roses curved round the wooden door – Kay's house, Seashell Cottage.

Sarah had stayed at Seashell Cottage when she moved back to Whitsborough Bay about fourteen months ago and I'd visited her loads. There was something about the cottage that had made me feel so welcome – a sensation I'd never experienced before.

He knocked on the door then pushed it open and stepped inside, calling out, 'Hello?'

'I'm in the lounge,' Kay called.

She was stoking the real fire when Ben pushed the lounge door open and I couldn't help smiling. I'd spent last New Year's Eve in this very room with Sarah, stuffing my face, drinking too much and trying to convince her that she should tell Nick how she really felt about him. And yesterday they'd got married.

Kay offered to make us some drinks but Ben insisted he do it while she finished tending to the fire.

'Does it feel strange being back here?' Kay asked, once the fire was roaring.

'Yes. But in a good way. I loved staying here with Sarah. Slept like a log every night. You have a lovely home, Kay.'

Her expression was wistful as she sat down on the armchair. 'Thank you. I'm going to miss this place.'

'You're selling up?'

She bit her lip and glanced towards the lounge door. 'Maybe. Maybe not. I shouldn't have said anything. Can you not mention it to Ben or Sarah until I make my decision?'

I nodded. 'Your secret's safe with me.' Secrets were always safe with me. I wanted to ask more because Sarah had always said that Kay loved Seashell Cottage and would never move on, but Ben burst through the door balancing three mugs on a tray and the conversation turned to the wedding.

When we waved goodbye an hour later, I took one last look at the cottage and a surprising thought popped into my head – if Leeds had been commutable from Whitsborough Bay, I'd have been straight in there with an offer to buy Seashell Cottage. Only Leeds wasn't commutable, so it wasn't an option. Shame.

5

New Year's Eve

'Oi! Saint Ben! Will you remind me again why I let you drag me here?' I gulped back the last couple of mouthfuls of cheap, warm Chardonnay out of a paper cup, shuddered, crumpled the cup and tossed it in the direction of the overflowing bin in the corner of Pete's dining room.

Ben smiled. 'Because, Irish, you're desperate to get your mitts on this, aren't you?' He reached into his jeans pocket and pulled out the king. I tried to snatch it out of his hand, but he was too quick.

'You know it doesn't work like that. King's still mine if you don't make it past midnight.'

'Bollocks. You're a mean boy.' I gave him a playful shove as he put the king back in his pocket. 'By the way, can we put it on record that this is the crappiest house party ever?'

'It's not *that* bad,' Ben said.

We both gazed around the large dining room. The table, pushed against the fireplace, housed empty tubes of Pringles, cremated sausage rolls, some wilted sticks of celery and about thirty or so discarded beer cans. In one corner of the room, a couple were eating each other's faces. In the opposite corner, another couple were having a domestic about who'd forgotten to renew the Sky subscription. Slumped on the floor between them, snoring loudly, lay a scruffy-looking twenty-something with 'I'm a twat' written across his forehead along with a Poirot-style moustache and glasses.

Ben laughed. 'I wonder how long it takes to remove permanent marker pen.'

'I think the clue is in the word "permanent".'

'Okay, it *is* that bad,' Ben admitted. 'Really bad. I'm sorry, Irish.'

'Home time?' I didn't want to lose the challenge, but this was torture. A chilli I could cope with; the house party from hell on the worst evening of the year was another matter.

Ben looked at his watch. 'It's only eleven-twenty. Pete will be insulted if we don't stay to at least see the New Year in.'

'Seriously? Pete's been throwing up in the bathroom for the last hour. I don't think he'd know if *everyone* left before midnight.'

'Five past midnight, Irish. I promise. Please.' He looked at me with big, sad, puppy-dog eyes.

'You know that stupid expression gets you nowhere.'

He widened his hazel eyes even more and pushed out his bottom lip.

'Jesus. Stop it. I submit. I'll stay, but only because I've already suffered three hours of this so I may as well do another forty minutes and embrace the stupid midnight thing. And win the king.'

'It'll be a worthy win.'

I poked him in the ribs. 'I hope you realise that the next challenge will be something you're going to *really* hate, just to piss you off.'

Ben grabbed two cans of lager from a box on the table and passed me one. 'Get one of these down your neck and quit moaning. I'm going to check on Pete. I won't leave you alone for long.'

'You'd better not.' I sighed as Ben left the kitchen. Everyone else seemed to be enjoying themselves – well, everyone apart from Pete, the arguing couple and the body on the floor. Why couldn't I? That was an easy one. New Year's Eve was the day my life changed forever, thanks to *them*.

I sighed again and swigged on the warm lager. I really should have stuck to my guns and ignored Ben's stupid challenge this time.

Stomach rumbling, I peered into the tubes of Pringles, but they were all empty.

'Excuse me, but have you got a sticking plaster?' I turned round to see a tall man with a wild mop of dark hair beside me.

'No. Do I look like the sort of person who carries a first-aid kit in case of emergency?'

'Oh. It's just that I scraped my knee falling for you.'

I stared at him for a moment. On any other night, I'd have cringed at the cheesiness but turned on the charm offensive anyway. But this wasn't any other night. This was New Year's Eve. 'Please tell me you didn't just say that bollocks. You must be very pissed.'

He shook his head. 'Not pissed,' he slurred. 'Just intoxicated by you. I think you're the most—'

I put my hand up in a 'stop' gesture. 'Can I just stop you there?'

He waited expectantly. 'You were going to say something?'

'No. I just wanted to stop you there before I join Pete in the bathroom.'

He looked confused. He wobbled a bit and grabbed the table for support, knocking the empty Pringles tubes over in a domino effect. 'If I were to ask you out on a date, would your answer be the same as the answer to this question?'

I opened my mouth to hurl another insult, then smiled. I'd give him his due for that one.

'That's actually quite clever. Not so cheesy. I'm Clare.'

'I'm Taz.'

'What sort of name's Taz?'

'Short for Tasmanian Devil.' He gave a little growl.

I shrugged. 'Not getting it.'

'Because of the hair.'

'Ah. You'll be a friend of Pete's?'

'No. I've come with a mate who knows Pete. You?'

'Same. My friend works with him.'

Taz picked up a burned sausage roll, squinted at it, then tossed it towards the bin in apparent disgust. Wise decision. It sounded like a stone when it hit the wooden floor.

'I've got a serious question for you,' he said. 'Was your dad an alien?'

I bristled at the mention of Da, even though I knew the line.

'Because there's nothing else like you on this planet,' he finished.

I squirmed. If I hadn't felt stone-cold sober, I'd probably have engaged in a little flirting with Taz and maybe tried to out-cheese him, but not tonight. I was on a countdown to midnight, then I was out of there.

Giving Taz what I hoped was a polite yet dismissive smile, I said, 'Will you excuse me? I could do with some fresh air.' I stepped over the 'dead body' and headed into the kitchen then outside, firmly closing the door out to the garden behind me in a clear message that I didn't want Taz to follow. I'd probably pissed him off by not responding to his lines, but who cared? I didn't invite him to talk to me; *he* was the persistent one. Being a lone female didn't make me fair game.

In the dim light emitting from the kitchen window, I could just about make out the shape of a swing in the middle of the lawn. With my back towards the house, I sat down on it, keen to shut out the sights and sounds of a hideous evening.

I shivered as a cool breeze wrapped around me. Granted, it was mild for the time of year, but it certainly wasn't the weather for sitting on a swing in the dark wearing an LBD and no coat. I only managed about five minutes before having to admit defeat. Shivering, I stood up and took a few steps towards the house, then smacked straight into someone.

'Sorry.' I stepped backwards and looked up. 'Taz? How long have you been there?'

'A few minutes.' He made no attempt to move. He just stood there, staring at me.

I shivered again... but not from the cold this time. 'I'm just going in.' I moved to step round him, but he sidestepped in the same direction. I moved the other way, but he mirrored my move. 'That's not funny, Taz. Will you not let me past? I'm freezing. I want to go in.'

'Why did you walk away when I was talking to you?'

Crap. I *had* pissed him off. 'I needed some air, but I've had plenty now. Anyway, I didn't just walk away. I excused myself first.'

I tried to step round him again, but he grabbed my arms, his rough hands digging into my bare flesh. I tried to wriggle free, but he tightened his hold and leaned closer, his breath smelling like a mix of whisky, cigarettes and pot.

'You're all the same, you women. Prick teasers. You want a guy to tell you how beautiful you are but when he does, you throw it back in his face.'

I wriggled again. Christ, he was strong. My heart started racing and I felt sick. 'You're the one who approached me.' I tried to keep my voice calm and steady. 'I didn't ask you to come over.'

'But you wanted me to. They all do.'

'Well, *I* didn't.' With all my strength, I sidestepped again, but I couldn't shake him off. He pushed me towards the side of the house and pinned me against the wall by my wrists.

'Stop trying to fight it. You know you want it.'

'I don't—' He rammed his hand over my mouth before I could utter another word. The back of my head scraped against the rough bricks as I tried to wriggle free.

'Enough talking. It's time for action.' He ground his crotch against me and I scrunched my eyes shut, willing it to stop. *Help me!* But I couldn't speak. I could barely breathe.

'You like that, don't you?' he sneered.

He took his hand off my mouth and immediately thrust his lips against mine, ramming his tongue down my throat. Seizing my opportunity, I bit down hard. He released his hold with a yelp and I drew my knee up between his legs. Crying out again, he dropped to the ground, clutching himself.

'You were right. It *was* time for action,' I yelled, as I legged it into the kitchen and slammed the back door.

'Clare? What's happened?' Ben ran towards me.

'We need to go. Now.' I glanced towards the garden, shaking.

'Who's out there?' Ben grabbed my hand. 'Clare? Who's out there?'

I glanced towards the door again. 'Not now. Where are our coats?'

'Was it Taz?' Ben's jaw tightened.

'How...?'

'Right. That's it. Is he still out there?'

I nodded slightly. Ben grabbed the door handle.

'Ben. No. Leave it.' But I was too late.

'Taz? Where are you, you piece of shit?' he yelled.

I ran after him. 'Ben!'

Taz had made it to his feet and was leaning against the same wall to which he'd pinned me moments earlier. He looked at Ben, then leered at me. 'Realised what you're missing and come back for more? No wonder you came looking for me if that's what you've been shagging. A dirty bitch like you needs a *real* man.'

'Don't speak to her like that.' Ben's fists were clenched by his side. My stomach churned. He'd never hit anyone in his life. He'd never win against Taz. The man was huge. And strong.

'Why? What you gonna do about it?' Taz squared his shoulders as he sauntered towards us.

'This.' Ben tried to punch him but Taz pre-empted it and grabbed his arm, bending it backwards. Ben gasped with pain.

'I think you were trying to do this.' Taz smashed his fist into Ben's face. 'That's how real men hit.' He let go of Ben, who fell onto his knees and then forward onto his hands.

'As for you.' Taz spat on the ground beside me. 'You're nothing special. Pretty minging, actually. I felt sorry for you. That's all.' Then he disappeared into the kitchen, slamming the door.

I ran to Ben and put my arm round him. 'You're not minging,' he said. 'You're beautiful.'

'I don't give a shit about that. Are you hurt?'

He looked up. I could see in the dim light that his cheek was badly swollen and his eye was already closing.

'We can go now, if you want,' he said. 'You were right. It's a pretty shit party.'

A nervous laugh escaped from me. 'We'll get some ice on this first. Then we can go. Can you stand up?'

He staggered to his feet with my help. 'Irish?'

'Yes?'

'Happy New Year! But the king's still mine, I think.'

'Yes, Ben. The king's still yours.'

6

'Are you awake?' Ben poked his head around the door the next morning.

'I am if you have coffee,' I mumbled from under the duvet in my old room. 'I'm still asleep if you don't.'

'After living with you, I don't think I'd dare appear without coffee.'

I reluctantly pulled back the duvet and squinted at him, then sat upright, eyes wide open. 'Jesus, Ben! Your eye!'

'You should see the state of the other guy.'

'I did, and I seem to remember that he got off scot-free.'

Ben handed me the mug and sat down on the edge of the bed. 'It looks worse than it feels, although I do have a banging headache.'

'I'm not surprised. Will you not put some peas on that again?'

'I forgot to put them back in the freezer last night.'

'Ice?'

'I forgot to refill the tray.'

'Eejit.'

Ben tried to smile but winced. 'I suppose you think I was an "eejit" for coming to your defence last night?'

'You were and always will be an eejit, Saint Ben. I like that you tried, but will you just remember that you wouldn't be sporting that shiner if you'd listened to me and we'd left that party when I said.'

'I know.'

'An apology would be grand.'

'I'm sorry, Irish. As always, you were right and I was wrong.'

'I *almost* believe you.' I stuck my tongue out at him. 'By the way, what made you think it was Taz who'd upset me last night?'

Ben curled his lip up. 'I've met him before and can't stand the guy. He thinks he's God's gift, but he's really aggressive towards women when he's had a drink. Pete hates him too. He threw him out before he started throwing up. I didn't know he'd come back until I saw the look on your face and I just knew. Sorry.'

'Not your fault. Now, will you get your fat arse off my bed so I can have a shower?'

Five minutes later, I stood under the steaming water. An image of Taz pinning me to the wall filled my mind, just as it had done when I'd tried to fall asleep. I gently stroked my throbbing, bruised wrists. He'd been so strong. What would I have done if he'd kept his hand on my mouth instead of kissing me? I shuddered, knowing I'd have been powerless to stop him. Fear made my breathing quicken. I closed my eyes as the water flowed over me and tried to push aside the feeling of my head scraping against the wall, the rancid smell of his breath, the strength of his grip.

I delved deep into my memory banks, keen to dredge up a happy memory instead. A meadow. A ruined farmhouse. Strong arms round me, wanting me, protecting me. But there was something else there. Something wrong. Something...

Despite the hot water, goose bumps prickled my entire body. I turned off the shower, grabbed my warm towel off the radiator and quickly rubbed myself dry. *What the hell was that?* I shook my head. Nothing. It was a delayed shock response to what had happened with Taz. I didn't need to think about it anymore. I got away. I was safe.

* * *

Ben's black eye looked even blacker in full daylight. I knew it wasn't my fault but I couldn't help feeling guilty. 'Thanks again for last night.' I nudged him playfully as we walked around his local park after lunch. 'You can add "rescuing damsels in distress" to your saintly repertoire. I'll never be getting the king back, at this rate.'

He indicated that we should sit on a bench. I slumped beside him and sighed.

'Are you okay?' he asked. 'You're not yourself today. I know you don't like New Year but it seems more than that.'

'That feckin' eejit Taz attacked me,' I cried, sitting up.' Does there need to be more?'

Ben shook his head. 'No. It's just that you seemed to be fine before your shower and you've been jumpy ever since.'

'Have I?'

'Yes. If I didn't know better, I'd have said that either Norman Bates or the closet monster had been waiting for you in the bathroom.'

I shrugged. 'Taz scared me but nothing happened, other than a scraped head and some bruises. Something did happen in the shower, though, and I can't explain it. I was looking at my wrists and there was something, but I don't know what. Like a dream or...' I knew I wasn't making sense. I shrugged again. 'I don't know. I really don't know.'

'I'm not going to push it, but you just need to say the word and I'll be here for you.'

He meant it. I knew that. Sarah had always said he was a great brother – always looking out for her – and he'd done the same for me. I could trust him.

'I know you said it was a money thing but I still can't believe Lebony didn't come home for Christmas or New Year,' I said, eager to move the subject away from me. 'Did you even see her last year?' As far as I could tell, she spent most of her time abroad on humanitarian projects and hardly any time with Ben. Apparently, her parents both worked for the Red Cross so it was in her blood.

'Yes,' Ben said. 'She came back to the UK for her grandma's eightieth birthday in April. Remember?'

'Vaguely. But Jesus, Ben, what sort of relationship is that?'

He gave me a wry smile. 'I think the common terminology is a long-distance one.'

'Duh. I know that. I just mean that there's long-distance and then there's what you and Lebony have.'

'I know it might seem strange to some people, but the relationship works for both of us. She gets to travel the world doing good, and I get to pursue my hobbies without feeling guilty that I don't give her enough time.'

'What hobbies?'

'Hospital Radio, the Samaritans, the Food Kitchen.'

'Jesus, Ben. You work for a charity and you spend all your spare time volunteering. Don't you ever do anything for you?'

'Those things *are* for me. I get a lot of satisfaction from them.'

'But you'd still get that sense of satisfaction if you ditched one of them and did something for you.'

'Like what?'

'I don't know. Take up base-jumping or something.'

'And a sensible suggestion would be...?'

I shrugged. 'Going to the gym, reading a book, playing football. Whatever it is that men in their late thirties do.'

'I *do* go to the gym. Can't you tell?' He flexed a non-existent bicep muscle at me. 'And late thirties? You cheeky nowt. I'm the same age as you.'

'And I look so much better for it.' I nudged him playfully. 'Well, if the distance thing works for you both, hats off to you. I still can't believe she was so chilled about me living at yours. Most women I know would not like that.'

Ben smiled. 'Lebony isn't like most women. She trusts me and I trust her. That's probably why the distance has never been an issue.'

We sat in companionable silence watching couples and families wander around the park, enjoying the public holiday and the crisp weather.

'I've got something for you,' Ben said.

He passed me the king.

'We agreed you'd keep it,' I said, frowning.

'The deal was that you had to stay till midnight. By the time you'd iced my eye, it was after twelve. And after what Taz tried to do to you...' He shook his head. 'He's yours. No argument.'

I took the king and placed him in my coat pocket. 'Thanks.'

'You're welcome.'

My phone bleeped a few minutes later. I dug it out of my bag.

✉ From Elise
I know you hate New Year, but Happy New Year
anyway! I have the most amazing news. I'm moving
in with Stevie! I have you to thank for that. I
really do owe you big time. Hope you're having
fun whatever you're doing xxx

I grinned. 'I don't believe it. He actually did it.'

'Who did what?'

'Stevie asked Elise to move in with him.'

'As a lodger?'

'No. As his live-in girlfriend.'

'Really? I didn't know they were seeing each other.'

'They weren't.'

Ben frowned. 'I'm all for a bit of romance, but how do you suddenly go from not dating to living together?'

'It's a long story. Maybe I'll tell you one day.'

'And since when did you and Elise become such good friends? You seemed really pally at Sarah's wedding.'

'Also a long story, and maybe I'll tell you that one day too but I can't just yet so don't you be asking me.'

Ben shrugged. 'I've no idea what's going on but that's the story of my life.'

I lightly punched him on the arm, then winced as my wrists hurt. 'Poor baby. Let's walk again. I'm getting piles sitting here.'

'Attractive,' Ben said.

'You know I'm irresistible to all men, women and small furry animals,' I quipped.

The sun – ahead of us and low in the sky – warmed my face as we walked along the River Aire. Despite the traumatic start to the year, the walk and company were doing me good and the news from Elise had really made my day. The woman deserved a decent break. I'd collared Stevie at Sarah's wedding and suggested that Elise needed a 'grand gesture' to show he was serious about her. I'm not sure what I had in mind, but they didn't come much grander than moving in together. I looked forward to hearing the full details.

How would Sarah react? To my knowledge, she had no idea that Elise was pregnant or in love with Stevie, so that was going to be a shock when she got back from honeymoon. The fact that I – Elise's former archenemy – knew both things already wasn't likely to go down well. I'd seen her glance across at us during the wedding with a look of confusion on her face, as if not able to comprehend how we'd turned from enemies into friends. For my part, I'd grown up. For Elise's, she'd needed someone, and I happened to be the someone who'd discovered her secret and promised to keep it. That hadn't been difficult. After all, I was better than anyone at keeping secrets.

7

January the second fell on a Thursday, so most of my team at work had taken that day and Friday as holidays, excited at the prospect of a five-day weekend so soon after the Christmas break. Had I? Bollocks to that. Why prolong the torture of New Year into yet another day and let it eke into your weekend too? I was up and working on my laptop by 6.30 a.m., thankful for a return to normality. Working was my domain, my comfort zone, the place where I was completely in control. Eejits like Taz couldn't get me at work. And I couldn't think about them, either. I was far too busy and important.

I was surprised when my phone rang at about half seven and my manager's name flashed up on the screen.

'Mike? I thought you weren't working today.' I stood up and wandered over to the full-length window looking out over Leeds city centre. The view from the fourteenth floor of my rented apartment in Orion Point was spectacular. I wasn't sure if I liked it best in darkness, like now, with twinkling lights, or in bright sunshine when I could see for miles.

'I'm not meant to be, but we've got a problem. I need you to clear your diary next week.'

I loved that Mike was always straight to the point; none of the pointless chitchat that so many of my colleagues seemed to favour.

'Should be possible. Why?'

'What about this weekend?'

I turned away from the window, a sinking feeling in my stomach. 'No plans yet.'

'Good. Fabrian phoned. His dad died yesterday.' Fabrian was my European equivalent, who'd announced at our last team meeting that his dad was seriously ill and would be lucky to make it to Easter.

'Poor Fabrian. You want me to cover for him?' I hoped Mike would say a simple 'yes', but I knew that he'd have waited until Monday to have that conversation, which meant bad news was on the horizon. Please don't let him say...

'You need to go to Ireland. Specifically, Cork.'

'No, Mike! Not Cork. Can't Rick do it?' Rick was my equivalent in the south.

'He's skiing.'

Bollocks! 'Surely there's someone else?' I sat down heavily at the dining table before my shaking legs gave way.

'There's nobody else, Clare. It needs to be you.'

'Can't it wait until Rick's back? He's covered for Fabrian before.'

'No. You know this is a key account and we've been teetering close to losing it. There's no way this meeting is getting delayed. You have to go.'

Cork. Of all the bloody places in Europe where we had clients, why the hell did Fabrian have to have meetings next week in Cork? I could have happily jetted off to Paris, Barcelona or Rotterdam. But Cork?

I closed my eyes and took a deep breath. I knew from the tone of Mike's voice that if I refused, he'd be issuing me with my marching orders. 'When will I need to go?'

'Saturday. There's a charity ball and we're hosting a table for them. You'll have Sunday to yourself. Maybe you can catch up with some family if you've still got any there.'

Family? Yeah, right. 'When can I fly back?'

'Fabrian had two days of meetings scheduled so I'd say Wednesday afternoon or evening, in case anything runs over.'

'Okay.'

'We're counting on you, Clare. Some serious bridge-building is needed and I know you'll be perfect for the job. Margaret's working today so I'll get her to email you the details and sort out your tickets. Let me know how it goes.'

I bid him goodbye and ended the call. Pushing my laptop out of the way, I slumped forward and lay my head on the table. Jesus. Cork? Why me? Could this shitty New Year get any worse?

* * *

I felt sick during the train journey from Leeds to Manchester on the Saturday morning. I felt even worse during the flight from Manchester to Cork. I must have looked it too, as the old lady in the seat next to me reached into the storage pouch, handed me a sick bag and asked me if it was my first time flying.

'No. It's not the flight. I love planes,' I said. 'I just don't love the thought of who lives at the other end.'

'Oh. Boyfriend trouble?' Her eyes widened with curiosity. She had one of those kind faces – the sort of trustworthy person with whom you instantly felt at ease. She reminded me of Sarah's Auntie Kay.

'Parent trouble,' I admitted. 'They threw me out when I was sixteen and we haven't been in touch since.'

'So this will be the first time you've seen them in, what, a decade?'

I smiled. 'Thanks for the compliment, but it's been about seventeen years.'

'You have a very youthful face, but your eyes tell of a greater maturity than your years.' She tilted her head to one side and stared at me thoughtfully. 'Yes, you've known some hard times, so you have.'

I swallowed on the lump in my throat and coughed. 'It was a long time ago. Anyway, I'm being an eejit because I'm not even going to see them. I'm here for business and I've got no intention of visiting them. Ever.'

The woman was silent for at least ten minutes. I kicked myself for saying too much. She was probably only being friendly. She didn't need to know my life story. This was more than I'd ever shared with Sarah, so why open up to a stranger on a plane? *Seriously, Clare, learn when to shut up!*

'My parents threw me out too,' she said, eventually. 'I was sixteen, just like you.'

'Really? Why?'

'I fell for a Protestant. You'd think I'd fallen for Hitler, the way they carried on.'

'Did you ever see them again?'

She shook her head. 'My da was killed in a fire at the factory where he worked ten years later. I went to his funeral, but Ma gave out big time, so she did. I think she'd gone a bit funny in the head because she blamed me for the accident. Seems it was the onset of Alzheimer's. I took pity and tried to see her but the nurses said I distressed her so I stayed away.'

'What about your man? Your Protestant man?'

'Oh, he's grand. We're still together. Four children, seven grandchildren and one great-grandbaby. I won't be having any regrets about him, but I do wish I'd confronted my da before he died, to understand why he cut me off without even listening to me. We all have to face our past sooner or later. This trip could be too soon for you but maybe later?'

I shook my head vigorously. 'No chance. My family are dead to me. Sorry if that sounds harsh.'

'Throwing you out was harsh. But people can change. Sometimes.'

The captain announced our approach to Cork airport. We fastened our seat belts and prepared to land. People change? Not my parents. But was she right about facing my past? I shivered and pulled my jacket more tightly across my body. Perhaps. But not this weekend. The incident with Taz had been bad enough without facing my past as well.

* * *

The hotel in Cork was nice. Comfortable. Warm. Yet I felt anything but comfortable knowing how close I was to my former home. I shuddered as I stared out of the window, my hands wrapped round a mug of coffee. *It's only four nights. You can do this. You're here for work and that's all you need to think about. Not them.*

The charity ball that evening couldn't have gone better. I cast aside all thoughts of Ma and Da and schmoozed like a champion. Mike had been right: I *was* the best person for the job. Even if Rick had been available, he wouldn't have had them eating out of his palm the way I had. Monday and Tuesday weren't going to be any problem. In the past I'd handled clients who were far more disgruntled. So why couldn't I sleep? I turned over and looked at the digital alarm by the bed: 03:17. Bollocks.

I peeled back the duvet and padded over to the drinks tray. Coffee wasn't going to help me sleep. Hot chocolate instead? I flicked the kettle on, then pulled on the fluffy hotel dressing gown.

Clutching my hot chocolate a few minutes later, I stood by the window and looked out at the lights of Cork reflecting in the River Lee – very pretty and a stark contrast to the ugly thoughts in my head.

By the time I'd finished my drink, I knew how I was going to spend my Sunday. Ireland mainly held bad memories for me, but there was one place that held only good ones and I felt compelled to pay it a visit.

* * *

The first thing that struck me as I drove down the familiar roads towards Ballykielty was that absolutely nothing had changed. Trees were bushier, hedges were thicker, but there were no new housing estates or businesses to be seen. It was like entering a place where time stood still.

I slowly drove through the village, tutting with disbelief at the familiarity of it all, then turned round and doubled back slowly. As I gazed out the windscreen, I realised I was drawing curious glances and hit the accelerator, cursing my stupidity. I hadn't meant to actually drive into the village. What if someone had recognised me? I shook my head. There was no way they would after all these years. To them, I'd just be a blonde in a hire car who'd got lost. Hopefully.

Driving out of the village, I took a right at the crossroads instead of going straight over towards Cork. A few hundred yards later, I pulled into the entrance to Farmer Brady's field and got out of the car. My hands were shaking so much that it took several attempts to unlatch the gate. I had to skirt around three fields and through a copse before I came to it.

Looking at the dilapidated building in the middle of the meadow, I felt like a teenager again. A tree had sprouted out of the chimney and there were a few more loose piles of stones round the building, where it had crumbled, but it was still *our* place.

Butterflies swarmed in my stomach as I stepped through the doorway. Sunlight filtered through the broken roof tiles creating dust bunnies and an ethereal sense. I half-expected Daran to tap me on the shoulder, then swing me around in a circle while showering me with kisses, like he used to. I stood for a few minutes with my eyes closed, taking it all in, my right hand wrapped tightly around the king in my coat pocket – trying to draw strength for this challenge that I'd set myself to acknowledge the past.

Opening my eyes, I took a deep breath, brushed away some grass and mud and sat down on the pile of stones that Daran had sat on when he first confessed his love for me. My eyes focused on something light-coloured in the corner of the room. *It can't be...* I stood up again, cautiously picked my way across stones and twigs and tugged at the piece of material. It was dirty and damp, but it was definitely *our* blanket. I closed my eyes, smiling, remembering Daran's gentle touch.

Suddenly, a shiver ran through me, and a flash of something sped across my mind. I dropped the blanket, gasping for breath. What the hell was *that*? My wrists throbbed and my head thumped. What was happening to me?

I stumbled back across to the stones and sat down heavily as a film of sweat covered my body. My eyes darted around the farm-house – *our* farmhouse. And I knew at that moment that it hadn't been only ours, and that the memories there weren't all happy ones. But what...?

'So the rumours were true. You *are* back.'

I leapt up off the stones. *Shit!* 'Da?'

8

Nineteen Years Earlier

'We have a very special guest for Mass this morning,' Father Doherty announced to the congregation at the start of the summer holidays. 'Daran McInnery is from Wicklow and has been studying in Cork. He's interested in becoming a priest and has asked to spend some time shadowing me while God and he decide if this is the right path for him. Daran, do you want to say a few words? They're a friendly lot. I'm sure they'll make you feel very welcome. Step up here, why don't you?'

I stopped playing with my long, blonde plaits and reluctantly looked up, expecting to see yet another old man with an expanding waist and diminishing hair. I certainly didn't expect to see a man in his early twenties with a full head of dark hair, a slim physique and a dazzling smile. Murmurs and giggles rippled through the congregation.

Leaning over to my best friend, Orla Brennan, I whispered in her ear, 'I'll bet you anything you like that the Black Widow will be the first to make sure he feels welcome. Very, *very* welcome.' I glanced across at Mrs Shaughnessy. Widowed when she was only twenty-one and never remarried, she had a reputation as a maneater. All the men in the village seemed to fancy her although that was not surprising. With her shiny, blonde hair and flawless, youthful complexion, she looked like a woman in her late twenties, although she was actually forty. I felt a bit guilty for giving her the nickname because she was always really nice to me but Ballykielty wasn't exactly the most exciting of places. Orla and I had to get our kicks somewhere.

Orla giggled a little too loudly. A sharp dig in my back made me yelp. I didn't dare turn round and look at Da in the pew behind me. I didn't need to. I'd seen that disgusted expression in his dark eyes so many times that it was etched on my mind forever so I kept my eyes forward. Father Doherty gave me a stern look, but Daran McInnery smiled.

And that dazzling smile was what started it.

During the summer, Da commented that he'd never seen me so eager to go to Mass and perhaps I wasn't going to turn into a huge disappointment, after all. Well, with someone like Daran McInnery to gaze upon, who wouldn't want to go? For the first time ever, I felt captivated by the words of the Scriptures. Watching him speak with such passion made my heart beat faster. I hung onto every single word he uttered. Even that eejit Jamie Doyle, from two years above me at school, couldn't break my concentration, despite tugging on my plaits and trying to tickle my ribs with his grubby, scabby hands.

In mid-September, the village held a céilí in honour of Father Doherty's thirtieth year with our parish. Despite it being Father Doherty's event, Daran McInnery was the centre of attention, with a constant queue of fawning women begging him to dance. I'd been right about the Black Widow; she was by his side constantly. Medusa herself would have been proud of the stony stares she gave to any woman with whom he danced.

I leaned against the wall of the barn, playing with a loose thread on the hem of my dark-purple floral dress, kicking at some loose straw with my purple canvas pumps, and watching. Always watching.

After a hissed lecture from Da on being a 'miserable, sulky little brat' who had better 'stop bringing shame to this family and accept the next invitation to dance', I was forced into dancing with that gobshite Jamie Doyle. His breath smelled of alcohol and he kept 'accidentally' placing his hand on my backside instead of my waist, and standing on my feet with his huge size-twelves. God alone knew why, but my da seemed to think the creepy git was potential husband material for either my sister, Nia, or me. Yuck. Over my dead body. Nia seemed to like him, though. I'd have thought that being in the same class as him would have put her right off. I wished, not for the first time, that I were much older. Closer to Daran McInnery's age, perhaps.

I danced with a couple of boys from my class, and with my da and my brothers, but I couldn't take my eyes off Daran. It seemed to me as though he was watching me too. Every time I danced, I could feel his eyes on me. And I liked it. A lot.

'Are you enjoying yourself, Father?' I asked, as I passed him on the way to dance with one of my brothers.

'That I am,' he responded, those green eyes burning into mine. 'But I'd be enjoying myself even more if you'd do me the honour of the next dance, Miss O'Connell.'

I smiled. Yes! Success! 'I might be free a little later, Father.'

'I'm not a priest, yet, Clare. It's Daran.'

I'd only just turned fourteen but I'd been an early developer and felt more like an eighteen-year-old. Being the youngest with four serious, boring siblings had made me grow up fast. My twin brothers, Keenan and Éamonn, were four years older than me and Nia was two years older. They were all devout Catholics. My other sister, Aisling, was six years older and at university in Limerick. She acted all serious when she came home for the holidays but, having spotted her unpacking some very sexy matching underwear, I liked to imagine that she drank alcohol and danced topless while she was there and only pretended to be nun-like to keep the peace with Da when she visited Ballykielty.

I tried to be more like my siblings. Being constantly scolded was no way to live but I couldn't help it – there was an extroverted, fun-loving, boisterous woman inside me who refused to conform. I wasn't convinced by the whole religious thing either, especially as

Ma, Da and my siblings seemed to think Catholicism was code for 'no fun'. Daran McInnery seemed like fun, though, and I was very aware that I'd developed a huge crush on him – my first serious, stomach-flopping, heart-racing crush. It was killing me to play it cool.

'Would you be free for that dance now?' Daran asked, three dances later. 'Or are you too much in demand?'

'I'm hugely in demand, especially with that eejit Jamie Doyle, but I think you've waited long enough.' I took his hand and a tingle ran through my body at his warm touch.

The music started and I sent up a prayer of thanks for a dance where the couple had to maintain close contact throughout. My heart raced as we placed our arms round each other's waists and moved round the room in a circle formation, changing direction and spinning when directed. Every time he gazed into my eyes and smiled, I melted. No man had ever affected me like this. I knew at that moment that I was in love.

I didn't want that dance to end and nearly whooped out loud when Daran suggested we get some juice and go outside for some fresh air.

'What are you planning to do when you finish school next year?' he asked as we wandered away from the village hall with our drinks. 'Will you be going to university?'

'University?'

'You must be in your Leaving Cert year, are you not?'

Not quite. I chose my words carefully. 'I'm studying hard. I'd like to be a midwife eventually. Babies are so cute and the thought of being the one who helps bring so many of them into the world must be such a blessing and so rewarding.'

'That's a grand vocation to want,' he said.

'My da doesn't think so.'

'Why not?'

'He believes a woman's place is in the home, being a good Catholic wife, and producing a baby every two years or so, just like my ma.'

'I'm sure he only wants what's best for you.'

'Da only ever wants what's best for him and best for God.'

'Perhaps what's best for God is best for you too.'

I pondered his statement. 'I want to challenge you on that, but I can't think of an example of something that has displeased me but would have pleased God, so perhaps I've been unfair on him.'

Daran laughed. 'Unfair on your da or unfair on God?'

I smiled. 'Both... I think. Are you from a large family?'

'The oldest of eight. My father died young so I spent a lot of time helping my mother with my brothers and sisters.'

'I'm sorry about your da. That must have been hard.'

'It was, but my siblings were a great distraction.'

'Father Doherty said you're only looking into the priesthood.'

He nodded. 'I planned to become a religion teacher and I could have started teaching this term, but I couldn't help feeling that God had another path in mind for me, perhaps as a priest or an overseas missionary. The priesthood's a big commitment. My priest in Cork is a good friend of Father Doherty so he arranged for me to spend some time with him to explore whether it's right for me. Here I am, exploring away, trying to work out what I want to do with my life.'

We stopped at a bench and sat down. The moon lit Daran's silhouette. He looked like a model rather than a priest and I longed to reach out and touch the curl of hair that kept blowing across his forehead and into his eyes. I sat on my hands instead. 'If you became a priest, you wouldn't be able to have a family of your own. Wouldn't you miss that?'

'A person can't miss something he's never had. Right now, I want God in my life more than I want a family of my own. Or at least I think I do. That's why I'm not rushing into any decisions. If I do join the priesthood, I'll be taking a solemn vow of celibacy and that's how my life will be.'

'Doesn't your mind ever wander and think about what it would be like to kiss someone and to press your body against theirs and make babies?'

I heard him gulp, but I couldn't see enough of his face in the darkness to discern his reaction. His shaky words conveyed his emotions, though. 'Emm... well, er, Clare. It's like this... A priest...

Well, it's just that... Okay, I sometimes *think* about it. Thinking is different from acting on... er... carnal desires. I... er... I think we'd better go back inside. I've cooled down now.'

How I resisted the urge not to reach up and kiss him at that moment, I'll never know.

9

Present Day

'What in the name of God are you doing here?' Da growled. 'I thought we'd made it clear that you were *never* to come back.'

I cursed my stupidity. Damn stranger-hating village. Should have known I'd be spotted. *Be brave. Be confident. You're not sixteen anymore. You can handle him.* 'It's great to see you too, Da,' I said, squaring up to him and standing tall. He looked old. And grey. And tired. I could take him.

But his strong, sharp voice still had the power to make me tremble. 'What do you want, girl? Why are you back?'

'I'm in Cork on business.'

'Business? Is that what you call it these days?'

My stomach twisted at the clear insinuation in his words. At least he'd stopped short of calling me the hurtful names he'd used seventeen years earlier. Unable to think of a clever quip, I stared at him and hoped he couldn't see me shaking.

'I hope you're not here to seek forgiveness,' he snarled. 'What I said back then still stands. You're dead to me, Clare. And to the rest of your family. You won't be welcome here again. Ever.'

He stared at me as if expecting a challenge. For years I'd dreamed of what I'd say to him if our paths crossed again. The scenes in my mind had ranged from a Harry Potter-and-Lord-Voldemort-style stand-off with fireworks and demons – ending with me striking him down, of course – right through to an emotional reunion where he begged for my forgiveness and welcomed me back into the fold with open arms, and pretty much everything in between. But none of my scenes involved me standing in the ruined farmhouse, shaking like a small child who'd just seen a ghost, completely dumbstruck.

'I expect you'll be leaving as soon as you've finished your trip down memory lane?'

I nodded.

'Good. Don't be coming back.'

'I won't,' I muttered, cursing myself for not being able to stand up to him.

He turned to go, then stopped in the doorway. I shivered as he turned his dark eyes on me. 'He never loved you, you know. He just used you.'

'Daran?' My heart dropped into my stomach as I whispered his name.

Even in the gloom, I could see his face redden at the mention of Daran. 'Some priest in training he turned out to be. He was getting up close and personal with most of the parishioners. You just happened to be the youngest and stupidest.' Then he turned and left.

I sank to the floor. Daran wasn't like that. It was just Da striking out. Again. And it had worked. Seventeen years on and he still had power over me. Bastard.

10

Eighteen Years Earlier

After the céilí, I made it my mission to introduce Daran to the stunning countryside around our village. Well, someone had to. He seemed keen to accept my offer. As we walked across the fields and through the woodland, I'd chat to him about his family and his life in Wicklow. I'd also talk about my family, how Ma hated me, how I was always in trouble with Da, and how I felt I didn't fit in with any of their expectations of what a good Catholic girl should be. I also confessed that I was a Junior Certificate student, not Leaving Certificate.

I knew it was cruel, given the career choice he was exploring, but I repeatedly painted a picture for him of what family life should be like – drawn from books and TV, rather than what I personally experienced from my own dysfunctional family – and what the love of a good woman, instead of just the love of God, might feel like. He laughed at first, but then he started to open up and talk about the family he'd dreamed of having before he'd started to think seriously about the priesthood.

Our favourite place on our walks was a ruined farmhouse in the middle of a meadow. It was so peaceful and so beautiful, with woodland on three sides and open fields on the fourth. Butterflies danced amongst wildflowers and birds chirped in the trees. I liked to imagine it was our home, although I didn't dare mention it to Daran in case I scared him off. I knew the boundaries. In all our conversations about family, I took care never to share my secret that he was the man who featured in my dreams.

He only ever asked me about boys once, roughly a year after the céilí. It was late September, a little after my fifteenth birthday, and we'd spent a few days basking in an Indian summer. Lying in the meadow outside our farmhouse, we'd been spotting shapes in the fluffy clouds that bounced across the cornflower sky.

'Why do you spend all your spare time with me, Clare?' He turned onto his side to face me. 'Do you not have a special boy in the village? Jamie Doyle, perhaps? He seems pretty keen on you.'

'Jamie Doyle's an eejit. He's not for me.' I shuddered at the thought, picturing his greasy, red hair and the way he always seemed to have white foam in the corners of his mouth as if he'd contracted rabies.

'He's not for you, is he not? Is there someone else who holds your heart, then?'

I turned onto my side too and gazed into his eyes. 'Yes, there is. There's someone who holds my heart so tightly that I don't think it could ever, or would ever, want to love anyone else.'

His eyes widened. 'And does he feel the same way about you?'

'I think he does, but he's torn because he has another love too. I keep trying to convince him there's space for us both in his life, but he's not ready to accept that. Not yet anyway.'

'Maybe he just needs time.'

'That's what I'm hoping.'

Daran turned onto his back again, staring at the sky. I hoped I hadn't said too much, but surely he'd have left if I had. I turned over and lay on my back again too. As I came to rest, my hand lightly touched his. He didn't pull away. We lay there in silence, hands touching, while my heart thumped faster and faster.

* * *

One Saturday afternoon towards the end of February, thick snow encased the meadow and weighed down the branches of the trees to the point where many had broken under the pressure. My heart leapt as I spotted footprints in the deep snow leading up to the farmhouse. Daran was early. Grand. I grinned as I stepped easily into his larger prints and danced across them, my breath hanging in the cold winter air.

'Daran?' I called as I approached the entrance. No answer. 'Daran?' I hesitated for a moment. What if the footprints weren't his? What if someone else had found our farmhouse?

'Daran? Is that you?'

'Yes,' came a hoarse whisper. 'I'm here.'

'Thank the Lord!' I walked through the doorway. 'I was starting to think that... Oh, sweet Jesus, what is it?' I ran across to him. He was slumped on a pile of rocks with his head in his hands. He looked up. His eyes were red and tears streaked his face. 'Daran? Are you sick?'

'I don't know what to do, Clare. I'm so confused.'

'Can I help?'

He shook his head. 'You're the problem.'

'Me. What have *I* done?'

'You've been you. Beautiful, funny, intelligent you.'

My heart thumped at his words. Did this mean...? I hardly dared hope.

He rubbed his cheeks and looked into my eyes. 'I can't stop thinking about you. I love you so much and every fibre of my body, mind and soul wants to be with you. I know it's wrong, yet it feels so right.'

He loved me? He really loved me? 'That's because it *is* right.' I knelt down beside him on the cold floor, grabbed his icy hands and kissed them, my heart bursting with joy.

He moaned softly at the gentle touch of my lips. 'You're too young.'

'I'm sixteen this year. And I'm very mature for my age. You know I am, Daran.'

'I know, but you're still only fifteen now, Clare. You may not look or act like it but, technically, you're still a child and I'm eight years your senior. I'm a qualified teacher who's considering becoming a priest. Neither of those scenarios allows for me falling in love with a fifteen-year-old. I made a vow to God to serve Him, whichever career path I took.'

'You can still serve God and be with me.'

'But I couldn't be a priest.'

I kissed his hands again. 'You could do missionary work. That was one of your options, wasn't it? I could go with you. I know it's hard for you, but it's hard for me too. I love you too, Daran. I want to be with you forever. I want to kiss you and hold you and make babies with you.'

He let out a shaky sigh. 'I can't believe I'm going to say this, but I think I want all those things too. With you. Which means I can't become a priest. I didn't expect...'

'You didn't expect to fall in love, but it happened. We can't control who we fall for.'

'But your age...'

I placed my fingers across his lips. 'My age is just a number. I'll be sixteen on September the fifth. I'm officially an adult then and I can do anything an adult can do. *Anything.*'

He shook his head. 'Not in Ireland you can't. The age of consent here is seventeen.'

'Perhaps, but it's just a number which changes in different countries, so don't start thinking we'd be doing something wrong because, elsewhere, it wouldn't be wrong. Other countries class me as an adult.'

He stroked my cheek. I closed my eyes as I trembled at his touch.

'What about God?' he asked.

'It's not me or Him, you know. You can have us both in your life. He won't abandon you for choosing me instead of the priesthood, Daran. He'll bless you for choosing love instead.'

Daran wiped his eyes. 'You make it sound so simple.'

'It is! You love me. I love you. You love God. That's all there is to it. We can make this work. We really can. Besides, if He really was calling you to be a priest, you wouldn't have spent eighteen months living in Ballykielty exploring it, would you? You'd have joined the seminary and started your studies.' I stroked his face and he leaned into my hand with his eyes closed. He looked so serene, so perfect, that I couldn't help myself. I leaned forward and gently kissed his lips. His mouth parted slightly as though he were about to speak, but no words came out. I expected him to pull away, but he didn't move. I kissed him again and again until he started to kiss back, gently at first, then more urgently. He entwined his fingers in my long, loose hair as he kissed my lips, then my neck.

Finally, he pulled away. 'I'm sorry, Clare. I shouldn't have done that.'

'You should.'

'No. I shouldn't,' he said firmly, guilt etched across his face. 'Because my thoughts were taking me much further than a kiss and I can't allow them to do that. Not yet. I'll walk you back to the village. Now.'

I cried myself to sleep that night, although the words 'not yet' gave me hope that, one day, he'd change his mind. And I'd be waiting for him.

* * *

Three agonising days passed with no word from Daran. I went to our farmhouse every evening and waited for hours. On the fourth evening, he appeared in the doorway, unshaven, dark bags under his eyes.

'I've barely slept,' he said. 'I thought it would be easier if I stayed away from you.'

I remained slumped on the pile of stones, terrified that he'd come to end it before it had even started. 'Easier for whom? You or me?'

He shrugged. 'I don't really know.'

'Has it been easy for you? Because it certainly hasn't been easy for me waiting here for you night after night, not able to come round to your house in case anyone sees me, worried that something might have happened to you.'

'Something *has* happened to me. I've made a decision. I finally know what I want to do with my life.'

My heart sank. He'd chosen the priesthood. 'You're leaving, aren't you?' I asked, my voice cracking.

Daran took a few steps towards me. 'Why would I go and do something stupid like that when all I want to do is be with you?'

In a fraction of a second, I was in his arms, the place I'd dreamed of being since the day he'd been introduced to our congregation. As he kissed me and ran his hands through my hair and down my back, I knew he'd been worth the wait.

11

Present Day

'How were the meetings?' Ben heaved my case into the boot of his old Focus early on Wednesday evening.

'Grand, thanks.'

He slammed the boot shut. 'Did you charm the pants off them?'

'Of course.'

We got into the car and belted up.

'So you saved the day?' Ben asked.

'They're still a client.'

'You might want to tone down the enthusiasm a bit.'

I gave him a half-smile. 'Sorry, Ben. It's been a tough trip.'

'Because it involved going back to Cork?'

I sighed. I couldn't lie to Ben. 'Yes. Because it involved going back to Cork.'

Ben started the engine. 'Remember, I'm here if you ever want to talk about it.'

'I know. I appreciate it.'

He manoeuvred his car out of Leeds train station. 'In the morning, I'm off to Birmingham with work and I won't be back till the end of next week.'

'Oh.' I felt quite uncomfortable at the thought of Ben not being around for a curry and a gossip.

'You won't be back for the weekend?'

'Unfortunately not. I need to work then too. You can phone me if you want to talk, though.'

'Seriously, Ben, I don't need to talk about New Year or Ireland, or anything else. I really don't. Stop raising your eyebrows at me. I'm grand. Honest. What is this obsession with people wanting to talk all the time? Sometimes, things just need to be left alone.'

'Okay. Message coming through loud and clear.'

I stared out of the window in silence for the rest of the journey. If I'd opened my mouth to speak, I might have begged him to stay because, for the first time ever, I felt as if I might actually need to talk to someone about my past. And if I started talking about it, I might never stop.

* * *

I abandoned my suitcase by the door of my apartment, headed straight for the fridge and poured myself a glass of wine. A very large one.

Unlocking the patio door, I stepped out onto the balcony and sat down, breathing in the icy night air. The cold metal of the chair under my legs made me shiver but I needed to be outside. Hopefully the wind and the cold might help clear the fog in my head.

I took a glug of my wine, then another. What a hideous start to the year. Could anything else go wrong? Staring out at the cityscape, I tried to focus on the sounds of a distant siren, honking horns, laughter, music – anything but the confrontation with Da, his suggestion about Daran's infidelity, and whatever the hell had happened in the farmhouse right before he'd appeared.

Could Daran really have slept around or had Da just said that to torment me? I wouldn't put anything past him.

A knock on the door made me jump. I reluctantly stepped back inside. 'Who is it?'

'Lydia from next door. I've got a recorded-delivery envelope for you.'

Bollocks. I couldn't face anyone. 'I'm just out of the shower. Thanks for taking it in but will you leave it outside and I'll get it shortly?'

'Okay.'

I stared through the peephole. When I was confident Lydia had gone, I yanked the door open, grabbed the envelope and quickly shut it again.

The large, brown, cardboard envelope was franked from the London head office. Inside was a white A4 envelope with my name and the London head-office address typed on it. A compliments slip paperclipped to it stated, 'This arrived for you'. Removing the compliments slip, I ripped the envelope open and removed a stiff sheet of A4 cream paper with a fancy letterhead on it giving the address of a solicitor's in Truro. My stomach churned. There could only be one reason why that a solicitor's firm in Truro would be contacting me.

Dear Ms O'Connell

At Bowson, Higgs & Crane, we represent the estate of Mrs Nuala Sheedy, who passed away on 18th October. Our Lady of the Portal & St Piran Church in Truro has been the sole beneficiary of Mrs Sheedy's estate. However, Mrs Sheedy requested that this letter be passed on to you, her great-niece.

We are unaware of the contents of the letter. However, if we can be of further assistance to you, please do not hesitate to contact the office and ask for me, quoting Mrs Sheedy's name.

Yours sincerely,
Angela Crane.

I was right. So, the old bat was dead. How did I feel about that? Like I needed a drink! I poured another large glass of wine, then leaned against the fridge, sipping on it. What was in the letter? A plea for forgiveness, perhaps?

Setting my glass down on the worktop, I retrieved Great-Aunt Nuala's letter from the bottom of the solicitor's envelope. A drawing of some rosary beads draped over a Bible filled the bottom-left corner of the small, peach envelope. How very Nuala. I stared at the envelope.

'Do you know what, Great-Aunt Nuala, I don't want to hear it. It's been a long few days. I'm off to my bed.'

I retrieved my suitcase and tossed the letter onto the coffee table as I walked back through the lounge towards my bedroom.

But sleep wouldn't come. Every time I closed my eyes, I pictured that damned peach envelope and Great-Aunt Nuala's immaculate script. What if it wasn't what I expected?

'For feck's sake,' I cried, hurling back the duvet and storming into the lounge to get the letter.

Crawling back into bed, I ripped open the envelope.

12th June
Dear Clare,

I'm dying. The doctors have given me until next spring, at a push, but I don't mind. I'm 76 and more than ready to meet both the Lord and my husband, who joined Him far too early.

As you'd expect, I've spent a lot of time in Confession, preparing for the end. I have a lot to confess and my priest, Father Finnegan, has been very generous with his penance. I feel blessed and forgiven for all but my greatest sin. I have confessed this to Father Finnegan, but I cannot meet the Lord without confessing to you.

Reaching the end of the page, I slumped back against the pillow. 'Exactly as predicted. Please forgive me, Clare, for I have sinned, but only because you sinned first.' I ran my fingers through my bob. 'I'm a bloody eejit for expecting anything else.'

I sighed and reluctantly turned over the page, bracing myself for a load of religious babblings.

This is going to come as a huge shock to you and I can do nothing to soften the blow: Shannon did not die. It was a lie.

I sat upright, gasping for breath. WTF? I reread the sentence again and again, my heart beating so fast, I thought it might burst. *She isn't dead? What? How?* I rubbed my eyes and blinked a few times before reading the rest.

She was adopted as planned, but by a different family from the one you met, so you could never trace them if you ever had doubts about her 'death'. It was your father's idea, but I am equally to blame, as I willingly played my part, believing I was doing the right thing.

You were so young, Clare, and you'd committed such a cardinal sin against God and the Holy Catholic Church, but Father Finnegan – and old age – has helped me realise that the future of your baby was not my choice, or your father's choice, to make. It should have been your decision, despite your youth. I now accept that we were very wrong to force you into giving up baby Shannon. We were even more wrong to tell you that she had died, poor little mite.

I don't expect your forgiveness. I would find it hard to forgive anyone who had done such a wicked thing to me. I do, however, hope to belatedly repair the damage we've done. Your father knows nothing of these actions. I lost touch with my nephew five years ago when I received my diagnosis, confessed my sins and realised the error of my ways.

I enclose a photo and all the details I know in case you wish to track her down. I believe Shannon would have turned 16 today. Perhaps she is ready to meet her birth mother? Whatever you decide, may God be with you.

I have one more confession. Daran McInnery wrote to you many, many times via your priest, Father Doherty. At my insistence, he destroyed the letters. Your sister Aisling also tried to make contact. I returned her letters, unopened. I know now that I had no right to do either of these things, not that this will bring you any comfort.

I go to my Maker with my conscience at peace now and hope that one day you can perhaps understand, even if you can't forgive. At the time, I genuinely did believe it was best for you, Clare, but I realise now that your father and I were thinking of ourselves, not what was right for you and your daughter.

God bless you on your journey, should you wish to find young Shannon.

Great-Aunt Nuala

I dropped the letter. *Jesus Christ! She's alive? After all these years,*

Shannon's alive? They lied to me? Why would they lie? I'd agreed to the adoption.

My hands shook and my heart raced as I snatched up the letter again and scanned it for an answer: '... *so you could never trace them'.* What difference would it make if I had? I closed my eyes tightly and muttered, 'Same as keeping her in the first place. Same reason I was banished to Cornwall. Disgrace to the family. Damn them. Damn them all. She was *my* baby. It was *my* choice. *My* body. *My* choice.'

I opened my eyes again and scanned over the names and dates of the family who'd really adopted Shannon, then reread the letter. 'Photo. Where's the photo?' I rummaged through the sheets of the letter. It wasn't there. *Stay calm. It'll be here. Think. The envelope! It'll still be in the envelope. So where the feck's the envelope?*

I found it on the floor and relief flowed through me when my fingers touched something inside. I sat on the floor, leaned against the side of the bed and gazed at the image. A pretty, blonde baby with green eyes and pudgy cheeks grinned at the camera. She must have been about five or six months old. I turned the photo over. A scribble in blue biro on the back stated:

Shannon at 6 months. Thank you for our beautiful gift.

I flipped the photo back over and stroked her face with my fingertip. 'I'm sorry I didn't keep you. I wanted to. I can remember the day you were born, as if it were yesterday. And the pain when they took you away was not a patch on the pain that I felt when they told me you'd died. Because, while you were alive, there was hope that we'd find each other one day, then we'd track down Daran and be a proper family. He'd have wanted that. He loved me and he was true to me, whatever Da says. I'm sorry, Shannon. I'm so sorry they gave you away.'

For someone who'd barely shed a tear about my past in seventeen years, the outpouring of emotion was overwhelming. I gasped for air as my body shook and tears rained down my cheeks, soaking my PJs.

I needed to talk to someone. Desperately. But with Ben out of town and Sarah still on honeymoon, who could I turn to?

12

✉ To Elise

Do you have any plans this weekend? I need to
talk to someone. Is there any chance I could meet
you in Whitsborough Bay? Please!

✉ From Elise

Are you OK? Do you want to talk now? I've got 10
mins till break's over. Just tried to call you
but got voicemail. Worried about you! No plans
for the weekend xx

✉ To Elise

Sorry for not answering. Don't want to discuss it
on the phone. Please don't worry. I'm fine. Just
received some unexpected news and I need to talk
through my next steps with someone. And no, I'm
not pregnant! Can we meet somewhere quiet at
10.30am on Saturday?

✉ From Elise

How about The Starfish Café a couple of miles
down the coast? It's lovely and really quiet

first thing. Google it for directions. It's easy
to find. See you then, but call me if you need me
before xx

I arrived at The Starfish Café shortly before ten. A heavy frost had
settled overnight and blankets of snow covered the higher ground.
Thankfully the café opened minutes later so I didn't have to sit in
the car with the heating on full blast.

Sitting at a window seat, I slowly stirred my latte, staring out at
the grey sea pounding the distant shore, as I wondered what to say
to Elise. Where could I start to talk about a past that had been
buried for seventeen years? A past that I'd refused point blank to
ever discuss with Sarah, even though I trusted her implicitly.

Elise was right next to the table before I even noticed her. 'Elise!
Sorry. Miles away.'

She unwrapped a long, fluffy turquoise scarf before sitting down
opposite me. 'You look like you've got the weight of the world on
your shoulders.'

I sighed. 'I may well do. I'm hoping I can unburden some of the
pressure on you.'

'Unburden away.'

I stood up. 'Let me get you a drink first and then I'm going to tell
you a little story that will make your hair even curlier than it is
already.'

At the counter, I ordered Elise a hot chocolate and a piece of
shortbread. As I placed them in front of her, I searched for the right
words. 'I found out something this week that has completely
thrown me and I need some advice on what to do next.' I sat down.
'To get the advice, I'm going to have to talk about my past and, as
I'm sure you already know, I *never* talk about my past, so this is
going to be really difficult for me.'

Elise snapped her shortbread in half and wiped her fingers on a
napkin. 'I'm all ears. Just like you were for me last year.'

'Thanks. Okay, here goes...'

* * *

'You must have been terrified, being pregnant at sixteen,' Elise said, when I'd told her the first part of my story – my relationship with Daran.

'I was. Not of having the baby, but of telling Da. I knew he'd go ballistic so I kept it quiet. I had no sickness or fatigue so there were no physical signs of pregnancy. My parents found out, though.'

'How?'

'I honestly don't know. Could have been anything. I got home from a walk with Daran on New Year's Eve to find Ma, Da and Father Doherty waiting for me in the living room, looking very serious. A suitcase and a couple of boxes stood in the middle of the room. Da ordered me to put on the clothes that Ma had laid out on my bed, then come back downstairs immediately. His voice was calm, but his face was puce. I knew that he knew and I swear I nearly wet myself with fear. As soon as I got to my bedroom, I could see it had been stripped bare of my belongings. My drawers and wardrobe were empty and the black woollen dress and thick tights that I wore for funerals were laid out on my bed.'

My eyes filled with tears as I relived that memory. Those faces staring at me. Judging me. Hating me. I didn't want to start crying again so I stared out the window at the sea while I composed myself. Elise remained silent, waiting for me to continue.

'I changed as slowly as I could but eventually had to go back downstairs to face the firing squad. Ma wouldn't look at me. She just sat in the chair, arms folded, lips pursed, shaking her head. It was Father Doherty who spoke. He wasn't angry. He just sounded disappointed. He wittered on about sinners and threw out a stack of quotes from the Bible. I wasn't listening. I was too scared to concentrate. Then Da asked who the father was. I couldn't tell them. They'd never have understood so I said, "I don't know", which was like lighting the touch-paper. Da obviously assumed I'd been sleeping around. For a God-fearing man who never swore, I heard words spew from his mouth that I'd never even heard before. I was called everything, from a harlot to a temptress to the village bike to Jezebel herself, before he told me I'd brought disgrace on the family and I was no longer his daughter.'

Elise gasped and reached for my hand as my tears started to flow.

'He said he never wanted to see me or hear from me again. I know he was upset and ashamed, but what parent says something like that to their youngest daughter?'

Elise shook her head. 'No parent should ever behave like that. It's appalling. Parents should be supportive, not judgemental. I'm so sorry, Clare. What happened next?'

'I was sent to live with Da's Aunt Nuala in Truro. There was no talk of me returning. Father Doherty seemed shocked at that part and tried to convince them to have me back after the baby was born, but they both refused. It got pretty heated. He started talking about forgiveness, but Da just hurled everything he'd said about sin back at him. He couldn't win. I got a letter from Ma a month later telling me that they knew who the father was. Apparently, Daran had been asking after me and they'd noticed he seemed overly surprised and concerned that I'd moved to the UK to help an elderly relative. Daran was removed from the county and given strict instructions never to contact me or he'd face legal consequences for having sex with a minor. Apparently, my parents didn't judge or blame him because I'd clearly been – and I quote – "the harlot who'd chased and hounded a celibate man until he was powerless to resist your advances". That was the last contact I had with either of them.'

Elise looked at me with tears in her eyes and whispered, 'Oh, Clare, I don't know what to say. I had no idea you'd been through anything like this. I knew you weren't close to your family, but I never imagined this.'

I wiped my tears and blew my nose. 'Nobody knows. Not even Sarah. It hurts too much to think about it. It's one of the reasons I don't do Christmas and New Year. It reminds me of being with Daran, then having our happy bubble burst on New Year's Eve.'

'I don't blame you,' she said. 'So what happened to the baby?'

'It was a baby girl. Shannon. She was born on the twelfth of June. She was beautiful. Absolutely beautiful. But I only got to hold her for a few minutes before they took her away. Da and Great-Aunt Nuala had arranged for her to be adopted. I'd had to sign some paperwork to give her to the Flannerys – a good Irish Catholic family from Exeter. I kept telling myself it was for the best, but best for whom? Me? Shannon? Or my prejudiced family? I tried to convince Great-Aunt Nuala to let me keep her, but she gave me an ultimatum: give Shannon up and she'd put me through school, college and university, or keep her and she'd throw me out with no money.'

'What sort of ultimatum is that?' Elise cried. 'It didn't give you any real choice.'

'I know. I knew I couldn't support Shannon because I had no money, no qualifications, no job and no prospect of getting one. I needed to start again with English qualifications two years behind everyone else and I figured that, if I let her get the right start in life with a family who could provide for her, I could try to find her once I got my education and a job. I knew I could never fully be her mother, but perhaps I could still be in her life.'

'And you never found her?'

'I never looked. They told me she died a few hours after being born. Post-birth complications or something. But I got this letter on Wednesday.'

I reached into my bag and passed Great-Aunt Nuala's letter to Elise. She scanned down the contents and I watched as her jaw dropped open. 'And you thought she was dead for, what, sixteen-and-a-half years?'

I nodded. 'This is her at six months.' I passed Elise the photograph.

Elise smiled. 'There's no doubting she's yours. Absolute image of you. She's beautiful.'

'I know. So now you know the huge skeleton in my closet. Only, it turns out it's not really a skeleton, but a young woman now. And while I'm confessing everything, I have another biggie that you may as well know. I hope you believe me that I wasn't the village bike at age sixteen, as my father so nicely put it, but I want you to know that I've never been the village bike since then...'

She shrugged. 'I don't judge. I know I've made snide comments in the past, but I haven't meant them. How many men you've had sex with is up to you.'

I laughed. 'That's just the point. I haven't had sex with any. Well, obviously I did with Daran, but he was my first and only.'

'But why...?'

'Why do I make out that I sleep around?' I wet my finger, picked up some sugar granules off the table and dropped them into my empty cup. 'It's easier that way. I created a persona to protect myself from my past, based around the person my parents clearly thought I was. If you make out that you don't do relationships, people want to know why. If you make out that you don't do relationships because you prefer one-night stands, people don't question it. They see it as a lifestyle choice. Which begs the question, why don't I do relationships? Quite simply, it was because I loved Daran so deeply that nobody else stood a chance. Every moment we were apart hurt.' My tears started again. 'Sorry. I can't stop crying now. It's like a dam has burst.'

'Are you going to try to find Daran?' Elise asked.

I shook my head. 'No. I thought of him constantly for years after I moved to Cornwall. I'd dream about how different things could have been if I'd told Daran I was pregnant or if I'd stood up to Da. The thing is, I don't even remember why I didn't tell Daran. I've been racking my brain and it feels like there was a reason, but I just can't put my finger on it.'

Elise shrugged. 'It was a long time ago and you've been through so much since then.'

'I know. It's so strange, though. It's not the only thing I can't remember. There's so much of our time together that I remember so vividly yet there are other things... well, it's like there's a thick fog hanging over parts of my past and I can just see shapes, but I can't convert them into anything tangible.' I smiled at Elise. 'Sorry. That sounds like absolute bollocks, doesn't it now? Hindsight's a great thing. I know now that I should have stood up to my da, but the man terrified me. He still terrifies me. I saw him on Sunday and I was completely defenceless all over again. I didn't put up a fight on Sunday and I didn't put up a fight when I was sixteen. Back then, I let him put me on a plane and send me to England, away from Daran. I wrote to Daran every other day until Shannon was born. I sent the letters to Father Doherty and begged him to pass them on.

I'm assuming he didn't, since he destroyed the letters that Daran wrote. The only thing I *do* know is that we could have been really happy together if I'd been a bit stronger and pushed a bit more. But I can't try to recover what we had nearly two decades later. I just can't.'

Elise shook her head again. 'What a waste.'

I sat back in my chair and looked out the window again. 'Father Doherty used to say Confession was good for the soul. I do admit that I'm feeling a little relieved just now.' I looked back at Elise. 'What should I do?'

She took a deep breath. 'Crikey. Where do I start? That was a lot of unexpected information that I can't believe you've been carrying around for half your life.'

'I know. And now I expect you to solve all my problems.' I smiled. 'Thanks for listening.'

'You're welcome. You've been there for me and baby bean so it's the very least I can do. Firstly, I'd say don't beat yourself up about any of this. You couldn't have prevented what happened. Making you put Shannon up for adoption was cruel, and to tell you she'd died was unforgivable.' She rubbed her own stomach, as if to reassure her baby that she was safe from imminent adoption. 'Secondly, I suggest you drop the sex-mad persona and just be you. If you don't want a relationship, you don't have to have a relationship, but you don't have to make out that you have a different one every week, either. Thirdly, I think you should confront your parents. I don't mean you have to fly to Ireland to see them, especially as it sounds like things with your dad didn't go well on Sunday. You could write to them instead. You don't even have to post it, but I think it would do you the world of good to get down on paper what you think of them, to help box it off and move on.'

'Did you do that to your mum?' Elise had a very volatile relationship with her alcoholic mother, who, even before the drinking, had resented the disruption that Elise and her sister had created by being born.

Elise nodded. 'My counsellor, Jem, suggested it. I've written loads of letters in my time. I've never sent any. Mind you, when I saw her between Christmas and New Year, I gave her a piece of my mind, then walked out on her, so I think I've finally had my opportunity.'

'Good for you.' I pondered on what she'd said. 'That's all good advice, so it is. Anything else?'

'I think you should start looking for Shannon.' Elise smiled. 'But you'd already decided to do that, hadn't you?'

I smiled too. 'Was it that obvious?'

'The way your eyes lit up when you spoke of her was a big clue. I don't think you really needed my advice, did you? I think you just needed to tell someone, after all these years.'

Very astute. 'The advice was good, though. An added bonus, perhaps. I liked the bit about ranting at the parents. I really will do that, but on paper, like you suggest. I never want to set foot in Ireland ever again. I didn't want to go last week, and I definitely didn't want to go to Ballykielty, but I felt drawn to *our* place. Never again.'

'Are you sure you don't want to find Daran? What if Shannon wants to know who her dad is?'

'Christ! It never even crossed my mind. If I find Shannon, I'm not expecting it to be easy. If she takes after me in personality as well as looks, she'll be a tough cookie and will give me a hard time for abandoning her. Quite rightly so. She might not want to hear the sorry story of my past. I really hadn't thought beyond her reaction to me, but you're right: she might want to know about Daran. I don't think I'm ready to find him yet, though. It's going to be emotional enough finding Shannon. I think adding Daran into the mix will tip me over the edge.'

'Do you fancy a walk along the beach and we can talk some more?' Elise asked. 'Unless you feel you're talked out.'

'I've been quiet for half my life and now that I've finally opened up, I feel like I could talk for Ireland. Are you sure you can cope?'

She smiled. 'Anything to help you get through this. But bean needs another shortbread first.'

'And I need a strong coffee.'

13

Seventeen Years Earlier

I gazed round the farmhouse at my handiwork and smiled. I'd liberated a couple of rectangular straw bales from a nearby field, opened one up and spread the straw across the corner of the room that I'd come to think of as 'kissing corner'. I'd found an old picnic rug tucked away at the back of the shed at home. Resting on top of a thick blanket of straw, it would be perfect for what I had planned. The second bale acted as a table. Having only turned sixteen that day, I knew there was no chance of being served alcohol anywhere local, so we'd have to pretend with fizzy white grape juice out of plastic picnic beakers.

I'd chosen my outfit carefully to avoid awkward clothing-removal disasters. The short, cream summer dress had buttons all the way up the front, which could be swiftly undone to reveal a cream and red lacy bra-and-panties set that I'd liberated from Aisling's drawers, the little minx. Surely Daran wouldn't be able to resist it.

As a good Catholic, he was a firm believer in 'no sex before marriage', but I could tell with each passing day and every touch that holding back was getting harder and harder – literally! I was determined to change his mind.

'I'm so sorry I'm late. I was worried you might have gone.' Daran picked me up and spun me around, kissing me, as he always did. After he'd admitted his feelings for me in February, he'd told Father Doherty that he didn't think life as a priest was the right path for him, but he was still just as committed to learning about and serving God. Father Doherty had been very understanding and had asked if he'd like to stick around and continue to help him out in return for further guidance on the Catholic faith. Daran jumped at the offer. After Easter, he also secured a position teaching religious studies at my comprehensive. Naturally, we had to keep our relationship quiet or he'd have been dismissed. Fortunately, Orla Brennan was seeing a Protestant in Ballyshelty, so we provided constant alibis for each other. She didn't know who I was seeing, just that he was older than me and that our relationship wouldn't meet with anyone's approval. She was convinced he was married and I let her continue to think that.

He cupped my chin and gave me a gentle kiss on the lips. 'I'm sorry, Clare, but I've only got about an hour and a quarter.'

'And I've got to go out for that meal with the parents anyway. Oh no, I haven't. That's what normal parents would do to celebrate the birthday of a child they love, whereas mine have barely acknowledged the day. Ma tossed a card at me. No gift. Just a card.'

'I'm sorry they're so cruel to you. It breaks my heart to see it.'

I shrugged. 'I'm used to it. Anyway, I don't want to waste any of our precious time talking about them. Seeing as time is tight, we'd better get on with things.'

Daran nodded his head towards the 'table' and makeshift bed. 'What's this? Are we moving in now?'

'It may or may not have escaped your notice, but I have reached the grand old age of sixteen today. I'm an adult and I'm ready to do everything that adults do.'

He wrapped his arms round me. 'We've talked about this and you know that I can't do that.'

'Are you trying to convince me or yourself?'

He laughed. 'Me! You know I want you but it's not how I was brought up.'

'I respect you for that, but—'

'And you're not the age of consent.'

'Also a good point and if this were just a casual thing, I wouldn't even consider taking that step. But it's not a casual thing, is it? I love you, Daran. I want to be with you till the end of forever. For me, this is the next logical step. You've already got my heart, my mind, my soul. The only thing you don't have is my body and I want you to have that too. I'm more than ready. Aren't you?'

He fixed his green eyes on mine. I could tell he was struggling to find more reasons not to consummate our relationship and the age of consent thing was such a flimsy excuse. Since he'd started teaching, he'd talked a lot more about the different religions he'd studied for his degree. They all had different views on relationships, sex and marriage, and, even though I knew his love for God was unfaltering, I also knew he was starting to question whether everything about the Catholic faith was right.

'I want to give you your birthday present,' he said.

I grinned. 'I didn't see you bring anything in.'

'My gift isn't big in size, but it's big in meaning. Close your eyes and hold your hands out.'

I did as he instructed. I could hear his shallow breathing, smell soap and shaving balm, feel the light touch of his fingers, as he gently placed something into the palm of my left hand. A shiver of longing ran through me at his touch. It took a hell of a lot of willpower not to drop whatever he'd given me, hurl myself at him and rip his clothes off.

'Open your eyes,' he whispered.

I opened them, looked down and gasped. 'A Claddagh ring?' I picked up the shiny, silver ring with my right hand. It was a simple yet beautiful design with a heart-shaped sapphire.

'It's your birthstone. I'm sorry that it's only sterling silver and a fake sapphire. I promise I'll buy you a better one as soon as I can.'

I shook my head. 'There's no need, Daran. It's absolutely perfect.' My heart raced. I had to ask the question. 'Which way will I wear it?'

He took the ring from me and smiled so tenderly that I feared I might cry. Not wanting to make an assumption, I put my right hand out towards him – right hand, the point of the heart towards the wrist, meaning 'in a relationship' – but he shook his head. He lifted my left hand to his lips, gently kissed it, then slipped the ring onto my fourth finger, with the point of the heart towards my fingertips. A perfect fit. I stared at him, then the ring, then at him again.

Daran got down on his bended knee in the straw. 'When I came to Ballykielty, I never imagined I could love another human being as much as I love God. Then I met you. You showed me a future I'd never considered and you taught me that I can be committed to God's work but also have a family. I love you, Clare, and I want to be with you till the end of forever too. Will you marry me?'

I did cry at that point. My lips trembled and great, fat tears splashed down my cheeks.

Daran leapt to his feet and wrapped his arms around me. 'Was it too much?'

'No. It was perfect, and the answer's yes.'

He stepped back so he could look into my eyes. 'Really?'

'Really. They're happy tears. Honestly.' I wiped my cheeks and passionately kissed my fiancé.

'I think we're ready for the next step,' I whispered, nibbling his ear.

'I'm still not sure.'

I moved my kisses down to his neck, untucked his shirt from his jeans and ran my nails up his bare back. 'We're engaged, aren't we? That's nearly married.'

Daran's breathing quickened. 'Nearly married isn't the same as married,' he whispered.

'I'm just as committed to you right now as I will be when we're married, so what's the difference?'

With shaking hands, I undid his shirt buttons and opened it wide. He gasped as I kissed his chest and my kisses went lower and lower. I wanted to unzip his jeans and continue my kisses down there – the way I'd read in a Jackie Collins novel that Orla Brennan had stolen from her older sister – but I wasn't brave enough. Instead, I worked my way back up to his neck, then gently steered him towards the makeshift bed. He didn't protest as we lay down on the rug and I slipped his shirt off.

'I'd like to give you an engagement gift,' I said.

Holding his gaze, I undid the top two buttons of my dress, revealing my bra. His breathing quickened even more, sending a ripple of electricity through my body. 'I want you, Daran.' I undid the rest of my buttons and he gasped.

'Clare! That's playing dirty.'

I giggled. 'That's what I'm hoping for.' I slipped out of my dress completely and reached round to unclasp my bra. I eased it off my arms and let it slip to the floor. 'I think you might be a bit over-dressed,' I said.

Daran propped himself up on one arm as he lightly traced his other hand down my face, neck and arm, gently skimming my breast and sending another fizz of pleasure through me. 'I do want you too, Clare. You have no idea how much.'

'Then why wait? We love each other. We're engaged. I don't know what else I can say to convince you it's okay to do this.'

When Daran didn't respond but continued to stroke me, touching more of my breast with each hand movement, I knew he didn't need much more convincing. I'd done enough talking. Actions spoke louder than words, didn't they? I reached down and, with fumbling fingers, undid the belt and zip on his jeans. He didn't protest. I slipped my hand inside, hoping I'd learned enough from a combination of biology books and Ms Collins to do things right.

Daran groaned as I touched him through his underwear. This was potentially the point of no return. 'Do you want me to stop?' I whispered. 'Because I will if you *really* want me to. It's just that I don't think you do.'

I caressed him and he groaned again.

'Will I stop?'

'No! Don't stop. Oh, Clare! That feels so... I've never done this before. It might be quick.'

'If it's quick, it's quick. We can always do it again. Lots of times, I hope.'

Daran kissed me. 'Are you sure this is what you want?' he asked.

'Yes! You?'

'May God forgive me, but yes. I really, really do.'

'Then you're wearing too many clothes.'

He wriggled out of his jeans and we lay side by side in only our underwear, gazing into each other's eyes. I lifted my hips up and wriggled out of my panties, then carefully pulled his boxers down and gasped. From the research I'd done, he *really* wanted this.

I straddled him and slowly lowered myself down, letting out a little squeal as he entered me.

'Are you okay? Does it hurt?'

'A bit. Ow! Oh, but it feels good too. Oh my God. Daran! Are you okay?'

'I'm incredible.'

* * *

I collapsed against Daran's chest a few minutes later, trembling from the new sensations. 'Are you okay?' I asked again, feeling him trembling too.

'I'm in shock. I've never... you know... even as a teenager... so that was... that was...' He shook his head. 'Why was I even considering a life in which I'd never get to do that?'

'I take it you enjoyed it.'

'Immensely.'

I snuggled against his bare chest. 'I know you won't like this, Daran, but I'm going to go on the pill. I know someone in Ballyshelty who knows someone who can get me it. I've already got the morning-after pill from them for what we've just done. I know it's not the Catholic way but—'

'It's your body. It's your choice,' he said gently. 'Sure, I can hardly preach about the Catholic way after what I've just done.'

'No regrets?' I asked, looking into his eyes.

'Just one.'

My heart thumped. 'Dare I ask?'

He smiled. 'That it didn't last longer. It will this time, though.' He pulled me closer and kissed me, then rolled me onto my back so he could trace kisses down my body from tip to toe, then back again. By the time he entered me for the second time, I was burning with desire for the man I loved, who now had my heart, mind, soul... and body.

14

Present Day

'Are you sure you'll be okay?' Elise asked, as we stood by her lime-green Beetle in the car park of The Starfish Café. 'You're welcome to stay with Stevie and me.'

I smiled as I shook my head. 'I appreciate the offer but I'm not being a gooseberry.'

'You won't be. Stevie won't mind.'

'Thanks, but no thanks.' I rubbed my hands together. 'It's feckin' freezing. Get yourself home and get your lovely man to warm you up. I need to get back to Leeds and plan what to do next.'

Elise opened her car door. 'You're sure?'

'I'm sure. Be off with you!'

'I really don't think you should be alone at a time like this.'

I laughed. 'You know me. Hard as nails. It takes more than my past catching up with me to knock me down.'

Elise raised an eyebrow at me.

'Go!' I cried. 'That's an order.'

'You're not as hard as you like to make out and you don't need to pretend you are.'

My throat tightened and tears pricked my eyes. I hugged Elise, whispering into her hair, 'Thank you for today.'

'Any time,' she whispered back. 'I mean that.'

We released each other and she eased herself into the driver's seat. 'Go and find your daughter. Keep me posted. I'm here for you.'

'I know.' I waved her off and walked back to my car. I started the engine and turned the heating up full blast but didn't set off. I actually felt quite shaky. Seventeen years. I'd kept my past hidden for seventeen years; more than half my lifetime. But, Christ, it had felt good to finally share it with someone.

Elise had been amazing. She'd listened and she hadn't judged. She'd asked lots of questions, but she seemed to have a gift for asking the right ones; the ones that made me think about what I wanted to do, instead of the sort that were clearly about getting the juicy gossip from the situation and – let's face it – 'sixteen-year-old gets pregnant by former-priest-in-training-turned-teacher' is scandalous stuff. We'd talked for hours and it had done me the world of good. It felt as though the cobwebs on the skeletons in my closet were being blown away. If I'd known that a chat to a friend could have so easily lightened the burden I'd carried for so long, I'd have done it long ago.

I took a swig from a bottle of water in my bag, ran a brush through my tangled hair, then pulled out of the car park. It was fine; I could do this. I was fine on my own. I was used to it.

But as I got closer to Leeds, a feeling of unease overcame me. Bollocks. Elise had been right. I really didn't want to be alone. What choice did I have, though? I could hardly turn round and drive an hour-and-a-half back to Whitsborough Bay and ask to stay the night. Elise and Stevie needed to make the most of their moments together before the baby arrived. If only Ben hadn't gone away for work. I didn't feel the need to talk – I'd done enough of that with Elise – but I did feel the need for company. An evening stretched out in front of the TV with him, a film, a takeaway and some trivial banter would have been perfect. Instead, I had a sparse, soulless, rented apartment and silence to return to. I pictured Ben's cosy lounge and knew what I was going to do.

* * *

There were no lights on at Ben's house, but I still rapped loudly on the door knocker a few times, just in case his plans had changed and he'd unexpectedly returned home for the weekend. When I felt confident that the house really was empty, I let myself in with the spare key that Ben had suggested I hang onto as long as I pinkie-promised him not to break in and steal the king whenever it was in his possession.

I hadn't realised I was quite so tense until I shut the door behind me and a wave of relief washed over me. A small two-up two-down mid-terrace, with film posters on the walls rather than pictures, and piles of books, CDs and DVDs everywhere, Ben's place was homely and safe. It would be my haven for the evening and I'd head back to Orion Point in the morning.

I dumped my handbag in the hallway, wandered through to the kitchen, filled the kettle and popped a bottle of wine into the fridge for later. I went upstairs and poked my head round Ben's bedroom door, just in case, but his room was empty. In my former room at the front of the house, I drew the curtains, then undressed and pulled on a pair of fleecy pyjamas and slipper socks that I kept there.

Thirty minutes later, I was curled up on the sofa with an Indian takeaway, a glass of wine and a film. It had definitely been the right decision to come to Ben's. It was just a shame that he wasn't there.

* * *

Sunday dawned and I still couldn't bring myself to go back to my empty apartment. Even though Ben's house was empty too, it felt different.

I had a long soak in the bath, put on a pair of Ben's PJs and his dressing gown, and retreated to the sofa to watch back-to-back films.

A text came through shortly after I'd had some lunch:

✉ From Sarah
We've landed safely! At Manchester station
waiting to get train home. Can't believe nearly 3

weeks are over already. Should be home by 5.
Catch up soon xx

    I tapped in a response:

✉ To Sarah
Welcome back from honeymoon! Hope you had an
amazing time. Loads to tell you. If you're not
too tired, give me a call when you're settled xx

When 5 p.m. arrived, my stomach did a somersault. Sarah would be home now and could call at any moment. I distracted myself by preparing dinner but once I'd eaten it, I couldn't stop fidgeting. I kept picking up my phone, putting it down, picking it up again. Despite half-expecting her call, I still managed to jump when Sarah's name flashed up on the screen. She was my best and oldest friend. It was ridiculous that I felt nervous about speaking to her.

While walking along the beach with Elise yesterday, she told me that she'd confessed to Sarah about her pregnancy before Sarah left for her honeymoon. Apparently, they'd had a huge argument about keeping secrets. If she'd reacted that badly to a secret Elise had kept from her for five months or so, how was she going to react to something I'd kept from her for the thirteen years since we'd met on our first day at Manchester University?

As I accepted Sarah's call, I toyed with whether I should be opening up to her face-to-face but it could backfire on me. Best get it done now.

* * *

It was the world's worst phone call. I'd imagined all afternoon how it would go and nowhere in my imaginings had I called her a 'selfish eejit', yet that's exactly what I did. I lost it. I'd gone for the pleasantries first – how was Canada/what was the best thing you did/favourite place/was it cold? and all that malarkey – but she gave really brief answers before changing the subject to Elise and Stevie. They'd just visited and told her they were moving in together. She was thrilled they'd got together but worried that they were moving in too soon. And, speaking of moving in together, her Auntie Kay and Philip were also setting up home. Philip was selling his house and Kay was putting Seashell Cottage on the market so that they could buy somewhere together. She seemed really shocked and upset about Kay selling up. As promised, I didn't let on that I knew anything about it, but I didn't get why Sarah was so bothered. It was Kay's decision, not hers.

I should have left my confession for another time. I should have accepted that she'd already had an overload of surprise information that evening and was never going to be able to process what I said. Yet, I blurted it all out. It was the first opportunity to tell her, and I didn't want her getting upset later that I hadn't opened up to her as soon as I'd made the decision to talk about my past.

I'd like to say she was supportive but all I got was, 'What made you confess all this to Elise? When did you two become the best of mates?'

We argued. Nasty things were said by both of us that couldn't be unsaid. She slammed the phone down on me in tears.

In bed that night, I lay there staring at the ceiling, replaying our conversation, and I felt sick. I could see her point. We'd been friends for thirteen years and during all that time, I'd point-blank refused to speak about my past, yet I'd confessed everything to Elise who I'd only become friendly with over the past couple of months. That had to hurt. But surely Sarah could see that it was down to the timing. If she hadn't been on her honeymoon, of course I'd have opened up to her rather than Elise. I just hoped we could put it behind us and move on. I needed my best friend more than ever right now.

15

I sat at the dining table back at Orion Point on Monday morning, staring at Shannon's photo and the list of information about her and her adoptive parents that had accompanied Great-Aunt Nuala's letter. Elise had been right: I was always going to try to find her.

I was meant to be working from home but I couldn't concentrate. Between the letter and the call with Sarah, my mind was on anything but sales figures and promotional strategies. Coffee.

I closed down my spreadsheet, opened Google and typed in: *how would I find a baby given up for adoption?* I scanned down the list of results. 'UK Birth Adoption Register' – seemed like a good starting point. I clicked into it. 'Information on what to do if you were adopted in the UK'. No. I wasn't the one who was adopted. Ah, 'Information on what to do if you gave a child up for adoption in the UK... Unfortunately, under UK law, it is illegal to try to make contact with an adopted child, at least until they turn eighteen years of age.' *Feck. She's only sixteen.*

I scrolled further down the page, clicking on various related websites, but nothing seemed helpful. Then I spotted a link to an adoption-search message board. Interesting. I clicked on it and waited a moment for it to load. A stack of messages appeared and I started scrolling through, but it was going to take forever. There had to be some sort of search facility. It wasn't in an obvious place but I found one and entered her name: Shannon O'Connell... No! Shannon Kitteridge. I triple-checked the spelling on Great-Aunt Nuala's note before I pressed 'return'. Surely there couldn't be many Shannon Kitteridges out there? A page full of messages loaded and my heart leapt, then sank again. All Shannons. No Kitteridges. Bollocks!

I tapped my fingers on the keyboard, then returned to Google and typed in: *Shannon Kitteridge*. A record of a Shannon Kitteridge living in Bognor Regis came up. With shaky fingers, I clicked on it and the first thing I noticed was the age guide of '65-plus'. Bollocks again! I returned to my Google search, but there was nothing. Absolutely nothing. I slumped back on the sofa, arms folded. What next?

As my eyes scanned the table, I clocked the letter from Bowson, Higgs & Crane. They'd offered to help, hadn't they? I reread the letter. It was probably just a polite standard line in all their correspondence, but what the heck? I dialled the number and quoted my great-aunt's name.

'Hello, Ms O'Connell, this is Angela Crane. I was your great-aunt's solicitor. Am I right in thinking you've received her letter?'

'Last week. You said to call you if you could help me...?'

'Of course. What's your query?'

'It's a long shot...' I explained about the content of the letter.

After I'd finished, Angela said, 'Unfortunately, under UK law, it's illegal to search for a child you've given up for adoption until they've turned eighteen and are therefore classed by law as an adult.'

'I'm aware of that, and Shannon won't be eighteen for another eighteen months. Is there anything else that can be done?'

'I'm assuming you've Googled her name?'

'Yes.'

'And those of the adoptive parents?'

'Muppet! I never thought of that. Thanks, Angela.' Before she could respond, I hung up and quickly typed in the names of Paul and Christine Kitteridge, plus Northampton, where Great-Aunt Nuala had said they lived.

The search revealed several newspaper articles. I'd found them. 'Ooh. They're both dead.'

I called Angela again.

'I think we got cut off,' she said, a little sharply.

'I'm sorry. I hung up in my excitement. Are you by a computer?'

'Yes. Why?'

'I know this may seem a little unusual, but can I ask you to Google something and see what you make of it? You can bill me for the time I've taken up.'

There was a pause and a sigh. 'Okay. You have my attention, but only because my ten o'clock has failed to show. What do you want me to Google?'

'Paul and Christine Kitteridge of Northampton.' I heard her tapping on a keyboard. 'Click on the article a few results down that says, "Tragic couple leave daughter" and tell me what you make of it.'

The line went quiet. As I waited impatiently for her to speak, I scanned down the article again. They had to be the same family.

'Hello, Ms O'Connell. It would seem that these are the same people who adopted your daughter. The problem is, it gives no indication of where she went next. Foster care is most likely, as it says that neither Mr nor Mrs Kitteridge had siblings.'

'So, what do I do next?'

'All I can suggest is that you make contact with Social Services in Northampton. They may not be able to help, given the law, but they'd be your best starting point. Because Shannon's adoptive parents are deceased, it puts the law into a different context, but the law is there to protect the child as much as the parents, and the fact still remains that Shannon is under eighteen. I wish I could help further but I'm not a specialist in this area. Would you like me to recommend someone who is?'

My heart sank. It was over. Well, for now anyway. 'I might come back to you on that.'

Angela gave me her email address in case I did want a recommendation, then wished me luck again before hanging up. I reread the article. Shannon's adoptive mother had been active in fundraising for heart disease after losing both parents to it but had died prematurely herself after a massive heart attack, leaving behind an adopted ten-year-old daughter. Three years later, her adoptive father dropped dead from an aneurysm. Absolutely tragic.

I shook my head, sent the article to print and emailed a copy to Elise to get her take on it. I was still sulking too much to share it with Sarah. My head throbbed and I felt emotionally drained. Very emotionally drained.

* * *

'Hi, Elise,' I said, turning down my music in the car on Saturday morning.

'Are you driving?' she asked.

'Yes, but I'm on hands-free. I'm actually on my way to Whitsborough Bay. Thought I'd pay a surprise visit to Sarah and see if we can get things back on track.' I'd decided that, with everything else that was going on, I didn't need the stress of falling out with my oldest friend right now.

'Do you fancy meeting me first to chat about the article you sent me?'

'You don't mind me taking more of your time?'

'Of course not. That's what friends are for.' There was a pause. 'There's also something I need to tell you.'

My stomach lurched. 'Are you okay? Is the baby okay?'

'We're both fine. It's something else, but it's not a conversation for the phone. Could you come to the house?'

'Sounds serious. I'm pulling into a lay-by. You can give me the postcode for my sat nav.'

* * *

Half an hour later, I pulled up outside Elise and Stevie's home – Bramble Cottage in Little Sandby. I gave Stevie a quick hug. He made drinks, then muttered some excuse about work before heading upstairs.

'Spill,' I said, sitting down on the sofa. 'I can't stand the suspense.'

'Please don't be mad at me. I know you said you didn't want to find Daran but it was such a romantic story, and curiosity got the better of me, so I Googled him.'

My heart thumped and I felt a little light-headed. I slumped back in my seat. 'Elise! What did I say to you just last Saturday?'

'I know. I was being nosy and I had no plans to share my findings with you. Only, I think you should know what I found out.'

I sighed. 'If you're going to tell me he married a nun and spawned the next von Trapp family, I'm really not interested.' I realised as I said it that I absolutely didn't want to hear that he'd got married. That was what *we* had wanted. It wasn't right to think that he'd done that with someone else.

Elise bit her lip. 'After he left your village, he went to Thailand to do some sort of missionary work.'

'And he shacked up with a ladyboy?' It felt inappropriate to say it, but after a decade and a half of trying not to think about Daran, discussing him like this was a bit overwhelming, and humour was the only defence mechanism I had in me.

Elise shook her head. 'He was there in 2004.'

'So?'

'Christmas, 2004.'

'So?'

'Boxing Day, 2004. Thailand.'

My hand went to my mouth. 'The tsunami?' I whispered.

Elise nodded. 'I'm so sorry, Clare.'

My mouth went very dry. 'He's dead?'

'I found this article online.'

Elise handed me a crumpled piece of paper, but my eyes couldn't seem to focus on the words. 'What does it say?'

She perched on the edge of the coffee table. 'Do you want me to read it to you?'

I reached for the Claddagh ring I now wore on my right hand and twisted it around my finger. Somehow, I found the strength to nod.

Catholic Online

16th January 2005

A service was held yesterday in St Mary's Pro-Cathedral in Dublin to commemorate the thousands who tragically lost their lives during the tsunami that hit Thailand, Indonesia and the surrounding area on 26th December 2004, or during the days that followed.

Among those specifically remembered was humanitarian Daran Seamus McInnery. Mr McInnery had been working tirelessly with local communities in Sumatra for three years, having previously supported community work in Counties Wicklow and Cork.

Mr McInnery was the eldest of eight siblings. His three sisters and four brothers all attended the service, along with his mother. His father had passed away shortly after his youngest sister was born.

I felt as if I were swimming in glue, unable to move or breathe or think straight. I listened to Elise's fuzzy words, my mind saying over and over, 'It might not be him,' but the facts were there: the middle name, the communities in Ireland, the seven siblings, the deceased father. It was definitely him. The last thing I heard was Elise shouting for Stevie to help her. Then the room went dark.

'Do you know what would happen to us if anyone ever found out?' Daran kissed my forehead as he wrapped his arms more tightly around me. I leaned back into his embrace.

'What could they do? Order us to stop being in love?'

'They could order it, but it would never happen. I know I've said it before but I really will love you until the end of forever, Clare. I hope you know that.'

'And I'll love you longer than that, you great big eejit.'

'I'm serious, though,' he said. 'There'd be consequences. Big ones. For both of us. They'd send me away. You too.'

I stroked his strong forearms. 'Then I'd jump in me da's car and chase after you.'

'You can't drive.'

I lay in Daran's arms in silence, trying to imagine life without him. 'I really would follow you,' I said. 'To the ends of the earth.'

He kissed my forehead again. 'You know where I'd really like to go?'

'Where?'

'The Far East. Places like Thailand, Malaysia, China, Vietnam, the Philippines.'

'Why there?'

'It sounds daft, but I had a dream many years ago where I was standing on a beach in Indonesia and it was like paradise on earth. A small boy came up to me and asked me to help his family. He led me to a village, where he lived in a shack – corrugated iron and bits of wood hammered together. It was a world away from what I knew, yet I felt God's presence more strongly than I'd ever felt it before.'

'I could come with you,' I said. 'Let's leave this place. Run away. Be together where nobody knows us and nobody will judge us.'

Daran turned my face gently and kissed me. I melted into his kiss as always. 'I want to take you up on that right now. I really do. But you need to finish school first. Do you hear me?'

'Why?'

'Because an education opens doors. It's only two more years. It'll fly by. You'll see. But finish your education. Do you hear me, Clare?'

* * *

'Do you hear me, Clare? Can you hear me?'

'Daran?' I whispered.

'It's Stevie. You fainted.'

'Drink this.' A glass was pressed against my lips and I took a sip of cold water, then another. I opened my eyes. Elise and Stevie were both crouched on the floor in front of me.

'You had us really scared there,' Elise said. 'I was about to call for an ambulance. Should I still do that?'

I took another couple of sips of water. 'Bollocks to that. I know I like drama but that's going a bit far, even for me. You know, Daran told me he wanted to go to the Far East to help the communities there. I was going to go with him when I finished school. I'd forgotten about that conversation.'

Stevie handed me the glass. 'I'm sorry.'

I sighed. 'I'm sorry too. He was a very special person.' I took a few more sips of water. 'I can't believe he's gone.'

Elise took my hand. 'Did I do the right thing in telling you?'

I nodded. 'Can I read it myself?'

Elise handed me the article. I read it over and over again and shook my head as tears streamed down my cheeks. Still the same words. Still the same message. Still gone. I wiped my tears again and looked at Elise. 'Hard as it was to hear, I'm glad I know. I told you last Saturday that I hadn't thought about Daran much over the last five years or so, and I really haven't. But this week I haven't stopped thinking about him. I'm sure I'd have searched eventually, so I'm glad I know.'

'What are you going to do now?' Stevie asked.

'You're not the only one who's been going mad on Google. I found out this week that Shannon's adoptive parents are dead. Seems there's a lot of it going around. I'm going to call Social Services on Monday and find out my options for tracking her down, especially as she's officially an orphan now. After that, there's something very important that I need to do.'

'What's that?' Elise asked.

'Go back to Ballykielty and confront my da.' I winced as I felt my nails digging into my palms, but I couldn't unclench my fists. 'I thought about writing that letter you suggested, Elise, but it wouldn't be enough. I need to look him in the eye. I'm owed an apology and I'm owed a hell of a lot of answers. When I saw him a couple of weeks ago, I crumbled before him, but I didn't know that Shannon had lived or that Daran had died. I hold him personally responsible for both of those things and, even if I get no answers, I want him to know what I think of him.'

16

Elise opened the door to Sarah's shop, Seaside Blooms, and the little bell tinkled. She'd rung Sarah to explain what had happened.

Sarah put down the bouquet she was making and rushed over, looking very worried. 'Are you okay?'

I nodded. 'I'm grand. Embarrassed, but grand. I don't think I've ever fainted before.'

'We've had a pretty chilled afternoon,' Elise said. 'I got Gary to pop round and give her a once-over, but he says she's fine and should just rest for a bit.' Elise's ex was a GP, a handy person to call on in circumstances like this.

'Am I okay to stay at yours tonight?' I asked Sarah.

'Of course. You know you're welcome any time. Cuppa?'

'Coffee, please.'

'Are you stopping?' she asked Elise.

'I've got some things to do so I'll love you and leave you. Take it easy, Clare.' She hugged me then left the shop.

'So, what happened?' Sarah asked. 'Elise said it was something to do with Daran, but she didn't say what.'

I was about to tell her but the door opened and several customers came in. 'You need to get on with your work,' I said. 'Do you mind if I have my drink out the back? I'll tell you everything when we get back to yours.'

* * *

After dinner at Sarah's, Nick went to the pub with Stevie, leaving Sarah and me to talk. I opened up to her properly for the first time ever. I told her about my brothers and sisters, how strict Da was and how Ma had always acted as if she hated me. I talked in detail about the Mass where I first saw Daran and how our secret relationship had developed. The more I spoke, the more the memories tumbled out.

'You're really going back to Ireland to confront your dad?' she asked, when I'd finished. 'Do you want me to come with you?'

'You'd do that?'

'Of course. You've always been there for me. I want to be there for you.'

'Thank you. That means a lot, but this is something I need to do on my own. I may need you when I get back, though.'

'I'll be here. When are you going?'

'I might fly out on Thursday night and confront them on Friday. If I chicken out, I've still got Saturday.'

'You're absolutely sure you don't want some moral support?'

'I'm sure. Besides, you've got a business to run. I know you're the boss but you've been away for three weeks already. Another few days would seriously be taking the piss, wouldn't it now?'

She laughed. 'You might have a point.'

It was after 3 a.m. before we finally called it a night. As I brushed my teeth, it struck me how great a friend Sarah had been over the years and how much I'd taken her friendship for granted. It must have been really difficult to deal with my mood swings and my refusal to talk about the past, yet she'd put up with it for thirteen years. I vowed never to take our friendship for granted again.

17

'What the hell are you doing here? You're not welcome.'

'Hello, Ma,' I said.

Her pale-grey eyes flashed with hate and bitterness. Her dark hair, streaked liberally with grey, was pulled back into a bun that emphasised the hard angles of her jaw and cheekbones. Frown lines creased her forehead. There was no evidence of laughter lines. My stomach churned and my first instinct was to turn round, jump into my hire car and speed back to Cork. But my need for answers was greater than my fear. Somehow, I mustered the strength to keep my shoulders back, my head held high and my voice steady. 'I'd like to say it's great to see you but that would be a lie.'

'You cheeky... What do you want?'

'I want to speak to Da and I'm not leaving until I do.'

'He's not here.'

'We both know that's a big fib. I saw him at the window just now. You might as well let me in because I'll only stand here and make a scene if you don't.'

'You wouldn't.'

'Is that a challenge?'

I stood on the doorstep, arms folded, holding her stare.

'Let her in, Maeve,' shouted Da from the living room.

Ma turned her back on me and yelled, 'She's not welcome here.'

'I didn't say she was welcome. I said let her in, woman, before the neighbours see her.'

Ma shook her head and narrowed her eyes at me but stepped back and held the door open.

'You'll not be wheedling your way back into his affections, you know. He hates you.' She practically spat the words.

I took a deep breath as I followed her into the living room. I didn't want to be part of their lives but hearing that Da hated me still hurt.

'So, you came crawling back.' Da glared at me.

I couldn't help looking round me. The wallpaper had changed and there might have been a new carpet but everything else was still the same, from the gold-coloured sofa with tassels around the base to the huge-backed TV, to the dresser covered in decorative plates depicting Jesus and Mary, and wooden crucifixes.

'You're not the prodigal daughter, you know.' He folded his newspaper and tossed it onto the floor before standing up. 'There's no forgiveness in this house.'

'I never expected to be welcomed back. And I wouldn't want to be. As for your forgiveness, I don't want it and I don't need it.'

'I'm not going to invite you to sit,' he said.

'I don't want to sit.'

'And you needn't think I'll be offering you any tea,' Ma said.

'All I've come for is some information, then I'll be out of your lives forever.'

Da scowled at me. 'As far as we were concerned, you were already out of our lives forever. Yet somehow you're here for the second time this month.'

'I want to know why you were so quick to disown me.' How I kept my voice calm, I'd never know.

Ma let out a high-pitched sound like a hysterical laugh. Da shook his head. 'I should have thought that would be obvious,' he snapped. 'You brought shame to your family and damaged a good man's name with your whoring ways.' The bitterness with which he spat out the last words cut through me. The years hadn't softened him at all.

'We were in love.'

He stamped his foot on the floor like a child having a tantrum. 'Blasphemy.'

'It's *not* blasphemy. Daran was young, I was young and we loved each other.'

'You seduced him, so you both had to pay the price.'

'Why were you so quick to believe it was *me* who seduced *him*?'

'I used to watch you, and how men and boys reacted to you. You weren't studious like Aisling or plain like Nia. You were precocious and curious. As a toddler, it was refreshing. As a growing woman, it was dangerous. Your ma and I always knew you'd let us down. You brought shame on our family name.'

'How? How could I have caused shame when nobody knew about the baby?'

'It wasn't just the baby,' Ma cried. 'It was everything about you. The way you dressed, the way you spoke, the way you flicked your hair. Everything about you said "harlot" and, to be sure, look what you became – Jezebel herself.'

Watching her eyes flash with hate and the colour in Da's cheeks darken with each word, I realised it was pointless and that they weren't worth it. Why had I thought for even a second that we might have a sit-down conversation tinged with regret and sadness, instead of a slanging match? Clearly, their opinion hadn't changed since the day they'd disowned me. It seemed that time had deepened their hatred instead of easing it. 'Seventeen years haven't mellowed either of you, so I'll be going soon. Before I do, I want to know two things.'

Da crossed his arms. 'The first will be...?'

'Why did you get Great-Aunt Nuala to say that my baby had died?'

A flicker of something flashed across his eyes. Doubt, perhaps? 'The baby *did* die,' he declared, holding himself upright and strong.

'Bullshit,' I snapped. 'Shannon's alive, and you know it.'

He visibly flinched when I used her name. He probably hadn't realised I'd named my daughter. His granddaughter. 'How do you know?' he snapped.

'Nuala wrote to me on her deathbed. She couldn't live with the guilty secret on her conscience. She told me why *she* went through with it. I want to know why *you* did. I was giving her up for adoption. I wasn't about to return to Ireland with my baby in tow to bring shame on you all, so why take it that step further?'

'Because.'

'Because what?' I was struggling to sound calm now.

'Because I had no choice.'

'That's bullshit too. Why did you do it?' I yelled. 'Why did you tell such an evil lie?'

'Because.'

'That's not an answer, and you know it. Why?'

'Because I wanted you to feel what I was feeling.' He uncrossed his arms and clenched his fists by his side. I sensed it was taking all his willpower not to strike me.

'What does that mean?'

'The day I found out about your treachery, you became dead to me. I wanted you to know what it felt like to lose a child.'

'I wasn't dead.'

'You were. You are. I told you back then that you were dead to me and I meant it. Now leave this house and, this time, don't ever return.'

I stared at him, wanting to say more, but my legs were shaking, my heart was racing and I was desperate to leave. After all these years, he still terrified me and I hated that he had that power over me. Ma was less terrifying – possibly because there'd never been any love lost between us – but I still squirmed in her presence.

'I'll go,' I said, hoping my voice sounded confident. 'And don't you worry, there's nothing for me here anymore without Daran. I won't be back.'

He followed me to the door. 'Like I give a damn what you do with your life. You're not my daughter. I don't care about you or anything that happens to you. Why is that so hard to get through your thick skull?'

I opened my mouth to speak but I couldn't form any words. Ma appeared by his side, arms crossed, eyes narrowed.

'Not that I'm remotely interested,' Da said, 'but what was the other question?'

'What?'

'You said you had two questions to ask me. What was the second one?'

'It was... em...' I tried to stand tall and force out the words, but the two hateful pairs of eyes boring into me were too much. And it didn't matter. I had planned to ask him how he lived with himself knowing what he'd done, but I could see the answer right in front of me. Quite easily. He hated me and when he'd said I was dead to him, he'd really meant it.

He planted his hands on his hips. 'Great second question, Clare. I bet you're really glad you flew here to ask that. I think we're done here, so we are.' He pointed to my hire car parked outside the house. 'Get in that thing and get out of here. I never, ever, *ever* want to see you again. Is that clear?'

I nodded. Crystal clear.

I made it four miles outside Ballykielty before I had to pull over and give way to my emotions. Facing him again had been terrifying, and I'd managed to let him intimidate me and throw me out yet again. I hadn't had the last word. I hadn't stood up to him. For Christ's sake!

As I dabbed my eyes and blew my nose, a battered silver Micra pulled up in front of me and a woman with shoulder-length dark hair got out and strode towards my car. *Oh Christ, who's this now? Someone to escort me to the airport and make sure I don't bring more embarrassment to the village?*

She knocked on the window. I reluctantly wound down the window, preparing myself for a torrent of verbal abuse at best, or a slap at worst.

'Clare? Is it really yourself?' asked the woman.

'Who's asking?'

'Your big sister.'

I did a double take. 'Aisling?'

She nodded and her face crumpled as the tears fell.

I clambered out of the car and she rushed at me, hugging me tightly. 'Can you forgive me for not coming after you? I'm your big sister. I should have protected you, but I did nothing. It doesn't mean I haven't thought about you every day since you left. I failed you, so I did. I'm so very sorry, Clare.'

I relaxed into her arms. 'I don't think there's anything you could have done. I don't think he'd have let you.'

She released me from her embrace but kept her hands on my shoulders and stared into my eyes. 'I can do something now, though. Can we go for a drink?'

'You're sure you want to be seen with the enemy?'

'Enemy, my arse. You're my sister.'

I followed Aisling in my car as she drove through various villages to the outskirts of Cork and a pub called The Burnt Whiskers.

'I'm friends with the owner,' she said as we walked across the car park. 'Nobody from our village comes here. We'll be safe to talk properly with no risk of Ma or Da appearing.'

'How on earth did you know I was here?'

'My friend Niamh lives over the road. She saw you arrive and phoned me. I was in the supermarket and I abandoned my trolley and sped over, praying I hadn't missed you.'

For the next three hours, we talked non-stop. Aisling had been approaching twenty-two and was completing the final year of a science and teaching degree at Limerick when I was banished to England. She'd come home for the Christmas holidays but was at a New Year's Eve party when it happened. She'd woken up the next morning to find my bedroom empty and was told that I'd decided I wanted to study in England.

'It was the oddest thing,' she said. 'They never breathed a word about it. I had to ask why your room was empty. When I say "empty", I mean completely empty. There was no furniture or anything.'

I gasped. 'They'd gutted my room?'

Aisling nodded. 'It was like you'd died and all trace of you had been wiped out. The thing about studying in England made no sense. You'd have had to go back a couple of years at school. Why would you do that? Da went mad at me for questioning him. I was told it was none of my business and I should drop the subject or I could get the next train back to Limerick and see how I managed the rest of my degree with no financial support.'

'That was harsh.'

'He's a harsh man, Clare, as you've experienced first-hand. I tried to quiz Nia about it. She told me that Father Doherty came round, she and the twins were sent out to visit friends, and when they came back, you were gone and your room was empty. I asked her whether she thought your sudden departure was something to do with your secret boyfriend but—'

'You knew I was seeing someone?'

'Someone kept stealing my underwear and I couldn't imagine it was Nia or Ma.'

I clapped my hand over my mouth. 'Jesus! I'm sorry. I had no money to get my own. I didn't mean to keep them.'

She laughed. 'It's fine. I found it quite funny. Anyway, Da chose that very moment to walk past and overhear me. He got really jittery and insisted that you'd never had a boyfriend and had always wanted to study in England. One more word and I could join you.'

'I'm sorry you got into trouble.'

Aisling smiled. 'Don't be. I could handle myself by then. Moving to Limerick was the best thing I ever did because I got free from his control and found out who I was. I discovered I had a voice and opinions and a life that wasn't controlled by him and the Church. But I also wasn't stupid. I needed his financial support to finish my degree so I dropped the subject at home. I did my Miss Marple bit out of earshot and discovered that Daran McInnery had been whisked away from the village and nobody seemed to know why. Rumours ranged from his ma being ill to an inappropriate relationship with a married woman, but a million little things suddenly made sense and I just knew that he was your secret boyfriend and that both of you leaving wasn't a coincidence.'

'Did you say anything when you'd made the connection?'

She laughed. 'I must like to live dangerously because I confronted Da. He denied it, of course, but his eyes gave him away. You might remember that I'd always been close to Father Doherty. I might have made out that Da had confirmed the relationship. Believing I knew everything, Father Doherty mentioned the baby. I'm so sorry for what Ma and Da did to you, so I am.'

'Father Doherty was there too, you know.'

Aisling nodded. 'He told me. He also said it was the worst thing that he'd ever experienced. Da had led him to believe that you'd have the baby, it would be adopted, then you'd come home and continue as before. He had no idea they were going to cut you off forever or he'd never have helped them.'

'To be fair, he did try to stop them but their minds were set. They told me I was dead to them and would never be welcome in their lives. Ever. Something they reminded me of again just now.'

Aisling closed her eyes and shook her head. 'You were sixteen. I know you were mature, but you were still only sixteen. What were they thinking?' She reached for my hand across the table. 'I want you to know that I wrote to you as soon as I knew but I had nowhere to send the letters. Father Doherty wouldn't tell me where you'd gone but he said he'd pass my letters on. I wrote every week for six months, then every month for six years.'

'What made you stop writing?'

'More like who. A package arrived with all my letters unopened and a letter from Great-Aunt Nuala. She admitted that you'd stayed with her in Cornwall and you'd gone to university but she had no idea where you were anymore, so I might as well save myself the postage. I should have tried to find you but I was married by then; I had a baby, and life just got in my way.'

'You have a child? I'm an auntie?'

She smiled. 'Twice over. Torin is ten and Briyana is eight, but I'm separated from their da. He lives in Manchester now.'

'Oh no! I'm sorry.'

'Don't be. Finn and I were friends who tried to make a marriage work, which was fine until he met someone he wanted to be more than friends with. You can imagine what Da had to say about that.'

'I bet he thought it was your fault.'

'Of course. Apparently, I didn't know how to keep my man happy so it was no wonder he looked elsewhere.'

'Sounds just like Da. What about Nia, Keenan and Éamonn? Do they know what happened to me? Do they care?'

She shrugged. 'There was no point in talking about it at the time. Keenan and Éamonn were like mini versions of Da and Nia was too scared to talk about it. She married someone just like Da, poor thing. She isn't allowed to wear make-up, to work, to have an opinion or do anything that would make her a real person. I don't really see much of her, but I do see the boys from time to time.'

'Did any of them know about the baby?'

She shrugged. 'I don't think so. If they did, they never mentioned it. Father Doherty told me the baby died. I'm sorry about that.'

'She didn't die,' I said. 'They lied about that too.'

Aisling cried when I told her about Great-Aunt Nuala's letter and my findings about Shannon since then. 'Just when I think that man can't get any lower... Oh, Clare, you must have been to hell and back. And poor Daran. I liked him.'

My heart raced at the mention of his name. 'We were going to get married. He gave me this, although I wear it on the other hand now.' I stretched out my hand with the Claddagh ring on it.

'It's beautiful,' she said. 'He must have really loved you to give up joining the priesthood, which makes the whole thing even more tragic.' She bit her lip. 'Oh Christ! You do know about him...?'

'Yes. A friend Googled him and found out about Thailand. Discovering that he died and Shannon lived made me determined to confront Da, which is why I was at the house today. I wanted answers. Fat lot of good it did me. I let him get to me again and bollocksed the whole thing up. Stood there like a right eejit, quaking in my boots.'

'I'm sure you didn't bollocks it up. Did you get any answers?'

'Yes. I didn't like them, but at least I got them.'

'Then it's mission successful or mission partly successful, isn't it?'

I smiled at my sister. 'I suppose so.'

'Purely selfishly, I'd say it was very successful because, if you hadn't visited them, I'd never have found you and I'm absolutely thrilled to finally catch up.'

'Thank you. Me too.'

'If your man, Daran, had still been alive, would you have tried to pick things up with him?'

I shook my head vigorously. 'No. It's been too long. I still love him, I always will, but there'd have been so many regrets niggling away that I don't know if we'd have made it. I thought about him constantly for years, though. I ached for him. I wrote long letters to him and posted them without Great-Aunt Nuala's knowledge. I didn't know where to post them, though. The only place I could think of was care of Father Doherty. Ma had threatened to call the Guards if I tried to contact him, but they obviously hadn't knocked all of the rebellion out of me, as I wrote anyway. I have no idea if Father Doherty delivered them. I suspect not because Great-Aunt Nuala said she told him to destroy the letters that Daran sent him for me. I wonder if he did.'

'Only one way to find out.' Aisling knocked back the last of her orange juice and stood up. 'Let's go now.'

'Where?'

'To see Father Doherty and ask him about the letters.'

My eyes widened. 'He's here?'

Aisling pulled her coat on. 'He's in a retirement home about ten minutes away. I visit him every few weeks. He sometimes asks about you, but I've never been able to tell him anything. He'll be delighted to see you.'

'Really? I know he tried to convince Da not to disown me but he still believed I was a sinner.'

'I think you'll find that old age and retirement have had a profound effect on our former priest. Come on.'

As we stepped out of the pub, she turned to me. 'Are you ready to face your past now?'

Was I? I'd already made one failed attempt this morning with the parents but, as Aisling pointed out, I *had* got some answers, even if I didn't like them. I'd also had an unexpected serendipitous moment in finding a sister who'd never stopped caring and trying to find out what had happened. Could Father Doherty hold more answers?

'Your kids?' I said, grabbing her arm. 'Who's got your kids?'

'Don't you be worrying yourself about that. They're with Finn's parents. They stay there every Friday night which is great because it means they don't miss out on time with their nice set of grandparents. So I'm free all night. Are you ready?'

I opened the door of my hire car. 'I'm ready. Bring it on!'

18

'Are you sure it's okay for me to turn up unannounced?' Seeing Father Doherty had seemed like a good idea in the pub but now, in the car park of the retirement home, it didn't seem such an enticing plan. I'd already faced two of my demons and it hadn't been pleasant. Was I strong enough to face the third?

'And here was me thinking you were a strong, confident woman,' Aisling said.

'I am. I'm just thinking of Father Doherty. I don't want him to drop dead of a heart attack at the sight of me.'

Aisling laughed and grabbed my hand. 'I think you'll be pleasantly surprised. He had a stroke round about the time Daran died. It seemed to really mellow him.' I followed her along a carpeted corridor until she stopped outside a door with the number thirty-six on it and a simple wooden cross. 'Are you ready to face himself?'

I drew a deep breath. 'As ready as I'll ever be.'

She knocked on the door, then turned the handle. 'Father Doherty? Are you home? It's Aisling.'

'Aisling? Come in, child, come in.'

She pushed the door wide open and we stepped into a small hallway. We walked past a couple of closed doors then into an open-plan lounge/diner/kitchen. He was reclining in an armchair by the window with a glass of sherry on a table beside him and classical music playing.

'I've brought someone to see you.' Aisling pushed me forward. 'Someone from your past.'

He looked in my direction expectantly and frowned. He removed his glasses, opened his mouth, replaced his glasses, then closed his mouth. Still staring at me, he pressed his feet on the recliner to bring the chair to an upright position, then shuffled towards me. 'It can't be,' he said. 'Is it yourself, young Clare?'

I nodded.

He reached out his hands and took both of mine in his, then brought them to his mouth and kissed them. 'I always prayed that I'd have a chance to meet you again one day and now the Lord has delivered you to me. Come and sit. Please.'

I looked at Aisling and she nodded encouragingly. I sat down on a two-seater sofa next to Aisling as Father Doherty shuffled back to his armchair.

'It really is you?' he said.

I finally found my voice. 'It really is me, Father. How are you?'

'Blessed,' he said. 'Blessed to see that you have grown into a fine young woman after everything your parents and I did to you. I have dreamt I could make amends for so many years and now here you are like an angel of mercy, so you are.'

'I'm confused, Father,' I said. 'You seem pleased to see me.'

'Of course I am, my child.'

'Why?'

'Because you've never been far from my thoughts for nearly two decades. I've longed to make sure you're well and to ask for your forgiveness for the part I played in your exile. Tell me, how is the child? She'd be, what, sixteen now? Does she look like you?'

'You don't know, do you?'

'Don't know what?'

'Why do you think my da sent me to Cornwall?'

'So you could have your baby away from the gossip and rumours in the village and give her a better start in life.'

I looked at Aisling but she shrugged and mouthed, 'I thought he knew.'

I took a deep breath as I looked back towards Father Doherty. 'Da arranged for Shannon to be adopted, but they told me she'd died shortly after she was born.'

'She died? Oh no, child. That's too tragic.' He closed his eyes.

'She didn't really die, though, Father,' I added quickly. 'It was just a ploy to stop me finding her. She was adopted by another family, which I only found out a week ago when I was sent a confession letter that my Great-Aunt Nuala wrote before she died.'

He opened his eyes. 'Oh my goodness! I should have realised something was afoot when your da didn't want to talk about his grandchild. He told me that he was in touch with you and had offered you the chance to return, but you loved it in Cornwall and wanted to stay.'

More lies. How could someone who claimed to be such a devoted Catholic lie as easily as breathing? I sat forward. 'Can I ask you a question, Father?'

'Of course.'

'What happened to the letters I sent you for Daran? Did he ever get them?'

He sighed, then stood up and shuffled out of the room. I heard the sound of a cupboard opening, then he reappeared holding a cardboard box. 'Here.' He handed the box to me.

I opened the lid. On the top lay a large bundle of letters in various pastel-coloured envelopes, tied together with a piece of string. 'My letters. You kept them. I take it Daran never saw them?'

'I'm sorry, child. Daran was a good man from a good family. I wanted to protect him, and them, from scandal. If word had got out that he'd impregnated a minor...' He shook his head. 'I'm afraid your da threatened to contact the Guards if I acted as any sort of conduit between the two of you. I felt I had no choice. What good would it have done for anyone if he'd been arrested? It could have ruined both of you, and I only wanted what was best for you and the child.'

I pulled out another bundle from underneath. 'These are for me. This is Daran's writing. You didn't destroy them?'

'Your great-aunt asked me to, but I couldn't do it.'

I stared at the bundles of letters, my emotions in turmoil. 'Did Daran know you had letters from me?'

'Yes.'

'Did he know his letters never made it to me?'

'Yes.'

'Then why did he write?'

Father Doherty looked at me with watery eyes. 'For the same reason that you wrote to him for all those years.'

I gently placed the bundles back in the box. It had been my way of keeping our love alive. It had also been my way of coping. If I hadn't been able to hide away in my room for hours and write, I'm not sure I'd have got through it. It was comforting to know that Daran had done the same. It was further evidence that Da's claims that I hadn't been the only one were absolute bullshit. He wouldn't have written so many letters if I'd meant as little to him as Da had tried to make out. And he wouldn't have given me the Claddagh ring. I twiddled it again.

'We were going to get married,' I said. 'He proposed to me on my sixteenth birthday. He gave me this.'

'I know.'

I stopped fiddling with it. 'He told you?'

'He asked me to hear his Confession. Oh, child, you do know what happened to him, don't you?'

I nodded.

He sighed and shook his head. 'Tragic. Absolutely tragic. I blamed myself for my part in him being in Thailand that day.' He leaned forward in his chair. 'He really loved you, you know. All I could think of in that memorial service was how I should have been strong and asked God what to do about the two of you, rather than being led by your da. If I'd done that, things could have been very different.'

We sat in silence for a while. I riffled through the letters although I didn't open any. I didn't feel strong enough.

A glass of water was pushed into my hands. I hadn't realised Father Doherty had got up. I sipped it slowly.

'We should go,' I said. 'Can I have these?'

'The letters are yours, my child. I'm sorry Daran's are with you too late.'

'You weren't to know. I blame my da for all of this. Not you. So if it's forgiveness you want, you have it. Although part of me wishes you had passed on our letters, I have no doubt that Da would have called the Guards on Daran. What good would that have done anyone? You did the right thing in the circumstances.'

A flicker of what I could only describe as peace passed over the old man's face. 'What you do next is entirely up to you, Clare, but I implore you to draw a line in the sand and move on. What's done is done and we can't change the past, but you have a chance for a new future. Find Shannon and don't waste a further thought on your father. He'll be judged by the Lord when the day comes. You don't need to waste the energy on judging him yourself, so you don't.'

Aisling and I hugged him goodbye, then left his flat and walked to the car park in silence.

'Thank you,' I said to her, when we reached the cars. 'I'm glad you made me do that.'

'I told you he'd changed,' she said. 'What happens next?'

I shrugged. 'I don't know. I feel drained.'

'I'm not surprised. Will you be reading the letters, do you think?'

I screwed my nose up. 'Not sure I'm strong enough for it today. I never cry, but I've barely stopped since finding out about Shannon. If I start on these today, it might completely break me.'

Aisling smiled and patted my arm. 'The main thing is that you have them. You'll know when the time is right. Will you go back tomorrow?'

'Probably. I booked a Sunday flight in case I bottled seeing the parents today, but the deed is done so I'll see if I can change it for the morning.'

'I understand if you want to head home after what you've been through today, but I'd love it if you'd stay. I know a couple of kids who'd be thrilled to spend a day with their long-lost Auntie Clare.'

'They know about me?'

Aisling grinned. 'Not the full family scandal, but they know I have a baby sister who lives in England with whom I lost touch. They'll be thrilled.'

'You're sure it wouldn't be too complicated?' I asked.

'It would be a pleasure.'

'If I spend the day with you, I have one condition.'

'Name it.'

'We don't talk about the past. I've had my fill of history today. Tomorrow I just want to focus on getting to know my big sister, my nephew and my niece.'

'You're on.' She flung her arms around me. 'Jesus, Clare, I'm so glad you came back. The rest of the family may be bloody eejits but I want my baby sister in my life.' Her voice cracked. 'I hope you want me in yours.'

The tears started again. 'Of course I do. You're the only family I have.'

'You get three of us for the price of one. Not bad, eh?'

As I drove back to my hotel, I glanced at the box of letters on the passenger seat and shook my head. What a day. Of all the ways I'd played it out in my mind, I hadn't expected to end it having gained a sister, a nephew and a niece. For the first time since I was sixteen, I had a family. I had real-life blood relatives who wanted me in their lives. Most unexpected.

19

'Will you stop passing me from one department to the next?' I snapped on Monday morning. 'I've been on the phone for forty minutes and I'm going round in circles.'

'It's illegal for a mother to try and find out about her adopted child before they're eighteen,' said the woman on the end of the phone.

'You are the eighth person to tell me that this morning and, as I said to the other seven, I'm very aware of the law already. However, I would like you to listen to what I'm saying to you about the circumstances of my enquiry, instead of repeating the words that I've already found online. Will you do that? Please?'

There was a pause and a sigh. 'Okay, Ms O'Connell. I'm listening.'

At last!

'I see,' she said, when I finished. 'Quite an unusual set of circumstances.'

'I know. Thank you for listening to them.'

'You're welcome. I'll tell you what I'm *not* going to do, Ms O'Connell. I'm not going to pass you onto anyone else. I'm also not going to lie to you. I don't know the protocol in this case, as it's unusual. What I *am* going to promise you is that I'll personally find out what we can do in these circumstances. May I take your phone number and assure you that I will call you in an hour's time? I suspect I won't have an answer in an hour, but I'll definitely call you to update you on my progress. Would that be acceptable?'

'That would be far more acceptable than any other offer I've had today,' I said. 'Thank you.'

'My name's Valerie Sinclair. I'll call you back within the hour.'

And she did. But only to tell me that she'd hit a few brick walls and was unable to get hold of the people she needed to speak to. She asked me to leave it with her and promised me she'd come back to me by the end of the week. Let the waiting commence.

I put the phone down and made myself a coffee, glad that I'd booked a long weekend off because my mind was on anything but work.

Despite the hideous confrontation with the parents, the weekend had ended up being pretty special. I'd had a long soak in the bath, then ordered room service on the Friday evening, before falling asleep in front of the TV. I met Aisling, Torin and Briyana for lunch on Saturday, then spent the day with them. The avoid-the-past pact worked well. Despite the six-year age difference, Aisling and I seemed to have loads in common. She was a strong, confident woman who also had a fragile relationship with our parents because she wasn't afraid to challenge their views and opinions. A biology and chemistry teacher from Monday to Thursday, she devoted her weekends to her kids. Torin and Briyana were a joy to be around: funny and vivacious yet polite at the same time. And they seemed to immediately accept me in their lives.

All too soon, it was time to fly back to the UK, start my search for Shannon and hope that she wasn't harbouring a sixteen-year-long hate vendetta towards the woman who had abandoned her at birth.

* * *

I sighed as I pressed the intercom button at around seven on the Friday night of that week. 'Yes?'

'Ah! You *are* alive. Can I come in?'

'It's not really convenient, Ben. Sorry. You should have phoned first.'

'I tried, but someone has been ignoring my calls.'

'Sorry, but I have loads to do. I'll call you next week.'

'Okay.'

I returned to the dining table and the pile of letters from Daran. A two-day work trip to Newcastle, followed by a day in Edinburgh, had provided a welcome distraction but now, with no news from Valerie Sinclair and no plans for the evening, I felt that it might just be the right time. I hoped that the years apart really had helped me get over him and I wasn't about to rekindle strong feelings that had lain dormant but not forgotten.

A knock on the door made me jump. Peering through the spyhole I saw Ben looking at his watch and reluctantly pulled the door open. 'I thought I said it wasn't convenient.'

'And I thought that was rude, so I decided to ignore you. Someone was leaving so they let me in. What are you doing?' He walked past me and into the apartment.

'Won't you come in and make yourself at home?'

'I fully intend to,' he said, heading for the sofa. Then he stopped and turned round. 'I'll stop now. You know I'm nowhere near that cheeky. If it really is inconvenient, I'll leave, but I'm worried about you. I haven't seen you since before my trip to Birmingham. You haven't returned my calls or texts so I wanted to come round to say that I'm here if you want to talk about what happened at New Year, what happened on your trip to Ireland, or anything else for that matter. Or if you just want someone to share a curry and a cold beer with.' He looked so sincere and so keen to help.

'How did you know I'd been to Ireland again?'

Ben shrugged. 'I didn't. I was talking about after New Year.'

'Oh.'

'You've been again? When?'

'This weekend just gone.'

'Oh. Two trips to Ireland in the space of two weeks sounds like a story…'

Feck it. It was time to let Ben in too. 'Why don't you sit down?' I said. 'You're making the place look a mess.'

I curled up on the other end of the sofa from Ben. 'I went to Ireland at the weekend to confront my da about why he kicked me out when I was sixteen. I know the fact that I was pregnant with the local trainee priest's baby wasn't exactly welcome news, but sending me to Cornwall and telling me I was dead to him was a bit harsh, don't you think?' I watched Ben's expression carefully. If he was surprised or shocked, he gave nothing away.

'Definitely a story,' he said. 'Do you want to tell me it all from the beginning?'

* * *

'I may be able to help you find Shannon,' Ben said, when I'd finished.

'How?'

'You know what I do for a living?'

'Saintly stuff?'

'Ha ha. What do I really do?'

I shrugged. 'Fecked if I know. Something for a charity. I think.'

Ben laughed. 'Yes, I do work for a charity. We help find missing persons and I focus particularly on young people who have probably run away from home. Consequently, I have a strong relationship with Social Services, adoption agencies and various other parties that could help.'

'You really find missing people?'

Ben nodded.

'Why didn't you tell me?'

'I swear I've told you loads of times.'

I studied Ben's face and realised that, although I'd spent a lot of time in his company over the years, I'd never bothered to really take the time to talk to him. It was always good craic being out with Ben, but that was mainly because we took the mickey out of each other all night. I felt a pang of regret for all the times I must have switched off or cut him short. Was I really that bad a person? 'I'm sorry,' I said.

'For what?

'For not listening to you. Tell me more about your job. And I'm not saying that just because I want to know how you can help me. I'm genuinely interested.'

As Ben talked about his job and the families he'd reunited over the years, I was filled with admiration. I'd jokingly called him Saint Ben but it turned out he really was a saint; someone who genuinely did good and made a massive difference to the lives of others. It must be amazing to feel like that. My own career in PR seemed pretty insignificant. A few hours' work from me could increase a client's Twitter following, put a positive slant on a bad-news story and increase the cash in the shareholders' pockets. A few hours' work from Ben could reunite a family, take a teenager off the streets or save a child from abuse. They simply didn't compare.

'If your contact comes through with information first, you keep the king,' Ben said. 'But if I get answers first, I get him.'

Bollocks. I suspected I was going to have to hand the king over. Right now, information on Shannon was far more important and I had every confidence in Ben that he was going to come through for me. He always did.

Shortly after he left, a text came through:

✉ From Aisling
Saw Da this morning. He banned me from being in touch with you. I told him where to stick his opinion. The kids can't wait to see their Auntie Clare again and I'm dying to spend more time with my baby sister. This time in 3 weeks, we'll be with you. Hurray for mid-term break! Any news on Shannon yet? xxxx

✉ To Aisling
No news. Hoping next week will bring something. Not a very patient person ;-)

I smiled at the thought of Aisling and the kids coming to stay. I wouldn't have predicted that at the start of the year.

Returning to the letters, I picked up the first envelope in the pile from Daran and stroked my finger lightly over his curvy writing, a lump blocking my throat. I shook my head and returned the letter to the box. I wasn't ready, after all. I wasn't sure if I ever would be.

Valerie Sinclair phoned me first thing on Monday with an apology. She'd been off sick all week, but she said she'd definitely get onto it and come back to me by the end of the week. Ben rang at the end of the day to tell me that he'd had some good conversations but had come up with nothing concrete yet. He also promised a deadline of the end of the week. He was definitely going to win the king.

20

'I've got news.'

I buzzed Ben in on the Thursday and stood with the door wide open, waiting for him to come up in the lift, my heart thumping uncontrollably.

'What is it?' I asked, ushering him into the lounge area. I could tell by the anguish in his eyes that it wasn't good news.

'I'm so sorry.' He took hold of my hand and shook his head. 'Shannon was in a serious car crash a few days ago. She's alive, but she's in a bad way.'

I could hear ringing in my ears and Ben's face blurred in front of me.

'I think you'd better sit down,' Ben said, putting his arm round me. 'Head between your knees. Take some deep breaths.'

He led me to the sofa and I did as instructed, taking deep gulps of air until the ringing subsided and my vision returned. I sipped on the glass of water he gave me. 'What happened?' I asked.

'She was on the M1 when a lorry jackknifed and hit the car she was travelling in. Apparently, she's in a coma.'

'Are you sure?'

He reached into his jeans pocket and pulled out a couple of sheets of A4 paper, which he unfolded and handed to me. 'I'm sure.'

I scanned the words on the computer printouts of newspaper

articles about the accident but found myself struggling to take it all in. 'Jesus wept! The driver was her boyfriend? And he's...?'

'Okay, I think.'

'Where on the M1 did it happen?'

'Close to Junction 43.'

My eyes widened. 'Junction 43? But that would mean...' I couldn't bring myself to say the words, in case I was wrong.

'It would mean that they were rushed to Jimmy's. Your daughter's in Leeds.'

* * *

'Can you not drive any faster? I knew I should have driven.'

Ben indicated to change lanes. 'You don't know the way, which is why I'm driving and, no, I can't drive any faster. There's a red light, in case you hadn't noticed. And stop biting your nails.'

'I can't help it. I'm full of nervous energy.'

The lights changed and Ben did his best to accelerate, but the flow of traffic wouldn't allow him to get up to more than 20mph. He gave me a sideways glance. 'You know I'm normally an optimistic person, but you do realise we probably won't be able to see her, don't you? Stop biting!'

I sat on my hands. 'I know, but I can't sit in that apartment knowing she's in the same city as me and doing nothing about it. I'd be climbing the walls.'

'As long as you're prepared for the reality.'

'It's worth a try.'

My stomach twisted and turned as the car edged ever closer to St James's University Hospital, affectionately known as Jimmy's. What if we were too late? What if she'd already passed away? No. I mustn't think like that. It could have gone the other way. She could have come out of her coma. How amazing would that be? But what if she refused to see me? How would I feel if I'd been given up for adoption and my biological mother turned up sixteen or seventeen years later? Would I want to see her?

'Are you ready?' Ben took my hand as we dashed across the car park. He'd already found out that she was in the Intensive Care

Unit. I gripped his hand tightly as we made our way up lifts and down a maze of corridors.

'What now?' Ben whispered.

'Would I be right in thinking they only let family in?'

'Yes.'

'Piece of piss, then. I'm family.'

Before Ben could protest, I marched up to the nurses' desk. A large, matronly woman with curly, grey hair looked up. 'I've just heard that my daughter's been in an accident,' I announced.

'Name?'

'Shannon O'Co... Kitteridge. Shannon Kitteridge.'

'You're her mother?'

'Yes. I've been abroad. I've just got back or I'd have been here sooner.' I hated the way the lies tripped off my tongue but, over the years, I'd got used to telling white lies to hide the truth about my past. I heard Ben gulp beside me.

'And you are...?' she said, glancing at Ben.

'Shannon's stepdaddy,' I said.

'I'll need to get a doctor to speak to you before you can see her. Give me a minute. You can take a seat over there.' She pointed to some plastic chairs nearby, then picked up a phone.

'What if she's calling Security?' Ben hissed once we'd sat down.

'We're hardly a threat, are we?' I whispered back. 'We're sitting down like good children, patiently waiting for the doctor.'

'I don't like telling lies.'

'Neither do I but needs must. Besides, the only lie was about you being her stepfather. I *am* her mum, even if only biologically.'

Six or seven excruciatingly slow minutes passed while we waited. Eventually, a petite woman appeared, holding a clipboard. 'Mrs Kitteridge?' she asked, barely glancing up from her paperwork.

Ben and I both stood up. 'Clare,' I said, avoiding another lie or an awkward explanation.

'I'm Dr Maahi Kaur. I'm treating your daughter.' She flicked through a few sheets of paper on the clipboard, then tucked it under her arm and looked at me for the first time, with a gentle smile. 'There's no mistaking the family resemblance.'

My stomach did a somersault. Shannon looked like me? I knew

from the photo of her at six months old that she'd inherited the blonde hair, but I had no idea how she'd developed.

'And you're the father?' Dr Kaur asked, turning to Ben.

His cheeks reddened slightly. 'Stepfather.'

Dr Kaur nodded. 'Shannon has been in a serious RTC. She's suffered a severe head trauma, broken arm and broken ankle. The ankle and arm will mend, but the head trauma is the greatest concern. In cases like this, it's vital to do our best to reduce any swelling that could cause damage to the brain. She's therefore in an induced coma to allow this to happen.'

Brain damage? I gripped onto Ben's arm. I had questions. Lots of questions. I needed to be strong. 'How long is she likely to be in a coma?'

'It's hard to say. The swelling has gone down, which is a positive sign, but her young body has been through such a lot that we don't want to bring her round too quickly.'

'She will pull through, though?'

I held my breath as I waited for Dr Kaur's response.

'We would expect so. She's young, healthy and strong. She's definitely a fighter. What we can't say is whether there will be any lasting damage until she comes round. All head traumas carry risks. We do our best to reduce those risks, but there are no guarantees. Do you have any other questions?'

I shook my head. I probably did. I probably had loads. For now, I just wanted to see my little girl.

'Nurse Wilson will direct you to Shannon. Please ask her if you think of anything else.'

'Thank you,' I whispered.

We followed Nurse Wilson down a corridor and into what appeared to be a private room.

'All the tubes and monitors can look scary,' she warned. 'She's actually doing better than you might think from looking at them all.'

But I wasn't looking at the tubes and monitors. I was looking at the baby girl who'd grown into a beautiful young woman. Long, blonde hair was scraped back from her forehead. Bruises and small cuts covered her face, but I could still see that she was the spit of me when I was her age. It was uncanny.

'I'll leave you to it.' Nurse Wilson shuffled out of the room.

'The doctor was right,' Ben said. 'She's just like you.'

I stared at Shannon for a while, searching for any similarities to Daran, but it was hard to tell among the injuries and tubes. *Please let her be all right. Please. Please don't let me find her, then take her away from me.*

'How does it feel, seeing her after all these years?' Ben whispered.

'Like I'm in a dream. I can't get my head around it. She was a tiny baby, and now...' I shook my head. 'Do you think she'll be okay?'

'I thought the doctor sounded positive.'

'Did you? I hope you're right.'

I stared at Shannon again, unsure whether to talk to her or touch her hand. I turned to Ben. 'I don't know what to do now that we're here. I feel like an intruder.'

'In what way?'

I started to bite my nails again and Ben gently slapped my hand away. 'If Shannon had wanted to find me, she could have. I know that I have no legal right to look for her until she's eighteen but she could have searched me out at any point and she hasn't. As far as she's concerned, I'm a stranger who abandoned her at birth and wants nothing to do with her. I don't have a right to be here, Ben, staring at her while she's in a coma fighting for her life. She doesn't get to choose whether she's ready to meet me or not. It's not fair on her. In typical "me" style, I've barged back into her life without thinking through the consequences. I've lied to a nurse and a doctor, and I've dragged you into that lie.'

'Don't worry about me. I wanted to come. What do you want to do, then?'

'I think we'd better go. I really shouldn't be here.'

'No, you shouldn't,' said a man's voice. 'So why the hell *are* you?'

21

I spun round, heart thumping, to face a broad-chested Zac Efron lookalike of roughly seventeen or eighteen, leaning on a pair of crutches. He shook a dark fringe out of his piercing, blue eyes. Just like Shannon, his face was covered in tiny cuts and bruises, and he had some Steri-Strips across his right cheek. He had to be the boyfriend.

'Hi. My name's—'

'I know who you are,' he snarled.

'You do?'

'My leg may be busted, but my eyes still work.'

'Clare O'Connell.' Too many years in PR kicked in and I walked towards him with my hand outstretched.

'Callum.' He showed no sign of returning the handshake, although, to be fair to him, his movement was somewhat impeded by the crutches. Could I have been any more of an eejit? I let my hand dangle by my side again and shuffled backwards. 'Shannon's fiancé,' he added.

'Oh! Congratulations.' It seemed a bit of a cheesy thing to say in the circumstances, but what was the protocol for the first time the absent mum meets the fiancé of the daughter she thought was dead?

'How did you find her?' he asked.

I glanced towards Ben.

'I did some research,' Ben said.

'Who are you, like? The police?'

Ben shook his head. 'Just a friend. I'm Ben. Hi.'

Silence.

'We came as soon as we found out,' I said.

'Really? How kind of you to rush to your daughter's side in her hour of need. Except, it's not her first hour of need, is it? It's not like you gave a shit when her parents died and she was in and out of foster homes. She needed you then. She doesn't need you now. She's got me. I'm her family now. I'm, like, all she needs.'

Ouch. 'I'm sorry she's had it tough. But there's a good reason why I've only just appeared.'

Callum flicked his hair out of his eyes again. 'Don't tell me. Let me guess. You've been living overseas? No, that's not it. Erm ... You've been working on your career and it's taken this long to earn enough to buy a home for you and Shannon?' He shook his head. 'No, that's not it either. I know! Your husband and kids wouldn't understand if you admitted that you'd shagged the local priest and got knocked up at sixteen?'

I gasped. 'You know about Daran?'

'Shannon's family – her *real* family – didn't keep secrets from her. She knew she was adopted and why, and she got it. What she didn't get was why you never tried to find her when her dad died. She wrote to you every week for months and—'

'I didn't get any letters.'

'Liar! You ignored her at first, like, but then you wrote back, telling her that you were happily married with two little kiddies and you didn't want a mistake from your past to ruin your perfect life. Can you imagine what that did to her? She'd just lost her parents and now her biological mother had rejected her for the second time.'

I felt sick. Great-Aunt Nuala. She must have written back. Or Ma. Or Da.

'Where did she send the letters?' I whispered.

'I don't bloody know. Does it matter, like?'

I shrugged. 'Probably not. Any of them could have done it. The point is that I never got any letters and I certainly didn't write to Shannon.' I stood up a little straighter. 'You've said your piece, Callum, and now it's my turn. I want you to sit down and rest your leg, though.'

'I'm fine here and I'm not interested in your excuses. You can leave.'

I folded my arms and fixed my hardest stare on him, reminding myself that he wasn't Da; he was an angry teenager who'd been through a traumatic experience and I didn't need to be afraid of him. 'I'm not going anywhere till you've heard me out. Sit down.'

'No!'

'Bollocks to you. Stand, then. I don't care. But you *will* listen. If you still want me to go after you've heard me out, I'll go, although please know that I'll be back. Now that I've found her, I'm not walking away that easily.'

Callum looked as if he were about to object but sat down anyway in the seat next to the bed, no doubt grateful at being able to relieve some of the pain.

'Right. Good. Glad you've seen sense. You said that Shannon's family never lied to her. Well, Shannon's very lucky because mine did nothing *but* lie to me. There's an exceptionally good reason why I never tried to find her, and it has nothing to do with being married with kids, because I'm *not* married and the only child I have is right there fighting for her life. The reason why I never tried to find her is that, until three weeks ago, I believed that she'd died two hours after she was born. How's that for a good excuse?'

Callum's mouth opened and he looked from me to Ben and back to me again, as if searching for signs that I was winding him up. 'You've just made that up!'

'I wish I had.' I yanked open my bag, rummaged for a moment, then thrust Great-Aunt Nuala's letter into his hands. 'Imagine my surprise when this arrived.'

Callum looked at the letter and shrugged. 'You want me to read this?'

'Be my guest. You can see first-hand what a delightful family I have.'

I watched Callum's eyes widen as he read the letter, then went back to the beginning and reread it. He put the peach sheets back into the envelope and handed it to me, keeping his eyes on Shannon the whole time. He took hold of her hand and kissed it. 'I think I should tell them. You would if you were awake and you'd just read that.'

My heartbeat quickened. What could he possibly tell us? If it was something serious about her injury, Dr Kaur would have told us already, wouldn't she?

Still holding Shannon's hand, Callum twisted round and looked at me. 'I need to show you something.'

He lifted the crutches up and heaved himself out of the seat. 'Follow me.'

'Where are we going?'

'You'll soon find out.'

'But what about Shannon?'

'Not being funny, but she isn't going anywhere, is she?'

In silence, Ben and I followed him along a corridor, down in a lift, along another corridor and up in another lift.

'Back so soon?' A young redheaded nurse with a Geordie accent looked up from some paperwork as Callum hopped towards the nurses' station.

'Are we okay to...?'

She nodded. 'Oh, aye. You know your way.'

'Thanks, Kelly.'

I followed Callum into a small room containing four plastic cribs. He stopped by the first one on the left and nodded towards the sleeping baby.

'Shannon and me have a little surprise for you. This is Luke. Your grandson.'

22

'Sweet Jesus!' I looked over at Ben as he fastened his seat belt. 'I wasn't expecting that. You really didn't know?'

'Of course not!' He started the engine. 'You don't seriously think I'd keep something huge like that from you, do you?'

I shook my head. 'No.'

Ben reversed his car out of the parking space. 'Where to now? My place? Your place? The pub?'

'The offie, then yours. Can I stay over?'

'Of course.'

I watched his profile as he concentrated on finding the exit of the hospital car park, noticing the way his cheekbones tightened and his nose wrinkled each time someone pulled out in front of him. I'd have beeped my horn and screeched expletives but Ben was definitely more in control of his emotions.

'I'm glad you were with me,' I said. 'Tonight was above and beyond. Thank you.'

He glanced in my direction. 'Any time. And it wasn't above and beyond. It's what friends do for each other. Besides, you're going to need a lot more looking-after going forward.'

'What do you mean?' I stared at him as he waited to pull onto the main road. 'You can pretend you're concentrating on the traffic till the cows come home, Saint Ben, but you'll have to explain a comment like that.'

Ben grinned. 'I'm sorry. I can't help it. I know it's completely inappropriate, given how poorly Shannon is, but I can't not acknowledge that you're a grandma. Granny Irish. That's hilarious!'

'It's not! It's bloody terrifying!'

'I can't help picturing you with a blue rinse, brogues and a shopping trolley. A tartan one. Ooh, and a Yorkshire terrier tucked under your arm.'

'Ben!'

'Perhaps one of those plastic headscarf things and horn-rimmed specs dangling from a chain.'

'Christ, Ben! Could you be more stereotypical? Next you're going to suggest I'll have yellow teeth and smell of wee.'

'If the cap fits...'

'Ben! If you weren't driving this car...'

But I had to admit, it was pretty funny. Thirty-three years old and already a grandmother. Imagine Ma and Da's faces if they knew! It would be all 'like mother, like daughter'. Maybe I'd feel brave enough to confront Da again one day and tell him. I shuddered. It wasn't going to happen. The man still terrified me. There was no way I'd be able to face him again, even though the expression on his face would be priceless.

Oh my God! I'm a grandma. The enormity of it hit me. The daughter I thought had died at birth was really alive and she'd had a child. I thought I'd finally found a family in Aisling and her kids, which had been amazing after so many years all alone. Now my family had grown again with two generations directly descended from me.

As I'd gazed upon Luke in his crib, I'd felt that same outpouring of love for him that I'd felt for Shannon in the brief moments I'd held her before they whisked her away. Shannon and Luke already meant the world to me, but would they feel the same way about me?

'Do you think Callum meant what he said about wanting me to be part of Luke's life?' I asked tentatively.

'Of course he did. I know he was angry when he first saw you, but wouldn't you be, in his situation? He clearly loves Shannon and, in his eyes, you'd abandoned her when she most needed you. Now he knows that's not true. He seems like a really decent lad.'

'I know. She's picked well there.' I stared out of the window for a while, my mind whirring. 'What will I do if Shannon's not as understanding as Callum when she wakes up?'

'You'll work that Irish charm and bring her round in time.'

'And what if she doesn't come round?' My voice cracked as I asked the question I feared the most.

'I'm sure she will. You'll just need to be patient with her.'

I shook my head. 'No. I meant what if she doesn't come round – as in what if she doesn't wake up?'

Ben's hesitation was miniscule but it was enough to send my stomach plummeting to my feet. 'She will,' he said.

'What if she doesn't?'

He stopped at a red light and turned round to look at me. 'Then we'll cross that bridge together. Come on, Clare. This isn't like you. You're always the strong one. I know this evening has been a hell of a shock, but you've got to think positively. Shannon's made it through the worst part already. I know she's not out of the woods yet but she's well on her way. She's already battled her way through the thick forest of thorns and now she's just got a little copse to navigate through.'

Despite everything, I had to laugh at his analogy. 'Did you just make that shite up?'

He smiled. 'Yes. Did you like it?'

'It was dire. But I get it, and you're right. I guess I'm just not feeling so strong at the moment. It's been a hell of a year so far.'

'Then it can only get better, can't it?'

I hoped he was right.

'I know what will make you happy,' Ben said, as we paused at another set of lights. 'Although he's still in your possession, the king's now mine, isn't he?'

'Feck.' I delved into my bag to retrieve him. 'I thought you said you were going to make me happy?'

'I hadn't finished. Officially, I'm the recipient of the king for finding Shannon before your contact, but I want to give him straight back to you.'

'Why? What have I done to make me king of the moment?'

'What have you done? You absolutely rose to that challenge. You dashed straight to the hospital, not caring whether or not you got a bad reception. You blagged your way in; you turned around your daughter's hostile fiancé. And you let me get away with a load of ageist jokes. Definitely king of the moment. Although, you do realise I'm going to go all out to win him back, don't you?'

I relaxed back in my seat. What would I do without Ben? Somehow, he always managed to make things seem better.

23

✉ To Elise and Sarah
Sorry to do this by text. I wanted to update you both and I don't have the energy for a phone call tonight so please don't call me back. Three pieces of news. Great news: Ben found Shannon and I saw her tonight! Bad news: she's been in a car crash and is in an induced coma while her body recovers. She should pull through OK. Unexpected news: I'm a granny. Yeah, I know! Ben's already done all the jokes. Will call tomorrow night or over the weekend xx

✉ From Elise
Oh my goodness! That's a lot of information in one text. Sitting on my hands to stop me from picking up the phone to find out more. Wonderful news about finding Shannon, although I'm so sorry to hear the circumstances. Keeping everything crossed. She has a baby? I'm assuming we're talking a baby, given her age…? Boy or girl? Sorry. Too many questions! Won't be offended if you don't text back. Speak tomorrow. Hugs xxx

⬚ To Elise
Ha ha ha. It's OK. Definitely a baby! Luke.
Shannon & her fiancé Callum were on their way to
Gretna Green to get married before he was born.
Hit by jackknifing lorry. They had to deliver
Luke by C-section. Miracle he's still with us &
healthy. I promise to call tomorrow with full
details. At Ben's now. Need a bottle of wine and
time to get my head round it all xx

⬚ From Sarah
OMG! You've certainly had a busy evening. I'm
here for you when you're ready to talk xx

I lay in my old bed in Ben's spare room that night, with the lights off and the curtains open, watching the rain pelting against the window. Despite the best part of a bottle of wine swimming round my bloodstream, I couldn't relax and switch off. Vivid memories swirled around my head of Shannon being born and placed in my arms for a few brief moments, before the midwife whom Great-Aunt Nuala had hired reached forward and took her away, whispering that it was for the best that I wasn't given any time to get attached. No time to get attached? What did she think had been happening during the nine months she'd been growing inside me? The next time I saw her was this evening – a grown woman lying on a hospital bed, her poor young body cut, bruised and hooked up to machines, believing that her own mother had rejected her at birth and then again years later. If she'd inherited any of my fire or my ability to hold a grudge, she certainly wouldn't accept me with open arms.

My heart ached for all the missed years, and a streak of hatred towards Da flowed through me again. When I'd reluctantly agreed to the adoption, I'd always known I was unlikely to see her until she turned eighteen, and that I'd have to live with the hope that we could be reunited, knowing that it might not happen if Shannon chose not to get to know me. That had been hard enough. What sort of monster would take that glimmer of hope away? I just didn't get it. He must have really hated me to do that, but why? Why did my own father hate me so much? I accepted that Daran and I getting together could be seen as scandalous in a small, narrow-minded community like Ballykielty, but he'd covered it up and he'd sent me away. He'd made it clear I wasn't welcome back and I'd had no intention of returning. He'd removed his problem and he'd punished me for what he perceived to be my crime. So why punish me further by telling me she'd died?

I picked up my mobile from the bedside table and looked at the time: 3.17 a.m. *Sleep. I need sleep.* Reluctantly, I rolled out of bed and closed the curtains. Maybe a bit less light would help. I needed to stop focusing on Da because, for every moment I wasted thinking about him, I was letting him control me, and he'd done that for far too long. I needed to stop thinking about the years spent without Shannon and focus on the future with her. Which meant a future with Luke. I smiled at the thought of that tiny little boy dressed in his hospital-loaned blue babygrow, curling his hand around my little finger and kicking his dumpy legs. I might not have had a chance to be there for my own baby but I had an opportunity to be there as my grandbaby grew. Daran's grandbaby.

As I lay on my back, staring at the ceiling and twiddling my Claddagh ring, I imagined Daran looking down on Shannon and Luke, and smiling at the legacy he'd left behind. *Christ! Looking down on them? I don't believe in all that bollocks.*

'Do you believe in God?' Daran had asked me, about a month after my sixteenth birthday. 'I mean, *really, truly* believe in God.'

Although the day had been mild for early October, the darkness had brought a chill to the air. We were going to need to rethink our farmhouse love nest very soon. I shivered slightly and pulled a blanket over us as I stroked my hand across his bare chest. 'You won't be hurt, whatever the answer is?'

'Nothing you say or do could ever hurt me, Clare.'

'Even though you believe in God and love Him with all your heart?'

He kissed the top of my head. 'Not with all of my heart. I did. But then I met you, and you took my breath away and stole my heart.'

I reached up and stroked his face, then gently kissed him, my body full of love and longing for this man who had chosen me over the priesthood.

'One more time, then I'll answer your question. But, for now, just know that I really and truly believe in you and the fact we're meant to be together. Always.'

'You'll be wanting my answer,' I said, as I lay beside Daran later, panting.

He laughed. 'You can get your breath back first. And you don't have to answer the question if you don't want to. I think I know the answer and I'm fine with it, so I am.'

I propped myself up onto my elbow. 'Amazing kisser. Incredible in bed. Will you be adding psychic powers to your list of skills?'

Daran propped himself up on his elbow too so he could look into my eyes. 'You really think those things about me?'

'Of course. Of the forty-seven lads in the village I've slept with, you're definitely the best.' I winked and he grinned.

I lay back and stared at the dilapidated ceiling. 'I'd better answer your question. The truth is that I don't like religion. It's been rammed down my neck by my parents and God has been used as a bribe and a threat.'

'In what way?'

'If we were naughty, we'd be told that God was watching and would punish us. If we hurt ourselves, we'd be told that it was God getting His revenge for our wicked thoughts or actions. We were made to believe He was judging us and that we needed to constantly work harder to make Him happy, as though He were always displeased. I found myself wishing He didn't exist. I hated the idea of this grumpy, old man watching over us, tutting every time I got a word wrong in my school spelling test or slopped gravy on my shirt.'

Daran held me closer and stroked my hair. 'Is that what you still think?'

I sighed. 'When I met you, you talked about a different God who cared, and understood, and forgave. What I'm struggling with is how two people can interpret the same God so differently.'

'I don't know your da very well but he strikes me as a man who hides behind religion to control others and manipulate them into doing what he wants them to do. The God I know and love doesn't sit in judgement. He guides and supports us through good times and challenging times. If you want to imagine Him watching over us and tutting, I think it's safe to say that it's your da he's tutting at – not you.'

'I like that thought.' A cold breeze ruffled my hair and I pulled the blanket more tightly across my body.

'It's too cold to stay here,' Daran said. 'We need to get you dressed and back home, where it's warm.'

'I know a way we can warm up,' I said.

Back in Ben's room, I finally drifted into sleep, thinking about that night with Daran.

* * *

I glanced at my watch after we'd warmed each other up that night in the farmhouse. 'Jesus, Daran! It's half eight. Weren't you meant to be meeting Father Doherty at eight?'

His eyes widened. 'I'm going to have to run. Are you up for it?'

'You be going. I'll blow the candles out and tidy up a bit.'

'You'll be okay on your own? You've got a torch?'

'Yes, and I'll be grand. I've been here in the dark on my own a million times. I'm perfectly safe.'

'I love you.'

'I love you too. Now, run! And make sure you get that straw out of your hair.'

Daran kissed me, then ran across the farmhouse, pulling on his jumper with one hand and trying to knock straw out of his hair with the other. I finished pulling on my clothes and hunted around for my running shoes. As I bent over to tie the laces, a feeling of unease crept over me. Heart racing, I slowly turned round to face him.

'That was quite a show the two of you put on again. You know what's going to happen now, though, don't you?'

'Clare! Are you okay?'

I squinted under the bright light. 'Ben?'

'You were crying for help.'

My heart was thumping, I was drenched in sweat and I was crying. 'Bad dream.' I pushed my hair out of my eyes and wiped my wet cheeks.

Ben knelt on the floor beside me. 'Can I get you anything? Some water, perhaps?'

I nodded. He held my gaze for a moment, then squeezed my arm gently. He flicked the bedside lamp on, putting the main light off as he left the bedroom.

Sitting up, I hugged my knees up against my chest. I'd been dreaming about Daran and the night he'd asked me whether I believed in God. That had actually happened. It was a real memory, not a dream. But what about what had happened next? *That* hadn't happened. Why had I gone from dreaming about Daran and a real event into a horrible nightmare? Because that's what it was. A nightmare.

Wasn't it?

24

✉ To Callum
Looking forward to seeing you all again tonight.
Do you need anything? Does Luke?

✉ From Callum
I'm OK but would be cool if you could get some
clothes and nappies for Luke. His are all
borrowed from hospital. Laters

✉ From Ben
Good luck tonight. Are you sure you don't want me
to get my Samaritans shift covered?

✉ To Ben
Don't you dare! You've done enough already. I'll
call you tomorrow

Looking at the pile of carrier bags in the boot of my car, I chewed on my thumbnail and hoped I'd chosen well. I'd dashed around several high-street stores in Leeds city centre at lunchtime, realising I knew absolutely nothing about babies and what they wore. Tiny Baby, Early Baby, New Baby, First Size, Newborn, 0-3 Months, Less Than

5.5lb, 5-7lb. And don't get me started on the nappy choices... Argh!
Who knew there were so many options for what appeared to be
exactly the same thing? No wonder so many new mums suffered
from postnatal depression. As if having a new life to take care of
wasn't scary enough, a trip to the shops was certain to tip them over
the edge! I'd finally settled on a combination of Newborn and 0-3
Months clothes, a similar size in super-absorbent nappies, and a
bottle of pretty much everything in the Johnson's Baby range. It'd be
grand.

I lifted the bags out of the boot, shoved a fluffy, cream teddy
bear under my arm and headed into Jimmy's to meet Callum on the
maternity ward, as agreed, before going to see Shannon.

Luke was awake. God, did we know it! My shoulders tensed as
his cries pierced through me.

'Jesus!' I said, when I'd greeted Callum and been introduced to
Kelly, the nurse gently rocking Luke. I recognised her as the same
nurse from the evening before. 'He's got a good pair of lungs on
him.'

Kelly smiled as she reached for a bottle of milk and gave it a
shake. 'Are youse ready?'

Callum had propped his crutches against the wall and was
settling into a chair beside Luke's crib. He draped a cloth over his
arm. 'Ready.' Then he looked at me. 'Unless you'd like to...?'

I shook my head quickly. 'You're settled now. And your little
man is starving, so I wouldn't want to delay him.'

Callum reached out for Luke, then the bottle. 'In that case, you
can be on nappy-changing duty.'

Bollocks. Was it too late to ask to feed him instead?

'I'll leave youse to it,' said Kelly. 'Just shout if youse need owt.'

'Thanks, Kelly.'

'How's Shannon?' I asked when Kelly left. 'Any
improvements?'

'They reckon there've been some, but it's still too early to bring
her round. Luke'll probably fall asleep after he's fed and changed.
We'll go and see her then.'

'And what about you? Are you okay?' Callum looked paler than
he had yesterday.

He wrinkled his nose. 'Aches and pains everywhere but it could be a lot worse. I've been very lucky.'

I watched Callum's natural ease with admiration. 'You look like you've been doing this all your life.'

'There were babies in some of my foster families. I got used to them.'

I took a seat beside him. 'How long were you in foster care?'

'Since I was six.'

'What happened to your parents?'

'My mum's dead and I don't know who my dad is. I don't think my mum knew, either.'

'Sorry.'

He shrugged dismissively. 'Shit happens. One of her many loser boyfriends liked to beat us both up. My teacher spotted it and I ended up in care but Mum stayed with him and he got her into drugs. It was a bit of pot at first, but it got more serious when he started dealing.'

Callum paused to wipe away some milk that had dribbled down Luke's chin. 'When I was eleven, she overdosed, and that was that. I hadn't seen her for, like, two or three years. She was so spaced that there was no point. I can't remember how she was before the drugs.'

'Sounds like you had a tough childhood.'

Callum shook his head. 'It wasn't so bad. My foster families were cool. And if I hadn't been in care, I'd never have met Shannon.' His eyes lit up at the mention of her name. He stroked Luke's head. 'And we'd never have had you, would we? I know you might think we're young to have a baby, but I had to grow up a lot quicker than most kids my age. Shannon says I act like I'm thirty-eight instead of eighteen. Says she's going to buy me a pipe and slippers.'

I smiled. As if I'd judge anyone for having a baby young. I wanted to ask more. I knew first-hand what it was like to be abandoned by your family but I had no idea what it was like to be brought up by strangers. How had that affected him? How had it affected Shannon? How would it affect how she felt about me?

'So, what's in the bags?' Callum asked, lightening the mood.

'Ah, yes! I got a bit carried away.' I jumped up and began unpacking bags, showing Callum the various sleepsuits and outfits

I'd bought. I picked up the teddy. 'And this fella is baby-safe and washable. His name's Philbin, apparently. Strange name for a bear. You can change it if you want. I'm sure he won't mind.' I placed the bear at the end of the cot.

Callum laughed. 'I'm not going to steal his identity, poor bear. Philbin it is.' He handed me Luke's part-empty bottle and held his hand under Luke's chin while he rubbed his back. Luke released the most enormous belch, making me giggle.

'Good boy,' Callum said. 'Ready for more?' He popped the bottle back into Luke's mouth and looked up at me. 'Shannon'll be gutted. She wanted to feed him herself but, like, we don't have much choice.'

At the mention of breastfeeding, a flashback hit me of my own swollen breasts post-birth and no baby to feed. Tears pricked my eyes and I blinked them away.

'What's Shannon like?' I asked.

His eyes lit up again. 'She's awesome. She's really brainy. Got top grades at school. She had a place at sixth form but deferred a year when we found out about Luke. She's a great friend and, like, dead funny. She can go quiet and likes to be on her own when she's got stuff to think about. She's ace at giving advice, even if she's not always good at taking it. She's feisty and opinionated and, now that I've met you, I know where she gets that from.'

'Feisty and opinionated? Me? What would possess you to say something like that?'

Callum laughed. 'No idea.' He removed the bottle from Luke's mouth. 'Nice work, Luke. Let's hear some more burps, then Grandma can change your nappy and dress you in some of those new clothes that don't smell of hospital.'

He passed me the bottle and manoeuvred Luke into burping position again. 'Do you mind me calling you "Grandma"?'

'No. Although, I'd be lying if I said it was going to be easy getting used to it. I do feel a bit young to be a grandmother, but I guess that's what happens when you have a child young and they have a child young too. I'm fine with it as long as Shannon is. I'm conscious that she might not want me in her life.'

'She probably won't at first, but she'll go quiet and spend some time thinking about it, then she'll decide it's right for her and right for Luke. Anyway, I'm his dad and I want you to stick around. I've never had a proper family, like, and neither has Shannon since her dad died. If there are real family members who want to be involved – ones who aren't into drugs – then I want them to be around Luke.' He blew his fringe out of his face and wrinkled his nose. 'You do want to stick around, don't you?'

'Of course I do. As I said last night, I'd always hoped I'd see her again when I agreed to the adoption. I never wanted to give her up in the first place. With no money, no home, no family and no education, I didn't have many options. I thought adoption would be best for her.'

Callum nodded. 'It probably was. I didn't know Paul and Christine, but Shannon said they were awesome parents.'

Luke produced a couple of loud belches. 'Nice one!' Callum said. 'High five!' He placed his fingertips against Luke's palm. 'Let's give you to Grandma for a change.'

Bollocks. I was going to have to tell him. 'I feel like a right eejit saying this, Callum, but I don't know how to hold a baby.'

He frowned. 'Really?'

'Yes. Really.'

'You've never held a baby before?'

'Never.'

'You don't have friends or family with babies?'

'No! Why's that so hard to believe? I don't have any family. Actually, I have my big sister Aisling now, but her kids are school-age. I wasn't in contact when they were babies. I don't have a huge circle of friends and none of them have had kids yet. My friend Elise is pregnant, so I guess I'll hold hers at some point, but I genuinely haven't held a baby since Shannon was born. Back then, a midwife placed her in my arms but whisked her away minutes later saying...' My voice caught in my throat and tears filled my eyes. 'Anyway, I don't know what to do. Can I watch you instead?'

'Slight problem with that plan.' He jerked his thumb towards the crutches behind him. 'You'll have to do it. Don't look so scared.'

'What if I drop him?'

'We'll just have to hope he bounces.' Callum laughed. 'I *am* joking, you know. How about you get out everything you need and then I'll pass Luke to you?'

'You don't think we should call Nurse Kelly instead?'

'Oh dear, Luke, looks like Grandma is a fraidy cat. She's scared of a six-pound, three-ounce baby.'

'I'm not scared of *him*. I'm just scared of... Okay, you've made your point. What do I need?'

How hard was it to remove a baby from his clothes, change a nappy and re-dress him? Jesus! How was it that I could negotiate incredibly tough business deals with stroppy chief execs and instigate challenging recovery plans when a client had experienced a PR disaster, yet I couldn't remove a baby's arm from a sleeve?

'I don't think he's had a dump, so you've got it easy with your first change,' Callum said.

'Easy? There's nothing easy about any of this.' I wiped the sweat off my brow with the back of my hand.

He laughed. 'It'll get easier. I promise. Oh, and you might want to—'

I screamed and stepped back, spluttering, as a flow of warm urine spattered across my face and down my white shirt.

'Oops! Too late.'

I grabbed at the sleepsuit that I'd removed, wiped my face and dabbed helplessly at my top. 'Did he do that deliberately?'

'It often happens when baby boys are exposed to the air. I was about to say that you might want to put a tissue over him, just in case. Sorry.'

'You're sure it wasn't a dirty protest for my incompetence?'

'I'm sure.'

I turned back to Luke. 'Right, you! Listen and listen good. When you're older and you bring girlfriends home, I'm going to be telling them all about how you peed on your grandma the second time she met you. You'll pay for this, young man. You mark my words. This'll come back to haunt you, so it will.'

Callum laughed again. 'If it's any consolation, it happened to me, like, the first time I changed a boy's nappy. Think of it as Luke marking his territory. You're now officially his property.'

When I'd finally sorted everything out, I was able to sit down and have a cuddle. It was my first opportunity to relax and properly look at my grandbaby. As I stroked his chubby cheeks and bald head, an overwhelming sensation of love and protectiveness enveloped me, just as it had that brief moment I'd held Shannon. Tears rushed to my eyes and my throat tightened.

'It's pretty special, isn't it?' Callum said.

I nodded, not daring to speak.

'You said you got to hold Shannon?'

A couple of tears sprang loose as a feeling of déjà vu hit me. 'Only for a minute or so before they took her away.'

'Must have been rough.'

'It was, but I managed to hold it together, convincing myself that she had a far better life ahead of her than I could give her. Then they told me she'd died. I lost the plot at that point.' I took a deep breath, shuddering again at the memory of that horrendous moment. I'd cried pretty much solidly for a fortnight. Great-Aunt Nuala told me to toughen up and accept my penance at first, then she got worried and called the doctor, who prescribed some happy pills. I didn't need tablets – I needed my baby. Disgusted by their lack of understanding, I flushed the tablets away and vowed never to let them see me being weak again. Until I got the letter from Great-Aunt Nuala, that had been the last time I properly cried.

'Tell me more about how the two of you met,' I said. 'You said it was in a foster home?'

Callum nodded. 'When her dad died, Shannon was thirteen. Her mum... adoptive mum... had died three years before. She had no aunties or uncles, like, so she was sent to an emergency foster family – the Hendersons – which was where I was placed. They're this awesome couple. Completely bonkers. They couldn't have kids of their own so they started fostering. She'd inherited the family business – a large guesthouse on the outskirts of Northampton – and quite a lot of money, so they ran it as a sort of children's home.

'I'll never forget the first day I saw Shannon. I'd been with the Hendersons for a couple of years and, as the longest-standing foster kid, I was always the one who welcomed newbies and helped them settle in. I got home from school one day and Mrs Henderson told me that we had a new girl who'd gone to explore the grounds. I couldn't find her at first. I was worried she'd done a runner, like, but I eventually found her in the treehouse talking to two wooden boxes. Turns out they contained the ashes of Paul and Christine. Her dad hadn't been able to bring himself to say goodbye and scatter her mum's ashes, and she was glad about that because it meant she could scatter them together when she found a permanent home. She knew her stay with the Hendersons was temporary because they didn't have space to keep her, but she had a plan. She was going to...'

'She was going to what?' I asked, when Callum stopped and looked away.

'She was going to contact her real mum and hopefully go to live with her.' He grimaced. 'Sorry. I'm not saying that to have a dig.'

'It's grand,' I said brightly, my stomach twisting with guilt. 'Go on.'

'Well, as you now know, she wrote loads of letters to you but heard nothing back at first. She moved around a lot, but she was really positive about it because she was convinced she'd find her birth mum and live happily ever after together. Sorry. Again, that's not a dig. Anyway, we became, like, best mates and often met up on weekends. She was so much fun and nothing seemed to get her down. She threw herself into everything she did: schoolwork, friendships, dance classes, learning the guitar. I struggled at school so she helped me with my maths and science. She taught me to play the guitar, although I refused to let her teach me ballet.' He paused and smiled. 'Didn't think a pink tutu was quite the look for me, like. Anyway, I found myself wanting to be with her all the time and I soon realised I wanted to be more than friends. I'd never had a girlfriend before, and I had no idea whether she felt the same way about me, so I kept quiet.

'When you wrote to her and said you wanted nothing to do with her – or at least when we thought it was you who'd written – she was gutted. It was like someone had taken a fire extinguisher and put out her spark. She'd moved to yet another foster family that week and claimed that nobody loved her or wanted her in their lives. I told her that I did. She said I was only saying that because we were friends and that I only needed her in my life to get through my school exams and would dump her after that. I had a go at her, telling her exactly how I felt about her. She had a go back at me, asking why the hell I hadn't said anything before then, because she felt exactly the same way and hadn't dared make the first move. We were inseparable after that.

'I passed my exams, thanks to her, and I started a plumbing apprenticeship. I wouldn't have had the courage to apply if it hadn't been for Shannon, but she's one of these people who believe you can achieve anything. She says the only barriers you face are the ones you put up for yourself.'

I felt a surge of pride in my daughter, who sounded wise beyond her years.

'When we found out about Luke, she was so excited. We'd talked about getting married and having kids at some point. It was earlier than expected, but she prayed about it and said it was God's plan that we have children sooner.'

I felt my pulse race and my stomach churn again. 'She prayed about it?'

'We both did.'

'You're Catholics?' I was aware that I was saying the words through gritted teeth, but I couldn't help it.

'Shannon is, and I'm a Methodist.'

Of course she was. As if Great-Aunt Nuala and Da would allow her to be placed with a family who weren't practising Catholics. Great. Just great.

'Our faith was one of the many things that united us,' Callum continued. 'And I have to say, I don't know how I'd have got through the past few days without God's love and support.'

'Luke's asleep,' I said, relieved of the opportunity to shift the subject away from religion. 'Will I put him in his cot?'

Somehow I managed to lay Luke in his cot without waking him up. Miracle. I shoved the shopping bags in the cupboard before reaching for my coat and bag. 'Will we go in to see Shannon now?'

'In a minute. There's something I need to ask you first. Actually, it's...' He winced and clutched his stomach.

'Are you okay?' I asked, rushing to his side.

He exhaled slowly then gave me a weak smile. 'Bit of stomach ache. Nothing to worry about.'

'Are you sure? Should I get Kelly?'

Callum shook his head. 'It's nothing. Honestly. Where were we? Oh yeah, there's something I'd like you to do for Luke and me, if you can.'

'Okay.'

'You might want to sit down for this one.'

My stomach twisted again. I sensed that a request for something a little more significant than shopping for nappies and sleepsuits was on its way. 'O-kay.'

'I don't think it's fair on a healthy baby like Luke to be stuck in hospital. I'd like you to look after him.'

25

'You're sure he wasn't winding you up?' Ben took another slurp of his coffee and pulled his duvet more tightly around his body as he curled up on one end of his sofa. I felt a bit guilty. After lying awake all night worrying about Shannon and thinking about Callum's proposition, I thought I'd been generous in waiting until nine before banging on Ben's door, instead of turning up at six like I'd wanted to. With everything that had happened, I'd forgotten about his nightshift at the Samaritans. I offered to come back later, but he insisted on getting up so I could update him.

I shook my head. 'No. He was deadly serious. I understand his logic. Shannon's incapacitated and even when she wakes up, she's likely to have weeks, if not months, of recovery ahead of her. He can't do much on his crutches. Apparently, he's also got a couple of cracked ribs so he's on strong painkillers. Meanwhile, poor Luke has started his life stuck in hospital, with limited human contact.'

'How did you leave it with him?'

'That I'd think about it. Seriously, Ben, I did *not* see that one coming. I don't know what to do, which, as you know, is very rare for me.'

Ben smiled. 'Rare? I'd suggest non-existent. Okay, let's start with the basics. What stopped you from saying yes immediately?'

'Only a-trillion-and-seven things.' I started counting them off on my fingers. 'One: I have no idea what to do with a baby. Couldn't even change a nappy yesterday. Two: I have a full-time job with frequent travel. Three: I rent a one-bedroom apartment with a "no children or pets" policy. Four: Shannon might not like it. Plus a-trillion-and-three other things. Stop laughing at me.'

Ben put his mug down on the carpet. 'Sorry. It's just that you're so cute when you get all stressed like this.'

'Cute?' I threw a cushion at him. 'Kittens are cute. Babies are cute... sometimes. I'm not.' I looked around for something else to throw.

'I concede!' Ben raised his hands in the air. 'Cute might have been the wrong choice of adjective. It's just that you're normally so in control and it's reassuring to see that you occasionally have vulnerable, clueless moments like the rest of us.'

'You should have seen me in the hospital with Luke yesterday. Jesus, was that a picture of clueless vulnerability or what?'

Shrugging the duvet off, Ben reached for his mug and stood up. 'Sorry, I need a top-up. You?'

I shook my head. 'Still on this one.'

He returned a few minutes later with another drink. 'Where were we? Oh yes, a-trillion-and-seven reasons not to say yes immediately. Let's just ignore all those issues for the moment. What's your gut feeling? What do you *want* to do?'

'I want to be looking after Luke. Of course I do! He's my grand-baby. But—'

'Don't revert to the objections yet. Let's focus on the positives. That was a pretty strong declaration that you *want* to do it. Aside from the fact that he's your flesh and blood, why do you want to look after Luke?'

I took a swig of my coffee as I thought for a moment. 'Because I missed out on looking after Shannon when she was a baby. This would be like getting a second chance. I want to do it for me and I want to do it for Shannon.'

'Then you should do it. I'm not sure about the trillion-and-three objections you didn't list, but we can definitely overcome the four you did.'

'What? The four absolutely enormous objections?'

'The only barriers in your way are the ones you put up for yourself.' Ben frowned. 'Why are you looking at me like that?'

I smiled. 'That's the exact phrase Callum used in the hospital yesterday. Apparently, it's the phrase that Shannon lives by.'

'It's a sign! Alleluia!'

Ben was saved from having anything else thrown at him by my phone ringing.

'Hi, Callum,' I said.

'How soon can you get here? Shannon's taken a bad turn.'

* * *

Ben pulled up at the entrance to Jimmy's. 'You go to her. I'll park and find you later.'

I leapt out of the car and power-walked to the ICU. As soon as I entered the waiting room, I spotted Callum slumped in a plastic chair, pale-faced. A cold chill crept over my body. I was too late. My feet felt as though they were rooted to the spot.

Callum looked up. 'Clare!'

'Is she...?'

He ran his hand across his stubbly chin. 'She's critical... infection from one of the lines... don't really know... couldn't take it in.' His speech was slurred and he appeared to be struggling to focus his eyes on me.

'Callum? Are you all right? Callum? Shit! Nurse! Help!' I tried to catch him as he fell towards the floor, but he was too heavy. '*Help!*'

* * *

Ben put his arm round me as we walked back to his car a little after eight that evening. 'They'll both pull through. The doctor said so. Callum's had a successful op and Shannon's over the worst.'

I relaxed against him, grateful for both the physical and emotional support. 'I know. It was just a hell of a shock. Hadn't they both suffered enough already?'

Callum's appendix had ruptured, or burst, or whatever it is they do, so he'd been rushed to have that removed while another team of doctors fought to stabilise Shannon. It had been a terrifying day.

'It makes one decision for me, though. I'm definitely going to look after Luke.'

Ben squeezed my shoulder. 'But you'd already decided that, hadn't you?'

I nodded.

'You know you're welcome to move back in.'

'Thanks, but I can't do that to you and Lebony.'

'I've already told you that Lebony has no problem with you living here. She sends her best wishes, by the way, to you and your new family.'

I was about to make a snide comment but it struck me that I could use all the best wishes in the world right now. *Please let Shannon and Callum be okay.*

26

✉ From Elise
Is everything OK? I've tried to call several
times but it goes straight to voicemail. Getting
worried. Hope all's well with Shannon and Luke xx

✉ From Sarah
Where are you? You didn't call on Friday so I've
been texting and calling you but no response.
Hope you're OK. Can you call me? xx

✉ To Elise and Sarah
Really sorry. Phone's been off. Been at Jimmy's.
Shannon took a bad turn, then Callum collapsed
with appendicitis, but they're both over the
worst. Traumatic couple of days. On my way back
from Northampton with their belongings. They were
meant to be moving into a rented house when they
got back from Gretna Green. Eejit landlord's
given it to someone else and their foster places
have been filled so, on top of all the other
bollocks, they're homeless! Also got Luke's cot,
buggy and a pile of other baby crap cos he's

going to be staying with me. Don't ask! Not
worked it out yet. Promise I'll call for a catch-
up soon but got lots to sort out. Off to London
tomorrow. Not sure my boss is going to appreciate
the immediate 'maternity' leave request! Hope
you're both OK xx

✉ From Sarah
OMG! Let me know if you need any help with
anything. Keep me posted xx

✉ From Elise
Stevie and I are on our way to Leeds. Sounds like
you're going to need help unpacking and putting
up a cot. He's just made ours so he's pretty
useful. We've packed the tools! Text me your
postcode xx

'Why do you keep looking backwards?' Ben asked, as we headed up
the M1 towards Leeds shortly after lunch on the Sunday.

I twisted back round in my seat to face forward. 'My last experience of moving was when I relocated to Leeds. My stuff filled a
small lorry. It seems a bit sad that there are three of them and their
stuff doesn't even fill a Transit van.'

'It's a big van, though,' Ben said. 'Bear in mind that you had
some furniture and they don't. And you've had twice as long to
accumulate stuff. How much did you have when you were their
age?'

I pictured the suitcase and a couple of boxes in Ma and Da's
lounge, ready to be banished with me. 'Not much.'

We travelled in silence for ten minutes or so.

'The Hendersons seemed like nice people,' Ben said. 'It was
good of them to store Shannon and Luke's things for them.'

'Yes, but they shouldn't have had to store the stuff. Bloody landlord evicting them. Who does that?'

'Hey! We've been through this already. He was a friend of the
Hendersons, and Callum explicitly instructed him to rent it out to

someone else. Callum doesn't know when they'll be out of hospital and there's no point him paying rent while he isn't working. It was his choice, Clare. *His* choice. Besides, you can't evict someone who hasn't even moved in. They haven't lost any money. They've got their deposit back. So uncross your arms and feed me some wine gums. Not green ones, though.'

I pushed a green one into his mouth and he grimaced. 'You're a mean girl, Irish. Very mean.'

'Yeah, but you still love me, so you do.'

He glanced across at me briefly. 'If you say so.'

* * *

Elise and Stevie were already waiting on the pavement outside Orion Point when Ben pulled up right outside the entrance and put on the hazards.

'I'm not going to be much help lifting and carrying,' Elise said, 'but I can keep everyone in drinks.'

'All help is appreciated. Thank you, both of you.'

'What floor are you on?' Stevie asked.

'The fourteenth.'

'Please tell me there are lifts and that they work.'

I laughed. 'Thankfully, yes.'

We filled the lift with the first load, then Elise and I travelled up together while Ben and Stevie emptied the van. I left Elise in the apartment in charge of drinks and travelled back down for the next load.

'Surprise!' The lift doors opened to reveal Sarah and Nick.

'Jesus! You scared me! What are you two doing here?'

'We figured you might need some help, but it looks like someone beat us to it.'

'The more the merrier,' I said, trying to ignore the slight edge to Sarah's voice. 'Thank you. It means a lot.'

Sarah put her arms out. 'I know you don't do hugs often, but I'm thinking now might be a good time for one.'

I nodded, tears suddenly pricking my eyes. 'It's been a shitty few days.'

'I bet it has,' she said.

'Excuse me! Any chance of getting to the lift?' There was no mistaking the anger in the woman's voice.

I let go of Sarah and wiped my eyes. 'Sorry.' I stepped aside. 'We're just moving some stuff in.'

'So I see.' The woman was in her mid-to-late forties, immaculately dressed from head to toe in winter-white Ralph Lauren. Her glossy black hair was pulled back into a chignon, and a slash of raspberry across her lips matched the raspberry-coloured Mulberry bag she carried. Wow! I'd always thought I was stylish, but I looked like something out of the Matalan sale next to her. Actually, in my present house-moving gear of jeans and an old T-shirt, I probably looked like something from a jumble sale.

'I'm Clare, fourteenth floor. I think you might live above me.'

She looked me up and down and I swear her lip curled in disgust. Without offering her name in return, she looked pointedly in the direction of the flatpack cot resting against the wall. 'You rent from Daryl Smithers, don't you?'

I nodded. 'How did you know?'

'Daryl's a friend of mine. A good friend.' She stepped into the lift and gave me a frosty stare. 'I trust the cot is a gift and you're not about to move a baby into the building because I do believe that would be a breach of your rental conditions?'

Holy crap! 'Of course. Just a gift.'

'I thought so.' The lift door closed.

Sarah whistled. 'Delightful neighbour you've got there.'

'And a hideous problem I've got now.'

'Why's that?'

'My lease strictly states, "no pets and no children".'

'Oh. What are you going to do?'

'Move Luke in and hope he turns invisible and never cries. Yeah, I know. I'd better start packing because I'm about to be evicted.'

Ben dumped a couple of suitcases next to me. 'You're not still angry at Shannon's landlord, are you? He didn't evict them.'

'I know. I was just telling Sarah about it, though.'

Ben pointed towards the pile of belongings in the lobby. 'That's everything except Callum's bike, which I'll store in my shed, so I'm going to move the van. Stevie and Nick are moving their cars to the visitor spaces.'

'Okay.'

'Why didn't you tell him about that woman?' Sarah said, as soon as the door had closed.

'Because I know him too well. If he gets wind of me being kicked out, what will he do?'

'Offer you his spare room again?'

'Exactly. Only, it wouldn't just be me this time, would it? It would hardly be fair to lumber him with a newborn baby too. I'll just have to find somewhere else to live. If the Ice Queen grasses on me, that is. Hopefully I'll be able to get away with it.'

Sarah smiled reassuringly, but I knew that she knew the Ice Queen was going to have her eye on me and would be running straight to Daryl the minute she got so much as a sniff of a dirty nappy. Bollocks!

* * *

I'm one of those annoying people who don't get nervous. I thrive on the pressure of deadlines, challenging targets and awkward negotiations. Yet I found myself actually trembling the following morning as I slowly made my way down the corridor of our London HQ to meet with Mike and our HR manager, Sabina. I felt exactly the same way as when I'd confronted Da, which was ridiculous, as I'd always had a good relationship with Mike. Some of my colleagues found him difficult but I loved his direct, straight-talking, no-nonsense approach. Unfortunately, he was embarrassingly old-school when it came to women and careers. I swear he'd only promoted me because he was certain I'd never settle down and have children. I therefore suspected he'd take my news as an act of disloyalty and treat me with the same contempt he'd shown to my colleagues, although I hoped that the results I'd delivered would have earned me enough brownie points to get the flexibility I needed.

I could hear raised voices as I approached the meeting room. Through the glass panel next to the door, I could see Mike pacing up and down, looking like a bear with a sore head. Sabina kept shaking her head and indicating that he should sit down and, I suspected, calm down. Bollocks! Taking a deep breath and standing tall, I knocked on the door, then entered the lion's den.

Sabina smiled warmly. 'Come in, Clare. Take a seat. Would you like some water?'

'Yes, please.'

Sabina poured me a drink from an iced jug on the table. 'Mike was just about to take a seat, weren't you, Mike?' Her voice was friendly yet firm.

Like a chastised child, Mike pulled out a seat, sat down and glowered at me.

'Thank you for coming, Clare,' Sabina said. 'I understand that you emailed Mike last night requesting a discussion about going on maternity leave. Is that correct?'

'It is.' I wished Mike would stop glowering at me.

'And I understand that your request is to start that leave with immediate effect? Is that right?'

'Yes.'

Sabina smiled. 'Okay. We'll explore the details in a moment. Before we do, Mike and I are a little concerned. As employers, we have a duty of care to ensure that all of our employees are safe at work and, for pregnant women, there are procedures we'd normally follow. I'm very conscious that we haven't been able to follow these because we had no idea you were pregnant, Clare.'

'Oh. Well, I'm not pregnant.'

Mike's eyes widened. 'You've already *had* the baby?'

'No. My daughter has.'

His eyes widened even further and he leaned forward. 'So, what the hell are *you* requesting maternity leave for?'

Sabina stared at Mike and gave a little cough. 'I think you'd better explain, Clare.'

I tried to stick to the bare facts, but it was still very uncomfortable laying my past out on the table when I'd never opened up to Mike or any of my colleagues about my life before Prime PR.

'I'm sorry to advise you that you're not eligible to take maternity leave,' Sabina said, when I'd finished. 'That's only available to mothers who have either given birth or who have adopted a child.'

'Oh.' I could have kicked myself for not Googling maternity rights first. Awkward.

Mike pushed his chair back. 'That's that, then. No maternity leave. Can we focus on business instead?'

Sabina frowned at him. 'There are other options we can explore, though. Clare's facing a unique scenario and as her employer, we want to try to find a way to support her.'

'She can take some holiday leave, then. In March. Late March. The next six weeks are pivotal for the new Elatryx product launch.'

'Late March? I need time off *now*, Mike. Six weeks' time won't work for me.'

'And right now doesn't work for Prime. You and your team have loads of work on, and I expect you to deliver. You can't take maternity leave. Sabina said so. I've offered you holidays. I think that's very reasonable. I'd grab the offer if I were you.'

'There *are* other options,' Sabina insisted. 'We need to explore them.'

I was still trembling. I had a horrible feeling that this was going to end badly. I tried to keep a friendly tone to my voice as I offered a compromise. 'I don't mind working from home for a week or two to finish things off and do a handover.'

'How's that going to work?' Mike demanded. 'The odd day at home is fine, but it's not sustainable. What about meeting clients? Are you going to strap the baby to yourself and take him with you? Leave him in the car and hope he doesn't cry? Dump him—'

'Mike!' Sabina snapped, stopping him from digging himself a deeper hole. She turned to me. 'That sounds like a reasonable compromise and a great starting point. We can explore how practical it is in a moment. Before we do, how long do you think you might need away from work?'

I tried to avoid eye contact with Mike. 'Hard to say. It depends when Shannon regains consciousness and how much support she'll be needing. Callum will be off his crutches eventually, but he won't be able to cope with a baby on his own. Plus, they have nowhere to live. Could be three months but could be six or more.'

'Six or more? You've got to be fucking kidding me!'

I flinched at the volume of Mike's voice and the expletive.

'Mike!' Sabina cried again. Her face was pale and I would have bet my life that, like me, she was trembling. 'I suggest you remember that this is a place of work and that one of your team has come to us with a very reasonable request. Unexpected? Yes. But she could hardly plan for something like this, and it's our job to find a way of making this work for both parties. How about we take a break for ten minutes while everyone calms down, then we can return and discuss the request without the expletives?'

Mike shook his head. 'As far as I'm concerned, the meeting's over. She—' he pointed at me '—needs to think about where her priorities lie. The way I see it, there are two options: holiday or the highway.'

I stared at Mike for a moment in astonishment and all I could see was the control freak, awkward bastard, bullying manager my colleagues saw. As if in a film montage, I recalled the snide comments, withering putdowns and public humiliations for failure to meet targets. I recalled the long hours, the no-praise culture, the extensive travel and being forced to go to Ireland when it was clear I didn't want to. He was just like my da! A feeling of calm swept through me. I smiled, nodded and stood up.

'What are you grinning at?' Mike demanded. 'This isn't funny. You've let me down, Clare. I thought you had it in you to go far. Believe me, it's the last time I promote a bloody woman.'

Sabina gasped. She opened her mouth to speak but I beat her to it.

'No, Mike. Not funny. Quite tragic, actually. It's tragic that you are a prehistoric, misogynistic bully. It's tragic that I used to look up to and respect you, when you're really not worthy of that respect. It's tragic that you think a woman has to work fifty times harder than any man to impress you. It's tragic that you'll probably walk away from this with no consequences and you'll take it out on the team I leave behind. The exceptionally talented team, that is, who work their arses off every day and would appreciate a thank you once in a while.'

'They get a bonus. That's their thanks. Ungrateful little—'

'I haven't finished! You asked me to think about my priorities. For the last eight years or so, Prime PR has been my life. It's been my number-one priority, and I've more than shown that through the accounts I've won and the millions in revenue I've generated. My priorities have now changed. I have a daughter, her fiancé and a grandbaby who need me and, if I'm honest, I need them too. Holiday or the highway? It's a no-brainer. I'll take the highway. I'll put that in writing, hand over my laptop and leave the building. Thanks for being so supportive.'

Mike's face was purple. I half-expected steam to come out of his ears, like a cartoon character. Sabina, on the other hand, looked as if she was having to stop herself from leaping up and cheering.

'I take it you're resigning with immediate effect?' she asked, eyes twinkling.

'She can't,' Mike yelled. 'She's on three months' notice. She has to work it.'

Sabina nodded. 'Contractually, she does. But given that she mentioned her potential case for constructive dismissal...'

'What? She never mentioned that.'

Sabina frowned. 'Sorry, Clare, am I having a senior moment and getting my wires crossed with a different meeting? You did just say that you felt you had been given no choice but to tender your resignation, given the refusal of your manager to consider any other options for your request, didn't you?'

I nodded. 'That's right. I think a tribunal would be very interested in the sex discrimination discussion too...'

* * *

'Well, that went well,' I said to Sabina, after Mike stormed out of the room, slamming the door. 'Thank you for doing that. I hope you won't be in trouble.'

She smiled and shook her head. 'I got offered a new job on Friday. I'm just waiting for the contract to come through, then I'll be handing in my notice too.'

'Congratulations!'

'Thanks. I can't wait to get away from Mike. Everyone else at

Prime is lovely, but most of my challenging cases have been because of him. Mind you, it's all been great employment law experience.' She gathered her papers together and stood up.

'I can't quite believe I'm leaving,' I said as we walked back to my hot desk. 'It wasn't the outcome I expected, but it feels right.'

'What will you do afterwards?' she asked.

'I don't know. I've been saving for a house deposit for years so I'm financially sound. I can focus on my family for however long they need me.'

'Then I'd say make the most of your time off and really think about what you want out of life. I reckon you'd be brilliant at running your own PR business.'

'Really?'

'I've always thought that. You're passionate, driven, focused, organised, great with people and brilliant at self-promotion. You'd be an amazing success.'

It wasn't something I'd ever considered, but I liked the idea. I liked the idea a lot. 'Maybe I will.'

She smiled. 'I bet you will. But enjoy your family for now. It's a lovely story being reunited after all these years. I hope Shannon recovers quickly.'

'So do I, Sabina. So do I.' I sat down on my chair and switched my laptop on. 'I guess I'd better write my resignation letter, then.'

27

My cheeks burned and tears of frustration dripped onto Luke's jacket as he screamed, his face bright red and his hands balled into tiny fists, flailing about angrily. It was about 4 p.m. After saying my goodbyes and leaving the office – clutching my handbag and a carrier bag containing my mug and a few other personal effects – I'd caught the train back to Leeds, picked up my car and driven to a specialist baby shop. Mike's PA, Margaret, had pressed a piece of paper into my hand. 'I've written the essentials on here and the stuff that's a waste of money. I've got five kids and eight grandchildren. If you need any advice, please call me. I've written my home number on there too.' She grabbed me and pulled me into a bear hug. I just hoped that Mike didn't take out his fury at me on her, poor woman.

'I'm sorry, Luke,' I cried. 'I'm trying. I just can't seem to...'

'Are youse okay?'

I twisted round to see Nurse Kelly hovering near the boot of the car. 'Jesus! Are you a sight for sore eyes?' I wiped the tears off my cheeks.

A flicker of recognition crossed her face. 'You're our little Luke's nana,' she declared.

'Yes. And I'm an eejit. He's coming home with me and I never thought to read the car-seat instructions. I've faffed that much, I've made him cry.'

'Aw, divn't worry. They seem more complicated than they are. Youse'll soon get the hang of it. How's aboots I...?'

I stepped back, gratefully. 'Be my guest.'

She crouched down and lifted Luke out of his car seat. 'Ah! I don't think he's crying just because youse couldn't do the car seat. He's crying because he's got a stinky bot. How's aboots I do it quickly?'

How had I not realised? Great start. I lifted the changing mat I'd just purchased out of the boot and found some wipes, a nappy and a nappy sack. Incredibly, Luke's cries had stopped. Nurse Kelly was obviously one of those baby whisperers. I wondered if I could bribe her to come home with me and teach me her secrets. Or kidnap her.

After Luke was changed, in ridiculously quick time, she helped me fasten him back into his seat.

'Firstly, it needs to be the other way round. Aye. That's it. And you see them clips...?'

Five minutes later, we were on our way.

As soon as I pulled into my parking space at Orion Point, I realised I'd messed up yet again. I had a boot full of baby stuff that would probably take me a few journeys had I been on my own. Problem was, I wasn't on my own. I couldn't leave Luke in the car while I traipsed back and forth, and I couldn't leave him in the apartment either. Bollocks! I was going to have to do at least six journeys with Luke in his car seat, with every journey putting me at greater risk of bumping into the Ice Queen.

* * *

Luke decided to demonstrate exactly how many decibels his cries could reach at 2.37 a.m. My hands shook so much while I tried to mix his formula that I dropped the first bottle and what seemed like ten pints of formula covered the cooker, the worktops, the cupboards, the kitchen floor and my PJs. I threw some kitchen roll over the mess on the floor then made up another bottle. And all the while, Luke screamed. And screamed. And screamed. There was no way on this earth that the Ice Queen hadn't heard.

The very next day, I was served with my eviction notice. How had I suddenly become homeless and jobless, with a baby to look after and not the faintest clue how to do it?

* * *

'Are you absolutely sure about this?' I said to Ben the following evening.

He slammed the boot of my car shut. 'I'm sure. And I was sure the 786 previous times that you asked me.'

'It's a huge thing,' I protested. 'He wakes up in the middle of the night and his screams register high on the Richter scale.'

'Oh, well, in that case...' Ben opened my boot again.

'I'm serious, Ben. I know you'd do anything for anyone, but this is seriously above and beyond.'

He shut the boot again. 'I know what I'm letting myself in for, Irish, and I genuinely want to help.'

God knows what I'd done to deserve such a good friend. 'I promise I'll find somewhere else for us to live as soon as possible but thank you for now.'

'There's no rush.'

'You won't be saying that at three in the morning.'

He smiled. 'I mean it. There's no rush.'

'I have a thank-you gift for you.' I reached into the pocket of my jacket. 'You're about to rise to the biggest challenge of your life so far. King of the moment, Ben.'

He shook his head. 'No. You keep him. You've packed in the job you love and given up your apartment for a grandchild you never imagined existed. You're king of the moment, Clare. What you've done is nothing short of amazing.'

I pushed the king into his pocket. 'I'll be offended if you don't take him. What you're doing for us is "nothing short of amazing". I mean that and you know I'm not generous with the compliments. Or the hugs. But you definitely deserve one of these.' I wrapped my arms round Ben and squeezed tightly. He squeezed back and, for a brief moment, I found myself closing my eyes and melting into his arms. I'd never really got hugging before. Perhaps it was because Ma and Da had never hugged me. There'd been no physical displays of affection towards anyone in our family. Of course, Daran had held me, but that had been different. We'd been in love. There had been chemistry and longing. I hadn't understood the need to hug friends but, clinging onto Ben, I suddenly got it. It felt as if all the stresses of the past month or so were seeping out of my body and into his, making me relax and feel that I wasn't on my own.

Ben squeezed a bit more tightly and placed a gentle kiss on the top of my head, then suddenly let go. Damn! I'd been enjoying that.

'You'd better check on Luke,' he said. 'You grab that case and I'll bring the rest of your stuff in.'

Taking the case, I went inside. Luke was in the dining room, away from the chaos my belongings had brought to the lounge, snuggled in his carrier, lips pouting, eyes flickering, sound asleep. I wandered back into the lounge and surveyed the mess. Daryl Smithers had issued me an ultimatum: leave at the end of the month and lose my bond for breaching the terms of our rental agreement or leave within twenty-four hours and he'd return my bond and the rent I'd paid for February. I didn't have much choice. I didn't have time to seek legal advice, although, let's face it, I probably didn't have a leg to stand on because I *had* breached the terms of my rental contract. I reluctantly accepted his offer and asked Ben if I could take him up on his kind invitation after all. Ben's mate Pete – the host of the New Year's Eve disaster – had generously offered his garage as temporary storage for my bed and a few other bits of furniture, and had sent his brother and dad to collect it all in a van. I got the impression that he'd heard about what Taz had done and this was his way of making up for what had happened at his house while he'd been out of action.

Ben appeared with the last few boxes. 'Déjà vu,' he said.

'Except this time there's two for the price of one, and no allowance for a kitchen refurb. Not such a great deal.'

'Kitchen's already done, thanks to you,' he said. 'So the allowance wouldn't be needed anyway.'

'I'll pay you rent.'

He shook his head. 'There's no need.'

I planted my hands on my hips. 'Bollocks! I may not have a regular salary anymore, but I *do* have money. If you won't take payment, you might as well put all my crap back in the car because we'll not be staying.'

'Okay, okay. We'll work something out.'

'Grand. Glad that's settled. Now, go and earn that rent I'll be paying you by making me a coffee.'

Ben laughed. 'Definitely déjà vu!'

* * *

We settled into a routine over the next week or so. Ben continued with his day job with the missing-persons charity, but he temporarily stopped his volunteering shifts. How guilty did I feel about that?

'We'd better move out, Ben. It's not fair that you're changing your life for us.'

'You once asked me why I didn't do anything for myself. I said I already was. I get a kick out of helping others and it doesn't matter what form that takes. Right now, it's more important to me that I'm here for you and Luke. I want to do this more than I want to do my volunteering and that's my final word on the subject.'

'She's a lucky girl.'

'Who is?'

'Lebony, of course. I think they might have broken the mould when they made you.'

He held my gaze for a moment, then smiled. 'You do realise it's a façade? I'm really a selfish misogynist who's luring you into a false sense of security before unleashing my evil plan for world domination.' He touched his lip with his little finger, like Dr Evil from the Austin Powers films. 'Speaking of Lebony, I'd better go and Skype her. She'll be dying to know how Luke's getting on.'

So that was that. I was back at Ben's, playing mum – a role I should have been allowed to adopt more than seventeen years ago. I spent my days at hospital with Luke, visiting Callum, and sitting beside Shannon's bedside, hoping for positive news. Sometimes Ben would accompany me to the hospital in the evening and other times I'd go on my own and leave Luke in his capable hands. He tried to make out that he struggled with changing nappies, found it challenging to dress Luke, and had the frequent bottle-assembling spillage disasters that I had, but I knew he was only saying it to make me feel better. He was a natural with Luke. What did make me feel a little better was when I 'accidentally' forgot to warn him about the urine risk and Luke gave Ben the same welcome he'd given me. Hilarious!

Callum's recovery was slower than expected thanks to an allergic reaction to his medication, but Shannon was doing very well. She'd fought off the fever and the cuts and bruises had healed, leaving behind a few tiny scars that were only noticeable if you knew they were there. Dr Kaur assured us that her internal wounds had healed too. The swelling on her brain had reduced and, two weeks after the accident, they started talking about bringing her round. I was elated yet also terrified at the thought.

I'd become close to Callum and had learned so much about my daughter from him. I'd learned that her favourite colour was yellow because it represented hope and happiness and her favourite passage in the Bible was: 'And there I will give her back her vineyards and make the valley of trouble a door of hope' (Hosea 2:15). I knew that fairground carousels terrified her, yet she loved roller-coasters. She was allergic to cats, she'd once dyed her hair green by mistake, and she dreamed of running her own school of dance. Callum showed me videos of her playing the guitar and dancing. She was a versatile and gifted dancer but ballet was her favourite. I knew all of these things about her and had a snapshot into her life through the power of social media. I felt as if I actually knew her as a person, yet she didn't know me from Adam. Worse than that, she hadn't given me permission to explore her past and might not be impressed that I'd done so.

* * *

On Saturday morning, Aisling arrived. She'd flown to Manchester the evening before to drop Torin and Briyana off at their da's, then caught a train to Leeds first thing in the morning. She was going to sleep on Ben's sofa, having refused to let either of us give up our beds for her, but would check into a local hotel when she picked up the kids on Thursday.

'This is my big sister Aisling,' I said to Callum, on the Sunday afternoon. I'd left Aisling at Ben's when I'd visited the day before to give her a chance to settle in.

They exchanged greetings, then I passed Luke to his daddy for cuddles. When he was settled, Callum reached for my hand. 'Tomorrow's the day,' he said.

'Shannon?'

He nodded with vigour. 'They're going to bring her round.'

'Oh my God!' Aisling said. 'That's amazing news. Will she be okay? Do they know?'

Callum shrugged. 'They're hoping so, but there are no guarantees. You'll be here, won't you, Clare?'

'I'd love to, but I don't know if I should be one of the first people she sees.'

'I talked to Dr Kaur about it. Thought I'd better tell her that you've never actually met. She says that Shannon will be, like, very disorientated, and it's going to be confusing enough having a bunch of doctors and nurses staring at her without introducing anyone else, especially someone she doesn't know. She wants me to be the only one she sees at first. She's not likely to be awake for very long. When she wakes up again, Dr Kaur and I can prepare her to meet you. I'd still like you to be here, though.' Callum squeezed my hand.

'Of course I'll be here. Should I bring Luke?'

'Dr Kaur says yes. Shannon might ask for him and she doesn't want her thinking she lost him in the accident and we're fobbing her off. It's better that he's around just in case.'

* * *

I couldn't sleep that night. I curled up in my duvet, listening to the wind battering the windows, staring at my sleeping grandbaby, snug in his cot. Up until that point, I'd focused mainly (and very selfishly) on how Shannon might react towards me when she came round. I'd pushed aside the thought that she might not come round in the way we hoped. What if she had brain damage? What would that mean for Callum and for Luke? I lit up my mobile for a moment so I could see the time: 3.38 a.m. They were planning to take her out of the induced coma during the morning so, by lunchtime, we'd know either way.

Shannon's favourite verse from the Bible kept popping into my mind – God making the valley of trouble into a door of hope. She'd certainly walked through the valley of trouble. Could hers and Callum's faith in God bring a door of hope? I thought about Daran. He'd have liked that verse. It might even have been one of his favourites too. The more I thought about it, the more familiar it sounded. What would Daran have done in this situation?

I slowly eased myself into a sitting position on the edge of the bed, clasped my hands and bent my head. I sat like that for a few minutes, watching the steady rise and fall of Luke's chest. Then I did something I hadn't done since they told me Shannon had died. I closed my eyes and I prayed.

✉ To Elise
Hope all goes well with the midwife today. Let me
know. Off to hospital shortly. They're bringing
Shannon round this morning. Moment of truth x

✉ From Elise
Oh my goodness! Thinking of you all. I'm sure
she'll be OK. Please let me know as soon as you
can. Nervous about midwife. Praying my blood
pressure has gone down. Glad it's half term. I'm
exhausted. Bet you are too! xx

✉ To Elise
I am! I've forgotten what sleep is! Good luck xx

* * *

'Feeling brave?' Aisling asked, when I'd pulled into a parking space
at Jimmy's.

'Shitting a brick! But I have to put on a brave face for Callum.'

Aisling squeezed my hand. 'I know it's a cliché, but what will be
will be.'

'I know.'

'I prayed for her last night,' I said, as we walked across the car park. 'That's something I never thought I'd do again.'

'Must be contagious,' Aisling said. 'Because I did too.'

'Let's hope that there is a God, then, and that He was listening. Luke surviving that crash unscathed was a miracle. We need another one for Shannon.'

* * *

'You look done in,' Ben said, as we bathed Luke together that evening.

'I am. I feel like I could close my eyes and sleep for a year.'

'Why don't I have Luke in my room tonight and give you a chance to sleep through?'

I shook my head. 'I can't ask you to do that.'

'You didn't ask me. I offered, so quit it with the protests.'

'Ooh, I love it when you turn all alpha male on me.'

Ben laughed. 'I don't think anyone could ever accuse me of being alpha male.'

He gently sponged Luke's legs. 'When do they think you'll be able to speak to her?'

'Maybe tomorrow. Maybe the day after. I'm just so relieved that the early indications are good.'

Shannon had opened her eyes a little before ten that morning. Callum told me she'd been very disorientated, as we'd been warned. She knew her name and date of birth, she could remember a lorry veering towards the car, but she couldn't remember the actual impact. She'd then tried to reach for her stomach, no doubt panicking that something had happened to her baby. Callum had reassured her that they had a healthy baby boy, but she was asleep again before they could fetch him from me. She'd awoken again in the afternoon and had managed to stroke a sleeping Luke. Callum admitted that he'd cried seeing Luke finally being held by his mum. He showed me a photo of the moment, which made me cry too.

Ben lifted Luke out of the bath and wrapped a bright yellow hooded towel around him. 'Don't you dare pee on me again, young man, or I'll be lodging an official complaint with your mummy when she's ready for visitors.'

The hood on Luke's towel slipped down as Ben stood up with him. 'Ooh, look, Grandma! I think we might be growing some hair. And, if Uncle Ben isn't mistaken, I do believe we may have a little ginger baby in the family.' Ben kissed Luke's head, then pulled the hood up again. 'Are you okay, Irish? You've gone pale.'

'I'm... It's...' I sat down on the edge of the bath. It was there again. Shapes. Shadows. Swirls. Something. Exactly as I'd felt when I'd stood in the farmhouse before Da appeared. I shook my head, trying to dislodge the feeling. 'I'm just exhausted. Ignore me.'

'You look terrible.' Ben looked genuinely worried. 'I think you should go to bed right now before you keel over.'

'We need to move the cot. And I can't abandon Aisling.'

'Aisling will understand, and don't worry about the cot. I'll sleep in your bed and you can sleep in mine. I changed it on Saturday, if you can cope with almost-clean bedding.'

'You haven't made a crusty mess since then?'

'I don't even want to think about what you might mean by that. No, I haven't! Bed. Now.'

I nodded, kissed Luke's cheek, kissed Ben's too, grabbed a fresh pair of PJs from my drawers, then gratefully retreated under Ben's duvet.

Sleep overcame me pretty much instantaneously. As I drifted into dreams later, I was back at the farmhouse. And there was something in the shadows. Or someone.

29

'Are you decent in there? Can we come in?'

I opened my eyes as Aisling pushed open Ben's bedroom door and appeared with Luke cradled in one arm and a mug of coffee in her other hand.

'Morning,' I mumbled. 'Or is it afternoon already?'

She smiled as she put the coffee down on Ben's bedside drawers. 'It's just gone eight-forty. Ben's gone to work. He had a pretty good night with Luke and he says he hopes you got the rest you deserved. How are you feeling?'

'Still pretty tired,' I yawned, as I wriggled into a sitting position. 'I had bad dreams last night.'

'I'm not surprised. Your head must be mashed after all the disruption and worry lately.' She handed Luke to me for a cuddle. 'I've popped some toast in for you so I'll just get that. Quick shower and we should be at hospital for ten at the latest.'

* * *

'I don't know how you cope with the traffic around here,' Aisling said, as a driver cut me up on the way to the hospital. 'It's so busy.'

'D'you think so? I'm used to London traffic, so this is grand by comparison.'

'I couldn't do it,' she said. 'My blood pressure would be sky high.'

'Arse! Blood pressure. Elise. Can you get my phone out my bag and see if I've got a text from her?'

Aisling reached behind her for my handbag and found my mobile. After I gave her my pin code she declared, 'No texts.'

'Bollocks. Can you send her a text for me?' I dictated what I wanted to say, then explained the situation.

✉ To Elise
I'm hoping no news is good news. Let me know how it went xx

As we crossed the car park ten minutes later, my mobile began ringing and my stomach clenched as I saw the name.

'Stevie? Is Elise okay?'

'Not really. She's in hospital.'

I stopped walking. 'Jesus! Is the baby okay?'

'Hopefully. Elise's blood pressure was really high so the midwife sent her to hospital for monitoring. They did all sorts of tests and checks, and apparently she's got pre-eclampsia too.'

'Pre-what-ia?'

'Pre-eclampsia. I don't really know the details, but I know it's not good for baby or mum. It's fairly common, though, so they know what they're dealing with. She had another scan and bean's fine, but they'll keep monitoring it. She's putting on a brave face.'

'What if her blood pressure keeps rising?'

'They'll put her on medication.'

I swallowed hard as I formed the next question. 'What if this clampsie thing gets worse?'

There was a pause before Stevie said, 'We could be looking at a premature birth.'

I put my hand over my mouth. Poor Elise! 'How far along is she?'

'She'll be thirty weeks on Thursday.'

'Ten weeks early? Christ, Stevie, is that far enough?'

'I don't know. I'm trying not to think about it. I'm about to leave for the hospital again now, but I wanted to call you and Sarah first to let you know what's going on.'

'What did Sarah say?'

'I got her voicemail so I left a message. I'll try her again later. I'd better go.'

'Okay. Send Elise my love and keep me posted.'

We said our goodbyes and I hung up. I turned to Aisling. 'It never rains but it pours.'

* * *

Callum was waiting for us in the corridor outside the ward.

'What's wrong?' I asked, panic filling me as I took in the anxious expression on his face. 'She's okay, isn't she?'

'She's fine. Actually, she's doing really well.'

'So, why the serious face?'

'She wanted to see Luke so I had to explain why she couldn't.'

'So she knows?'

He nodded. 'The bang on the head hasn't knocked the feistiness out of her.'

'Feck!'

Aisling placed a comforting hand on my arm. 'It was probably just a shock since she thought you wanted nothing to do with her.'

'Did you tell her I didn't send that letter? Did you tell her I didn't even know she was alive?'

He shuffled awkwardly. 'I kind of didn't get the chance before—'

'Before what?'

He wrinkled his nose and shuffled a bit more on his crutches, suddenly appearing fascinated by his shoes. 'Before they had to sedate her.'

Aisling's grip on my arm tightened. I took a deep breath. 'That bad, eh?'

'Sorry.'

'No. It's me who's sorry. I never meant to cause trouble between you two.'

He shrugged. 'It was the shock. I told you that she's a thinker.

She'll strop and sulk for a while, but she'll think it through and she'll come round.'

So my worst-case scenario had come true. Actually, it was worse than that. She'd reacted so badly, she'd had to be sedated. I glanced down at my grandbaby. 'What do you want to do about Luke?'

Callum glanced down at Luke too. 'Same as before. We're both stuck in here and it's not the right place for him. I'm still on a ward so I can't look after him and it will be ages before Shannon can so she's, like, got no choice for the moment.'

'What about now? She'll want to see him when she wakes up, won't she? Do you want Aisling and me to stick around?'

He sighed and slowly shook his head. 'Maybe not. Maybe leave Luke with me for now and I'll ring or text you later about picking him up again. Don't stress. We'll get it all sorted. God will show Shannon that it's the right thing for Luke to be with you, like he showed me.'

I squirmed at the mention of God but didn't say anything. If He existed, He owed it to me to bring her round to wanting me in their lives. God had always seemed very real to me when I was with Daran. Everything had seemed very real to me when I was with Daran. But if God had loved Daran as much as Daran had loved Him, why had He taken him in the tsunami? Immediately, Daran's voice echoed around my mind with his answer: 'Yes, but what about all those He saved?'

* * *

I felt as if a part of me were missing when I left the hospital without Luke. Aisling draped her arm around me. 'She just needs time. It'll be grand.'

Would it be? I knew what it was like to hold a grudge.

'How about we go shopping?' she said, when I remained silent. 'Ben said there's a shopping centre near here. White Dove or something?'

Shopping was the last thing I felt like doing, but it struck me that when Aisling had booked her flight for the school holidays, she hadn't signed up to all of this. Granted, she'd expected to have to amuse herself during the day, as I'd have been working. Instead, I wasn't working, but she'd been subjected to disturbed nights, and days spent hanging around a hospital waiting room. The least I could do was treat her to a nice lunch and a bit of retail therapy.

'White Rose,' I said. 'It's about five or six miles from here. Shopping it is, then.'

A spot of shopping would probably do me the world of good.

* * *

I found myself in Zara an hour later, stroking a gorgeous, short, ivory wrap dress with embellished shoulders and waistband, and a low back, imagining how it would look with my nude Louboutins. 'What do you think of this?' I said to Aisling, holding it against my body.

'Absolutely gorgeous. I saw that in *Practical Parenting* last week. It's what all the mums wear when changing dirty nappies and burping their babies.'

It took me a moment to register what she'd just said. 'Jesus! What an eejit I am! When will I ever have a chance to wear something like this with Luke around?' I hooked the dress back onto the rail. 'Mind you, if Shannon gets her way, I won't be allowed to be part of Luke's—'

'Stop right there,' Aisling said. 'I won't be letting you wallow in this. Shannon's angry and that's understandable. When she calms down, Callum will explain what really happened. She won't suddenly become your BFF and start calling you Mum, but she *will* want to build a relationship. It'll be slow and there'll be hiccups but it *will* be a relationship. Callum will make sure that happens. You heard what he said. He's only going along with it just now because he doesn't want to jeopardise her recovery.'

Aisling steered me out of Zara and towards a coffee shop, where she ordered two large cappuccinos. I tipped a packet of sugar into mine. 'What am I going to do with myself all day if Luke is at the hospital with Shannon and Callum? And what if Callum recovers enough to move into a visitor's room so they don't even need me to have Luke overnight? I packed in my job to look after him and now I might not even get to see him.'

Aisling shrugged. 'I think it'll be a while before Callum's well enough to have Luke on his own overnight. But could you ask for your job back? Part-time, I mean, after you've done the hospital drop-off?'

I shook my head. 'I kept in touch with my boss's PA, Margaret. She says they've already replaced me.'

'That was quick.'

'Internal promotion. They've even backfilled his position.'

Aisling studied my face for a moment. 'If they'd granted you leave to look after Luke, you wouldn't have returned, would you? You're thinking of doing something else?'

I smiled at my big sister. 'How did you know that?'

'There's a twinkle in your eye. You're scheming something.'

'It's just a seedling of an idea at the moment and it might not grow. When I left, our HR manager said she could imagine me running my own business and the more I've thought about it, the more I like the idea.'

'I could see you as a successful young entrepreneur,' Aisling said. 'Doing what? PR still?'

I nodded. 'PR, marketing, social media... but maybe on a smaller scale. Local companies, rather than big corporates.'

'Sounds grand. Here in Leeds?'

I shrugged. 'That'll be the unknown element. I want to be near Shannon, Callum and Luke, if they'll let me. I'll follow them anywhere. Well, anywhere as long as it's not Ballykielty!'

Aisling laughed. 'Can't imagine why you wouldn't be dying to move in next door to Ma and Da. They'd make you so welcome!' She took a slurp of her drink. 'Have you heard from your man? Stevie, is it?'

'Jesus! I haven't checked my phone.' I dug it out of my bag. Sure enough, Stevie had texted me:

✉ From Stevie

Elise and bean OK but BP still rising Will give
it a few days before they decide on inducing
birth. Elise is bored but says she has another
story idea. Hope Shannon's OK xx

'Everything okay?' Aisling asked.

'Elise is in hospital but hopefully everything's okay.' I took a sip
of my coffee while I gathered my thoughts. 'If she's anything like
me, Shannon won't change her mind about seeing me within the
next few days. Do you fancy a trip to the seaside tomorrow after we
drop Luke off? I'd like to visit Elise. I know that means the inside of
yet another hospital, but I promise that the rest of the day will be
devoted to you.'

'Will you buy me an ice-cream?'

'It's February.'

'It's the seaside. Which means ice-cream.'

I laughed. 'Okay. There's a really cool vintage ice-cream parlour
on the seafront. Sarah took me there once. It does amazing
sundaes.'

'Sold,' she said. 'When we've finished these, what would you say
to us getting you some sensible baby-friendly clothes? We passed a
Penneys earlier. Or, what do you call it in England? Primark?'

'Wash your mouth out!'

'Have you been in Primark lately?'

'I've *never* been in Primark.'

'Then you don't know what you're missing. I love your clothes,
Clare. They're gorgeous and you always look amazing, but designer
skirts and dresses with three-inch heels are not practical with a
baby.'

True. I'd become increasingly exasperated with my wardrobe
since I'd started looking after Luke. I actually only owned one pair
of jeans and two T-shirts, and I felt so much more comfortable with
Luke when I was wearing them. Maybe it was time to change my
wardrobe.

'Sounds like I'm about to have the most dramatic makeover of
my life.'

Aisling nudged me in the ribs. 'It's just a transition into the world of parenting. It doesn't need to mean sweatpants and shapeless, beige sweaters. You can still have colour; you can still have dresses. You just probably don't want to spend as much on them. And you might want to invest in a few pairs of flat shoes.'

30

'Welcome to Whitsborough Bay,' I declared brightly as I pulled into a parking space on The Headland, opposite Lighthouse Cove. 'Looks like we've got the perfect weather for a trip to the seaside.'

We stepped out of the car and breathed in the fresh sea air. Fluffy clouds danced across a cornflower-blue sky and gulls squawked as they swooped down in search of discarded chips and doughnuts. I reached into the back seat for my coat and scarf. The sun felt warm against my cheeks, but it was still February and there was definitely a winter chill in the air.

'What do you fancy doing?' I asked Aisling. 'We've got three hours till visiting time. If we go left out of here, we can walk round The Headland. It's about thirty to forty minutes and it brings us out at North Bay. There's a couple of cafés and a bar that Sarah says does good food.'

'Sounds grand.'

'So,' Aisling said, when we'd crossed the road and set off, 'you and Ben? What's the story?'

I pulled a face at her. 'There's no story. He's a friend.'

'Is he now?'

'Yes!'

'You don't think that what he's doing for you goes a bit above and beyond friendship?'

I laughed. 'For most people, yes. For Saint Ben, no. He works for a charity by day and volunteers by night. Luke and I are his current volunteering project. He's just being a good friend.'

'Friend? You're codding yourself.'

I stopped and leaned against the thick stone wall between the path and the sea. 'What brought this on? Did he say something?'

Aisling smiled. 'No. But I've seen the way he looks at you, so I have.'

'Bollocks! He's got a girlfriend and he's devoted to her.'

'Ah, yes, the mysterious Lebony. Don't you think it's convenient that she's on the other side of the world?'

'Not really. In fact, not at all, poor Ben.' I shook my head and started walking again. 'You've been reading too many romance novels. Ben doesn't see me as anything other than a friend and, even if he did – which he doesn't – it would be bugger all use because I don't think of him in that way. He's my best friend's brother and he's a good friend and housemate. There's never been anything more and never will be.'

'You go on convincing yourself of that.'

'Aisling! What's got into you? Ooh, I know! You've seen me *looking* at him too. Men and women *never* normally look at each other so it *must* mean we're harbouring deep, secret desires for each other.'

'I'd say your man Ben is, but your feelings for him are a bit too deep for you to acknowledge just yet.'

'Bollocks! The reason I haven't acknowledged them is because they're non-existent.'

'That's what you think.'

I shook my head again. Where the hell had this conversation sprung from? 'Even if I did have feelings for Ben – which I don't – and even if he didn't have a long-term girlfriend – which he does – it would be pointless anyway.'

'Why?'

'Because I have no intention of letting anyone in ever again. I've been there and got the battle scars.' I twiddled my Claddagh ring as images of Daran filled my mind once more. 'It's too painful when it ends.'

'But that was an extreme set of circumstances and it only ended because of Da. If he hadn't interfered, you'd still be together now, wouldn't you?'

'I'd like to think so, but who knows? What if he'd started resenting me for taking him away from the priesthood? What if he'd started to hate sharing his love for God with me?'

'And what if he realised that the priesthood was never his calling and a life with you was? And what if he was such a wonderful person that he had plenty of love for you *and* God? From what you've told me, you were made for each other. You'd have made it.'

We wandered in silence for a moment, only breaking it to say 'good morning' to a dog-walker and an elderly woman pushing a buggy.

'Did you think you and Finn were made for each other?' I asked eventually.

'Of course I did.' She sighed. 'Fair point. *I* believed we'd survive forever, but we didn't.'

'There you go, then. It's all heartache and I don't believe it's worth it.'

'Lots of relationships end, but there's always a reason. For Finn and me, the reason was that we should never have got married in the first place. *I* thought we were made for each other; *I* was the one who believed in us and *I* was the one who loved him so deeply that I couldn't imagine life without him. Finn didn't feel the same. He certainly cared about me but as soon as he met someone who was the real thing, he was off and I couldn't blame him. I knew it would happen eventually.'

I frowned. 'Really?'

'On our wedding day, I kept expecting him to stop the Mass because he couldn't go through with it. When he didn't, I kept telling myself that I needed to do the right thing and stop the ceremony myself, but I selfishly couldn't. I managed to convince myself that he had to love me a bit if he was willing to go through with the wedding. If a seed of love was there, perhaps it would grow into something bigger. So we both said, "I do" and I spent the rest of our marriage wondering if each day was the day when he'd announce, "I don't".'

'Jesus, Aisling! You never told me that. From what you'd said, I thought you'd been happy together until the affair.'

'That's what I let everyone think.' She pulled a tissue out of her coat pocket and wiped her eyes. 'I played the part of the hurt wife who'd known about the affair but had turned a blind eye for the sake of the kids. I pretended I was relieved that it was out in the open and we could end the sham marriage and both start afresh. I never admitted that I'd been expecting him to leave from day one. I told him everything he needed to hear to keep the split amicable for the sake of the kids so that...'

'So that what?' I asked, when Aisling didn't continue.

'So that I could still have him in my life.'

I stopped walking again and looked at my big sister. 'Oh no! You're not still...?'

She sat on the wall, her body twisted so she could stare out at the twinkling sea. 'Pathetic, isn't it? He never loved me, he had an affair for three years, then left me for her. He left Ireland and moved to Manchester to be with her and, even though they split up and he didn't come running back to me, I'm still head over heels in love with the man and would do anything for him. I think that makes me the eejit, doesn't it?'

I sat on the wall beside her and took her hand in mine. 'No. I think it makes him the eejit for not realising a good thing when he had it.'

She dabbed at her eyes again. 'He is one. But I'm an even bigger one because, ever since he split up with *her*, I've let him... you know.'

'Friends with benefits? Jesus, Aisling, are you mad?'

'Madly in love?' She shook her head. 'I know! You don't need to lecture me. I lecture myself about it every day, so I do. Because of the kids, I was always going to have to see him, so it was going to be harder to try and get over him. I know that sleeping with him is taking me deeper and deeper into this mess, but he's so attentive when we're together that I can almost kid myself that he loves me. Almost.'

She adjusted her position and put her head on my shoulder. We sat like that in silence for five or six minutes, still holding hands, listening to the gulls, a gentle sea breeze tickling our faces with locks of our hair.

'I don't know about you, but I'm ready for that coffee,' Aisling said, squeezing my hand then standing up and stretching.

We set off walking again. 'What happened with Finn and *her*?' I asked.

'Ironically, it was the same as what happened with Finn and me, only he was the one in deep this time. Turns out she was a big, fat coward and thought that accepting a job in Manchester would bring a natural end to the relationship. Stupid cow hadn't counted on him following her. She strung him along, house-hunting and everything. They even put a deposit down on a new build. His money, of course. They exchanged contracts and then the day before completion, she dropped the bombshell that she didn't want to be with him anymore.'

'Bitch.'

'I know! He was devastated. There he was, stuck with a house they'd chosen together, miles away from his kids, and no girlfriend anymore.'

'Could he not have moved back to Cork?'

'His job had gone, not that he'd have wanted to return to it even if it hadn't. Going to Manchester was a good career move for him – better company, big promotion – and he loves his job, so he decided to make a go of it.'

'What about the two of you? Any chance?'

'I'd have him back like a shot, but only if I could be sure that he'd woken up one day and realised he loved me as much as I loved him. Chances of that? Zero to none.'

'I'm sorry.'

'Not your fault. We can't control who we fall in love with.'

I smiled. 'No shit. A potential priest would *not* have been top of my list!'

'And the opinionated, underage daughter of a stroppy, controlling, religion-obsessed bigot probably wasn't top of his list, either. Yet it worked because you both felt the same way about each other. That's why it didn't work with Finn and me, or Finn and *her*. It's why it didn't work with your friend Elise and her ex-husband...'

'That, and the fact that he's gay.'

Aisling laughed. 'True. And that's why it won't work between you and Ben. Yet. Because, at the moment, he's smitten but you're not. It'll grow, though. It'll definitely grow.'

'Seriously, Aisling. Do you want me to push you over the sea wall? Will you stop trying to matchmake Ben and me. We're just friends.'

'For now.'

'Forever!'

'Hmm. Anyway, I'll drop the subject for now. Would that be a coffee shop I can see ahead of me like a shimmering oasis?'

'It might be.'

'Then coffees are on me for talking about Ben. I should have realised it was too soon.'

I gently pushed her towards the sea wall. 'Final warning!'

As we continued to walk round The Headland towards the café, a feeling of unrest settled upon me. She was completely and utterly wrong about Ben, wasn't she? I certainly didn't feel anything for him, other than friendship and a tremendous amount of gratitude. He'd never given any indication that he felt anything for me, either, had he? I racked my brain. No! He'd always been clear about his devotion to Lebony and that was a huge amount of devotion to keep a relationship going across such a distance. Aisling was way off. Given her revelation about still sleeping with Finn, she needed to get her own love life under control, instead of inventing romances between other people that didn't exist. What was she thinking?

31

Aisling was keen to explore Hearnshaw Park so I left her there while I drove up to the hospital, although I did a bit of a detour through The Old Town. Parked close to Seashell Cottage, I sighed and shook my head. What was I doing there? Yes, I loved the cottage but I was only torturing myself by visiting it. Right now, I had no control over what the future looked like. It all depended on Shannon's recovery and whether she'd let me be part of their lives.

Elise looked tired but was upbeat. Her blood pressure had gone down again and her baby was in no immediate danger so all she could do was relax and hope nothing changed for the worse.

'What's this?' she asked, as I handed over a sparkly, lilac gift bag once she'd updated me.

'Stevie said you'd been working on your stories. I thought these might be helpful.'

She carefully emptied the contents of the bag onto her bed. I'd bought her a selection of notebooks, pens, a planner and Post-it notes in different shapes and colours.

'Clare, that is so thoughtful,' she said. 'Thank you.'

'How's the writing going?'

'I've come up with an idea for my tenth novel.'

'Tenth? That's amazing. If you want anyone to read them, send them over. I could do with the distraction. I don't know how long it'll be before I can see Shannon, and I can't stop thinking and worrying about her. Aisling is here at the moment, the kids will join us tomorrow, but I'll be on my own from Saturday afternoon with just my thoughts and my guilt for company.'

'How are things going with her?'

'When she heard I'd put in an appearance and had been looking after Luke, she had such a strong reaction that they had to sedate her.'

'Oh my goodness, Clare! That's awful.'

'Not the best. I felt so sorry for Callum having to deliver that little gem to me.' I coughed. 'I'm parched. Is there anywhere I can get a drink?'

Elise pointed. 'There's a water fountain and some cups over there near the nurses' station.'

When I returned to the ward with fresh water for us both, Elise had another visitor.

'Sarah!' I put the jug and cups down. 'Elise didn't tell me you were coming.'

'She didn't know. Auntie Kay offered to cover the shop so I could nip over. How are you? I didn't know you were coming to Whitsborough Bay.' Sarah might as well have added the missing words 'and that you clearly weren't planning to visit me afterwards' because her intention was very clear.

It felt just like the hideous phone call we'd had after Sarah returned from her honeymoon, and I absolutely didn't want to go down that road again, especially after we'd had such a good talk when I'd stayed over at hers. It was time to change the subject. 'How's the shop?' I asked.

'Fine. A bit quiet after the Valentine's Day rush, but it will soon be Mother's Day.'

'Are you okay?' I asked, noticing that Sarah's eyes had filled with tears.

She sniffed and dabbed at her eyes with a tissue from her pocket. 'Sorry. Think I'm getting a bit of a cold. Watery eyes. Do you mind if I have some of that water?'

I picked up the jug and poured her a cup. 'Are you sure you're okay? You don't look too good.'

'Just a bit tired. It's been busy at work. I'll go and find another chair.'

Elise caught my eye as Sarah headed towards the nurses' station. 'Is something wrong with her?' she asked.

I shrugged. 'Not that I'm aware of, but I'm not buying the "tired" thing. There's something else.'

'I think so too. Whatever it is, she obviously doesn't want to talk about it. Maybe she'll let us know later.'

'The nurse is going to bring one over,' Sarah said, returning to the bed. 'So, how's Shannon doing?' She looked from Elise to me, then back to Elise. 'Or have you already discussed this?'

'No,' I said. 'I only got here about ten minutes ago. So, the update is that she came round on Monday but was in and out of sleep. She was more with it yesterday and asked for Luke. Callum told her about me, and she hit the roof and had to be sedated. Physically and mentally, they're pleased with her progress so that's really positive. Doesn't look like the knock on the head has had any lasting damage. Emotionally, it's clearly not so good. It's going to be a long road and that's another reason to be angry with my da. That man has such a lot to answer for.' I unclenched my fists and tried to relax. The mere mention of him made my blood boil.

'I'm sure he'll answer for it one day,' Elise said. 'Changing the subject slightly, how's it working out with Luke?'

'It hasn't been without its challenges. I've lost my job and I've been evicted, I've got baby sick on most of my clothes, and I still haven't quite mastered feeding, burping or changing him. But the cuddles are worth it.'

'I still can't believe you're a grandma,' Sarah said. 'And that you've walked out of the job you loved to take on parenthood, just like that. That's such a huge commitment. Are you sure about it?'

'It's different and it's unexpected, but what sort of person would I be if I'd refused to do it? I'd have kept Shannon if I'd had any choice but I wasn't given one, as you know.' I winced at the sharpness in my tone.

'I didn't mean it like that,' Sarah said.

'Sorry. Ignore me. I'm seriously stressed by the whole Shannon situation. Do you want to see a photo of them?' I dug in my bag for my mobile and thrust it under Elise's nose.

She smiled. 'Aw, she's just like you. And Luke's a little baldie! How cute.'

'He's started to get hair now. Looks like he may be a redhead.' As I said the word, an involuntary shiver rippled through me and that strange feeling was there again. What the hell was it?

'Really? Is Callum a redhead?'

I shook my head. 'Callum's dark.'

'Maybe the red comes from further back in the genes.'

'Not on our side but maybe it does on Callum's.'

Elise handed the phone to Sarah, who took it without a word. I frowned as her eyes filled with tears again. She cleared her throat and handed it back. 'They're gorgeous, Clare. I can't wait to meet them.' She fished a tissue out of her jeans pocket and blew her nose. 'I think it's time I headed off.'

'But you've just got here,' Elise protested.

'I know. I'm sorry. I'm definitely coming down with something and I don't want you to catch it, Elise. It's the last thing you need right now.' She stood up and picked up her bag. 'Keep me posted. Both of you.' Then she left.

'Was it just me or was that really strange?' Elise said, as soon as Sarah had gone.

'Very strange,' I agreed. 'Although I think I was a bit snappy with her and I didn't mean to be.'

She nodded. 'I'm sure she'll understand it's not about her but about your situation. Do you think I should phone her later and ask her what's going on?'

I shook my head. 'You've got more than enough on your plate at the moment.'

'And so have you. I'm sure she'll tell us what's wrong if she needs our help. Remember how she was with Jason? It took her a year to admit that she wasn't happy with him and the first we knew of it was when she dumped him. She likes to work things through in her own mind.'

I nodded. I felt uneasy about it, though. What if she didn't think we were interested anymore? What if she thought we had each other now and didn't need her? Surely she wouldn't think that. It was childish and Sarah wasn't a childish person. She'd always wanted Elise and me to make our peace. Surely she was happy that we had.

But that feeling of uneasiness wouldn't go away.

32

✉ From Elise
Hi everyone. Baby's on the way! BP's continued to
rise and pre-eclampsia's getting worse so they
induced me early this morning. Waters have just
been broken and everything seems to be happening.
She'll be 31 weeks tomorrow so scared but excited
about early arrival. Been taking steroids to
build her lungs so hopefully she'll be OK. Stevie
or I will text with news and a name when she's
born xx

Jesus! Thirty-one weeks. Elise must be terrified. After visiting her in hospital the week before, I'd Googled it and it seemed that thirty weeks was the magic number for a high survival rate so the odds were in her favour, as long as there were no further complications.

I strapped Luke into his car seat. 'Are you ready to visit Mammy and Daddy?' He stared at me and blew some bubbles. 'I'll take that as a yes. When you're with your mammy today, will you ask her to stop sulking and accept that what happened when she was born was completely out of my control? I just want to see my daughter and try to make up for all the lost years.' Luke blew some more bubbles. 'Good boy! I knew you were the man for the job!'

I tried to relax as I drove to Jimmy's. Again. To drop Luke off. Again. To face Callum's slumped shoulders, the bags under his eyes and that apologetic expression. Again. It had been nine days since she'd woken up. Nine bloody days, yet she still point-blank refused to talk about me, never mind meet me. It broke my heart that she refused to let me in. If she had her way, I wouldn't get to see Luke at all and I certainly wouldn't be the one providing a roof over his head, but Callum had put his foot down. He'd moved into a visitor's room but the reliance on his crutches and the recovery from appendicitis meant he couldn't have Luke with him. Shannon wasn't well enough to look after Luke and the hospital had already done their bit so Shannon didn't really have a choice. I would remain as Luke's primary care-giver and she'd have to like it or lump it.

'Let's take it as a good sign that she only had to be sedated the once,' I said to Luke, as we drove towards Jimmy's. 'Did you have words with her and tell her that I'm not so bad?'

* * *

'You look exhausted,' I said to Callum, who was waiting for me on the seats near the nurses' station as per our demanding new routine: 10 a.m. drop-off, pick-up two hours later. So much for worrying that I'd have nothing to do all day and no time with Luke. All I seemed to do now was ferry him back and forth, desperately trying to fit in shopping, cleaning and washing in between.

'I had a bad night,' Callum replied. 'I think I'm also suffering from a lack of fresh air.'

'If you can get hold of a wheelchair, I don't mind pushing you around outside for a bit, if that would help.'

'Tempting, but I'd better take Luke into Shannon. She's been asking where he is.'

Argh! Must control temper. Must not snap. 'She's been asking where he is? I'm... what?' I glanced at my watch. 'Two minutes late. *Two minutes.* And that's only because your son decided it would be a good time to fill his nappy moments before we were due to set off. Only, when I say "fill his nappy", I don't really mean that. I mean his nappy, his dungarees and his T-shirt. Christ alone knows how something so small can generate so much. It was like a sewer had exploded in there. So I had to strip him, wash him and start again. Then, guess what? I realised that I had shit all over me too so I had to get changed. So I'm sorry I'm late by two whole minutes and have failed my daughter yet again. You'd better rush Luke to her side immediately and I'll be on my way, rushing home, then rushing back again so that Luke and I are out of your hair by dinnertime, exactly as demanded. I've left my job and been evicted, yet she still won't even grant me five minutes of her time. I get that she's angry. I get that she was let down. I get that I wasn't there when she needed me. What *she* needs to get is that I was forced to give her up, I was told that she was dead and I didn't write that letter telling her I wanted nothing to do with her.' Did really well controlling my temper there.

'Feeling better?' Callum asked.

I stared at the floor, feeling very sheepish. 'Yes. Sorry. I wasn't having a go at you. I just needed to vent. The whole situation's getting to me.'

He smiled. 'I'm surprised you didn't do it sooner. The reason that Shannon was wondering where Luke was had nothing to do with her being demanding or thinking you were late. It was about her being anxious and nervous and wanting to get it over with.'

'Get what over with?'

'She's had her sulking and thinking time, and she's ready.'

'For what?'

'To meet her mum.'

* * *

I was shitting a brick as I held Luke close to my chest with one arm and wielded the baby carrier with the other. I had no idea what to expect. Would she rant at me, releasing a lifetime of pent-up frustration? If she did, would I be able to control my temper, or would my frustration at Da project onto her and ruin any relationship before it had even started? Or would she give me a chance to explain?

And if she did, was 'I had no choice' a good enough excuse for agreeing to the adoption? I had, after all, had a choice. I could have said no and faced the consequences.

Shannon had been moved onto a ward with six beds in it, five of which were occupied.

'She's on the far left,' Callum whispered, as he hobbled beside me on his crutches.

I felt quite sick with nerves, my heart racing and my stomach churning as I approached my daughter. It took my breath away, seeing her sitting up for the first time, not surrounded by machines and wires. Her hair was shiny and fanned across her shoulders and there was colour in her cheeks.

'Hi, Shannon,' I said, my voice catching in my throat.

She looked me up and down, chewing on her lip, but she didn't speak.

I panicked and thrust Luke towards her. 'Somebody wants cuddles from his mammy.'

Shannon adjusted her position so I could settle Luke in her arms. She smiled at him and lightly kissed his head. 'Thank you.'

'You're welcome.'

Callum settled into the chair closest to us and nodded encouragingly towards Shannon.

'So, you're my birth mum,' she said. Her voice was low and gentle, devoid of any discernible accent. It threw me. For some ridiculous reason, I'd expected her to have an Irish accent like me. Of course she wouldn't have!

'It would appear so. How are you feeling?'

'Sore. Tired. Grateful to be alive. Speaking of which, Callum tells me you thought I was dead.'

I nodded. 'They told me you'd died shortly after you were born. That letter you got? It wasn't from me. I knew nothing about it until Callum told me.'

'He told me that too.' Her tone suggested she doubted it was the truth but the hopeful look in her eyes made me think she wanted it to be. She nodded towards a chair on the other side of the bed. 'You'd best pull up a pew and start from the beginning.'

'Okay. Thank you.' I moved round the bed and sat down. 'Right. From the beginning?'

'Yes please. But you might need to do it in two parts.' Her voice had softened. 'I get tired easily.'

* * *

I did manage to make it through the full story before Shannon's eyes started to get droopy. 'I'd better go,' I said. 'Will I leave Luke with you and come back later?'

'No. Stay,' Shannon whispered, before surrendering to sleep.

'Do you want to see if we can get that wheelchair?' Callum asked, reaching for his crutches. 'I could do with some air. Shannon will probably be out for an hour or so.'

Fifteen minutes later, Callum and Luke were bundled up in coats and blankets, ready for a push round the grounds. Luke was due a feed so one of the nurses had heated up his bottle in readiness.

'That seemed to go well,' I said, as we left the building.

'It went very well. I knew she'd come round.'

'What happens next?'

'With you and Shannon?'

'With everything: Shannon and me, the three of you, hospital, where you live. Everything!'

Callum adjusted Luke's hat to cover his ears better. 'You and Shannon will continue to talk and get to know each other. She might still have stroppy moments but the hardest part is over. Me and Shannon will get married at some point, but the priority is getting her better. And me. They think I've got a urine infection so I'm having more tests.'

I stopped pushing the wheelchair and moved round it so I could face him. 'No! Really? That's not fair. Haven't you been through enough already?'

'You'd think so, wouldn't you?'

'Is that why you had a bad night?'

'Yes.'

'That's bollocks. Sorry, Callum.'

He shrugged. 'Could be worse. At least I'm in the right place to get it sorted out.' Luke's face crumpled and he let out a loud squawk. 'Looks like someone's ready for his feed.'

I resumed pushing as soon as Luke was settled with his bottle.

'What else did you ask me?' Callum said. 'Oh yeah, where we'll live. I don't know. There's nothing left for us in Northampton. No home. No job.'

'What about your apprenticeship?'

'Gone to someone else.'

'No! Why did they do that?'

'Because I told them to. It wasn't fair to ask them to hold my place when I had no idea when I'd be able to return. Even when I'm better, Shannon won't be, so I'm going to need to be around for her and Luke. For now, this place is our home. I'm temporarily back on the ward being monitored so it's not costing us anything.'

'You know you don't need to worry about money, don't you? I have savings. I can help.'

Callum shook his head. 'There's no need. We've got the money back from the house we were going to rent, and Shannon gets, like, an allowance from her parents' estate. It'll be tight without me earning but we'll manage. Besides, we only need to scrape by till a year come June.'

'Why? What happens then?'

Callum twisted round to face me, frowning. 'Shannon's eighteenth, of course. She'll inherit half a million. Actually, it might be closer to £600,000.'

I stopped pushing. 'You're kidding?'

'Her parents... her *adopted* parents... were loaded. It all went into a trust fund until Shannon's eighteenth, with a monthly allowance till then. I'll get a job and keep working, you know. I'm no sponger. And Shannon still wants to go to college so I want to bring in some income while she's studying. I'd like to put some of the money aside for Luke's future.'

'From what I've learned about you, Callum, I know you're definitely not a sponger. So your challenge isn't money – it's location?'

Luke finished his bottle and we stopped so Callum could burp him. 'I don't know where we'll live,' he said. 'It'll depend on whether we need to stay close to Jimmy's or not. I don't know Leeds, but it probably wouldn't be in my top ten of places to live. Or Shannon's. Big cities aren't us. The Hendersons were out in the country and Shannon was brought up in a village.'

'If you could live anywhere, where would you go?' *Please don't say you want to move abroad, and definitely don't say you want to move to Ireland.*

Callum pondered for a moment. 'I don't really mind. It would need to be in the north. Shannon's inheritance sounds like loads but it won't buy us much down south. It would need to be a town or village. It would need to have a decent school for Luke. Shannon quite fancies living near the sea. I've never really thought about it, but why not try something different, after spending my whole life living miles from the coast? What I *really* want is to find somewhere that Shannon can properly call home. She's carried those wooden boxes around with her for years. I want her to find somewhere to scatter the ashes.'

'So, you want northern, coastal, not too big, reasonable house prices, decent schools and somewhere that feels like home?'

Callum ran his fingers through his hair. 'I said I didn't mind but it looks like I do, when you list it like that.'

'I know the perfect place.'

'You do?'

I smiled brightly. 'Yes. Whitsborough Bay.'

33

✉ From Stevie
She's here! Melody Hope. Born at 3.42pm by C-
section as her heart rate had started to drop.
She's tiny — 3lb 9oz — but mum and baby are doing
well. Melody's on the special care baby unit.
Elise is resting. Will report back with news
#prouddad #firstselfie

Tears filled my eyes as I clicked into the image attached. Stevie, wearing a surgical mask, blue paper gown and hat, was closest to the camera, the joy clearly radiating from his eyes. I could guarantee the grin beneath that mask was enormous. On the right, Elise's head rested on a pillow, her auburn curls hidden beneath a paper hat too, and a clear oxygen mask over her face, showing the biggest smile ever. Wrapped in a white towel, a tiny, red, wrinkly baby nestled between them, eyes tightly shut, fists in tiny balls under her chin.

'Hi, Melody Hope,' I whispered, gently touching her image with my finger. 'You be a good girl now and grow quickly so you can go home with your parents.'

✉ To Stevie
Beautiful name for a beautiful baby. Congratulations to you both. Send my love to Elise. Can't
wait to meet Melody xx

I finished folding the washing then slumped back on Ben's sofa. What a day! Shannon finally speaking to me. Elise having the baby. I hadn't realised I'd been so tense about those two events.

* * *

The sound of a key in the lock startled me.

'Were you asleep?' Ben asked, poking his head round the door.

I rubbed my eyes and sat up, 'I must have been. I swear I only closed my eyes for a moment.' I looked at the clock on the wall. 'Bollocks. I've been out for forty minutes. I'd better check on Luke. He'll be awake any minute.'

'I'll do it. I need to go up to get changed anyway.'

'Thanks.' I rolled my stiff shoulders and checked my phone for any more messages but there was nothing.

'He's still asleep,' Ben said, when he reappeared in a fresh T-shirt and jeans ten minutes later. He sat down beside me on the sofa. 'How was today? Is she still refusing to see you?'

'No. I was finally granted an audience.'

'Oh my God! How was it?'

'A bit awkward at times, but it was such a relief to see her. She looks—' I rolled my eyes as a loud squawk filled the room. 'No rest for the wicked. I'll tell you later. Have you got any plans tonight?'

'I've got to Skype Lebony at seven, then I'm all ears.'

As I made my way upstairs, I thought about my conversation with Aisling when we'd visited Whitsborough Bay. She absolutely had it all wrong. Ben messaged and Skyped Lebony on a regular basis. He was just as committed to making their long-distance relationship work as he'd always been. I was just a friend. In fact, I was almost certainly more like another sister to him. Aisling probably just liked to fantasise about happy-ever-afters for other people, given that she couldn't have her own, thanks to her little obsession with Finn.

'Has your Auntie Kay sold Seashell Cottage yet?' I asked Ben, after we'd put Luke to bed later that evening.

'I spoke to her at the weekend and she's had two viewings but no offers. The housing market's slow at this time of year. What makes you ask?'

I shrugged. 'I'm probably jumping way ahead of myself here. I was talking to Callum about what happens when they're both recovered. He said they'd like to settle in a town or village in the north and that Shannon fancies somewhere coastal. I suggested Whitsborough Bay.'

'You're thinking they might want to buy Seashell Cottage?'

'Not them. Me.'

Ben's eyes widened. 'You're leaving Leeds?'

'I'm jobless and I'm homeless. It's not like there's anything to keep me here, is there?'

'Thanks a lot.'

I shoved his leg. 'Don't sulk. You know I don't mean it like that. If I were to copy your sister and write the pros and cons on some Post-its, seeing you would be top of my reasons to stay in Leeds. Problem is, I'm not sure there'd be any other Post-its on that column. It's an amazing city but my priorities have changed. If they'll let me, I want to be where my family is and, from what Callum's said, Whitsborough Bay would seem a sensible place to settle.'

'Do you want me to have a word with Auntie Kay?'

'Not just yet. I don't want to be my usual impulsive self, put plans in place, then discover that by "north", they actually mean Scotland, or that they don't want me with them.'

'I'd miss you,' Ben said. 'You and Luke, that is. I've got used to having the little man around.'

'We'd miss you too, but it's not like we wouldn't see each other again. You are, after all, his step-granddaddy, or whatever lie it was we told the nurse on that first day.'

'We? What's with the "we"? I think it was you, young lady, who were the big, fat fibber that day.'

I laughed. 'I can't believe it was only four weeks ago. So much has changed in such a short space of time.'

'Feels like longer.'

'It certainly does.'

We sat in companionable silence for a while, listening to the clock tick and sipping on our drinks.

'Seashell Cottage?' Ben said, after ten minutes or so. 'I always imagined you'd choose to settle in a swanky apartment with a shiny kitchen, white walls and minimalist décor like Orion Point.'

'So did I. It had a spectacular view and it was a practical option for me when I was travelling but it never felt like home. Somehow it always felt like I was living in a hotel room whereas Seashell Cottage felt like home from the first time I stayed there when Sarah moved back to The Bay. I must have a thing for older properties because I get that same feeling of home here too.'

'Is that why you stayed here while I was in Birmingham?'

I gasped, as colour rushed to my cheeks. 'Jesus! How did you know that?'

'The old lady next door, Mrs Astell, asked if you'd moved back in or if you'd just been house-sitting while I was away.'

'I'm so sorry. I meant to say something. It was after I got the letter and told Elise everything. It was such a huge thing for me, opening up to someone after so many years of silence. I couldn't face going back to the flat on my own. I should have asked, or said something afterwards, but things went a bit crazy.'

'I'm not mad at you. I'm glad you like it here. I just wish I hadn't been away that weekend so I could have been here for you.' He smiled at me and his dark-brown eyes twinkled with warmth. For a moment, I thought I saw a flicker of something. No! Aisling couldn't be right about him, could she?

'You're a good friend,' I said, placing a slight emphasis on the word 'friend'.

'Any time.' He was still looking at me tenderly. Arse. I had to nip this in the bud.

'I don't think I've ever had a proper male friend before,' I said. 'Any male I've got pally with has always turned out to have another agenda of getting into my knickers, so it's so refreshing that we can have this, knowing that it will never be more than friendship.'

Ben grinned. 'You think I fancy you, don't you?'

I blushed again. Where the hell had *that* come from? I'd *never* blushed before and now I'd done it twice in one evening. 'No. It's just that—'

'It's just that your sister's planted the idea in your head and now you're overanalysing every comment, every glance and every touch.'

Realisation dawned. 'She said something to you too?'

'She quizzed me about it when you were in the shower one morning.'

'I hope you told her she was way off and you were very happy with Lebony.'

'What do you think?'

'Phew! I can relax again now.'

'Am I *really* that undesirable?'

I threw a cushion at him. 'Stop fishing for compliments. I suppose you're not too bad-looking, if you're into that whole "boy next door with sad puppy-dog eyes" kind of thing.'

'Ooh, don't push it with the praise.'

'What about me, anyway? How come you've never tried it on with me? Am I *really* that undesirable too?' I playfully flicked my hair and pouted. 'I thought I was irresistible to all men, women and small furry animals.'

Ben laughed as he stood up and reached for my empty mug. 'Just as well I'm immune to your charms then, isn't it?'

'How can that be?'

He shook his head at me, grinning. 'Look, you know I think you're gorgeous but I have a girlfriend, so let's just say that I can enjoy looking at the goods, I just can't sample them – which works out perfectly for everyone. No friendships are tested and no partners are made jealous. Win-win. Night, Irish.'

'Night, Saint Ben.'

As I lay in bed shortly afterwards, gazing across the room at Luke sleeping peacefully in his cot, I thought about my conversation with Ben. What must he have thought when he'd discovered I'd stayed for the weekend? How embarrassing! And even more embarrassing was the revelation that Aisling had interrogated him about his feelings for me. I didn't like to dwell on what she might have actually asked him. I'd be having words with her when I next spoke to her. What was her game? It could have gone horribly wrong, because I couldn't have continued to live with Ben if I thought he saw me as more than a friend.

34

✉ To Sarah
I'm coming over to visit Melody this afternoon. I
can't stay long as I need to be back for Luke. I
know it's a Saturday, but do you have time for a
coffee late afternoon?

✉ From Sarah
Would love to see you but Cathy & Jade are away
for the weekend so I'm really short-staffed.
I've had to send Briony home with a high temp
and Josh isn't very experienced yet. Mum's here
but we have a 60th birthday party to prepare for
so I might not be able to give you much time.
Sorry

✉ To Sarah
Sounds chaotic. I won't add to it. Catch you
soon x

'She's absolutely gorgeous, Elise. Congratulations, both of you.' I
hugged Elise and Stevie, then gazed into the incubator again. 'I'm
not convinced that the tube-up-the-nose fashion she's currently

sporting will catch on, but she's working the look pretty well just now.'

Elise laughed. 'With us as parents, I don't think she's ever going to be fashionable, is she?'

'Can I get you a coffee, Clare?' Stevie asked.

'You're a legend. Black, strong, no sugar, please.'

When he left the room, I turned to Elise. 'Does the twat know?'

Elise rolled her eyes. 'Daniel?'

'Unless there's a list of twats who could be the father?'

She shook her head. 'One's enough, thank you. I texted him yesterday.'

'Any response?'

'What do you think? Kay and Philip stopped by this morning with some gifts. Philip says Daniel's still going for the "it's not mine" approach. If that's the attitude he still wants to take, it's fine by me. As far as I'm concerned, Stevie's Melody's dad.'

'What if Daniel wants to be in her life later?'

'The door will always be open for him, but I'm not going out of my way to try and get him involved. I don't want or need any money from him so that should make things easier.'

Stevie returned with the coffee and I took a grateful gulp. Luke now only woke up twice a night for a feed and settled quickly afterwards, but I didn't. My mind would start whirring. Sometimes it was worries about the future, sometimes it was a list of chores I needed to do and sometimes it was a song or TV theme going around my mind on a loop. I never used to struggle to sleep. What was that all about?

'I come bearing gifts, as you might have noticed.' I unknotted a bin liner to reveal a shiny, pink 'It's a girl!' helium balloon, then handed over a packed gift bag.

Elise smiled widely. 'Thank you, but when have you had time to go shopping for all of this?'

'Luke and I went to a retail park for a spot of late-night shopping on Thursday. I've got all the receipts, if you don't like anything or already have it. Apologies that nothing's wrapped.'

'This is too much, Clare,' Elise said when they'd seen all the gifts. 'You must have spent a fortune.'

'It's grand,' I said. 'I'll admit I might have got a bit carried away, but it was exciting. It was quite therapeutic buying things for a baby girl when I didn't get the chance to do it for Shannon, and boys aren't quite as much fun to buy for.'

Elise started to carefully place everything back in the gift bag. 'How's it going with Luke?'

'I'm still a bit worried I'm going to break him when I change him but I don't feel as completely clueless as I did before.'

'I think most first-time parents are clueless,' Elise said. 'When my sister's twins came along, I realised I'd had hardly anything to do with babies. I could confidently hold one, but I didn't know how to change a nappy or make up a feed. Our Jess made sure I had plenty of practice on the twins.'

'Same here,' Stevie said. 'I've never been round babies either. The first time I held one of Jess's twins, I thought I was going to drop him, and I was convinced that I was going to hurt him when I tried to change his outfit one day. I'm still learning but I feel a lot more confident now.'

So it wasn't just me being an incompetent eejit? I'd assumed Elise would be a natural at it all, like Callum and Ben. I finished my coffee and dropped it into a nearby bin. 'So, have you had any other visitors?'

Elise nodded. 'Our Jess came yesterday afternoon and her husband dropped in that evening. My boss and his wife nipped in very briefly this morning before Kay and Philip, but that's it. Dad's flying over on Tuesday or Wednesday.'

'No Sarah?'

Elise glanced towards the incubator and shook her head. 'No. No Sarah.'

'She's texted,' Stevie said. 'She replied to the group text about Melody's arrival to say she was thrilled for us and hoped Melody would be home really soon but there was no mention of visiting. Are you going to see her while you're over?'

'I texted to say I could pop in after visiting time but I got this gibberish response about staff being on holiday, off sick or inexperienced. Who's Briony?'

Elise shrugged. 'Not heard her mentioned before.'

'Me neither,' Stevie added.

'Well, apparently Briony is ill, whoever she is. It seemed to me like she didn't want me there, but she didn't want to say it outright so there were all these excuses. You know how she babbles when she's nervous? Well, she was babbling on her text message, if that's possible.'

Stevie shook his head. 'I don't know what's going on with Sarah lately. I invited her to start running with me again but she's had an excuse every time. I've suggested cinema trips but she's turned those down too. I've hardly seen Nick, either.'

I looked towards Elise. 'Have you seen or heard from her since the awkward hospital visit?'

She shook her head. 'No. A couple of texts to ask if I was okay but nothing more.'

'There's something going on,' I said. 'Under normal circumstances, I'd drive over to the shop and drag it out of her, but I have too much going on at the moment and I don't have the energy to keep asking her what's wrong.'

'I feel the same,' Elise said. 'We've got bigger things to worry about right now and it's a bit easier for Sarah to come and visit us, rather than the other way round. I understand that a Saturday is difficult because of the shop but if she doesn't show up tomorrow, I'll be very unimpressed.'

A young nurse opened the door. 'Sorry to interrupt, but you have another couple of visitors and I'm afraid we only permit two at a time, plus parents.'

'Sarah and Nick?' Elise asked, sounding hopeful.

'Gary and Bob, I think they said.'

'Gary and Rob. Okay. Thank you. Could you ask them to wait a moment, please?'

The nurse nodded, then closed the door.

Stevie hugged Elise. 'She'll come soon.'

I picked up my bag. 'I'm sure she'll visit soon too. Gary and Rob have perfect timing because I need to get back to Leeds. I'll try to get over again soon.' I blew a kiss in the direction of the incubator. 'Bye, Melody. Hurry up and get out of that incubator so Auntie Clare can have hugs.'

In the car, I reflected on our conversation about Sarah, and how I was more likely to pick up the phone to Elise or Ben these days rather than her, despite that huge heart-to-heart we'd had. How had that happened? Had I pulled away from Sarah or had she pulled away from me? If Elise was feeling it too, surely it was the latter? But did I have the time and energy to do anything about it? No. Did that make me a useless friend? Did it mean I was taking her friendship for granted again – something I'd sworn I wouldn't do?

Could there be something going wrong with the shop or with her marriage already that she didn't want to face up to? Surely not. The shop was thriving, and she and Nick were besotted with each other still, weren't they?

An uneasy feeling settled over me as I joined the A1 towards Leeds. I *was* being a useless friend. I was all wrapped up in Shannon and Luke, and full of criticism for Sarah for not being more supportive, but what if she was facing something even bigger in her life that she needed my support on?

I drummed my fingers on the steering wheel. What could be going on in Sarah's life that was bigger than me discovering that my daughter hadn't really died at birth, that her father had been killed in the tsunami, that she'd been in a serious car crash and that she had a son who needed my care?

I pressed my foot on the accelerator. Sarah had occupied enough of my thoughts. I'd make another attempt to find out what was going on but I'd wait until next week. She knew where I was if she really needed me. Why should I be making all the effort?

35

I had no idea where the next two weeks went. Well, actually I did. They flew by in a frenzy of hospital visits and babysitting.

Callum's immune system was so low that he picked up another infection which wiped him out so he was on strict bed rest and hooked up to a drip. Meanwhile, Shannon continued to improve. Dr Kaur was very impressed with her. They'd got her up and about surprisingly quickly after they'd woken her up, but she still had a broken ankle and arm, which meant she was limited with her movement.

Five weeks after the accident, she was ready to put weight on the ankle. Her first steps were very tentative. Physically, I could see she was exhausted, as she clung onto the railing in the physio room. Emotionally, I could see that it was worse. I recalled the footage of her dancing and was pretty certain she was petrified she'd never be able to dance again. I didn't know how to broach the subject so I took Dr Kaur aside and asked her outright.

'The fact that she's a dancer will make her rehabilitation easier,' she assured me. 'Her legs will be used to hard work. Because of the accident the muscles have forgotten what that feels like and they're objecting to it. If she's determined – and I can see that she's that kind of woman – there's no reason why she won't fully recover and dance again to the same standard. The broken ankle has healed nicely because she's had complete bed rest and she didn't damage her legs in the accident. She just hasn't used them for a while.'

Shannon cried after that first intense physio session. She'd been strong in front of us but, when she was alone on the ward, the tears fell. I only knew because I realised I'd left Luke's teddy on her bed so returned to get it. She wasn't quick enough to wipe the tears away.

'I know it hurt today, but it will get better,' I said, passing her a tissue.

'And you'd know because you were in a coma and woke up to discover that your legs had forgotten how to work?' she snapped.

'No.'

'You're a doctor then, are you?'

I gazed at her and saw so much of me in her, desperate to strike out at anyone, in order to keep the pain at bay. 'You'll dance again,' I said. 'I know it.'

Another tear slipped down her cheek. She didn't need a pep talk from me. She needed her alone time to think.

'I'll see you tomorrow, Shannon. Don't give up. And don't forget that stuff about God making the valley of trouble a door of hope.' Without waiting for her reaction, I left the ward. Callum was adamant that her faith was strong. Maybe that was what she needed to get her through this. It wasn't my thing but if it worked for her, so be it.

The next day, she seemed a lot more positive and apologised for snapping. It was her first apology to me so things were looking up.

A week of physio did wonders for her. By the end of the second week, Callum was up and about again, encouraging and supporting her, and the improvements were incredible.

I visited Whitsborough Bay hospital twice during that fortnight. The first time was an evening so I texted Sarah a couple of days before, knowing the shop would be closed. I got another garbled message back about meetings and stocktakes and Christ knows what. I didn't bother contacting her the following week. I couldn't face a third rejection. While I was there, I drove round the Old Town and parked near Seashell Cottage. There was a 'for sale' board outside but thankfully no 'sold' sign on it. I was so tempted to knock on the door and tell Kay I wanted to buy it, but I needed to know where Shannon and Callum were going to settle before I could make any major life decisions like that.

Melody was doing really well, putting on weight and sleeping less. Sarah still hadn't visited and I could see how hurt Elise was about that. She'd sent several texts, each with a different excuse: she had a cold and didn't want to pass it on to Melody; she had a stomach bug and couldn't risk passing that on either; Nick had picked up the bug and she was worried about still being contagious. And so it went on. She'd posted a new baby card through their letterbox one evening but hadn't knocked. Stevie had actually been in and his car was on the drive, so he'd felt pretty miffed that she didn't seem to have five minutes to say hello and ask after Melody. Elise, who always tried to see the good in everyone and every circumstance, suggested that it might not have been Sarah who'd dropped off the card, but her words lacked conviction and I could tell she felt totally let down by Sarah's absence.

Shannon and Callum made a decision that it wasn't fair on Luke to spend so many hours cooped up in hospital, especially as that had been the reason why Callum had asked me to look after him in the first place. We therefore settled into a fresh routine of visits – one full day there without me, the next evening with me, a morning without me, another evening with me, then back to the start again. I liked the new arrangement. It was far better for Luke to get out in the fresh air, and it was good for Shannon and Callum to get quality time alone with him. It also helped my relationship with Shannon. I could tell her about the places Luke and I had been and she lapped up all the minute details like the colours of the leaves on the trees, the feel of the breeze on our cheeks, the cries of other children in the park and so on. I think she liked to imagine she was the one pushing the pram and behaving like a 'normal' mum.

On the Sunday, two weeks after Shannon had started her intensive physio, I was scheduled for an evening visit. A mild mid-March day had dawned, with blue skies and a warm sun.

'It's gorgeous out there,' Ben said, as he washed up after breakfast and I dried the dishes. 'Do you fancy making the most of a full day with Luke and taking a run through to Whitsborough Bay?

'To see Elise?' I asked. I clocked his frown and quickly added, 'Or Sarah?'

He reached for the tea towel and dried his hands, then leaned against the sink. 'You can tell me to mind my own business, but she's my sister so I have to ask. What made you say "Elise" first? You hardly ever mention Sarah these days.'

'I can't work out what's going on in Sarah World at the moment. I've tried to spend time with her but she seems to be avoiding me. She's avoiding Elise too. Don't think she wants to be our friend anymore.' I flinched. Even to my own ears, the reference to 'Sarah World' sounded extremely bitchy and the rest of the statement sounded downright childish. Clearly, Ben thought so too.

'Have you tried to find out what's going on in "Sarah World", as you so beautifully put it?'

I snatched the tea towel back off him and picked up a mug to dry. 'Don't get stroppy with me, Ben. It was just a flippant comment.'

He folded his arms and shook his head. 'I don't know what's going on between the three of you, and I don't really want to get involved, but I also don't want to hear any talk about you not being friends anymore. If you think my sister hasn't been there for you, it might be because she has things going on herself, and she could easily say that you haven't been there for her either.'

'Don't be cryptic, Ben.'

'I'm not being cryptic. I'm just making a point. I know you have lots on at the moment, and so does Elise, but perhaps Sarah does too.'

I put the mug and tea towel down and folded my arms as well. 'Is she sick? Is that what you're trying to tell me? I mean, properly sick, rather than just a cold?'

'No.'

'Problems with the shop?'

'No.'

'Problems with Nick?'

'No. It's not that either.'

'Then what is it?'

'It's... Sorry, Irish. I can't tell you. It's not up to me to say anything. But I really think you should—'

But at that moment, Luke woke up and screamed. The unfinished conversation hung in the air while I brought Luke downstairs, doing my best to avoid eye contact with Ben as I prepared the bottle. Eventually, Ben left the room, muttering something about taking a shower, and my shoulders relaxed. Well, that had gone well!

In true Saint Ben style, he came back downstairs fifteen minutes later, apologised for interfering and for lecturing me, and insisted that we still go to Whitsborough Bay and forget the conversation had ever happened.

* * *

'So, how's Lebony?' I asked, as I pushed the pram along the promenade at North Bay after a walk around Hearnshaw Park followed by a late lunch outside a beachside café. The sun had brought everyone out. Cyclists, dog-walkers and families jostled for space along the wide pathway, and the beach was as packed as on a summer's day. Many of the brightly coloured beach huts had their doors wide open, with children dashing in and out brandishing buckets and spades or body boards, and parents or grandparents making lunch or lounging on deckchairs with a book, e-reader or the Sunday papers. I smiled as I took in the scene, thinking how much Shannon and Callum would love living in Whitsborough Bay. It was so perfect for families.

'She's good,' Ben said, bending to chuck a rogue Frisbee back to a couple of teenagers on the beach. 'She's in France at the moment.'

'France? That's a little normal for her, isn't it? I thought she wasn't interested in anywhere that wasn't famine- or disease-stricken.'

'The charity she currently works for is French so she's doing some training with them.'

'Oh.' I wasn't really interested in hearing more about Lebony. I'd heard enough about her from Sarah over the years. Sarah didn't like her because she never seemed to have time for Ben, even when she was in the UK. Visiting him was like an afterthought. Sarah said she was too nice, too perfect and too passionate about changing the world, without being aware of the impact she had on those she left at home. I was inclined to agree and found myself disliking her too. And then I'd feel like a right bitch for thinking that, because we needed people like Lebony. So much was wrong with the world and I was full of admiration for anyone who felt compelled to do something about it – something more than making the occasional charitable donation. I guess, in that way, she was a lot like Daran. I just wished she'd either end it with Ben or spend a little more time with him. He always made out that he didn't mind and their long-distance relationship worked for both of them, but he got a sad, faraway look in his eyes when her name came up.

A couple moved away from a bench beside us and I indicated to Ben that we should sit down. I lifted Luke out of his buggy.

'You're imagining living here, aren't you?' Ben said after a few minutes' silence.

I smiled. 'Is it that obvious?'

'I see the way your eyes are darting about everywhere, as if you're seeing the place for the first time and sussing it out.'

'I laughed when Sarah moved back here. I couldn't understand why someone who'd lived in Manchester, then London, could possibly want to move back to a small town by the sea. When I first visited, I was pleasantly surprised. It was *very* Sarah, but it wasn't me. I still wanted my bright lights, big city. I couldn't imagine settling down somewhere like this.'

'And you can now?'

'Very much so. I thought I liked being surrounded by designer clothes shops, nice restaurants and trendy bars, but it turns out I prefer a night out at your local Indian, or a night in with a takeaway and a film. My expensive wardrobe suddenly seems impractical and uncomfortable, and I'd rather go shopping for clothes for Luke than anything for me. I think this young man might have completely changed me, in more ways than my wardrobe choices.' I pointed to my outfit – charcoal leggings, grey Uggs, a burgundy tunic top, nipped in at the waist, and a sparkly, silver scarf.

'I like the outfit, by the way,' Ben said. 'I like this new style a lot. I think it's more the real you, not that you didn't look amazing in your old outfit choices.'

'It feels more like the real me. I used to dress like this when I was younger, before I was kicked out. I consciously changed my clothes and cut my hair to separate myself from the past. I guess the real me couldn't really disappear.'

'And the real you is a small-town girl at heart? I actually think you started to change last year, before you knew about Shannon or Luke. When you lived with me first time round, I'd suggest going out to bars and restaurants but you were always keener to stay in or go local.'

I thought for a moment. 'You could be right. I hadn't—'

My phone began ringing, cutting me off. I pulled it out of my jacket pocket. 'It's Aisling. Do you mind...?'

'Be my guest.' Ben reached for Luke as I connected the call.

'Hi, Aisling, how's it going?'

'Not good. I'm sorry to do this over the phone, but Da's had a heart attack. A serious one.'

The squeals of children and the squawks of seagulls, which had been so loud moments ago, seemed to mute. The scene before me on the promenade and the beach paled and blurred as I fought to form any words.

'It's not looking good,' she continued. 'He's asking for you. I know you owe him nothing but...'

I took a deep breath. 'I'm in Whitsborough Bay at the moment so I doubt I'll be able to catch a flight tonight. Plus, I need to make arrangements for Luke. But I'll get there as soon as I can. Do you think he'll...?'

'I don't know. He's really sick.'

36

Rushing through arrivals the following morning, clutching a carry-on case, I kicked myself for not packing better. I didn't want to be in Ireland and I didn't want time away from Shannon, Callum and Luke, but more clothes would have been a good plan, in case I couldn't get away as quickly as I'd like.

I was already missing Luke and had hated saying goodbye to him at Jimmy's last night. Callum had finally been given the all-clear to stop using his crutches and was well enough to have moved back into a visitor's room. Ben had offered to request emergency leave to look after Luke but Callum had insisted he'd be able to manage now. Much as it hurt me to admit it, it would do them some good to be together as a three without me being around. Valuable family bonding time. After all, they hadn't exactly had a conventional start to family life.

Aisling was waiting for me in the arrivals lounge and looked exhausted. 'Am I pleased to see you,' she said, holding me tightly. 'Ma's driving me crazy. If she doesn't calm down, she'll take a heart attack herself, so she will.'

I followed her out to her car. 'So, what happened?' I asked, as we pulled out of the car park.

'It's been building up for ages. The man's a bloody eejit. He's been in a right state since your trip home, spouting on about sinners and repentance. I subjected the kids to a visit the weekend after you were here and Da commented on how much Briyana had grown since Christmas. She responded by asking him if he thought she'd grow up to be as tall and beautiful as her Auntie Clare.'

'Shite. I bet he hit the roof.'

'Ma spilled her cup of tea all over the carpet. Da turned purple and suggested we'd probably been there long enough. The poor kids could hear the yelling as we got back into the car and hadn't a clue what was happening. I visited again a couple of weeks ago without the kids and told them we'd seen you over the school holidays. I thought they'd better hear it from me rather than Torin or Briyana.'

'Did you tell them about Shannon and Luke?'

'No. I only told him we'd visited.'

'Did he turn purple again?'

She concentrated on the traffic for a moment as she guided the car out of the airport car park and towards Cork. 'I actually thought he was going to keel over clutching his heart at any moment. His mouth kept opening and closing, and no words came out. Ma called me a few choice words and threw me out. I haven't seen or spoken to them since.'

'Jesus Christ! I'm so sorry, Aisling. That sounds hideous.'

'It wasn't the best craic I've had, but it was inevitable at some point.'

'If that was two weeks ago, what happened to bring on the heart attack? Or was it just a build-up of rage?'

'It was a steady build-up but Keenan going round on Saturday night and announcing that he's getting divorced didn't help.'

'No! I thought you said he was a strict Catholic like Da.'

'I thought he was but I've spent so little time in his company since the kids were born that I had no idea how much he'd changed. He took Éamonn with him for support, which makes me think he must have changed too.'

'So I'm not the only sinner in the family, then?'

Aisling shook her head. 'Nope. Five kids, two divorcees, and one supporting one of those. Mind you, you still hold the crown for being a wicked harlot. Keenan and I are sadly no contest for you there.'

I laughed. 'I'm very proud of that. Will I have that carved on my gravestone? "Here lies Clare O'Connell. Wicked harlot. And proud!"'

Aisling laughed loudly. 'I'll have to outlive you now, just to be able to see that.' She shrugged her shoulders and rolled her head as if letting the tension ease away. 'You're a tonic, little sister. An absolute tonic.'

We drove in silence for a while until I realised she hadn't finished the story. 'You said you didn't think that Keenan's news had helped. Does that mean something else happened to bring on the attack?'

She nodded. 'So, we have him angry with you since, well, since forever. We have him furious with me for spending time with you. We have him livid with the twins, and then the straw that broke the camel's back was that he visited Father Doherty after Mass yesterday. I hadn't told him about you seeing the Father and him handing over the letters. He hardly ever visits Father Doherty so I didn't expect him to find out but I'm assuming he wanted his guidance on the divorce situation, so he pays him a visit, no doubt expecting support and understanding. Instead he gets a sermon on how wonderful you are and how he should seek forgiveness. He storms out, drives home and collapses an hour later.'

'Christ!'

'I know!'

* * *

We pulled into the visitors' car park of Cork University Hospital and walked towards the entrance. 'Why do you think he's asked for me?' I said.

'To clear his conscience.'

'Do you *really* believe that?'

She hesitated and lightly touched my arm. 'I want to. I really do.'

My stomach churned. She clearly thought exactly the same as me – he wanted to say his piece before he met his maker, and his piece wasn't going to be about making peace. It was going to be about him getting the last word in. Would I let him, or would I finally tell him exactly what I thought of him, knowing that it could finish him off?

I'd carefully selected my outfit. I didn't want to give them any ammunition to accuse me of dressing provocatively, so I wore a pair of tailored boot-cut black trousers, a ruched turquoise blouse that revealed no cleavage, and a pair of low-heeled boots. From the withering look Ma gave me, I might as well have danced down the ward wearing fig leaves on my privates and flowers in my hair.

She rose from beside his bed and narrowed her eyes at me. 'The good Lord alone knows why he's asked for you, you dirty harlot.'

'Hello, Ma. It's lovely to see you too.' My voice might have sounded confident but I didn't feel confident inside. I felt like a sixteen-year-old girl being judged all over again.

'Will we get some tea, Ma?' Aisling said, grabbing Ma's shoulders and steering her out of the ward.

I gasped as I took in the sight before me. When I'd last seen him just two months earlier, he'd looked older, of course, but he'd still been a big, strong, formidable character. Lying on the bed in front of me was an old man with grey skin and sunken features. If I'd walked into a room full of beds, I'd never have picked him out as my da. Wires connected him to various bleeping machines, and I wondered fleetingly what was keeping him alive – the machines or sheer willpower in wanting a final standoff with me.

I glanced at the chair that Ma had just vacated. Sitting would bring me down to his level. It would take me closer to him. It would imply a relationship – that I wanted to be close because I cared. I pushed my shoulders back and stood tall. 'You wanted to see me.'

His eyes flickered open and he turned his head slightly. 'You're here.' It was uttered as a statement – no relief, no sentiment. Just as well I hadn't sat down.

'I'm here. I thought Aisling might need me.' *Cheap shot but you deserve it. 15-love.*

'Why would she need *you*?' *Ooh. 15-all.*

'Because, try as you might to turn my whole family against me, she had the intelligence and integrity to bother to find out the truth.' *30-15, I believe.*

The beeps on the heart monitor quickened. He closed his eyes for a moment and exhaled deeply a few times until they steadied. I glanced towards the door, my heart racing too. Should I just leave? He meant nothing to me, but he was a human being and I didn't want to be the cause of his death.

'You found her.'

I turned back to Da. 'Who?'

'You know who.' The strong voice was back. Demanding. Accusing.

'Oh. Would you be referring to Shannon? My daughter? Your granddaughter? Did you know that was her name? Shannon Máire. Beautiful Irish name isn't it, for a beautiful Irish girl?' *40-15.*

He stared at me, his dark eyes flashing with the same contempt I'd seen in Ma's. 'You say that as if I'd care. You should know that she means *nothing* to me. NOTHING! You're *not* my daughter so she's *not* my granddaughter.' *Ouch! 40-30.*

I straightened my shoulders again and narrowed my eyes at him. 'Why did you ask for me?'

'To order you to stop bringing shame on this family.'

'To *order* me?' I slammed my handbag down on the floor in disgust. 'I don't take orders from you and haven't done since you threw me out.'

'Maybe not directly, but I've still controlled your life. I made you give up your bastard, didn't I?' *Deuce.*

'Oh, that reminds me. Did you know that my bastard had her own little bastard?' His eyes widened and the heart-monitor beeps quickened again. *Advantage, Ms O'Connell.* 'Yes, I thought that might shock you. A little boy called Luke and he's absolutely gorgeous. You might have sent my fiancé away from me and stolen my opportunity to be a mother to his child, but you can meet your God knowing that Daran McInnery lives on in his grandbaby. I may not have been a mother, but I'll be the best grandmother ever.' *Game, Ms O'Connell.*

'You're lying,' he said.

'No, that's what you do, Da. I'm nothing like you.' I picked up my bag and retrieved my mobile. I found a recent shot of Shannon cuddling Luke and thrust the image into his eyeline.

'Gorgeous, aren't they? My family, who, despite everything you did, I'm reunited with.'

'More shame on the family,' he spat.

'I don't know why you're getting so het up about it. You told me two months ago that I wasn't your daughter and you've just reiterated it now. You're absolutely right too. I'm *not* your daughter because I don't recognise you as my father. That means that you don't have a granddaughter or a great-grandson. I, on the other hand, have a family who love me unconditionally and, whatever challenges or issues Shannon or Luke face in the future, I'll be there for them without judgement or prejudice. Because that's what families do. But, hey, you'd know that if you'd ever been part of a loving family, wouldn't you?'

'Family? What do you know about family?'

'Loads of things, and none of it was learned from you. I'm not the one who brought shame on the family. You and Ma did that by your actions towards me before you knew about Daran, after you knew about him and every moment of every day ever since.'

He stared at me, breathing heavily, but I could see that the fight had gone out of his eyes. Whether that was down to fatigue or recognition that the words I spoke were true, I'd never know.

I put my phone back in my handbag and hoisted it onto my shoulder. 'What I suggest you do is forget about me from now on. Put your energy into getting yourself better and repairing your damaged relationship with Aisling and the twins, and Nia if you've damaged that too. They're your family. I'm not. So what I do from now on should make no difference to you.' I shook my head and turned to go. Then I turned back. 'I feel sorry for you, Pádraig O'Connell. I just hope your God can forgive you for your sins because I can't. Goodbye.' Without another glance, I strode out of the ward and out of the hospital. *Game, set and match, Ms O'Connell.*

37

The call came through at 5.47 a.m. the following morning as I lay fully dressed on top of my bed in The River Lee Hotel. 'He's dead, Clare,' Aisling said, in a tone that reflected relief rather than sorrow. 'I can't believe he's died on St Patrick's Day of all days.'

The significance of the date hadn't been lost on me either. 'I want to say I'm sorry...'

'I know. And I understand. Look, Ma's lost it so I can't talk just now. I'll call you later and we'll meet. Promise me one thing.'

'What?'

'You won't go home. I want you here. I *need* you here.'

'I promise.'

I lay back on the pillows, clutching my phone to my chest. 'Wherever you are right now, I hope you've found your peace,' I whispered. 'Because I don't think you ever found it in this lifetime, did you, Da?' A tear slid down my cheek, then another, and soon my cheeks were slick with moisture.

Why was I crying? Regret? I certainly didn't regret what I'd said the day before. I'd maintained my dignity while my parents had continued the name-calling. Tempted as I'd been, I hadn't told him what I thought of him – I wasn't that heartless – although I had deliberately given him facts that I hoped would hurt him. Relief? I tossed the feeling around my mind. Was I relieved he was gone? Not really because, although his actions from seventeen years ago had had a major impact on my life, I'd blocked thoughts of him from mind until recently, so he hadn't been on my radar enough for me to be relieved that he was no longer around.

I turned onto my side, staring towards the curtained window. What was it, then? Loss? I certainly wasn't going to miss him. You can't miss something you never had. Maybe that was it. Maybe I was mourning never having had a father, Shannon not knowing her father, and Luke not knowing his grandfather or great-grandparents. But at least Shannon had had her adopted dad, and Luke would have Ben. I sat up and wiped my cheeks. Luke would have Ben? Where had that come from? Ben was just a friend; he wasn't a father figure. Obviously, I'd meant Callum. I looked at the clock: 6.23 a.m. I needed some fresh air. I wasn't thinking straight.

✉ To Aisling
Hope Ma's calmed down. I'm out for a walk but I've got my phone with me. I'm here for you xxx

It was a few hours before Aisling called, suggesting that we meet up for dinner and saying she had a surprise for me – Keenan and Éamonn wanted to join us.

The pub was heaving with St Patrick's Day revellers. Green and white bunting and flags hung from the ceiling and the bar. All-day drinkers wearing leprechaun hats and ginger beards brushed shoulders with those who'd had to work the public holiday but had stopped off for a swift drink or two on the way home.

'Clare? Is that you? I barely recognised you.'

'*I* did. It's the eyes. I remember those green eyes.'

The four of us stood awkwardly in a small gap near the bar. Hug? Shake hands? What was normal in these situations?

I looked at Aisling for reassurance and she nodded encouragingly. 'I'd have recognised you two,' I said, 'but I must confess that I don't know which is which anymore.' As boys and young men, they'd been identical, although, being their sister, I'd never mixed them up. Now they'd both changed. You'd have put them as brothers, but not necessarily twins. One was freshly shaved, smartly coiffed and wore contact lenses. The other had greying hair curled up at the collar of his shirt. Glasses couldn't hide the dark circles under his eyes, which fitted well with a few days' growth on his chin. I suspected he was the soon-to-be-divorced Keenan. I was right.

'Quick! Grab that table!' Éamonn called, pointing to a table by the window about to be vacated by a gaggle of leprechauns. Aisling practically launched herself at it. We took our seats and an awkward silence descended on us again. The pub door opened and I half-expected a collection of tumbleweed to blow through and spin past us. I was about to make a flippant comment about that to try to break the ice when I saw Keenan remove his glasses and rub his eyes. At that moment, I registered what they'd been through that day and that the silence was more about that than it was about meeting me again. I might have detached myself from Da years previously, but they hadn't. They'd lost their father that morning and were probably hurting like hell.

'I'd ask "tough day?" but I'm guessing that would be a daft question,' I said.

Keenan gave me a weak smile. 'One of the toughest.'

'Look, I really appreciate you coming to meet me, but I understand if you'd rather not do the big reunion thing tonight. You all look exhausted.'

'We are,' Éamonn said. 'But it's nothing a bit of food won't fix. I'm starving. I need to order some food pretty damn quick. Apologies if that's rude.'

I smiled. 'I understand. I'm pretty hungry myself.'

'It's been a long time,' Éamonn said, after we'd ordered our meals. 'You look great, Clare. Aisling says you're a PR manager or something like that?'

I nodded. 'I was, but I'm taking some time off at the moment.'

'Oh. To do what? Are you going travelling or something?' Keenan asked.

I glanced towards Aisling, who shook her head and said, 'It's your news to share, but I think they'll be pleased.'

'What's going on?' Keenan said. 'Oh. You're pregnant?'

I laughed. 'Are you saying I'm fat?'

'No. Just...'

I laughed at his red cheeks. 'I'm so not pregnant. You have to be having sex with someone to get pregnant.' I laughed again at both their shocked expressions. 'Sorry. Way too much information to share with my brothers who I haven't seen for seventeen years. No. I'm not pregnant, but I am bringing up a baby at the moment. It might be back-story time...'

They listened in stunned silence as I told them my side of the story, from my relationship with Daran right through to reuniting with Shannon and looking after Luke. It took every bit of diplomacy I could muster to avoid painting Da in his true colours, but it wasn't right to speak so ill of him when he was only just cold, and I had no idea what their relationship had been like until the recent divorce debacle.

My twin brothers were obviously pretty astute, though. 'It's good to hear your side at last,' Éamonn said, 'and thank you for not dwelling on the part Da played. I think I can fill in the blanks.'

'Sorry. I tried.'

'We appreciate it.' Keenan rubbed a hand across his stubble. 'So, that would make us both... what? Uncles and great-uncles?'

I thought for a moment, 'Yes. Shannon's uncles and Luke's great-uncles.'

'That's pretty special,' Éamonn said.

'It sure is,' Keenan agreed.

Another silence descended, and I let it rest for a while so that they could chew over the implications of family lost and family found. I studied their pale faces. I could see so much of Da in them, in terms of physical looks, but there was something in the way they held themselves that reminded me more of myself: someone who'd taken a battering but was trying to prove to the world that they were strong and could take whatever else life threw at them. I saw it especially in Keenan. As if aware I was focusing on him, he said, 'I take it Aisling told you I'm getting divorced?'

'Yes. I'm sorry. I think it's time for your back-stories now.'

We spent the next three hours in the pub eating and chatting, until the live music started and it became impossible to talk. We dwelled very little on our childhood, instead focusing on the paths our lives had taken since. I liked them, but I didn't feel the same instant affinity with my brothers that I'd felt with Aisling, despite them being closer to my age, at four years older than me compared to her six. I knew I held some wariness towards them from what Aisling had told me about them being very religious and, despite the impending divorce, it was clear they did hold strong Catholic beliefs and were struggling to understand why I – shock, horror – had no man in my life to provide for me. I held my own, though, and made it very clear that I had been and always would be fiercely independent and if they judged that, then they needed to pause a moment and think about why I'd become that way.

When we said our goodbyes, I suspected we wouldn't become the closest of siblings, but a truce had certainly been called, and they clearly had an interest in getting to know their new family members.

'The wake's probably going to be Thursday and Friday and the funeral Saturday,' Aisling said, after the twins had gone. 'You'll be coming?'

'I don't know whether I should. I won't be welcome.'

Aisling shrugged. 'I can tell you right now that, from Ma's perspective, a dose of the clap would be more welcome than you at Da's wake.' She smiled and I laughed at the crudeness of her comment – the sort of thing I'd come out with.

'I half-want to come to make sure he's really dead. And I want to be there for you. But I don't want to turn it into a circus.'

Aisling pulled me into her embrace and whispered, 'You do what's right for you. Don't mind the rest of us.'

* * *

I caught a taxi back to the hotel, where a wall of sound hit me the moment the sliding doors opened. A St Patrick's Day event was in full swing in the bar, with live music and laughter. I hesitated for a moment in the lobby. Not that long ago, I'd have joined the party, not caring that I was on my own. I'd have chatted and flirted, then slipped away before any expectation that it would go further. At that very moment, though, I was aware of being alone and I didn't like it at all. Somehow, I'd gone from being fiercely independent and happy in my own company to someone who longed to be surrounded by my family and friends. My arms ached for Luke. I missed Shannon's sharp tongue, her zest for life, and the softness in her eyes when she let her guard down and allowed a moment of closeness to pass between us. I missed Callum's eternal optimism and his passion for his family.

Crossing the lobby, I caught the lift up to my floor. Without switching my light on, I crossed the bedroom and looked out over the River Lee. Yes, I'd admit it, I missed Ben too. As a companion, though, not anything else. I closed my eyes and pictured a typical Saturday night in his cosy terrace, curled up on the sofa with a take-away and a bottle of beer, watching a film, an easy banter flowing between us. I'd have done anything at that very moment to open my eyes and be there with him.

38

'Clare? Is that yourself? Come in, child, come in.' Father Doherty shuffled back to let me pass the following morning.

'These are for you,' I said, handing him a large carrier bag bursting with fresh fruit and vegetables. 'And because that's all very healthy, I have a little treat too.' I handed him a chocolate orange.

'My favourite,' he said. 'How did you know?'

'I asked the warden.'

He smiled but tears glistened in his pale eyes. 'I don't deserve your company or your kindness.' He lowered himself into his armchair and I sat on the sofa.

'You know I've forgiven you,' I said. 'Because you asked and you apologised. Which is more than I can say for the guiltiest party.'

Father Doherty nodded. 'I heard about your da. How do you feel?'

'I don't know. I cried when I found out but not because I'm sad that he's dead. I'm not glad, either. I'm not sure what I am.'

'You don't have to know at this moment. You may not know how you feel for a long time to come. He didn't ask for forgiveness, then?'

'I didn't think he would. He called for me so I jumped on a plane like an eejit. I suspected there'd be an ulterior motive and there was. He knew I'd been searching for Shannon and wanted me to stop bringing shame on the family.'

Father Doherty's shoulders sagged. 'He never did. Oh, Clare. I'm so sorry, child. What did you say?'

'I told him about Shannon's baby.'

His eyes widened. 'You found her and she has a baby? You have a family?'

'It seems that I do.'

Father Doherty listened attentively while I told him everything that had happened.

When I finished, he sat back in his chair and closed his eyes. He kept them shut for so long, I thought he'd fallen asleep.

'Father?' I whispered. 'Father?'

He muttered, 'Amen,' then opened his eyes. 'Sorry, child, but I felt a prayer was needed for your poor Shannon, who has had far too much suffering for one so young. I'm so happy for you. You've found your little girl, thanks be to God, and she has a child of her own. You may have lost one family, but you've gained another. I believe it's God's way of putting right for you the wrongs that others – including myself – have done to you.'

I was about to retaliate and say I didn't believe in God, but I stopped as a wave of comfort swept over me. Whether there was a God or not, I did believe in the concept of karma and that was essentially what Father Doherty had just described. Very comforting.

I drove back to the hotel a couple of hours later, abandoned the car I'd hired that morning and walked along the river into Cork. A dull, grey sky threatened rain, and a cold wind pushed my hair across my face and tickled my nose. I bought myself a sandwich and coffee and headed for Bishop Lucey Park, shivering as I sat down on a bench, feeling the cold metal through my dress. Office workers scuttled past on their lunch breaks. Women and the occasional man pushed babies and toddlers in prams and buggies. I watched for a while before digging out my mobile and calling Sarah. My conversation with Ben on Sunday morning was niggling at me. I wanted her in my life, I needed her in my life, and it was time to reconnect. Unfortunately, the only connection available was with her voice-mail so I hung up without leaving a message. 'Sorry I'm a lousy friend, hope your health - business - marriage - everything else is okay. By the way, my da's dead,' didn't seem like an appropriate message to leave.

I thought I might manage to catch Aisling on her school lunch break but I got her voicemail instead, so I left a message telling her that I was definitely going to the wake, even though I knew Ma would make a scene.

I looked at my watch. I hadn't caught Aisling on her lunch break, but was it worth trying Ben in case he was on his? No such luck.

'Hi, Ben, it's Clare. Just thought I'd let you know that the old git is dead. I'm going to the wake tomorrow and the funeral on Saturday, although I suspect my ma will throw me out of the wake and have Satan on hand to brandish a pitchfork at me if I turn up to the funeral. I expect I'll be back on Sunday afternoon, so maybe we can do a curry and get pissed or get pissed and do a curry. Or just get pissed, because I think I need to. I've texted Shannon and Callum to let them know. I know it's a big ask, but I'd be really grateful if you could visit them and let me know they're okay. Bye.'

I put my phone back in my bag and opened my sandwich. A woman in her late sixties ambled past pushing a buggy as I took my first bite. Assuming she was a relative, she was clearly the granny. I doubted anyone would imagine I was the granny when they saw me out with Luke. Next to the woman, an older man pushed an older lady in a wheelchair – possibly the great-grandmother. It was a shame that my ma would never get to enjoy that role, or at least not with my side of the family. *Christ! What about Daran's mother?* She'd lost her son, but did she have any idea that she had a granddaughter by him? If she did, she certainly wouldn't know that she also had a great-grandson. Father Doherty must have met her at Daran's memorial service. Perhaps he had her contact details.

With my lunch finished, I stood up. It was time to shop. I had a funeral and a wake to attend, and I hadn't packed anything appropriate.

39

I twisted and turned so I could see the black skater dress from all angles in the full-length mirror on the wall of my hotel bedroom. Not bad. Not that he deserved black, but I didn't want to make a scene by turning up in head-to-toe scarlet, especially as that's probably what Ma and her cronies expected. Mind you, I'd snuck in some colour to show I wasn't really in mourning. The dress had an Aztec-style embellishment in red, burnt-orange, turquoise and green across the waistband, and I'd teamed it with a red silk scarf.

I ran my brush through my hair, then, in another streak of rebellion, applied some bright-red lipstick. Picking up my handbag and coat from the bed, I took one last look in the mirror and nodded approvingly.

By the time I'd descended to the hotel lobby, my confidence had well and truly evaporated. I glanced towards the hotel bar to my right and had to fight the urge to walk right in, sit in a corner and drink myself into oblivion. Maybe offering Father Doherty a lift had been my way of ensuring I went through with it.

* * *

'Are you nervous, my child?' Father Doherty asked as I pulled out of my space outside his retirement home.

'I am, Father. The whole extended family will be there, along with most of the village, and I don't know who knows what. I'm a pretty strong person, but even the strongest would hesitate at being thrown into the lion's den.'

I could see him nodding in my peripheral vision. 'I wish I could offer some words of comfort and suggest you're exaggerating what it will be like...'

'I know.' I turned my head slightly and smiled. 'I've been through worse.'

'Hindsight is a wonderful thing,' he said. 'And I know that everything we do is all part of God's plan, but I do so wish that I'd known then what I know now and guided your father to show forgiveness and compassion, instead of stirring up accusations of sin.'

'Please don't punish yourself, Father. Even if you'd done that, I don't think he'd have listened.'

'Perhaps you're right.'

I laughed. 'If we're going to remain friends, I think you'll find I'm always right.'

Father Doherty laughed too. 'I'd like to be friends. You're a wise woman, Clare O'Connell.'

'Well, before he started spouting hell and damnation at me, I was tutored by a pretty good priest.'

'Thank you.'

'And, even though he decided against the priesthood, Daran taught me well too. He taught me so much about the world, about myself, about the person I wanted to be...' I tailed off, as the words stuck in my throat.

Father Doherty lightly touched my hand on the steering wheel. 'I know,' he said softly.

We left the city behind and headed into the countryside towards Ballykielty. I didn't like the silence. It gave me too much time to think about what I was about to face. 'I wondered something yesterday,' I said. 'Daran's mother. Did she know about me?'

Father Doherty paused for a moment before answering. 'I can't be certain, my child, but I know they were very close.'

'Do you have a phone number or an address for her?'

'No phone number but I think I have an address somewhere.

She's on a farm in Wicklow but I cannot remember where. My memory's not what it used to be. I'll have a hunt around. See what I can find.'

'Thanks, Father. I'd appreciate that.'

* * *

I linked arms with Father Doherty as we walked slowly along the laneway, which was packed with cars. I knew that he knew my grip was more for my benefit than his. I felt sick as we turned the corner and walked down the driveway of my childhood home.

Aisling was on door duty. She hugged Father Doherty, then me. 'Be brave,' she whispered in my ear.

'Does she know I'm coming?'

'Yes.'

'Does she know I'm here?'

'No. She's in the garden with Mrs Leary just now. Nia's in the kitchen, though. Will we go inside and reacquaint the two of you?'

I nodded and followed her. The living room was packed with people so I kept my head down, eager not to make eye contact with anyone, as I let my big sister lead me by the hand towards the kitchen.

'Nia,' Aisling called.

A petite woman with shoulder-length, mousy-coloured hair had her hands in the sink. She jumped and turned, dropping her dish-cloth onto the floor with a splat as she spotted me.

'Hi, Nia,' I said. 'Long time, no see.'

'Emm, hi, uh, Clare,' she stammered, pulling a shapeless, grey cardigan tightly across her tiny body. Her big, brown eyes kept flicking fearfully over my shoulder. 'You look a lot like I remember. But prettier. And taller. You're very tall, aren't you?'

I shrugged. 'Might it be the heels?'

'There are people out here needing tea,' boomed a man's voice from the living room. 'Stop gossiping and get on with your work, Nia. It's embarrassing having people desperate for some basic hospitality and knowing it's my wife leaving them parched and starving.'

I cringed. So that was Nia's husband? What an absolute prick, shouting like that and humiliating her in front of all those guests. My fists clenched by my side and I bit my lip. I wanted to march into the living room and give him an earful, but I could tell from Nia's expression that it would only cause her more problems.

'Sorry, Jim. It'll be ready in a minute.'

'I shouldn't have to remind you, Nia, should I?'

'No, Jim. Sorry, Jim.'

Nia swiftly retrieved the cloth from the floor, tossed it into the sink, grabbed the kettle and filled it.

'Charming,' I muttered.

'Shhh,' Aisling whispered.

The doorbell rang. 'I'm needed out front,' Aisling said. 'Nia, will you let Clare help you?'

Nia dropped a teaspoon onto the worktop, and it bounced and clattered to the floor. 'There's no need. Really. I can manage.'

But I'd already put my bag down, rolled up my cardigan sleeves and put my hands in the sink. 'Will you sort out the drinks while I finish this lot?'

Nia stared at me for a moment as if she were about to protest, then a flicker of something resembling relief passed across her face and she mumbled, 'Thank you.'

'Don't mention it.'

The only problem with being stuck in the kitchen was the clear view of the back garden. From the window above the sink, I could see Ma looking angry, pacing up and down on the lawn. In one hand, she held a tumbler of dark liquid – brandy, perhaps? – and in the other, she held a cigarette. I didn't know she smoked. As she talked – or shouted – the liquid sloshed over her hand. Mrs Leary, seated on the garden bench, kept making calming gestures with her arms. I'd liked Mrs Leary as a child. She'd been a teacher at school and had always been friendly. Had they turned her against me or was she trying to be the voice of reason?

'How many's she had?' I asked Nia, who'd wandered back into the kitchen with a tray full of empty cups and glasses.

'Ma?' She placed the tray down next to the sink and peered out the window. 'I lost count after number six.'

'Jesus!'

'Clare!'

'Sorry. It slipped out.' I loaded the dirty pots into the sink while Nia emptied a box of assorted shortbread biscuits onto a plate. 'The anger is because...?'

Nia stopped and looked at me with her eyebrows raised.

'Because of me,' I said. 'Of course. You think I should leave?'

'I, erm... I haven't really got an opinion on the subject.' She placed the last few of biscuits onto the plate and scuttled into the living room.

I picked up a tea towel when she returned and started to dry the pots. 'So, Nia, why don't you tell me about yourself?'

'What do you want to know?' She looked scared again.

'Anything. What you do for a living, for example?'

'Oh, I don't work,' she said. 'Jim likes me to keep house for him.'

Christ alive! The 1950s called and they want their protégée back. 'Hobbies and interests, then. What do you like doing?'

'I... uh... I cook.'

'Do you enjoy cooking?'

'Not really.'

'So, what do you enjoy doing?'

Nia shrugged. 'I don't really have any hobbies and interests. I go to Mass and I help out arranging the flowers for the altar every Sunday.'

'But you don't like either of them?'

She shook her head. 'Not really. But Jim says we need to be active at the church and I want to please God so...' She tailed off.

I decided to change the subject. 'How long have you been married?' I had to stop myself from adding '... to that arsehole'.

'Fifteen years.'

'Any kids?'

'No.' Her eyes seemed to plead with me not to explore that any further, before she turned away and busied herself loading some clean cups and saucers onto a tray. As I watched her, I wondered whether she'd been unable to have children. She was a timid little mouse of a woman, all skin and bones, hollow cheeks and wispy hair. She didn't look strong enough to grow a baby inside her.

'So, what's your name now?' I asked, when I couldn't stand the silence any longer, yet couldn't face going into the living room.

'Cullen.'

'Jim Cullen?' I wrinkled my nose. 'Is he from around here?'

'He is.'

'Where?' I expected her to say one of the surrounding villages.

'Ballykielty.'

'Really? Cullen. Jim Cullen. How old is he?'

'Same age as me.'

I shook my head. 'I don't remember anyone of that name.'

'Yes, well, you moved away a long time ago, so you did,' she said. 'I'm sorry. I can't talk. I need to make more sandwiches.'

Conversation over, I turned back to the washing-up. If a stranger had walked into the kitchen and seen us together, they'd never have guessed that she was my sister – my older sister, at that. We were nothing like each other in looks or temperament. I hated that I so clearly intimidated her. She'd always been quieter than me, but I remembered playing with her as a child and there being genuine affection between us. Yet another thing Ma and Da had taken away.

Outside, Ma had stopped pacing and had taken a seat on the bench with Mrs Leary. I noticed her glass was empty, which meant that she'd probably be coming inside any minute. And *that* meant that, if I wanted to do what I'd come to do – satisfy myself that Da really was dead – I'd better find him.

'Where's Da?' I asked Nia.

'In the small back bedroom.'

I gulped. That was cruel. 'My old room?'

She nodded. 'Sorry.'

I shivered. This was going to be very strange. With another glance out the kitchen window to make sure Ma wasn't on her way in, I wiped my hands on the tea towel. 'Wish me luck.'

I had to walk back through the dining room, then the living room, to get to the stairs. A wave of whispers and nudges followed me, along with a few clear statements: 'She's got a nerve showing up here.' 'Where's her respect?' 'She brought such shame on the family, don't you know.'

Head high, shoulders back. These people are small-minded and they mean nothing to you. I needed to see him, then get out of there. I glanced around the room brazenly. They weren't all hostile. I received a few smiles and a couple of nods. Which one was Nia's arsehole of a husband? There were only four men in the room including Father Doherty and all of them were fifty and above. Jim must have gone out. The men had probably retreated to the pub.

Aisling stopped me as I reached the door to the hall. 'You're not leaving, are you?'

'Soon,' I said. 'But I'm going upstairs first.'

'Will you be wanting company?'

I smiled weakly at my sister. 'Thanks, but I have to do this alone.'

My legs shook as I took each stair and slowly made my way towards the back of the house. Nothing seemed to have changed. The carpet was still green, although it had probably been replaced. The swirly brown and cream wallpaper was definitely the same. I passed the hot press and paused to take in the white, glossed door with height measurements of the five of us as we grew. Only there weren't five measurements anymore. Someone had scratched out mine. My eyes burned. I shouldn't have felt hurt or surprised, yet I did. Why not just paint over me? Why scratch me out? But I knew the answer to that – it was a cathartic act of scratching me out of his life. I could picture him sitting there for hours, carefully erasing me from his home and his world.

The next door was my bedroom door. It was wide open and the thin closed curtains fluttered in a slight breeze from the open window. A large mirror had been taken off its hook, turned round and propped against the wall. *Most of the traditions observed, then.* I heard the word 'Amen', then a couple of mourners appeared in the doorway. With barely a glance at me, they squeezed past and headed down the stairs. I hoped nobody was observing the tradition of sitting with the body constantly because I really wanted to be alone with him. I listened, but there was absolute silence, so I took a few steps forward and peered round the edge of the door. Empty. Except for the large, dark-wood coffin on the bed. I shuddered, then took another step closer.

I recognised his suit immediately – his Sunday best. He'd worn the same navy double-breasted jacket and trousers for as long as I could remember, so it shouldn't have surprised me that he'd never shelled out on another considering how tight he was with money. Rosary beads rested in his left hand. I recognised them from childhood too.

'Hello, Da.'

I half-expected him to sit up and demand to know what the hell I was doing in his house when he'd made it clear I wasn't welcome. But he just lay there. Still. Silent. I gently prodded him on the arm. Then a bit harder. Then harder still. I smiled and exhaled. It was safe to say that he was well and truly dead.

Staring at his body for a few more moments, I felt nothing. No sadness. No regret. And no fear. I didn't want to say a prayer, ask for forgiveness, or even tell him what I thought of him because, actually, I didn't think anything of him. In the same way he'd claimed I was nothing to him, I realised he was nothing to me. He wasn't my father – he was just someone I used to know. Someone who I'd never felt very fond of. Someone who caused me no end of pain. And, more importantly, someone who couldn't do that anymore.

I sighed. 'Goodbye, Da.'

Aisling met me at the bottom of the stairs. 'How was it?' she asked.

'Reassuring.'

She nodded. 'You'll be heading off now, won't you?' Her eyes showed sadness but I knew she understood why I couldn't stay.

'I've done what I came to do. Me being here's awkward for everyone. Is there any chance you could run Father Doherty home? I know it's a big favour but—'

'It's fine. I'll see him home safe.'

'Can you remind him to look for Daran's ma's address?'

She nodded. 'I'm assuming you won't be back tomorrow but you will come on Saturday? To the funeral?'

'I might slip in at the back and shoot away before the end, but I'll come. I promise. I bought a new dress so I might as well wear it. It's bright red, shows my cleavage and only just skims my arse. Appropriate, don't you think?'

Aisling giggled as she hugged me. 'A tonic, so you are. An absolute tonic.' She opened the door.

'Bollocks!' I said. 'I'm such an eejit.'

'What?'

'I won't be getting too far if I don't have my handbag with me, will I?'

I reached for the door to the living room.

'Don't go—'

But her warning came too late. I opened the door and came face to face with my mother.

40

'You!' she spat. Clumps of wiry, grey hair had escaped from her chignon and streaks of mascara down her face gave her the appearance of a coal miner. A very angry coal miner. 'I thought I made it clear that you're not welcome here.' She staggered then lifted the glass tumbler to her mouth. She frowned and staggered a bit more when she realised it was empty, then dropped the glass on the carpet, where it rolled under a chair.

'I didn't come to cause a scene,' I said, my cheeks burning as I took in the curious faces around the room. They'd all stopped talking, eating and drinking, and were watching. Intently.

'Cause a scene? *Cause a scene?*' She laughed – a hollow, chilling sound. 'You've caused a scene your whole life, Clare. From the day you were born, you caused a scene.'

I wasn't exactly sure what she meant by this, but a few nods and murmurs of 'You tell her, Maeve' from around the room suggested that others knew exactly what she meant.

'I'm going. I just need to get my bag from the kitchen.' I tried to sidestep her but she blocked me.

'Where do you think you're going, missy? This is my house. *My house!* And I don't want you in it.'

'I know that. But I can't leave without my bag.'

'I never wanted you, you know.' I felt my stomach clench at her words and heard an audible gasp go around the room. 'I thought two girls and two boys were enough,' she continued, 'but your da insisted on having you. The moment you were born with your blonde hair and big eyes, I knew you were trouble, and that's all you've been. You've brought shame on this family.' She lifted her hand towards her mouth, then must have registered she no longer had a glass in it. 'Nia! Bring me a drink. Now.'

'Don't you think you've had enough, Ma?' whispered Aisling.

'Siding with her, are you? I might have known she'd turn you against me.'

'Ma! You're being ridiculous. Clare hasn't turned me against anyone.'

'Nia! Drink!'

Nia scuttled into the living room, shot a terrified look at me, handed Ma a tumbler of brandy, then darted back towards the kitchen.

Ma took a couple of gulps, then exhaled. She was so close by this point that I could smell the fumes on her breath. I took a step backwards.

'You still here?' she demanded.

'I need my bag. As soon as I have it, I'll go. If you'll just let me past.'

'I'll get it,' Aisling said, but Ma blocked her way too.

'You see! You're siding with her. I knew it. She always gets what she wants. Just look at her. She's like a blonde Mary Magdalene. Bats her eyelashes and all men keel over and give her whatever she wants.'

'Ma!' Aisling cried. 'Stop it!'

Ma pointed at me, sloshing liquor over her hand. 'You were always his favourite, but I knew you were trouble. I warned him, but he never saw it until it was too late. When you left, you took a piece of him with you. He was never the same. *You* did that to him.'

'He threw me out. I had no choice.'

'You had lots of choices, but you chose whoring.' Another gasp went around the room. I flinched, but I'd heard it all before. Well, apart from being Da's favourite. I'd never have guessed from the way he treated me, even before Daran. And her not wanting me was new information too, although not surprising in the least. She'd never shown much tenderness towards any of us, but least of all towards me.

'Enough, Ma.' Keenan appeared by her side with Éamonn just behind him. They must have arrived while I was upstairs and been out in the garden.

She twisted around, slopping more brandy. 'Ah! Keenan. The other embarrassment. Soon to be divorced. Just like that one.' She twisted back around and pointed at Aisling.

'Don't be starting on Keenan and Aisling,' Éamonn said, stepping forward and taking the glass from her hand. 'Da's laid out upstairs and this really isn't the time or the place, is it now?'

'But he loved her more than me,' she cried.

I flinched again. Really? But I couldn't remember Da ever showing Ma any affection. Perhaps they'd stayed together to avoid the 'shame' of divorce but actually hated each other.

'Nia,' shouted Éamonn. 'Can you get Clare's bag for her, please?'

Nia appeared from the kitchen a few moments later and handed me my bag. 'Thanks, Nia,' I said. 'It was nice to see you today.'

'And you,' she whispered.

'Don't say that,' shouted Ma. 'Don't be making friends with her. She's an embarrassment to us all and I want her out of my house. NOW! Why's nobody listening to me? Why are you all on her side?'

'I'm going.' I turned towards the door.

'You're not welcome tomorrow or at the funeral,' Ma screeched. 'Don't you dare show your face. I'll call the Guards if you do. I'll have you removed. You ruined our lives, you little slut. I'll never forgive you for—'

I slammed the door on her shrieks and ran down the driveway as fast as my stupid heels would let me. I stumbled down the lane that ran alongside the house, where I'd parked the car, then leaned against the driver-side door, gulping in fresh air, waiting for the churning in my stomach to subside before I got in the car and left Ballykielty. For good. Forever.

Gradually, my heartbeat slowed and my breathing regulated

itself. For a moment there, I'd thought I might pass out. I unlocked the door and grabbed a bottle of water from the door compartment. I took a few greedy gulps, keeping an eye towards the end of the laneway, in case Ma decided she was ready to unleash another torrent of verbal abuse and I needed to dive into the car for safety. She'd said some nasty things in the past, but the venom with which she'd let go just now had been something else. Why did she hate me so much? I didn't buy that bullshit about Da loving me more, because he'd never behaved as though he did. I remembered my childhood and teenage years as being filled with lectures, punishments and expressions of disappointment.

I was about to get into the car when a figure appeared at the end of the laneway. Shit! I should have got away from the house and caught my breath outside the village borders. I squinted in the low sun. The figure was waving something. I shielded my eyes with my hand.

Was that Nia? And was that...? I put my hand up to my neck. Of course! I'd removed my scarf in the kitchen because it kept dipping into the washing-up bowl. I closed the car door and headed down the laneway towards her. She took a few steps closer to me too, then she stopped abruptly and looked to her right as a gruff voice shouted, 'Nia! What the feck are you doing? Get back in the kitchen, where you belong. Christ, woman, what the hell was I thinking when I married you?'

The sun in my eyes meant I couldn't see his face, but I could make out the silhouette of a large bulk of a man staggering towards my sister. So that was the gobshite of a husband, was it? Poor Nia.

'Sorry, Jim. It's just that... well, I... It was Clare. She left her scarf behind. I just wanted... She was leaving and...'

He grabbed at her arm and she yelped like a puppy. 'I'll give her that.' He snatched my scarf out of Nia's hand. 'After all, Clare loves it when I give her things, don't you, Clare?'

I took another step closer, ready to do battle with Nia's arsehole of a husband, but the sun dipped behind a cloud at that moment and I gasped. Jesus Christ!

He released Nia and shoved her roughly in the direction of the house. Running one scabby hand through his greasy ginger hair, he raised my scarf up to his nose and sniffed.

'You still wear the same perfume. I always did like that smell.'

I stared at him, then at Nia hovering awkwardly nearby. 'This is my husband, Jim,' she said. 'I think you knew him as Jamie.'

'Jamie Doyle,' I whispered, still staring at Nia. 'Cullen. You said your name's Cullen.'

Jamie laughed and I shuddered at the chilling sound. I knew that laugh. It reminded me of... What was it? I closed my eyes tightly, trying to think.

'The Guards took my da away again,' Jamie said, his voice dripping with bitterness.

I opened my eyes to see him lifting a bottle of whiskey to his mouth and taking a swig.

'Ma changed our names to wipe us clean of him, stupid cow. Couldn't change my blood, though. Bad blood runs through my veins, doesn't it, Clare?'

He lifted my scarf up to his nose again and inhaled deeply, closing his eyes momentarily. 'Brings back memories, so it does. Good memories.'

Memories? My breathing quickened. The shadows. The shapes. It was...

'Jim? What are you doing?' I heard fear in Nia's voice, but I couldn't tear my eyes away from Jamie's face. There was something so familiar...

'None of your business. Get inside, Nia.'

'But, Jim...'

'*Now!* Unless you want my fist to connect with your face again, you useless bitch.'

I wanted to yell at him to leave my sister alone but I couldn't seem to form any words. I couldn't move either. What was happening to me?

Gravel crunched as Nia turned and ran. Jamie took another glug of whiskey, then let the empty bottle drop to the ground with a smash. He slowly wound my scarf around his left hand, then twisted it around his right, before pulling his hands apart so that the material was stretched between them. He laughed that sinister laugh again. 'This would make a good gag, wouldn't it, Clare? Not that we really needed the one we used before. Who was going to hear screams from a deserted farmhouse in the middle of a meadow?'

Oh my God! Sweet Jesus. The shadows. The shapes. The fear. It had been him. It had been Jamie Doyle.

41

Seventeen and a Half Years Earlier

Daran pulled on his boxer shorts and jeans after we'd made love for a third time on my sixteenth birthday. The second time had been slow and tender, and the third more frantic and daring as we started to understand each other's bodies. 'I really don't want to leave you, but I have to get back to Mrs Murphy and see whether old Carrig is still with us. I promised her.'

'I wish you could stay here all night with me, but I understand. They need you.' I reluctantly picked up Aisling's bra and fastened it then pulled on my dress.

Seeing Daran glancing at his watch, I smiled. 'Go. I'll find the rest of my clothes and tidy up in here.'

'I can wait for you.'

'No, you can't. You're already late for a dying man. I won't be the one who stops you doing God's work. See you here tomorrow night?'

Daran held me tightly. 'I can't. Remember, I'm going away in the morning.'

I pouted. 'I was trying to forget about that. I don't know if I can last ten days without you.' Daran was going on a school trip to Jerusalem, returning via Vatican City.

'I wish I didn't have to go, especially after what we've just done. I'll be thinking of nothing else for the full ten days.'

'Me too. I'll miss you so much.'

He kissed me tenderly. 'I'll be counting down the hours. Happy birthday, fiancée. Don't forget that I'll love you till the end of forever.'

'And I'll love you for longer than that.'

'Don't stay long. It's a quarter to eight now, so you only have about half an hour till sunset.'

'I'll be grand. Ten minutes should sort things out.' I blew him kisses as he headed for the doorway, then disappeared into the meadow.

Five minutes later, I'd cleared away the drinks and was rummaging through the straw trying to find my panties. 'I always knew you were a dirty girl,' a voice sneered.

I leapt up. 'Jamie Doyle! What the hell are you doing here?'

'Watching you.' He took a few steps closer, his dark eyes boring into my skin.

'For how long?'

'Long enough.'

My stomach churned. 'Long enough for what?'

'To see you and the Father doing things a priest shouldn't even be thinking about, let alone doing.'

I shuddered at the thought of him being a voyeur. 'He's not a priest and it was private. You shouldn't have been watching.'

'And you shouldn't have been doing it.' He took another couple of steps closer. 'At least I know why you kept turning me down. You were already getting your needs serviced elsewhere.'

I backed away a couple of paces, my heart racing. 'I turned you down because I'm not interested in you in that way.'

'Why not?' He took another step closer. Too close. I could smell alcohol on his breath again and see that gross foam at the corners of his mouth.

I shrugged. 'I'm just not. I'm sorry, Jamie, but we can't control who we fall for. I need to be getting home now, so I'll say goodnight if you'll just let me pass.'

'You're not going anywhere.'

'Come on, now. You don't mean that.'

He took another step closer and reached out. 'Such beautiful hair.' He ran his fingers down a blonde tress and I froze. 'Don't ever get it cut. Because, if you did, I wouldn't be able to do this.' He grabbed most of my hair and yanked it, pulling me down onto my knees in front of him.

I squealed as my left knee scraped against a stone and pain shot through my ankle. 'You're hurting me, Jamie.'

'Considering what I saw during your last go with the Father, you quite like it rough. It's my turn now.'

'No, Jamie, don't,' I whimpered.

But he unzipped his fly and released himself. 'Suck,' he ordered, thrusting my head towards his crotch. I gagged at the unwashed aroma and tried to clamber to my feet, but he had one hand entwined in my hair and the other on the back of my head, holding me down and pulling me towards him. I couldn't move.

'You take my dick in your mouth and suck it or I'll tell everyone in the village about your dirty little secret. You'll be ruined and your beloved Daran McInnery will be shipped abroad where you'll never see him again.'

'You wouldn't do that.' I knew he would. Even if I did as he demanded.

'Are you prepared to take the risk?'

Finding some courage from God alone knows where, I pushed at his legs, but he held his ground and laughed. I slapped at them, but he laughed harder – a cold, sinister sound.

'I'll tell you something really funny, will I, Jamie? You put that thing in my mouth and I swear to God I'll bite it off.'

He looked down in horror. 'You wouldn't.'

'Are *you* prepared to take the risk?'

'You whore.' He released my hair and I tried to scramble to my feet, but the punch to my left eye sent me crashing to the floor. 'You asked for that,' he yelled.

I tried to scramble to my feet again, but my left ankle wouldn't hold and I fell to my knees again. Another punch knocked me onto my back. My dress flipped up and Jamie's eyes widened. Before I had time to move, he'd pounced on top of me. Pinning my arms above my head, he laughed as I screamed. 'You're in the middle of nowhere, slut. There's nobody to hear you. But just in case. Ah! What have we here? A pair of panties? Perfect as a gag.' He stuffed them into my mouth. 'We don't want anyone disturbing us.'

And he was right – nobody disturbed us, and nobody heard as I cried for help while I staggered across the meadow and fields in the darkness. Nobody heard as I limped through the village. Nobody heard as I crawled into bed at home shortly before midnight. Yet they all heard when I claimed I'd 'tripped' in the darkness. They heard that I was a 'clumsy eejit' while the nurse bandaged my twisted ankle and stitched my cheek back together. They heard that I wanted to get my beautiful, long locks cropped into a short bob because I 'fancied a change, now I'm sixteen and all grown up'. Because that was all they wanted to hear – the simple explanations muttered with fearful, downcast eyes and a tone that begged them to say, 'Are you sure?' But nobody really heard. Nobody asked. Nobody wanted to. Rape wasn't something that happened in a good God-fearing community like Ballykielty.

42

Present Day

I could hear whispering and opened my eyes but the room was in darkness. I was laid on my back in a bed. Fanning my arms out either side of me, I soon touched the wall with my left hand and the edge of the bed with my right. It was a single bed, which meant I wasn't in my hotel room. So, where the hell was I? I tried to sit up, but my head hurt and I quickly lay back on the pillow again. I reached out my right hand and touched some sort of bedside table, which thankfully had a lamp on it.

A dull, yellowish glow lit the small room. It was a very feminine room. Three walls were painted a dusky pink and the fourth was papered with a delicate flowery pattern. A white wooden wardrobe stood opposite the bed, next to a tall white bookcase packed full of romantic and historical paperbacks. A couple of framed cross-stitches of cottages hung on the walls. It wasn't a room in Ma's house. Oh Christ, what if it was a room in Jamie Doyle's house and he'd...? No! Surely it was too feminine and I imagined Nia had no say in the décor of their home.

The door opened and a shadow crept along the wall. My heart raced uncontrollably. I could have wet myself with relief when Aisling's voice said, 'Is that you awake, Clare?'

'Where am I?'

She shuffled into the room. 'Mrs Shaughnessy's house.' She placed a glass of water on the bedside cabinet.

'The Black Widow? Why?'

'She saw the whole thing. She's the one who called the Guards.'

I closed my eyes. 'What happened?'

She sat down on the end of the bed. 'Don't you remember?'

'I was about to leave, but Nia had my scarf. She... Jesus! Jamie Doyle!' I sat upright and grabbed Aisling's arm. 'You've got to warn her. She's not safe. He's violent.'

'I know. It's okay. The Guards took him after he knocked you out.'

'He knocked me out?'

'Mrs Shaughnessy says he struck you and you went down like a sack of spuds.'

Aware that my face was throbbing, I reached up and touched my cheeks, wincing as I felt the swollen skin. I gently moved my fingers and they made contact with what I assumed were some Steri-Strips.

'The doc came and patched you up.' She shook her head. 'You really don't remember him hitting you?'

'I remember him hitting me all right. On the night of my sixteenth birthday. Right before he raped me.'

* * *

Several hours then passed in a blur of visits from the doctor and the Guards. They took statements, they took photos, they took swabs from my nails and a sample of my saliva.

The incident in the laneway soon came back to me. Jamie had lunged at me, thrusting the scarf across my mouth like a gag and grabbing both sides of my head. Nia, who'd obviously ignored his orders to go into the house, screamed and hurled herself at him. Her tiny frame was no match for his bulk and he'd swatted her away as though she were a fly. Seeing my sister pushed to the ground, anger-induced adrenaline flowed through my veins and I finally unfroze. I tried to knee Jamie in the balls, but he was too quick and jumped back, knocking me off balance on my heels. As I staggered to regain my stance, he drew his fist back and hit me square on the cheekbone. I was already on an unsteady footing, so the force sent me to the ground and I hit my head. Dr Ellory suspected that the blow to my head hadn't actually knocked me out but that I'd passed out as a result of the trauma of remembering the rape.

The memory of what Jamie had done to me on my sixteenth birthday – which I'd somehow managed to bury deep in the recesses of my brain for nearly two decades – was now as vivid as if it had happened yesterday. Dr Ellory explained that it was normal for repressed memories to feel very recent at the point of their return. He suggested that Taz's attack at New Year had started to awaken them, which was why I'd been having bad dreams and seeing shapes and shadows. Then the sight of Jamie Doyle again, brandishing a gag and laughing that chilling laugh, had been the final turn of the key to unlock Pandora's box.

I discovered that, after I'd fallen to the ground unconscious, Mrs Shaughnessy had alerted the Guards before running across the road and into Ma's house, screaming for Keenan and Éamonn to help. Nia had staggered to her feet and launched herself at Jamie, kicking, screaming and biting. He'd grabbed her arms and bent one of them behind her back with such force that he actually broke it. Keenan and Éamonn had managed to rugby-tackle him to the ground at that point, and several of the mourners had kept him pinned there until the Guards arrived.

The whole time he was pinned to the ground, he screamed and shouted about what a whore I was and how I deserved to be attacked, and how Nia was just as bad, which was why he had to give her a damn good beating on a regular basis. I cried when Aisling told me that. Nia was tiny. What sort of monster would do something like that? But I pictured him pinning me down in the farmhouse and hurting me so badly that I knew exactly what sort of monster would do that. Jamie Doyle. A man whose father's bad blood flowed through his veins, exactly like he'd said.

* * *

'Are you sure you want to be alone tonight?' Aisling said, as she drove my hire car towards the centre of Cork the following evening.

I twisted round in the passenger seat to see out the back window, where Mrs Shaughnessy was following us in Aisling's car.

'Mrs Shaughnessy's been grand, but I can't stay there a second night. It's not fair on her and it's making me feel on edge.'

'Jim's locked up. He can't get to you.'

'I know. I was thinking more about Ma.' I'd made no objections to staying in Ballykielty the previous evening, grateful for the rest and the emotional support. But with each passing hour today, I felt increasingly agitated, expecting Ma to storm across the road and have another go at me.

'You could have stayed at my place.'

'I couldn't let Torin and Briyana see me like this. They'd have questions.' She couldn't argue with that. They'd want to know why their Auntie Clare's face was covered in bruises. How could we tell them their Uncle Jim had thumped me, then thumped their Auntie Nia, then had to be pinned down by their Uncle Keenan and Uncle Éamonn until the Guards arrived to arrest him? Oh, and now he was in custody being questioned, not just about that incident but about fifteen years of domestic violence and the assault and rape of a minor.

'I'm worried about you, on your own, after what you've been through.'

'You don't need to be. I could actually do with some time on my own to get my head around everything. Remember, I'm tough as old boots. It takes a hell of a lot to knock me down.' I could hear the shake in my voice. I felt anything but tough right now, but I definitely did want to be alone for a while.

Aisling gave me a sideways glance and I couldn't bring myself to catch her eye. One more sympathetic look and I'd crumble.

'You and I both know you're not and that what's happened to you would be enough to push anyone over the edge,' she said gently. 'But we also know that you're stubborn and nothing I say is going to change your mind, is it now?'

'No, but I appreciate you offering.'

We pulled into the hotel car park and exited the cars. I thanked

Mrs Shaughnessy for everything she'd done and was a little surprised when she pulled me into her arms and held me tightly. 'If you need anything... anything at all... you'll be sure to let me know, won't you?' She sounded as if she was about to burst into tears. I raised my eyebrows at Aisling over her shoulder but she shrugged, clearly as confused as me by Mrs Shaughnessy's reaction.

* * *

Twenty minutes later, I was in my PJs, curled up on the wide armchair overlooking the River Lee, sipping on a large glass of wine. I'd hesitated by the bar as I crossed the lobby, wondering if it might be more sensible to have a hot drink instead of alcohol. But I wanted the memories to be numbed.

Remembering that night meant I now had the explanation for something that had been bothering me – why I hadn't told Daran when I found out I was pregnant, and how I'd got pregnant in the first place when I'd taken the morning-after pill. After what Jamie did, it was more important than ever that I took that pill but I'd been sick several times that morning – probably from the shock – so it clearly hadn't made it into my system. As for not telling Daran about the baby, there was a very good explanation – I had no idea who the father was. I pictured Shannon. Looks-wise, anyone could see that she was my daughter. Personality-wise, she was very much like me too. I hadn't seen anything of Daran in her so far. Was there anything of Jamie Doyle in her? Jesus, I hoped not. What about the red hair on Luke? Had that been Jamie's genes that had skipped a generation? If that violent rapist was Shannon's father, did that make any difference to how I felt about her and Luke?

So many questions. No answers. I gulped down the rest of my glass, poured another and took a big gulp of that. I looked over at my suitcase and chewed my lip.

It was time.

43

I stuffed the last letter back into its envelope and shook my head slowly. He'd never known I was pregnant. Daran said he'd wondered and had even asked Father Doherty, but he'd categorically been told I wasn't.

I poured another glass of wine. Bollocks! That was the end of the bottle. The second bottle.

I'd cried and laughed and cried some more as I read through Daran's letters. His early ones were filled with regret that he'd been the cause of my exile, but no regret about our relationship. He poured out his ongoing love and devotion to me, and his longing that we'd be reunited once more. As time progressed, his letters became chattier. The expressions of eternal love were still there, but it was as though he were right next to me, chatting about his day and his hopes for the future.

When he moved to Sumatra, the letters had arrived less frequently. The love was still there, but there was also a resignation that we weren't going to see each other again. There was so much of God's work to be done over there that he couldn't ever see himself leaving, but he didn't think it was the right place for me.

I didn't need to read my letters to him, because I knew they followed the same pattern – hope followed by resignation that Da had succeeded and we'd never be together.

I rummaged in the pile for the second one he'd sent, scattering the others to the floor. He quoted 1 Corinthians, chapter 13, verse 13 – a verse from the Bible that is heard frequently during wedding ceremonies: 'And now these three remain: faith, hope and love. But the greatest of these is love.'

> *I think of this verse constantly. It's so perfect for us right now. I HOPE that you're happy and are being treated well, wherever you've been sent. I have FAITH that God will reunite us when the timing is right because He was the one who brought us together. He believes in us. And, of course, my LOVE for you will last until the end of time and beyond...*

The words, which were already blurred from the wine, became even more blurred as tears dripped onto the page. I swiped at them, determined not to cry. If I cried for what we'd lost and what could have been, they'd have won. Da would still be controlling my life.

A knock on my door made me jump. I glanced at the phone. I hadn't ordered a third bottle of wine, had I? I staggered over to open the door, bouncing off the bed, then overcompensating and ricocheting off the wall on my way.

'Ben! How...?'

'Aisling called last night. I'd have come then but there were no more flights.' He reached out his arms. 'I thought you might need a friend.'

'I need a friend,' I whispered. With his strong arms round me, the tears started again. 'He raped me, Ben. That bastard raped me.'

He stroked my back and held me tight. 'I know. I'm so sorry. I'm here now and nobody can hurt you anymore.'

* * *

At some point in the early hours, my eyes flickered open. My mouth felt as if I'd eaten sand, my cheeks were tight from unwashed tears, my eyes stung, and my head thumped. I focused on Ben, fully clothed on top of the duvet, and smiled to myself. My knight in shining armour. Again. Yes, I felt terrible, but I felt safe.

When I awoke again, Ben was sitting by the window, reading a newspaper. 'How are you feeling?' he asked, folding the paper and placing it on the table.

'Hungover.'

'I'm not surprised.' He nodded towards the two empty bottles on the dressing table.

I rubbed my head. 'Was I coherent last night?'

'You were a bit slurred and very upset but I got the gist.'

'Did I make an eejit of myself?'

He sat down on the bed next to me. 'You could never make an idiot of yourself. And, if you had, you'd have had every right to. You've had a heck of a few days. I'm sorry about your dad.'

'I'm not.' I looked away, reluctant to let Ben see the hate in my eyes. 'He wasn't a nice man.'

'What happens next?'

'It's his funeral today.'

'Are you going?'

I looked at Ben again. 'Ma ordered me not to.'

'So are you going?'

'I just said—'

'You just said that your mum told you not to. The Clare I know does her own thing – not what others tell her. In fact, the Clare I know is *more* likely to do something that she's told not to do.'

'What if that Clare is sick of fighting? What if they've broken her?'

Ben gently pushed a tress of hair behind my ear, revealing my bruised cheek. He looked at me with sadness in his eyes. 'No. She's not broken. She's been bashed about a lot, physically, mentally and emotionally, but she's not broken. She's too strong for that.'

'Do you really think so? I don't feel very strong at the moment.'

He smiled. 'That's because you're hungover, you're wearing your PJs, and you have a panda-eye situation going on with your mascara. I guarantee that you'll feel better after a shower.'

'Have the leprechauns turned it into magic water that'll take away the memories of what Jamie Doyle did?'

'Of course. I ordered it especially.' Ben put his arm round me and I cuddled into his side as he kissed the top of my head. 'You and

I both know that a shower is going to make sod-all difference to the trauma that your mind had managed to bury. Only time can do that. I know a great counsellor who specialises in this field and I'd urge you to see her. Your friends will get you through this, your family will get you through this, and you'll get yourself through this. You could choose to let your mum and that rapist win, but you're not going to, are you? Having seen you going after that king with such determination, I know how competitive you are. You're going to win this time, aren't you?'

'Yes,' I whispered.

'Sorry, did you say something?'

'I said, yes.'

'I think I might be going a bit deaf in my old age. I'm sure I heard a noise, but I couldn't quite make it out.'

I laughed. '*Yes! I'm going to win!*'

He hugged me tighter and kissed my head again before releasing me. 'And she's back in the room.'

'Thanks, Ben. I can't remember if I said it last night, but I'm glad you're here. So very glad.'

'You did. About twenty times, as it happens, but it's good to hear it sober. You don't have to go through any of this alone from now on. I know you kept Daran and Shannon secret from everyone for years. I know that your mind kept what that Jamie Doyle did secret from you for all that time too. But we know now and we're here to help you get through it. If you want to talk, we'll talk. If you want to focus your mind elsewhere, we'll do that. You know me. I can talk mindless bollocks any time you want!'

I laughed again. He really was an amazing friend.

'Go on, get yourself in the shower, because the only thing you're going to win looking like that is a Halloween competition for scariest make-up.'

I rolled off the bed and looked in the mirror. My eyelids were black with mascara and eyeliner smudges, and my cheeks were covered in black streaks. Add in the bruising and it was definitely scary. 'Jesus! Would you look at the state of me? I'm surprised you didn't jump on the first flight home last night.'

'Believe me, it was very tempting.'

I shook my head in disbelief at my reflection. Had I really let them do that to me? Ben was right. I *was* a fighter and I *was* going to win. It was easy to think of it as a façade that I'd built up to cope with my exile and Shannon being taken away from me but I'd *always* been strong and confident, even as a young child. It was who I was.

'I'd better get myself ready for a funeral, hadn't I?'

Ben smiled. 'Will you be taking a handbag?'

'Of course. Why?'

He reached into his pocket and took out the king. 'Because you're going to need somewhere to keep this.'

44

'Wow! You look amazing,' Ben said.

I smoothed down the sides of my straight black dress and adjusted the hot-pink belt. 'You'll notice I'm not fully embracing the black-for-mourning concept,' I said, indicating the belt and the matching pink stilettos.

'Why should you? You're not in mourning, are you?'

'No.'

'I think more people should wear sparkly pink stilettos for funerals.'

I reached for my coat. 'You're sure you don't want to stay here?'

'And miss the fireworks when your mum sees you? No chance!'

I laughed, but my stomach churned. Despite the splash of daring colour, and all the bravado, I was absolutely bricking it, and I knew Ben knew that I was.

When Ma had thrown me out on Thursday, I'd told Aisling I'd slip into the back of the church, but I'd changed my mind as I'd leaned against the car in the laneway. What was the point in attending? I'd already sought the reassurance I needed that he was really gone and I had no intention of crossing swords with Ma again. Yet, lying in the spare room at Mrs Shaughnessy's yesterday morning, I'd found myself wanting to attend. I'd thought about Daran and what he'd say. He'd have acknowledged that Da was a cruel man who, on the face of it, didn't deserve my forgiveness, but he'd also have reminded me that Da had thought his actions – however selfish or wrong – were the right actions for Shannon. It could be argued that my actions in giving up Shannon were selfish or wrong, but they were also the ones I believed were right for Shannon. She'd (sort of) forgiven me. Well, God would judge Da and decide whether or not to forgive him; I didn't need to. My role was to say goodbye and perhaps even feel sorry for a man whose narrow-minded views had pushed aside his chance of a happy, loving family.

Aisling had made it clear that she saw Ma and Da as infrequently as possible and took their only grandchildren to visit on even fewer occasions. From what I could gather, Éamonn and Keenan weren't exactly close to them either, and the divorce announcement hadn't helped their relationships. It seemed that poor Nia had been terrified of Da. Mind you, after what she'd probably been subjected to at the hands of Jamie Doyle over the years, Nia was likely to be terrified of most men, understandably so.

Nia. She was another reason I wanted to attend the funeral. Although she was older than me by two years, she seemed like a baby sister whom I wanted to protect. I needed to know she was safe and was going to be able to walk away from Jamie Doyle and start living her life at last. The funeral could be my only opportunity to talk to her.

* * *

My legs shook as I walked slowly along the path to the entrance of St Mary's in Ballykielty.

'Who's the winner?' Ben whispered.

I lifted my head and pushed my shoulders back. 'I am.'

'That's the spirit. So your mum doesn't want you here. What's the worst that can happen?'

'She creates a scene like at the wake and throws me out?'

'So what if she does? You'll have paid your final respects, you'll have shown support for your family – the ones who count, that is –

and you'll have held your head high, showing that you won't be bullied or intimidated by a lonely old woman.'

He was right. What was the worst that could happen?

Éamonn and Keenan stood in the entrance, greeting the mourners. Aisling had told me they'd both stopped by Mrs Shaughnessy's while I'd been sleeping and had been very concerned about me. Éamonn was deep in conversation with an elderly couple I didn't recognise, but Keenan looked up and spotted me.

'That's one of my twin brothers, Keenan,' I whispered to Ben. 'The other one's Éamonn. Oh bollocks, he looks angry.'

Keenan strode towards me. It took every ounce of strength not to turn on my pink heels and leg it. I stood my ground but was nearly knocked off my feet as he grabbed me in a tight bear hug. He didn't say a word, just squeezed me tightly. What could you say when you discovered that your youngest sister had been raped by the man who then married your next-youngest sister and had beaten her regularly?

Éamonn appeared by my side and tightly hugged me too. 'I'm sorry,' he whispered into my hair. 'We didn't know. We should have known. I'm so very, very sorry.'

When he released me, I could see pain and confusion painted across both of their faces.

'Don't be blaming yourselves for any of this. I never let on back then, and Nia never let on either. You weren't to know.'

They both nodded, but I could feel their guilt.

'Is Nia here?'

'She's at the front,' Éamonn said. 'With Ma and Aisling.'

Keenan's eyes widened. 'You're not going to...? Are you?'

'I'm not going to what, Keenan? Make a scene? Of course not! Oh, unless you'd call tap dancing on Da's coffin in my glittery pink stilettos making a scene.'

His eyes widened even further. Éamonn nudged him in the ribs. 'She's winding us up, you daft eejit.' Then he frowned. 'You are, aren't you?'

I smiled. 'It's tempting, but have you seen how straight and tight this dress is and how high my heels are? If I attempted to get up there, I think I'd end up laid out in a coffin myself.'

Stepping through the church doors again was like stepping back in time. My eyes were drawn immediately to the lectern, where I could vividly picture Daran speaking with so much passion for God's word.

St Mary's felt cold and strangely empty without him, despite the packed congregation. I ushered Ben into a pew at the back and slipped in beside him. Another couple of people squeezed in next to me, but I didn't recognise them and they paid little attention to me.

When the homily was delivered, I swear that the priest was talking about someone else entirely. If Keenan and Éamonn hadn't been outside, I'd have thought we'd walked into the wrong funeral. Loving father? Dedicated husband? Devoted to his family? Yeah, right.

'Pádraig's wife of forty-one years, Maeve, would like say a few words,' said the priest.

I found myself shrinking a little further into my pew. The church wasn't that big. If she went up the couple of steps into the sanctuary, she was bound to see me.

Ma, wearing a shapeless, ankle-length black dress, lace-up black flats and a baggy, long, dark-grey cardigan, slowly staggered forwards. Her long hair was pulled back into a severe bun, but she'd missed a bit. In fact, she'd missed a couple of bits. A long straggle of hair hung down the side of her face and another clump stuck out of her bun at a funny angle. She'd never bothered with her appearance much, but today she looked extra dishevelled, like a bag lady. I tried to feel sympathy. She'd just lost her husband so washing her hair and putting on nice clothes weren't going to be top of her priority list.

She lifted her foot towards the first step up to the sanctuary but somehow missed, falling forward and steadying herself just in time. A gasp went round the congregation. She regained her composure and somehow made it up the steps and across to the lectern, but as soon as she spoke, it was obvious why she'd lost her footing – the woman was blind drunk.

'Forty-one years,' she slurred. 'Forty-one long, long years. And for what? Look at them! Look at the state of them. Two divorces. Two! What a disgrace.'

A murmur went around the congregation. People started nudging each other and I shrunk down even further in my pew.

'Three of them incapable of producing offspring of their own. Wouldn't be surprised if those poncey twins prefer men to their wives, bloody disgrace to God and mankind.'

I closed my eyes, willing someone to shut her up, but everyone seemed rooted to their seats, no doubt shocked at what they were hearing.

'That one there!' She pointed to Nia, head bowed in the front row. 'That pathetic mouse of a woman with no idea how to please her man. No wonder he had to keep her in order. And don't even get me started on the other one. Biggest embarrassment of the lot. At least she's had the decency to stay away today after ruining the wake, the little whore.'

It seemed to happen in slow motion. Like a Mexican wave, heads turned from all directions to look straight at me. I could see Ma following the movement. And then she spotted me.

'You!' She pointed at me. 'I asked you for one thing, but you couldn't grant me that, could you? Had to waltz in here, showing off, and showing everyone up.'

Managing the steps without incident this time, she marched down the aisle towards me. Ben grabbed my hand.

Éamonn raced after her. 'Leave it, Ma. This isn't the time or the place.'

Keenan appeared by his side. 'Let's lay Da to rest. Clare'll go, won't you, Clare?'

I nodded, but I was trapped in the pew by the two strangers.

'I never wanted you,' she cried. 'Did you know that?'

I rose to my feet. 'Yes, because you decided to tell everyone at the wake and, even if you hadn't, it was obvious from how you treated me my entire life. You made it *very* clear that you never wanted me.'

'Is it any wonder, in light of where you came from? You're just like her, you know, with your big green eyes and your perfect blonde hair. Should have known you'd behave just like her too.'

'Just like who?'

'Her!' She spun round and pointed at Mrs Shaughnessy. 'Dirty Jezebels, the pair of you. Like mother, like daughter, so you are.'

Jesus, Mary and Joseph! I stared at Mrs Shaughnessy, who stood a little way behind Ma, open-mouthed and pale-faced. I took in her bobbed blonde hair and green eyes. Aisling and the twins were brunettes like Ma, and Nia had mousy hair like Da. None of them had green eyes. How had I never questioned it before?

'Is this true?' I asked her, although I knew at that moment that it was. I could see the similarity.

Mrs Shaughnessy nodded. 'I'm sorry, Clare. I wanted to tell you, but not like this.' Suddenly, her kindness made sense, her insistence that I stay overnight, the huge hug and the request that I call her any time I needed anything. And a million comments that Ma had made over the years now had context too.

'You and Da?'

'We loved each other.'

Ma turned on her. 'Loved each other? What a pile of shite. You were just a tart who offered it up on a plate, and he was an eejit who couldn't keep it in his pants. A leg-over with consequences, that's what you were.' She turned round and pointed to me again. 'Bet you weren't expecting that, were you?' She swayed in the aisle and grabbed hold of the end of a pew to steady herself.

'It wasn't like that,' Mrs Shaughnessy cried. 'It wasn't just one night.' She clapped her hand over her mouth, as though she hadn't meant to let that slip.

Ma turned to face her again. 'Yes, it was. That's what you both told me. One drunken mistake on what would have been your dead husband's thirtieth birthday.'

'No, Maeve, it wasn't.'

Ma looked her up and down, contempt written across her face. 'So he came back for more, did he? Once? Twice?'

Mrs Shaughnessy pushed her shoulders back. 'Twice a week for about twenty years.'

Another gasp went round the congregation. When they'd woken up that morning, I bet none of them had expected a sombre funeral would descend into a soap opera.

'You're lying,' screeched Ma.

Mrs Shaughnessy shook her head. 'I'm sorry, Maeve. We never meant to hurt you.'

The next moment, all hell broke loose. Ma let out a high-pitched shriek akin to a battle cry, then hurled herself at Mrs Shaughnessy, kicking and screaming, trying to throttle her.

The priest, who'd maintained a dignified distance until that point, sprinted down the aisle, begging them not to fight in God's house – a place of peace and forgiveness. Keenan and Éamonn tried to drag Ma off, but she was like a woman possessed, with the strength of decades of betrayal pushing her on. Mrs Shaughnessy didn't fight back. Poor woman probably thought she deserved it.

* * *

'I'm sorry you had to find out like that.' Mrs Shaughnessy leaned back in her armchair and winced as I placed a bag of frozen mixed vegetables against her neck. Ma had really gone for her. I could actually see handprints and nail imprints. Just as well Ma kept her nails short as long ones would have definitely punctured the skin.

'Were you ever going to tell me?' I asked when Ben appeared from the kitchen with hot drinks for us all. I took my coffee from him and sat beside him on the sofa.

'I wanted to tell you yesterday but you'd had such a shock already, it didn't feel like good timing. Obviously your da's funeral was even less ideal but what could I do? Maeve had already announced it in front of everyone.'

'Were you really with him for twenty years?'

'Yes. Right until the day he told me he'd banished you to England. He'd changed over the years but, that day, I didn't recognise him at all. The Pádraig I knew and loved would never have been so cruel. I demanded he bring you back or it was over between us forever.'

There was a distant look in her eyes, as though she was remembering what must have been as challenging a time for her as it had been for me. 'I'd better start from the beginning,' she said eventually. 'But, before I do, can I ask you one thing? I feel like a schoolteacher when you call me Mrs Shaughnessy. I'd rather you didn't call me The Black Widow either.' She winked at my shocked expression. 'It's Ellen.'

It turned out that Ellen's husband, Cormac Shaughnessy, had been Da's best friend – something I'd never known – but Ellen and Ma had never really hit it off. She said Ma was always very aloof towards her, which didn't surprise me at all. Ellen was nineteen and Cormac was twenty-three when they wed. At that time, Ma and Da had been married for a year and Ma was pregnant with Aisling.

Two years later, Cormac was killed in a farming accident, leaving Ellen a widow at only twenty-one. They'd bought a house over the road from Ma and Da and had been planning to start a family.

Ellen and Da were distraught, but Ma was very unsupportive. She told Da that he should get over it and focus on his own family instead but he ignored her and regularly visited Ellen. It started off as support as they both grieved, but soon developed into a genuine friendship. Da opened up about the difficulties he had at home and how Ma had become increasingly distant since Aisling was born.

On what would have been Cormac's twenty-sixth birthday – the first after his death – the pain was too much for Ellen. Da found her with a glass of brandy in her hand and fifty strong painkillers neatly lined up on her dining table.

'He asked me why I wanted to end it,' she said. 'I told him that I had nothing to live for. I had no job, no children, no husband and no friends or family in the area. He said he thought we were friends and that he needed me to stick around because he'd already lost one friend he loved, and he couldn't cope if he lost another.' She smiled at the memory. 'I could tell he meant "love" in a non-friendship way and I realised I felt the same. We had a few drinks, toasted Cormac's birthday and, well, one thing led to another...' Ellen blushed.

'Things at home were close to breaking point for your da. Maeve was struggling with motherhood and Pádraig could do nothing right by her. She was always so angry. He decided to leave her for me but she found out she was expecting the twins. I couldn't let him do it so I gave him an ultimatum – stay with his family and keep me or leave his family and lose me. Looking back now, I think your mother had postnatal depression, but it wasn't really a thing back then, so she went without the help and support she needed. The birth of the twins darkened her mood even further. When she fell pregnant with Nia, things hit rock bottom. She had a difficult pregnancy and a long labour. She nearly died; did you know?'

I shook my head. 'They never talked about things like that. All Ma would say was that Aisling screeched and gave her an instant migraine, the twins were the ugliest babies she'd ever seen, Nia was pale and weedy, and that she knew I was trouble the moment I was born. She was such a wonderful mother.'

'You poor treasures.'

'So, how did I end up living with them instead of you?'

'Like Maeve said in church, your da and I got a bit drunk on what would have been Cormac's thirtieth birthday and you were the result. I'd always wanted children so I was thrilled. Pádraig was too. He was adamant that he was going to leave Maeve for me but I couldn't let him walk out on four young children; we would either continue as before, or I'd do it on my own. He reluctantly agreed. I'd already built a reputation as a maneater to throw people off the scent so we thought the villagers wouldn't be surprised that I was pregnant with no man on the scene.'

It might have worked but somebody else had a long-term obsession with Ellen and, despite her repeatedly turning down his advances, he was determined to have her. He'd been watching her, had worked out her secret, and threatened to tell Maeve if she didn't give him what he wanted. Ellen called his bluff, but strange things started happening. It started off as small nuisances like silent telephone calls. It escalated to petty vandalism. Then it became scary – a dead rabbit was strung up on her doorknob with a note attached stating, 'It's you next.'

'I was terrified,' Ellen said. 'I got to the point where I was scared to use the car in case he'd cut my brakes.'

'Who?' I asked.

'A man you don't want to ever mess with,' Ellen said, eyes downcast. 'You know, they said it was an accident, but I'm convinced that he killed my Cormac. I'd been dancing with him at the céilí where I met and fell for Cormac. They worked on the same farm and, the next day, he attacked Cormac, accusing him of stealing his girl. Cormac laughed it off and said I wasn't property so I couldn't be stolen. He'd always been an awkward bugger to work with, but he made Cormac's life hell after that. Cormac would joke that if I ever got a call to say he'd been in an industrial accident, I should tell the Guards who to investigate.'

'Who was it?' I asked again, a coldness engulfing me. I knew the answer.

'Eoghan Doyle.'

'No way!' cried Ben. 'He's not...?'

I turned to Ben and nodded. 'Jamie Doyle's da. Eoghan Doyle was in and out of prison when we were kids. Theft, assault, fraud. When I was about fifteen, he was put away for manslaughter after a pub brawl. I'm guessing that's what triggered his ma to change her and Jamie's surname at some point after I left Ireland.'

'He's been in and out of prison ever since,' Ellen said. 'They never found any evidence back then to pin Cormac's death on him, but I'm certain it was him.'

She went on to explain that the vandalism and threats continued until Eoghan cornered her one night, held a knife to her throat and told her she could either let the world believe the baby was Ma's and hand it over at birth or she could keep the baby and be constantly looking over her shoulder, wondering if that would be the day her child would die.

'Could you not go to the police?' Ben asked.

'What could the Guards do? I had no proof to put Eoghan away so I'd have been putting my baby at greater risk. I'd have had to confess to the affair, ruining your da's family and my already delicate reputation. Besides, the Guards already thought I had a vendetta against him after I accused him of killing Cormac. I could have been the one ending up in trouble.'

'I don't get why he'd want you to give Ma the baby,' I said. 'What was in it for him?'

'The man was obsessed with me. I suspect that, after you were born, he was going to expect certain... emm... favours from me. Fortunately, he got sent to prison for fraud just after you were born. When he came out, he found someone else to hound.'

I had to ask the question. I knew she was a nasty piece of work, but could she really stoop so low? 'Did Ma know about Eoghan Doyle's threats?'

Ellen shrugged. 'They were quite pally but I can't be sure.'

'What does your gut tell you?'

'That he told her about you, they hatched the plan to get me to give you up and she asked him to make a few threats to make it happen, but that she had no idea how far he'd gone. She's a nasty, bitter woman is Maeve, but she's not evil. Not like the Doyles.'

The Doyles certainly were evil but, in my eyes, so were Ma and Da. I smiled gently at Ellen. 'I'm really sorry for everything you've been through. I know how it feels having your baby taken away from you. I've been given my second chance with Shannon and I'd love to have my second chance with you too. If you want me in your life, that is.'

She pressed her fingers to her lips and tears glistened in her eyes. 'I've always wanted you in my life, Clare. Always.' Then she frowned. 'Who's Shannon?'

'The baby I had when I was sixteen.'

'But Pádraig told me she'd died.'

'Ah! No. She's very much alive although I've only recently discovered this. Not only are you a grandma but you're a great-grandma too...'

* * *

The doorbell rang about twenty minutes later. Ellen got up to answer and returned with Aisling and an attractive fair-haired man of about the same age.

'I came to make sure you were all right,' Aisling said, looking from me to Ellen. 'Both of you.'

'We're grand,' I said. 'I've been finding out all about the skeletons in the family closet. 'How's Ma?'

'Asleep. Dr Ellory gave her something.'

I turned to her companion. 'My sister's being rude. This is Ben, a good friend of mine, and I'm Clare, youngest sister and trouble...' I stopped and shook my head as I looked at Aisling. 'Jesus! We're only half-sisters.'

'I don't care how much blood we have in common, you're still my sister and auntie to our children.'

I looked at her companion again. '*Our* children? Is this...?'

Aisling nodded. 'This is Finn, my ex-husband.'

'Lovely to meet you, Finn. Aisling didn't say you were coming.'

'That's because I didn't know he was coming, did I, Finn?'

'I thought she might appreciate some moral support,' he said. 'And I had to see if the old bugger had really gone.'

'I take it you were a big fan?'

'Founder member of his fan club, so I was.'

'Da had a go at him for not having the kids baptised immediately,' Aisling said. 'And for *allowing* me to work after I had the kids. And for bringing shame to the family by divorcing me.'

'Not forgetting the lecture I got for *permitting* you to go on a hen weekend to Ibiza and leaving me with the kids, which was, of course, woman's work.'

'He never used to be like that,' Ellen said, picking up the dirty mugs. 'I know he didn't always show it, but he really was a wonderful man. When you were babies, he was amazing with you all. He was like a mother and a father to you. She wore him down, though. He became tired and irritable. By the time he discovered you were pregnant, Clare, he was broken. He'd become nasty and bitter, like her.' She shook her head. 'The night he sent you away, he came to tell me what he'd done and why. I think he expected my support, but I was mortified. I demanded that he tell me where you were, so I could bring you back to live here and help you bring up the baby, or I could even bring up the baby for you, if that's what you wanted. He stamped and swore and blasphemed. I told him that he could either tell me where you were or he could walk out of my house and never return. He never returned and I never did find out where you were. It was...' Her voice cracked. 'Who's for tea and who's for coffee?' she asked, a little too brightly, darting into the kitchen before we could give our orders.

45

The four of us moved to the village pub for a late lunch, leaving Ellen with her memories and the huge news about the family she had no idea existed. I promised to see her again before I returned to England and she was keen to visit as soon as possible to spend some quality time with me and to meet Shannon, Callum and Luke. I already liked her and I suspected we'd become kindred spirits, united in having our daughters taken away from us, then being reunited with them years later.

I couldn't quite get my head around Ellen and Da being an item for twenty years. How hypocritical could one man be? After all the accusations he'd hurled at me about sinning, it turned out that Da had been the biggest sinner of us all! And what the hell had a lovely woman like her seen in him anyway? I didn't get it at all. That phrase about love being blind could be the only explanation.

'It was very lovely of you to rush to Aisling's side in her hour of need,' I said to Finn, after our plates had been cleared and we'd got another round of drinks. 'Not many exes would do that.'

Finn shrugged. 'She'd had a challenging relationship with Pádraig, but I knew she'd still be upset. I wanted to be there for her.'

I watched a tender look of adoration pass between them. My head might have been slightly fuzzy from a couple of afternoon drinks, but the love was definitely coming from Finn's direction as well as Aisling's. If I raised the subject, maybe they could both open up about their feelings. I thought about her meddling in my relationship with Ben based on non-existent looks. Well, this time there were definitely meaningful ones. Before I had time to think about the consequences, I said, 'You wanted to be here for her, or you were after another weekend of friendship with benefits?'

Finn nearly dropped his pint. 'You told her?'

'Yes. No. Yes. She's the only one who knows, though. I promise.'

'Perfect set-up you've got going there, Finn. Get to see the kids and have a shag every month or so, and date who you like in between. Whereas Aisling remains hopelessly—'

'Don't do this, Clare.' Tears pricked Aisling's eyes. Bollocks. I wasn't trying to upset her; I was trying to help her. But what did I know about love, anyway? I'd refused to let it in after Daran.

I smiled reassuringly. 'Sorry, both of you. Feels like it's all been about me for the last few days, so I'm resorting to dirty tactics to divert the attention.'

'Don't be doing it again,' Aisling muttered. 'Life's complicated enough without anyone else meddling, so it is.'

There was an awkward pause while everyone took a sip of their drinks. 'So,' Ben said, 'at the risk of keeping the attention on you a little longer, I have something you might like to see, and this is the first opportunity to show you.' He dug his phone out of his pocket and tapped the screen a few times. 'Let me just turn the volume up. Here we go.'

He handed me his phone. A close-up of Callum filled the screen. 'Hi, Clare,' he said. 'I'm really sorry to hear about your dad. Shannon and I wanted to tell you that we're thinking of you, and there's no need to, like, rush back from Ireland. Luke's fine. We're getting all the help we need at the hospital so you take your time and do whatever you need to do over there.' He grinned and gave a thumbs-up into the camera.

'She's going to think we don't want her to come back,' came Shannon's voice.

Callum turned away from the camera. 'I didn't say that. I just said not to rush back. I didn't say *don't* come back.'

'Well, she might think we don't want her to rush back and she might stay forever.'

'I hardly think she's going to—'

'Just give me that thing.'

Everything went blurry and I heard Shannon muttering, 'If you want a job done well, do it yourself.' Her face then appeared on the screen. She smiled and waved, 'Hi, Mum!'

I grabbed Ben's arm. 'Rewind it.'

'Why?'

'I think she called me Mum.'

He fiddled with the phone and handed it back to me.

'...well, do it yourself. Hi, Mum!'

Tears pricked my eyes. 'She did! She called me Mum. She usually calls me Clare.'

Aisling reached for my hand and squeezed it.

'What Callum was trying to say is that we know what happened and...'

I turned to Ben, eyes wide, my heart racing. 'They know?'

Ben shook his head. 'No! Not that. They know your mum had a go at you and asked you to leave the wake. That's all they know. I hope you don't mind.'

'That's grand. I just wouldn't want Shannon to know... other stuff. Sorry, Ben, can you rewind? I missed the rest.'

'...what happened and we hope you're okay. I've had a lot of thinking time while you've been away and I'm really sorry I've given you a hard time. Your mum sounds like a right cow, and I should be grateful that it's not hereditary and that you're really nice.'

'Really, really nice,' Callum shouted in the background.

A tear slipped down my cheek at that point.

'Anyway, I wanted to tell you that I'm going to make a special effort not to be so stroppy when you get back and you have permission to send me to the naughty step if I am.'

The camera moved away from Shannon and focused on Luke asleep in a cot next to her bed. 'Luke misses his grandma,' Shannon said, 'and apologises that he fell asleep before he could tell you himself. And I miss you too.'

'So do I,' Callum cried. The phone turned around and focused on him giving the camera a stupid grin, then returned to Shannon.

'If you need a few more days or even a few more weeks in Ireland, we understand. We know you have things to sort out. When you get back, there are things we want to sort out. We still want to get married, but we don't think we need to run off to Gretna Green this time. We'd like something small and I'd like you to give me away. We also need to decide where to live. I hear that Whitsborough Bay comes highly recommended. Neither of us has been so there are no guarantees, but if we do decide to make our home there, we'd like you to join us. If you want to, that is.'

Callum snatched the phone off her. 'What she meant to say is that you're still welcome to join us even if we don't move to Whitsborough Bay.'

'That's what I said.'

'No, it isn't! You said that she could join us if we decided to make our home there, which implied she couldn't join us if we settled anywhere else.'

'Bollocks!'

I giggled at the sound of Shannon using my favourite expletive.

Shannon snatched the phone back. 'Okay, so Mr Pedantic here has clarified things. I hope you'll join us wherever we settle. And we don't mean as a live-in babysitter or anything like that. I'm sure you'd want and need your own space. We just want you to be around. Luke needs his grandma and I need my mum.'

'Only if you want to,' Callum called.

'Yes, only if you want to. Which we hope you do. But, like, there's no pressure or anything. Well, not much.' Shannon looked to her right and frowned. 'Sorry. Got to go. Tablet time. Say goodbye, Luke.' The camera panned onto Luke, still fast asleep, then onto Callum.

'Thanks, Ben, for coming to visit and filming this. Give Clare a big hug from us all when you see her. Keep us posted.'

They both chorused, 'Bye,' then the video stopped.

I wiped at my cheeks, but I couldn't speak. They liked me, they wanted me to live wherever they lived and Shannon had called me Mum. After a very shaky start, today was shaping up to be the best day ever. I'd discovered that Ma – the woman I hated – was no blood relation to me; I'd discovered that Ellen Shaughnessy – a woman who'd always been friendly, despite knowing what I called her – was actually my mum, and I'd discovered that my daughter – the one who'd resented me all her life – actually wanted me around. I bet Daran was looking down and smiling.

46

✉ From Elise
I'm so sorry. Melody had a temperature spike and
I haven't touched my phone for days. She's fine
now, but I've only just heard your voicemail. I'm
sorry about your dad. I hope he was kind to you
at the end. How were the wake and the funeral?
I'll check my texts intermittently but I'm not
able to answer my phone on the baby unit.
Thinking of you xxx

I put my mobile back in my bag as Ben drove us back to the hotel
that evening.

'What did Sarah say?' Ben asked.

Shite!

'You didn't call her, did you?' Ben said, when I didn't answer.
'You left a message with Elise but you didn't call my sister. I don't
understand.'

'It wasn't deliberate. Elise had texted me with a Melody update
so I rang and left a message on Tuesday night. I didn't think to call
Sarah. You're annoyed with me, aren't you?'

'Not annoyed, but I *am* disappointed. I asked you to call her a
week ago.'

'I know. I'm sorry. I've had a lot on.'

'I know you have, but she could really use a friend right now.'

I twisted in my seat so I could see his face, albeit only occasionally lit by the street lighting. 'Seriously, Ben, stop it with the cryptic stuff. What's going on?'

'I'm not telling you. Call my sister.'

'Okay. I'll do it now.' I held the phone to my ear. 'Switched off.'

'Try again later.'

'Yes, sir!' I saluted him.

'Sorry. I don't mean to lecture you. I'll shut up about it now. What do you fancy doing tonight?'

'I could do with a long, hot bath, then a lie-down on the bed with a film.'

'Do you want some company? I mean, for the film, not in the bath!'

I laughed. 'Just as well. The bath's not that big.'

'Do you think the hotel will be full, with it being a weekend?'

'I doubt it, but why?'

'I need a room.'

I nudged him. 'Don't be daft. It's pointless you shelling out when I've got a king-sized bed. I think I can trust you for another night. I might even let you sleep under the duvet this time.'

* * *

A bath, followed by room service and a movie, was exactly what I needed. It felt more like our usual weekend together: safe and predictable. It would have been even better with an Indian or Chinese, but burgers and fries made a pretty good replacement. They came with gherkins, which Ben hates, so I challenged him to eat his and mine without gagging, vomiting or even pulling a disgusted face. All credit to that man. He rose to the challenge. I didn't mind passing the king back to him on the day I'd won it, because it felt good to be exchanging him for something light-hearted again.

I really needed that evening of stupidity, banter and a complete avoidance of talking about anything complicated, like my family or the rape. I knew I would need to address questions around Shannon's parentage, but I didn't need to do it at that moment. I already knew that I was going to seek the professional help that Ben had suggested because I suspected that, when I fully recovered from the shock about Ma and Ellen and everything that meant for my family, the rape would be the only thing I could think about. And it could destroy me. I didn't want to be that person. I wanted to get through it and I knew I couldn't do it alone.

The following morning, the bedroom phone rang as Ben and I were packing.

'Ms O'Connell, it's Cara on reception. There's a visitor for you. She says she's your sister.'

Aisling. 'Grand. I'll be down in five minutes.'

Only it wasn't Aisling in reception. It was Nia.

I cringed at the sight of her left arm in a sling. 'Nia! Hi.'

'Is there somewhere we can talk?'

'I could take you up to my room, but Ben's there. The bar's empty.' I indicated the entrance. Nia nodded and let me lead her to a table in the corner.

I winced at her black eye too. 'How are you feeling?'

'Sore. Not the first time. Won't be the last.'

'Nia! You're not taking him back, are you?'

She fiddled with a tassel on her scarf. 'What choice do I have? I've no job and no skills or experience, so who'd take me on? I've no home. The house is Jim's and I've no money of my own. I wouldn't want to move back in with Ma, not that she'd let me. I've no friends. Jim pushed them all away. I've got nothing, Clare. Jim says that, if I drop the charges, he'll keep a roof over my head and he promises not to hit me again.'

'Do you believe him?'

Nia didn't answer.

'Nia! Do you believe him?'

She shook her head. 'No. I'm scared of him, Clare. Really scared.' She looked up, her large, frightened eyes meeting mine. 'Were you scared?'

'I've never been so terrified in my whole life.'

'Did he hurt you?'

'Yes.'

'A lot?'

'Yes.'

She pressed her fingers to her lips. 'I'm so sorry. I didn't know. I knew he had a crush on you at school. He used to make out that you liked him too and he'd turned you down, but I knew you couldn't stand him. He said things about you over the years. Cruel things. Looking back now, they make sense but, you have to believe me, I had absolutely no idea that my husband had... I'm sorry, I can't even say the word. He's such a bad man.' She shook her head and lowered her eyes again. 'I'm so ashamed.'

'What are you ashamed for? He's the one who raped me. He's the one who should be ashamed. Unless... Jesus Christ! Did he rape you too, Nia?'

She played with the tassel on her scarf again.

'He did, didn't he?'

'It can't be rape if you're married.'

'Oh, Nia. It *can* be. Did he force himself on you when you said no? Make you have sex when you didn't want to? Force you to do other things?'

'Yes.'

'Then he raped you. Non-consensual sex, whoever it's with, is rape.'

Silent tears dripped onto the table. 'He hurts me,' she whispered.

'Then don't let him do it again. Escape from him properly. Come to England. Live with me. I know we barely know each other, but we have plenty of time to do that. We played well together as children. I'm sure we can get along nicely now that we're all grown up.'

'I don't have a passport.'

'Then get one.'

Nia pulled a tissue out of her pocket, wiped her eyes and blew her nose. 'Thanks for the offer, but I can't. I have no money. I can't sponge off you, and I won't be able to find a job.'

'Bollocks. Are no passport, no money and no work experience the only things stopping you?'

'Aren't they enough?'

'They're nothing that can't be overcome. We'll apply for a passport and I'll give you a job. I'm thinking of going freelance and could do with someone to help me set up my business. I bet you have loads of skills and just don't realise it.' I was completely winging this, but I'd do anything to get her away from Jamie Doyle before he laid another finger on her or, even worse, killed her. I wouldn't put it past him for taking out his anger on her at being questioned by the Guards.

'I'm not sure.'

'You don't need to make a decision right now but will you promise to think about it?'

She smiled weakly. 'Yes.'

'And will you promise not to take him back?'

'I don't know. I—'

'Nia! He's a nutjob.'

'Where would I go?'

'I'm sure Ellen would take you in.'

Nia smiled. 'That was unexpected news, wasn't it?'

'Just a bit. But it was a hell of a relief for me, and it explained so much about Ma's behaviour towards me when we were young.'

'I wish Mrs Shaughnessy were my real ma too. She's always been nice to me.'

'And she will be again. I can ring her if you want.'

Nia shook her head. 'I need to think about it.'

'You can think about my offer for as long as you like, but don't take forever to decide about that rapist. If you let him come back to you, it could be the worst – or even the last – decision you ever make.'

She stood up. 'I've got to go.'

'Give me your number before you do.'

I typed her number into my mobile and sent her a text to make sure I had it right. 'Please call me any time, night or day.'

'Thank you. And I really am sorry. That's all I came here to say. I didn't expect to tell you... you know.'

'That you'd been raped? I know it's a horrible, scary word because of what it means, but keep saying it to remind you of the horrible, scary thing that he keeps doing to you.'

'I suppose I should be grateful that we never had children. Imagine what he might have done to them.'

'Didn't you want children?' I asked, as we made our way out of the bar and into the lobby.

'I've always wanted kids, but Jim couldn't have them.'

I stopped dead. 'Why not?'

'He had a really bad case of the mumps when he was fifteen. It made him infertile, so it did.'

'You're sure he was fifteen?'

'Definitely.'

I grabbed Nia in a huge bear hug and squealed. I didn't care that everyone was looking at me. Shannon was Daran's daughter. There was no doubt about it.

47

'I hope nothing comes the other way,' I said to Ben as I drove down a narrow country lane early that afternoon. High bushes flanked the lane on either side so I'd need to do a hell of a long reverse to the nearest passing point if another vehicle appeared.

I hadn't been to Wicklow before. In fact, I'd hardly been anywhere in Ireland beyond Cork because Ma hated travelling. Wicklow was stunning, with rolling hills, lush green fields and, pretty villages.

'What was the name of the farm again?' I asked.

'Kylekerry Farm,' Ben said. 'There it is.'

I looked at the colourful sign, swinging slightly in the gentle breeze, announcing it as a farm, B&B, and equestrian centre.

Heart thumping, I turned the car onto a gravel driveway and drove about half a mile up a steady climb with nothing to see but meadows each side. The road then dipped revealing a pretty stone cottage, several barns and a collection of other outbuildings. Fields containing sheep, cattle and horses surrounded the farm. It was absolutely gorgeous.

'Are you nervous?' Ben asked.

'Very. I'm wondering if I should have rung ahead rather than just turn up.' Father Doherty didn't have Daran's mother's number but it was a working farm so I could easily have found it online. I hadn't known how to broach the conversation: *You don't know me, but I'm the woman your son gave up his plans to go into the priesthood for, and I wanted to tell you that you're a granny.* Was it going to be any easier face to face, though? From what Daran had told me about his mother, she wasn't likely to scream abuse and order me off her land, but I knew she'd been proud of him for considering the priesthood, so she might not react well to the woman who'd ruined his vocation for him.

I drove carefully into the farmyard, avoiding a striped ginger cat and a few hens wandering round, pecking between the gravel.

'Do you want me to wait here or come with you?' Ben asked. 'I won't be offended if you'd prefer to do this alone.'

'Will you come with me?' *I might need the moral support.*

A dog barked as we approached the large, wooden stable door. I rapped on the wrought-iron knocker, sending the dog into a frenzy. When the door opened, an excitable poodle ran out and playfully bounced round my feet.

'Sorry about that.' A slim woman in her early sixties with long silver hair in a side plait and twinkly grey eyes bent down to pick up the dog. 'This is Frodo. He loves visitors, don't you, boy?'

She tickled his belly, then looked up and smiled. 'Can I help?'

'I'm looking for Mrs McInnery,' I said. 'Is that you?'

'It is. Are you looking for a room?'

I glanced at Ben and he nodded in encouragement.

'No. I actually came to see you. I used to know your son, Daran.'

Mrs McInnery stopped tickling the dog. 'Oh my goodness! Clare? Is that yourself?'

'You know who I am?'

'Of course. My Daran showed me photos of you. What a beautiful young woman you've grown into. Come in! Come in! Kettle's just boiled and I've got some scones cooling. Do you like scones? I always say you can't beat them fresh out of the oven, so you can't.' She ushered us over the doorstep and my nerves steadied. Tea and scones were a good sign.

She led us into an enormous kitchen-diner. A Belfast sink, pale-blue Aga, and a large fridge-freezer broke up sturdy wooden units. A preparation island stood in the middle of the room, on which racks of scones and a chocolate cake were cooling. At the other end of the kitchen, a pair of two-seater sofas covered in bright-coloured blankets flanked an open fireplace, and between them and the kitchen was a large, solid dining table.

'This is my friend, Ben,' I said, as she directed us towards the table.

Mrs McInnery released Frodo, who ran towards a dog basket on the hearth, where he rolled around with a knotted rope between his teeth.

'Pleased to meet you, Ben,' she said, shaking his hand.

She turned to me. 'God told me this day would come. Come here, child.' She reached out her arms and hugged me. 'I'm thrilled He brought you to me on a day I've baked. Sit at the table while I get you a bite to eat.'

A few minutes later, she was back with a tray laden with scones, butter, jam and cream, plus a coffee for me and tea for herself and Ben. 'Tuck in! There are fruit and cheese scones.'

'Thanks, Mrs McInnery.' I reached for a cheese scone. 'This looks amazing.'

'You must call me Laurel. My poor husband has been gone these past twenty years, the Lord rest his soul. Being called "Mrs" doesn't feel right, so it doesn't. I'm just plain Laurel.'

'I hope you don't mind us turning up out of the blue, but I was in Ireland for my da's funeral and—'

'Oh, my treasure. I'm sorry for your loss. Was it unexpected, God rest his soul?'

'Heart attack. I'm... Well, we weren't close, so...'

'Daran told me. It's still a sad thing when a parent passes, even if the relationship is an estranged one. I'll pray for his soul and that the good Lord grants forgiveness.'

I wiped my buttery fingers on a piece of kitchen roll. 'How much did Daran tell you?'

'Oh, he told me everything, my treasure. I do know that yours was a loving relationship in every sense of the word and that the good Lord gave His blessing for it to be so. I know that your da found out and sent you away, and that my Daran tried so hard to find you. He wrote to you for years, but he had nowhere to send the letters.'

'I know. Father Doherty kept them. He gave them to me recently.'

'And how is the good Father? We send cards at Christmas, but it's been years since I've seen him. I never have cause to be in Cork. It's so far away and there's so much to do here.'

'Father Doherty is just grand. I've seen him a couple of times. He's the one who gave me your address.'

I reached forward for my drink, and the light must have reflected off my Claddagh ring because Laurel put her tea down and reached for my hand. 'You still wear it, my treasure.'

'Wear what? Oh! The ring.'

'Did he tell you I helped him choose it? He was so excited. I've never seen a man so in love. It warmed my heart.'

'He never mentioned it. It's beautiful. You helped him make a good choice.'

'You wear it on your other hand, though.' She frowned, then shook her head. 'Of course you do. You've been separated these past seventeen years. He'll be so happy that you still wear it.'

I smiled. 'I'd like to think he would be.'

'Oh, I guarantee he will be. Can I tell him? Or do you want to?'

'Tell him? What do you mean? By praying?'

'I could pray about it, but the conventional way would be when I next see him.'

I exchanged a confused glance with Ben. Was Daran haunting his mother? A shiver ran down my spine. 'We *are* talking about the same person, aren't we? Daran McInnery, the eldest of eight siblings?'

'Yes. I'll be seeing him tomorrow, but I bet he'd jump in the car and drive straight over if I told him you were here.'

'I don't understand. Daran's dead.'

'What?' Laurel leapt up from the table, slopping her tea over her hands. 'When?'

Jesus! What had I done? Was it possible she had Alzheimer's and I'd just told her that her son had died, when, in whichever year she believed she was in, he was very much alive? I cringed as I said the next words. 'In the Thailand tsunami of 2004.'

She sat down again and breathed out loudly before reaching for some kitchen roll to mop up the spillage. 'Goodness me, my treasure. You scared the life out of me just now. Daran didn't die in that awful tsunami, though many did, God rest their souls. Terrible tragedy. Just terrible. And the day after Christmas too.'

'But there was a memorial service and everything. Father Doherty went to it. He said you were all there.'

She nodded and closed her eyes for a few moments. 'That was one of the most painful days of my life. I thought that burying my precious husband was just about the worst pain I could ever experience, but a parent should never, ever have to lay one of their children to rest. I thought the blackness would never lift but I prayed to the Lord and, not only did He help me to see the light again, He returned my firstborn to me. Daran's alive and well and living five miles down the road from here.'

48

'Are you sure you don't mind flying back on your own?' I asked Ben an hour or so later.

'It's for the best. I need to be back at work tomorrow, and you need to spend time with Daran.' Ben's voice cracked as he added, 'You won't expect too much from seeing him, will you? It's been a lot of years. People change.'

'I'll be grand. I'm not really expecting anything. I'm still shocked that he's alive.'

Laurel told us that a man's body was found matching Daran's description and with Daran's wallet in his pocket so there was no reason to believe it wasn't him. Weeks later, one of Daran's colleagues was visiting a hospital and she recognised one of the patients as Daran. He had no idea who he was or how he got there but seeing someone familiar finally jolted his memory. He couldn't remember anything after entering the water but he could remember the lead-up to it. He'd been with a new recruit, demonstrating how to do some repairs on a shack. When he bent over, his wallet dug into him so he passed it to the recruit to put in his pocket until the demonstration was complete. Next moment, there were shouts and screams and they looked up to see a wall of water rushing towards them.

Laurel could have sworn they'd told everyone Daran hadn't

been killed so was surprised that Father Doherty didn't know. Aisling said he'd had a stroke around then, though, which would certainly explain him missing the news.

'Don't rush into anything,' Ben said, opening the driver's door. 'Take your time. Just let me know when you're coming home. Assuming you do come home, that is.' His dark eyes fixed on mine.

'Don't be daft. Of course I'm coming home. I've got a daughter and a grandson, and the possibility of an exciting new life and career at the seaside. I'm not about to give all of that up. And I need to win that king back, don't I?'

Ben smiled, then hugged me tightly. 'Take care of yourself. Ring me any time.'

I hugged him back, closing my eyes at the safety I felt in his embrace. 'Thank you for everything this weekend. You've been my rock. Now, release me because you're crumpling my lovely new Primark T-shirt.'

As I stood in the farmyard with my suitcase by my side and a black and white cat weaving around my ankles, waving goodbye to the hire car disappearing over the summit, I felt quite overcome with emotion. A stream of tears rained down my cheeks.

'He's a remarkable young man, isn't he?' Laurel said, appearing by my side. 'A true gift from God.'

I couldn't answer her. Without Ben by my side, I felt very vulnerable.

'Let's get you inside, my treasure. Get those tears wiped away before Daran arrives.'

'Did you tell him I was here?'

'No. I told him he had a very important visitor and that he and the children should get over here immediately.'

My heart skipped a beat. 'Children?'

'Ah, yes. I might have left that part out. You see, Daran got married and had three beautiful children. They're not together anymore, though.'

'Oh. What happened?'

'I think I'd better let Daran tell you that. Come on. Let's get you settled in one of the guest rooms so you can freshen up and change if you want to. Not that there's anything wrong with what you're wearing, of course. They'll be here in about forty minutes.'

* * *

Laurel settled me in a beautifully decorated guest room on the ground floor of one of three barn conversions.

I opened out my suitcase on my bed. *Christ! What the hell do I wear for my first meeting after seventeen years with the fiancé I thought was dead?* I finally settled on a cute, soft-lemon dress. It had a baggy bodice with spaghetti straps and gathers around the neckline. The flared skirt was covered in pansies, cornflowers and pretty yellow flowers. It made me think of the meadow outside our farmhouse. I wondered if Daran would make the connection. I slipped my feet into a pair of beige Converse and pulled a soft, cream cardigan on.

Staring at my reflection in the shabby-chic cheval mirror, I could vividly picture standing in front of my wardrobe at home, trying to see whether I looked innocent yet alluring on my sixteenth birthday, before I fully gave myself to Daran. I'd been wearing a pretty flowery dress back then, which I'd loved. If only Jamie Doyle hadn't ripped it and my blood hadn't smeared across it. I closed my eyes and shivered. This was *not* the time for thinking about him. He was *not* going to ruin this for me.

'Goodness me, aren't you a vision of summer meadows and sunshine?' Laurel said, smiling as I slipped back into the kitchen.

'Do I look okay? I didn't really have much else to wear.'

'You look perfect.'

My heart jumped at the sound of a car crunching on the gravel. Laurel squeezed my hand. 'That'll be them. Don't you be expecting too much. Neither of you are the same people who fell in love back then.'

'Ben said something like that too.'

She smiled at me. 'He's got a wise head on young shoulders, that one. He sees things.'

Frodo started barking again and jumping up at the stable door. 'Why don't you go through to the sitting room and out onto the patio. I've put some iced lemonade out there. I'll keep the treasures amused. You and Daran can talk.'

She pointed me in the direction of the sitting room. I heard car doors slamming and the squeals of young children. What was I doing here? How would he react after all these years? Would he even recognise me? I shook my head. Of course he would. Laurel had recognised me and she could only have seen me as a teenager in a handful of photos.

Sliding patio doors at the end of the room opened out onto a stepped terrace with stunning views across the farm. What an incredible place it must be to live, knowing that everything the eye could see belonged to them.

I looked at the wrought-iron chairs but didn't sit; far too much nervous energy for that. Pacing up and down the patio, I waited anxiously for Daran to appear. What would he look like? Grey? Bald? Or just as damned gorgeous as he'd been that first Sunday Mass when he'd stolen my heart?

The patio door slid open, and there he was. He'd filled out a little, his hair was receding slightly and he wore glasses, otherwise, he looked exactly how I remembered. My heart fluttered and a well of emotions threatened to overcome me. Daran was clearly shell-shocked. He didn't move or speak for several moments, and I found that I couldn't either.

Eventually, he said, 'Clare? Is that really you? Or am I dreaming?'

'It's me, Daran. It's been a long time.'

The next minute, we were in each other's arms, holding on tightly. Tears streamed down my cheeks and I could hear Daran sobbing too as he stroked my hair and my back.

'Where did they send you?' he said, when we finally separated.

'Cornwall. To my Great-Aunt Nuala's house.'

'I heard you'd gone to England but nobody mentioned Cornwall. Why did they do it? I know your da was angry that we were seeing each other, presumably because of your age and my vocation, but surely sending you away was a bit extreme.'

'It wasn't because we were seeing each other. It was because... Actually, I think you'd better sit down.'

* * *

Laurel was true to her word. She kept Daran's children entertained and out of our way so Daran and I could talk. We sat on the patio initially but I couldn't stop fidgeting so we went for a walk down the garden then across the fields.

He was stunned to hear about Shannon, especially as his suggestion that I might be pregnant had been so vehemently denied. I told him everything, from the moment my parents threw me out right up to the events of the last few days, including the return of my blocked memories.

'I should never have left you alone that night,' he said as we ambled side by side through a field full of grazing sheep.

'Don't do that,' I said. 'I'd been alone at night loads of times. You had a job to do and I told you to go. Jamie Doyle was determined. If it hadn't been there, it would have been somewhere else.'

'I remember you being distracted when I got back from the school trip. You said you'd had a huge argument with your parents and I believed you.'

'Why wouldn't you? My wounds had healed by then. Well, my physical ones had.'

'When we made love that first night after I returned, you cried. You said it was with happiness at having me back. But it was because of what he'd done, wasn't it?'

I nodded. 'I'm sorry.'

'Oh, Clare! You have nothing to be sorry about. And you've only just remembered that this happened?'

I nodded again. 'I didn't block it out immediately, because I remember not telling you about the baby in case Jamie Doyle was the father, which, thankfully, he isn't because he's infertile. I'm wondering whether the loss of Shannon was the trigger for putting it in a box and hiding it in the back of my mind.'

'Like one traumatic thing wiping out another?'

'Something like that. I'll ask the counsellor about it when I get home.'

'I can relate to lost memories,' he said.

Daran talked to me about his work in Thailand, before and after the tsunami, and what he could remember of the disaster itself. After the tsunami, he spent another four years in Thailand, helping rebuild communities, before returning to Ireland to live a low-key life. Soon after, he met a Finnish nurse called Freja. They married and had three children – two girls, now aged six and five, and a boy aged three. He awoke one morning to a note from Freja telling him that she'd gone back to Finland and he wasn't to follow her.

'Jesus, Daran! Why would she abandon her husband and kids just like that?'

'She never really took to motherhood. She found it difficult showing affection towards the children.'

'Yet you had three of them?'

Daran laughed. 'Still the same Clare – as blunt as ever. It's a valid point, so it is. I think she kept hoping she'd feel something different with each birth, but she just found it harder and harder. She said in her note that she couldn't stay when she knew she'd never have the whole of my heart. She said I gave too much of it to our children and what was left had been given away a long time ago, leaving none for her.'

I stopped and faced him. 'You mean, to me?'

He nodded. 'Until the end of forever, remember?'

My breath caught in my throat. As I stood face to face with Daran, looking deep into his eyes, the years seemed to melt away. We could easily have been standing in *our* meadow seventeen years ago. My heart thumped uncontrollably.

Daran reached out and tenderly cupped my face with his hand. 'We haven't reached the end of forever yet.'

He titled my head ever so gently as he moved closer and closer until his lips found mine. His kiss was so light and tender, and so full of love, that I couldn't help but respond. As I wrapped my arms round his neck and pressed my body against his, Ben's words came into my mind – *Don't rush into anything* – swiftly followed by Laurel's – *Neither of you are the same people who fell in love back then.* Was this a mistake? He was single. I was single. We were in a beautifully romantic setting. We were reminiscing about what might have been. The moment felt right. But was it just that – a moment? Could love really be rekindled after so many years apart, especially after what we'd both been through during those years?

Obviously sensing my hesitation, Daran pulled away. 'Sorry. Probably too soon, isn't it?'

I nodded. 'I'm a bit overwhelmed by everything. Until a couple of hours ago, I thought you were dead. Now you're right here and we're kissing, and you've got three kids and a life in Ireland, and I've got a home and family in England. Well, I don't actually have a home, but I will and... and I'm babbling and going to stop talking right now.'

Daran laughed and gave me a quick hug. 'You always did babble when you were nervous. I'm sorry if I'm the one making you nervous. I couldn't help myself.'

'You aren't making me nervous, as such. My feelings are. I don't know what to think or feel anymore.'

We set off walking again.

'Is it because of him?' Daran asked.

'Who?'

'The one who you said brought you here today. Ben, is it?'

'Christ, no! He's just a friend. Well, I say "just a friend", but he's so much more than that. Not in a friends-with-benefits way or anything. He's just been unbelievably supportive since... well, for pretty much the whole time I've known him.'

'Someone else, then?'

'There isn't anyone. Actually, there hasn't been anyone since you, Daran.'

'Anyone you've loved, you mean?'

'Anyone, full stop. A few kisses when I've let my guard down, but that's been it.'

'Really? Why?'

'Because the only two people I ever cared deeply about were taken away from me. Being sent away from you was heartbreaking, but I had our baby to focus on so I still had a little part of you, assuming she was yours. When I was told that she'd died, I'd never felt pain like it. I couldn't put myself through that again. So I didn't.'

We walked side by side in silence for a while.

'When do you have to go back?' Daran asked.

'Tomorrow, assuming I can get a flight from Dublin. It's pointless going all the way back to Cork.'

'Any chance you can stay a bit longer?'

I shook my head. 'I've been away for nearly a week already. I want to get back to Shannon and Luke. I need to explore where we're going to live and think about getting some work.'

Darren stopped and took my hand. 'You couldn't make it Tuesday, could you? I know it's a big ask, but I'd really like to see you again and I think tonight would be too soon for you. You need a bit of space to get your head around things, don't you?'

I considered for a moment. One more day? 'Okay. Tuesday it is, but I absolutely can't stay beyond that.' I glanced at my watch. 'Christ! We've been gone ages. Your kids will be thinking you've been kidnapped.'

'I heard rumours of chocolate cake, so they probably haven't noticed I'm gone.'

We turned and walked back towards the farmhouse. 'I like your dress, by the way,' Daran said. 'It reminds me of our meadow.'

'It reminded me of that too.'

We walked on a bit further and the farmhouse came into view. Laurel was pegging out washing on a lawn next to one of the hay barns. I could see three small children racing around, ducking between the sheets, presumably chasing Frodo, by the sounds of the excitable barks. How different their childhood would be from mine. They only had one parent, but he clearly adored them and made up for their lack of a mother. Laurel had told me that her children had all settled in the area and many worked on the farm so Daran's kids were surrounded by aunties and uncles and had a granny with a farm on which they could run riot.

'I see you're still wearing my ring,' Daran said.

I held out my right hand in front of me but dropped it quickly when I realised it was shaking. 'I've never taken it off, other than to swap hands, of course. If Great-Aunt Nuala had thought it was an engagement ring, she'd have confiscated it.' It had been the genuine reason at first, but I could have swapped it back at any point. Why hadn't I?

'Thank you for keeping it.'

'It was until the end of forever for me too, you know.'

'Was... or still is?' Daran paused by the gate.

I shook my head. 'I can't answer that at the moment.'

He smiled. 'Sorry. Far too pushy. I promised to give you time. Freja was right, though, my heart always was – and still is – yours.'

He pulled on the metal bar to open the gate and we stepped into the farmyard.

'Daddy!' Two dark-haired little girls rushed towards him.

'My princesses!' he cried, gathering them in his arms. 'Where's your brother?'

'Pretending he's a dog.' The taller one pointed to where a small boy was rolling around on the grass with Frodo.

'This is Clare, Erin, and Ethan,' Daran said. 'Girls, this is an old friend of Daddy's. She's also called Clare. Say hello.'

Both girls looked up at me, squinting.

'Your dress is very pretty,' Clare said.

'I like your hair,' Erin added. 'It's yellow like the sun.'

'Thank you,' I whispered, as they ran off to join Ethan and Frodo.

I turned to Daran, my eyebrows raised. 'You named your first-born after me?'

He bit his lip. 'Freja wasn't too impressed when she found out. We were planning to call her Katelyn and I changed it when I registered the birth. Freja went mad. She threw a vase at me.' Daran pointed to a faint scar close to his hairline.

'I'm not surprised. If I'd been her, I'd have thrown ten vases at you.'

'It wasn't one of my finest moments. It was probably the beginning of the end for us.'

Ethan launched himself at Daran's legs at that moment, and Daran picked him up and swung him in the air, ending the conversation. Poor Freja. I'd started off feeling bitterness towards a woman who could abandon her husband and three young children by leaving a note. Now I just felt sorry for her. The poor woman had been living under my shadow for the whole of her marriage. No wonder she'd fled.

49

The next day, I awoke a little after nine to the sounds of birds chirping and cows mooing. Sunlight streamed through my window. Rolling onto my back, I stretched. It had been the early hours before I'd managed to fall asleep, although I'd slept soundly once I'd finally managed to stop my mind from whirring.

I showered and dressed before crossing the farmyard to the main house. The top half of the kitchen door was open and the delectable smell of bacon and eggs wafted out to me as I approached.

'Good morning!' Laurel said, as I unlatched the bottom half of the door. 'The boys have just been in for their mid-morning snack and I'm about to put some more bacon on. Sit yourself down.'

'Can I help?'

'No, no!' She shooed me towards the table. 'You're a guest.'

I'd no sooner sat down than my phone started ringing. I glanced at the screen. Aisling. 'It's my sister. Do you mind if I take this?'

'Help yourself. Reception's not great in here. You're better in the yard. I'll wait till you're back before I put the bacon on.'

I accepted the call as I headed into the yard. 'Aisling! I meant to call you yesterday but things got a little crazy. I'm so sorry for interfering between you and Finn. I shouldn't have said anything. I thought I was helping but I should have engaged brain before mouth, as usual.'

'It's grand. I'm glad you interfered.'

I sat down on a wooden bench. 'Really? Has something happened?'

'Let's just say that it's taken two kids, a divorce, a few booty calls, as you put it, and a long-distance friendship to make my husband finally fall in love with me.'

'Oh my God, Aisling, that's amazing! But how?'

'After *she* left him, he realised that he was more upset about her getting him to move away from his kids than he was about losing her. He said he missed my company more than hers and, when the kids visited, he found himself looking forward to seeing me as much as them. He'd thought that love and friendship were two separate things and that our relationship hadn't worked because we'd started out as friends, but it struck him that he actually loved me because of our friendship.'

'So why didn't he say anything?'

'He was worried that I didn't feel the same way. He knew he'd hurt me and he'd expected me to shout and scream at him or beg him to stay. When I didn't, he assumed it was because I didn't really care. What you said in the pub and my reaction to it made him dare to hope.'

'Aw, Aisling. I'm so thrilled for you both. What happens next?'

'He had to be back for work this morning but it's the Easter holidays starting next week. The kids were going over anyway so we're extending our trip and I'm staying the whole time and, well, a move to the UK wouldn't be off the cards. We're not going to rush into anything, though.'

'I bet you'll be living there by the summer.'

Aisling laughed. 'I bet you're right. I'm so happy and it's all thanks to you. If you were still in Ireland right now, I'd come and give you a huge hug.'

'Actually, I am still in Ireland, only you won't believe where.'

A bell sounded in the background. 'Damn. Break's over. Tell me!'

'Daran's mum's farmhouse in Wicklow. And you won't believe

what's happened.' I ran my fingers through my hair, still struggling to get my head round the unexpected turn of events. 'Daran's not dead. I saw him yesterday.'

'Feck off!'

'I know! Shocker, eh?'

'Clare! This is huge. Look, I've got to go but we'll speak later, yeah?'

'Yeah. Enjoy your class.'

I hung up and sat back on the bench and closed my eyes. Had I really seen Daran yesterday or had it been a dream? But I could still feel his lips on mine, his hands in my hair, the closeness of his body. Definitely real. And very, very confusing.

* * *

I'd run out of clothes. I frantically rummaged through my suitcase. Seriously. Everything, whether clean or in need of a wash, was completely unsuitable.

'I've got a problem,' I said to Laurel, over a spot of lunch. 'I've got no clothes for tonight. Is there a town I can get to round here?'

She shook her head. 'Nowhere close with any decent clothes shops. I could put a wash on.'

'That's very kind but I don't actually have anything nice with me that I didn't wear for a funeral.'

Laurel smiled gently. 'I'm sure our Aoife will lend you something. I'll give her a ring and ask her to bring you some options.'

As soon as she arrived, Aoife gave me a huge hug. 'So you're the one who stole my big brother's heart. I can see why. Come on, let's get you fixed up. I've got just the thing.' She grabbed my hand and pulled me over to a bright-yellow van. She opened the passenger-side door and rummaged through a pile of clothes. 'You're welcome to look at the others, but I think this one's you.' She thrust a navy dress on a hanger at me. 'Do you have shoes? Ma didn't say to bring any.'

'I have shoes,' I said, holding the dress out in front of me. It had a ruched bodice and a short, flared, lacy overskirt. Not too casual and not too dressy. My nude heels would be perfect with it. 'I love it. Thank you.'

'You're welcome.' She closed the door and leaned against it. 'He's still besotted with you, you know.'

'I know.'

'If anything, absence has made the heart grow fonder for him. It doesn't mean it's going to be the same for you.' She moved round me, opened the back of the van, and lifted a vacuum cleaner out. 'The kids are staying with me so you won't be disturbed. Enjoy tonight. You'll look stunning in that.'

'Thank you for lending it to me.'

She picked up the vacuum, walked towards one of the barn conversions, then stopped and turned round. 'I love my brother, Clare, but I know what he can be like. Don't let him talk you into anything you don't want. Sometimes the past is called the past because it's already passed.'

I stood in the middle of the farmyard with a dress draped over my arm, wondering if I should have stuck to my original plan and caught a flight back to England instead of staying another night.

50

'Was it strange, seeing him again after so much time?' Ben asked, as we tucked into an Indian takeaway the following night. It felt so good to be home and back to normality.

'Actually, it was. Sunday was grand. We had years to catch up on so lots to talk about.'

'And last night?'

I pushed a chunk of chicken round my plate with a piece of naan bread while I found the right words. It had started so well. We'd continued to reminisce about our time in Ballykielty. Daran had reassured me that not going into the priesthood had been right for him. He'd still been able to do God's work overseas and continued to do so now in his local community.

I told him about Da's claims that he'd been unfaithful to me. Although I was convinced that it had been Da's vindictive lies, it was reassuring to look Daran in the eye and hear him declare emphatically that I had been – and still was – the only one for him. I liked the 'had been' part, but the 'still was' concerned me.

After eating, we moved to the sofa. He held me and kissed me, and it was lovely, but something was missing. He whispered again that he still loved me, and I so wanted to be able to say that I felt the same, but I really wasn't sure, which made no sense, because I'd dreamed of a moment like this for so long. Closing my eyes, I tried to focus on what it had been like when we'd been together in the farmhouse, hoping to recapture the passion and longing I'd felt for him back then, but my mind kept picturing Jamie Doyle instead. Looming over me. Laughing. Hurting me.

As Daran's hand slid up my bare leg and caressed my thigh, I froze. I was back in the farmhouse, pinned down by a man whose intentions were very clear. No! I had to stop thinking like that. This was Daran. He loved me. 'Pinned' was the wrong word. He was gentle. It wasn't forced. I could move. I could escape. I could say no. And I did. The moment his fingers touched my panties, I screamed.

Daran leapt off me immediately, absolutely distraught. He couldn't apologise enough for taking things too far, too soon.

'It's not that,' I whispered, sitting forward on the sofa with my head in my hands. 'I know it happened seventeen years ago but my memory has only just come back and it's like I was raped a few days ago. I'm sorry, Daran. I can't do this.'

He held me as I sobbed, then drove me back to the farm, apologising all the way. But it wasn't his fault. It was Jamie Doyle's for what he'd done. It was Da's for separating us. And it was mine for falling out of love with Daran and not being able to find the words to tell him.

'Clare?' Ben asked, bringing me back to the present.

'Sorry. Lost in my thoughts. It was lovely. He was lovely.' I put my unfinished meal on the coffee table. 'Can we watch a film?'

'Anything in particular?'

'Something that doesn't require much concentration.'

'Sounds good. I'll clear these away first. Another beer?'

'Another five, please.'

'It's like that, is it?'

'Be grateful it's not another ten.'

Ben stood up. 'I'll get you the number of that counsellor tomorrow.'

'Yes, please.'

* * *

I'd actually necked six bottles by the time the film ended and was halfway down my seventh. I felt more relaxed than I'd felt in a long time, grateful for the slight fuzziness in my head to numb the bad stuff.

'Great, big, steaming pile of shite,' I said, as the credits rolled.

'Really? I didn't think it was that bad.'

'It was.'

'Why did you hate it?' Ben asked, taking a glug from his bottle. Despite his protests that he had to work the next day, he'd managed to match me drink for drink and he was slurring his words.

'Plot was okay. Couple of holes. Nothing major. What was shite was the chemistry between the leads, cos there was shag all! Weren't they meant to be dating in real life when the film was made? No wonder they split up.'

'Didn't think they were *that* bad. Pretty steamy sex scenes.'

I nodded. 'Yep. But the rest of it had zero chemistry, especially the kissing. It was like watching my parents kiss. Actually, don't think I ever saw them kiss, but that's what I imagine it would be like. Complete lack of passion. Surely any half-decent actor can convince an audience that they're in love. I reckon that even I, with no acting training at all, could fake a passionate kiss and have anyone believe I was madly in love with the man I was kissing, even if I hated him.'

'I bet you couldn't.'

'You *bet* I couldn't? Are you challenging me to win the king back?'

'No! Just a turn of phrase, but if you want to see it as a dare, Irish, that's up to you. Not sure who you're planning to kiss, though.'

It absolutely was a dare. Well, if he was stupid enough to dare me when he was the only man around... I leaned forward on the sofa and planted my lips on his, and held them there for a few moments, fully expecting him to laugh and pull away when it got too much. But he didn't. Ah! I knew what he was up to. The eejit was challenging me to be the first to pull away, then he'd say I'd lost the challenge and he'd get to keep the king – faked chemistry or no faked chemistry. Bollocks to him. No way was he going to win that easily. I opened my mouth slightly and gently kissed him. He responded. Mr Daring! I parted my lips a little more and cheekily slipped out my tongue, then gasped as he did the same. Most unexpected and most pleasurable. His kiss became more urgent and his hands found their way into my hair. I let out a soft moan as something stirred in me that hadn't stirred for so long. It certainly hadn't stirred with Daran over the last couple of days. *Jesus, Mary and Joseph. What's he doing to me?* Playing me at my own game, of course. He was showing that he could fake passion and chemistry too. Right. He'd asked for it.

I wrapped my arms round him and held him tightly, kissing him with more fervour. We lay back on the sofa, legs entwined, hands running through each other's hair. I knew one of us had to break soon, because the point had definitely been proved and this was going beyond a stupid dare. But I didn't want it to be me.

As I ran my fingers through Ben's hair and down his back, all I could think about was ripping his shirt off, liberating him of his jeans and surrendering myself to him completely. I didn't feel afraid, like I had when I'd screamed the night before as Daran touched me. I didn't feel anxious. I just felt... oh my God! I felt absolutely everything. Every nerve ending fizzed.

Ben began to trail light kisses across my face to my neck and ears. A shiver of delight ran through me as I arched my body in response to his touch. Why were we still kissing? We didn't fancy each other. We hadn't been flirting. How had we got to this point? This wonderful, amazing point? Because of a dare. Because we were both too stubborn to stop. I was determined to win the king and Ben wanted to keep him. What a pair of eejits we were. It made no difference to me in my fiercely single status, but he had Lebony. Dare or no dare, this was surely being unfaithful, and Ben wasn't that kind of man. I had to stop it. I had to... *Oh Christ, Ben, just take me to bed!*

A shrill ringing broke us apart. Saved by the bell. Ben pulled away looking completely shell-shocked, as if he'd expected it be Lebony opposite him, not me. What the hell had I done?

'I'd better get that. Sorry,' he muttered, grabbing his phone and disappearing into the kitchen with it. I thought I heard him say, 'Hi, Lebony,' but that could have been my guilty conscience.

I stood in the middle of the lounge, trying to recover my breathing, feeling suddenly very sober. I ran my fingers through my dishevelled hair, shaking my head. *Feck! That was close. If his phone hadn't rung, we'd... Well, we might have... Surely not... No, one of us would have had the sense to declare that the dare had gone too far.* I just wasn't sure it would have been me. Feck, shit, bollocks! I grabbed my drink from the coffee table and slumped back onto the sofa, gulping the rest of it down in one.

When Ben returned to the lounge ten minutes later, he looked pretty sheepish. 'Sorry about that. I... er... you know I can't stand ringing phones.' He stood awkwardly for a moment, his hands in the back pockets of his jeans, nearly overbalancing as he rocked on the spot. 'Sorry.'

I needed to regain my composure and act normally. 'I think you need to give me something, don't you?' I held out my hand to him.

He gulped. 'You really want to do this?'

'Of course. I wouldn't have kissed you like that if I hadn't wanted it so badly.' I winked at him. 'Are you going to make me beg for it?'

'I... er... I don't know if this is such a good idea.'

'What do you mean? I won him fair and square. Unless you're going to try to make out that you didn't believe the fake chemistry.'

Ben closed his eyes for a moment and shook his head. 'The king. Of course. Well done. That was some pretty amazing acting.'

'Thank you. You were pretty amazing yourself. Hand him over, then.' I put my hand out again and Ben dropped the king into my palm. 'I'm seriously impressed with how far you took that, especially when you're the one with the girlfriend. I've no idea why she spends her time abroad, when she's got that on offer at home.'

Ben stiffened. 'Yeah, well, life doesn't always turn out the way we'd like it to, does it?' He turned and left the room.

Awkward. I waited. And waited. And waited.

It was a good ten minutes before Ben reappeared. 'Sorry about that. My mobile rang again while I was upstairs. It was Pete.'

'Pete who threw the crappiest New Year's Eve party in the history of the world?'

Ben nodded. 'He'd invited me down The King George tonight with some of the lads and I said no, in case you needed me. It's Pete's birthday and they're pestering me to come down...'

'Oh. So...?'

'Well, I said I'd go. I'd invite you but it's blokes only and, well, you've met some of them and they're not exactly... erm... It's just...'

I jumped to my feet. 'It's grand. You go. You were probably planning to before I demanded an Indian and a movie, weren't you? You should have told me.'

'You'll be okay on your own?'

'Of course. I'll unpack, then get to bed.'

Ben nodded. 'I'm at work early in the morning so I guess I'll see you tomorrow night.'

'Grand. See you tomorrow.'

It was only when he'd gone that I looked at my watch and realised it was 11.15 p.m. Who went out to join their mates at a pub at 11.15 p.m. on a Tuesday night, when they had to be up early the next day? I'd completely bollocksed things up with that kiss, hadn't I? He couldn't get away from me fast enough. If that had been Lebony calling the first time, I couldn't blame him for wanting out. That had been some intense kissing and he probably felt fifty shades of guilty. Ooh, speaking of fifty shades... I put my fingers up to my red cheeks. I had to stop thinking about that right now. All that had happened was that the trust and friendship I had for Ben had triggered some dormant feelings. Not for him – just for a relationship. Although kissing Daran, the former love of my life, hadn't had the same effect, which meant... *Stop it! It was a one-off and, while extremely pleasurable, it will never happen again.*

51

'We've got amazing news,' announced Shannon, the moment she spotted me approaching the following day. Callum was seated beside the bed, cuddling a sleeping Luke. Seeing my family together like that, smiling so warmly at me, I could have cried again but with happiness this time.

'Amazing news would be very welcome,' I said.

'They're letting me out.'

'Oh my God! That certainly *is* amazing. When?'

'Friday.'

'Jesus! So soon? And that's Good Friday, isn't it?'

'I know. Very good Friday for me. Apparently, I've made great progress,' she said, grinning.

'Oh, Shannon, I'm so thrilled for you. I bet you can't wait to get out of here.'

'We're so excited. It's been a tough couple of months but we can finally start our lives as a family now.' She gazed lovingly at her fiancé and son, then her expression darkened. 'How was the funeral?'

I sighed and shook my head as I perched on the edge of her bed. 'Not quite what I expected. Ma was plastered, had another go at me, and revealed the reason why she hates me so much and it affects you too. It turns out I'm not actually her biological daughter, which means you're not her granddaughter.'

Shannon's eyes widened but she didn't say anything.

'Apparently my da was seeing Ellen Shaughnessy, our neighbour over the road, for twenty years and it turns out that she's my real mother and your grandma.'

'Oh. Wow! That's unexpected. What's she like?'

'She's lovely, Shannon. Really lovely. And I can't tell you how thrilled I am to discover we're not really related to Ma because she's a very wicked woman. Ellen is dying to fly over to England to meet her new family but she doesn't want to rush you. Whenever you're ready.'

She exchanged glances with Callum. 'I'd love to meet her as soon as we're out of here and settled.'

I took a deep breath. 'I've got some even bigger news. It's about your da.'

'He's not the trainee priest?'

'It's definitely Daran. But it turns out he wasn't killed in the tsunami like we thought...'

* * *

I had a lovely day at the hospital with my family. Shannon squealed excitedly when I told her that Daran was dying to meet her and would fly over next week if she felt ready. Her squeals woke Luke up, so he added his own louder squeals to hers.

She was desperate to know all about our relationship and how it felt seeing him again after so many years. I gave her the edited highlights, deliberately leaving out any mention of what had happened between us on Monday night.

'We wanted to talk to you about moving,' Callum said over lunch. 'We've done some research and we think that Whitsborough Bay looks pretty decent. Neither of us have been there before so we want to explore before we commit to living there so we've booked a holiday cottage for two weeks from Friday in a place called Little Sandby.'

Little Sandby. It rang a bell. 'Oh! That's where my friends Elise and Stevie live.'

'Is it nice?' Shannon asked.

'I've only been there once but it's a really pretty village.'

'We'd like you to stay with us. If, like, you're free,' Callum said. 'There are three bedrooms so Ben can stay, or Shannon's dad when he comes over next week. Luke'll sleep in our room.'

'I'd love to stay. Thank you. So what happens if you like the place?'

'Then we find somewhere to rent until we can buy next June, when my inheritance comes through,' Shannon said. 'Do you think we'll like it, Mum?'

My heart melted as she called me that. 'Yes. I think you will. But if you don't, we'll find somewhere else that's right for us all.' I didn't really care where it was, as long as we were together, although I couldn't help hoping they'd love it. The more I thought about it, the more Whitsborough Bay felt like home. And Seashell Cottage was the place I wanted to settle. I only hoped I wasn't too late and it hadn't sold already.

Luke was going to stay with Callum at Jimmy's until Shannon was discharged. It didn't make sense to disrupt the routine and bring him home with me, so I said my goodbyes and choked back the tears when Shannon hugged me.

As I drove through Leeds later that afternoon, I found myself hoping that Ben wouldn't be late home from work so I could share the news with him – and so I could apologise for taking the dare too far the night before. My body fizzed again as I thought about lying on the sofa, kissing him. Why did it keep doing that?

The house was in silence, but that was fair enough, as Ben didn't usually get home till after six and it was only half five. I dumped my handbag on the kitchen worktop and looked round at the steriliser, bottle warmer, empty bottles and teats. I might as well start packing, although I'd maybe start upstairs.

Four hours later, I'd packed most of Luke's possessions and had even managed to disassemble his cot, despite not being able to find the instructions. There was still no sign of Ben. My stomach growled in protest at the late hour without food, so I padded down-stairs and made some cheese on toast.

✉ To Ben
Where are you? Getting worried! Hope you're not
avoiding me after last night. Pleasurable as it
was, I promise not to force you to repeat
it! ;-) xx

✉ From Ben
Forgot to say. Working really late. Back about
midnight. Don't wait up

I frowned. Those last few words sounded like an order, i.e. he absolutely didn't want me to wait up because he was avoiding me. No! It was just a text. People are curt in texts. I shook my head. *I* was curt in texts – Ben wasn't. Bollocks. I should never have got drunk and thrown myself at him like that, dare or no dare.

I picked up the number of the counsellor he'd left me on the kitchen worktop. It was a Leeds landline. If we were moving to Whitsborough Bay, a Leeds-based counsellor wasn't going to work for me. I'd call her in the morning, though, and see if she could recommend anyone on the coast instead.

I'd just turned towards the stairs when my phone rang and, as soon as I saw the name on the screen, I cursed myself.

'Daran! I'm so sorry. I completely forgot.' I was meant to have FaceTimed him at eight. How had I forgotten that?

* * *

I lay in bed, watching the clock, and listening for the sound of Ben's key turning in the lock around midnight. I hated that I hadn't seen him that day. Having previously found his home a haven, even when on my own, it had felt empty and lonely without his easy banter.

Even though I'd had a good chat with Daran on the phone, I'd found myself wishing it had been Ben who I was talking to about my plans for the future. But that was only because Ben would have been excited for me about the move, whereas Daran suggested that if I wanted the coast and the countryside, I couldn't go far wrong with Wicklow.

It was obvious from our conversation that there was no way Daran was ever going to move to England, and I was certainly never going to move back to Ireland.

I knew I didn't love him at the moment, but I still cared for him deeply and he was the father of my child. Could my feelings come back? And, if they did, would they be strong enough to bridge the distance? A long-distance relationship worked for Ben and Lebony. Could it work for Daran and me?

As I drifted off to sleep, the last thought on my mind wasn't whether we could make it work. It was whether I *wanted* it to work for Daran and me.

52

I switched my phone back on as I left Jimmy's the following after-noon. I had the packing to finish before we moved the next day and I felt quite giddy with excitement at the thought of the fresh start with my new family. Especially a fresh start in Whitsborough Bay.

A beep indicated a missed call from Ben from a little after 11 a.m. followed by a text advising me that I had a voicemail. Phew! He was still speaking to me then, then. He hadn't been around when I'd awoken that morning and I couldn't shake the feeling he was avoiding me.

Crossing the car park, I dialled into my voicemail: *Clare. It's Ben. My dad's just phoned. Auntie Kay's been in a coach crash. It's on the news. There are fatalities. We don't know if... We're hoping she's... Oh God! I can't bear to think about it. I'm going to Whitsborough Bay. Mum and Sarah are in bits. They need me... I'm sorry I didn't come home till late last night. I hope you were okay. It was... It doesn't matter. Look, call me when you get this, if you can.*

I ran across the car park, jumped into the car, attached my phone to the hands-free system with shaky hands, then sped towards the A1. As I waited impatiently at a red light, I speed-dialled Elise's mobile. Voicemail. 'Elise. It's Clare. Call me on my mobile the minute you pick this up. I'm on my way to Whitsborough Bay. We need to see Sarah.'

She rang back less than ten minutes later, panic in her voice. 'Has something happened to Sarah?'

'No. Yes. Sort of. I don't know much. I've just picked up a message from Ben. Kay and Philip are in Italy on holiday, but their coach crashed and he doesn't know whether Kay's...' I couldn't bring myself to say the word 'dead'. '... one of the survivors.'

Elise gasped. 'Oh my goodness. I can't believe it. What about Philip?'

'Ben didn't say. I'm assuming they don't know about him either.'

'I only saw them a couple of days ago. They were so excited about the trip. How's Sarah?'

'Not good, by the sounds of it. I've just set off now. Do you want to go to Sarah's directly or will I pick you up?'

'Can you pick me up? Stevie will be here in about an hour so he can stay with Melody.'

I hung up after making arrangements to ring her when I arrived at the hospital car park. My heart raced. Poor Ben. And poor Sarah. Ben was close to Kay, but Sarah had an exceptional bond with her auntie.

As I headed north, I cursed myself for being so lax at keeping in contact with Sarah. She probably thought I didn't care. I did. I just wasn't very good at dealing with other people's problems when I had so many of my own to sort out. And it wasn't as if I hadn't tried. I'd made a couple of attempts to visit, and I'd called her on the day of Da's funeral when I was with Ben. I hadn't tried again, though. I should have. I'd promised Ben I would.

'Do you think she'll be pissed off at us for turning up together?' I asked Elise, as I rang the bell at Sarah's parents' house.

'No. I think she'll appreciate that we're here.'

Ben opened the door and my throat constricted as I took in his pale face and red eyes. 'You got my message.'

'I came as soon as I heard it,' I said, reaching my arms out to him. He hugged me, then Elise, and ushered us into the hall.

'Any news?' I asked.

He shook his head and opened the lounge door. Sarah's dad, Chris, was pacing up and down, talking in hushed tones on the phone. Sarah was curled up on the sofa, watching him intently. I frowned. She'd lost a lot of weight since I last saw her, and not in a good way. She actually looked quite frail. I glanced at Ben. He'd warned me something was up but he'd insisted she wasn't ill. Had that been a cover-up?

At that moment, Sarah looked up and spotted Elise and me. She stood up. 'What are you two doing here?' was all she managed, before she broke down in tears.

'Did you think we'd let our best friend go through something like this on her own?' I said, giving her a hug. Elise put her arms round her too, and the three of us stood in the middle of the lounge, clinging onto one another.

Chris put the phone down. 'That was Adrienne from the tour operator. They've been able to confirm that Philip *isn't* one of the fatalities, although that doesn't mean he's not injured. They still can't tell us anything about Kay.'

'That's ridiculous,' Ben cried. 'The crash happened last night. How can they not know who's dead and who's alive?'

'Apparently, the crash site was between two hospitals, so passengers have been taken to one or the other with no particular logic. It's chaos out there.'

Ben sat forward in his chair. 'So, how can they confirm the nationalities of the dead on the news, yet they can't confirm the names?'

'I don't know, son. She's trying her best to find out more.'

'Where's your mum?' Elise asked Sarah.

'Asleep. She was beside herself. I called your Gary and he gave her something to settle her.'

'I'd better go and check on her.' Chris left the room.

'How are you holding up?' I asked Sarah.

She crumpled again. 'She can't be dead.' Big, fat tears tumbled down her cheeks.

I sat down beside her and held her tightly. 'I'm sure she isn't. She'd have been sitting next to Philip and he's alive, which would suggest they weren't in the part of the coach that took the greatest impact. I reckon they *do* know who the dead are and they're letting those families know first. I really think that, if she'd been one of them, you'd have heard by now.'

The doorbell rang. 'Do you want me to get that?' Elise asked.

Sarah nodded.

Elise returned moments later accompanied by a tall, slim woman with long, blonde, tousled hair, the sides of which were swept back in fishtail plaits. She looked very tanned, despite it only being late March, and was dressed for summer in a tight coral-pink T-shirt and floaty white skirt. There was something familiar about her. Oh Jesus, she had to be...

'Lebony!' Ben cried, returning from the kitchen.

She rushed across the room, arms outstretched. 'Oh, Ben! I'm so sorry.'

Ben gave way to his grief as he held onto her and she stroked his back. I felt as if I was invading a very private moment but I couldn't take my eyes off the pair of them. I had to admit that Lebony was beautiful and, seeing them together, they looked so right. I was still staring at them when they finally pulled away and Ben composed himself.

'Er... This is Lebony. Lebony, this is Clare, and I think you've met Elise before.'

'Yes, I have, and she answered the door just now. Hi, Elise. Hi, Sarah,' Lebony said. 'And hi to you, Clare. Ben's told me so much about you. I feel like I know you already. I'm only sorry we've had to meet under these circumstances.'

'It's good to meet you too, at last,' I said. My voice sounded strange, as though I was struggling to say the words.

Ben sat back down on the armchair and Lebony perched on the armrest with her arm round his shoulder. We all jumped as the phone rang.

'I'd better let Dad get it,' Ben said. 'It was quick, though. I hope that doesn't mean bad news.'

We could hear pacing up and down the landing, then Chris ran down the stairs and burst through the door. 'She's alive! She's injured. They don't know the details but apparently it's not critical. Adrienne's going to call me back as soon as she knows more. I think I need a cup of tea after that.'

'I'll make it.' Lebony jumped up and took drinks orders from everyone, then disappeared into the kitchen.

Chris slumped onto the second armchair, looking exhausted but happy. 'I can't wait until your mum wakes up so I can tell her Kay's safe.' He smiled at Elise and me. 'Thank you both for coming over. You're such good friends. After what Sarah went through with the baby, this was the last thing she needed.'

'What baby?' I said.

'Oh no!' Chris put his hand over his mouth. 'Didn't you know? I'm sorry, Sarah. I didn't mean to... I think I'd better see if Lebony needs any help.' He jumped up and scuttled out of the room.

'Sarah...?'

She started sobbing again. 'Ben, I can't...'

'Do you want me to tell them?'

She hugged her legs to her chest and nodded.

'Shortly after getting back from Canada, Sarah discovered she was pregnant. She didn't want to say anything till she'd had her twelve-week scan and knew the baby was okay. At about ten weeks... Is that right, Sarah?'

Sarah nodded.

'At about ten weeks, she started bleeding so was taken into hospital, where they discovered she had an ectopic pregnancy. She had to go in for surgery to remove the foetus, but they had to remove one of her fallopian tubes too.'

'Jesus Christ!' I cried. 'Why didn't you say anything?'

'I couldn't... so ashamed... my fault.'

'Of course it wasn't your fault,' Elise said. 'These things happen.'

'No. My fault.' An agonised sob escaped from her.

'It *isn't* Sarah's fault,' Ben said. 'Sadly, these things *do* happen. However, Sarah and Nick wanted to spend a few years together before they started a family. She was a bit upset to discover she was pregnant so soon. When she started bleeding, she blamed herself for not wanting the baby, and now she can't seem to stop blaming herself.'

I took Sarah's hand in mine. 'You can't blame yourself, but I know how easy it is. At first, I blamed myself for Shannon dying because I thought God was mad at me for taking Daran away from the priesthood.'

'I might never be able to have children,' she whimpered.

'I thought Ben said they only removed one tube.'

'They found some scarring on the other one. They're running tests at the moment.'

Sarah blew her nose. 'I'm sorry I haven't been there for you both, but I couldn't be around babies and talk of babies. I know it's selfish but—'

'When you visited me in hospital before Melody was born and Clare was there...?' Elise asked.

Sarah nodded. 'I shouldn't have come. I thought I'd be okay, but I'd just found out that morning and I was booked in for my op that afternoon.'

No wonder she'd acted so strangely. What must have been running through her mind, seeing Elise and me all excited about Luke and about Melody's impending arrival, when she knew she was losing her baby? 'I wish you'd told us.'

'Yeah, like you told me about Daran and Shannon, and Elise told me about her pregnancy and having the hots for Stevie?'

Awkward.

'Do you know what I think?' Ben said. 'I think you should all go for a long walk and talk. Really talk. Get all your secrets out in the open and start supporting each other through some of the shit you're going through right now, because I know that you, Clare, need your friends around you to help you through the latest revelations.'

'Why? What's happened?' Elise asked.

'What hasn't happened?' I sighed. 'I hate to say it, but Saint Ben is right. Who fancies a walk along the beach?'

Elise and Clare muttered their agreement. 'You'll call me if there's any more news?' Sarah asked, looking at Ben. 'And will you tell Nick where we are when he gets back from walking Hobnob?'

'I will.' He stood up. 'Dad! Lebony! It's safe to return.'

* * *

'We need absolute and complete honesty,' I said, as we piled out of my car and crossed the road, ready for a walk round The Headland to North Bay. 'It's going to hurt at times, but I think that the only way we can get this friendship back on track – bearing in mind that the dynamics have changed and it's a three-way friendship now instead of two pairs – is if we explore how we've all felt over the past year, when we've encountered certain hurdles or discovered certain secrets. Is everyone up for it?'

I don't think I'd ever talked so much in my life. Or listened so intently. We got it all out in the open, exploring the friendship shifts, the secrets, the lies, the misunderstandings and the lack of communication. We laughed, we cried, we had awkward moments where one or the other could happily have run off down the beach, but we got through it.

I'd thought before that being in our early thirties automatically made us 'mature adults' but it didn't – it was the harsh realities of life that had been thrown at us all over the past couple of months and talking about how we'd struggled to deal with them, that had matured us.

Despite me setting the 'ground rules' about absolute honesty, I didn't breathe a word about Ben. There was nothing to tell, after all. If I told them about that kiss, who would it benefit? It had been a stupid dare which hadn't meant a thing and it wasn't worth the risk of word getting back to Lebony and damaging her relationship with Ben. Some things were better off being kept secret.

53

I lay on my back on the sofa in the semi-darkness of Sarah's parents' lounge. Sarah had insisted on staying there that night in case there was more news, given that we'd heard nothing since before our walk. Nick had joined us for a takeaway, then gone home to tend to their dog and cats. He offered me their spare bed but I insisted I was happy with a sofa and a duvet. Elise returned to the hospital and, as far as I knew, Lebony and Ben were upstairs.

That had been one hell of a conversation on the beach. A long-overdue one. Christ, we'd been through a lot recently. I felt like a right cow for not taking Ben seriously when he'd suggested – several times – that there was a reason for Sarah not being in touch. There certainly had been. I should listen to Ben more. He spoke so much sense.

Ben. I pictured Lebony and him clinging onto each other when she'd arrived. Tightly. Tenderly. She wasn't what I'd expected. I'd seen photos, of course, so I knew what she physically looked like, but I hadn't been prepared for her personality. She was so bubbly, so helpful, so damn friendly. She'd heard all about what I'd done for Luke and said I was an inspiration for leaving my job and taking him on without question.

I'll admit that I wanted to dislike her. I knew that Sarah had mixed feelings about the woman; she liked her as a person but hated her for spending so much time away from Ben. I wanted to hate her too. But I couldn't. Why did I want to hate her? Out of support for Sarah? It had to be. Ben was just a friend, so what difference did it make to me who he chose as a girlfriend? If he wanted to see someone who lived overseas for forty-eight weeks of the year, that was his decision and he could live with the consequences. Sod all to do with me.

I kicked off my duvet and padded barefoot through the dining room and into the kitchen, gently closing the doors behind me. I made a strong black coffee, then turned all the lights off except the one on the cooker hood. The clock on the oven informed me it was 04:12. Far too early for the glare of spotlights. I sat at the small, round table, blowing on my coffee and reflecting on the events of the previous day.

I heard a slight noise upstairs and suddenly my mind was in overdrive, imagining Ben and Lebony on the bed together, kissing, undressing each other, caressing... Only, it wasn't Lebony I was picturing with Ben anymore – it was me. Why was I picturing that?

The door from the hall opened and a dark figure stepped into the kitchen. I don't know who was more shocked, but I was the only one holding a cup of coffee. And then I wasn't.

'Shit! I'll get a cloth.' Ben dived towards the sink and I numbly looked down at the dark liquid trickling off the edge of the table onto the tiled floor. How had that happened?

'Did it scald you?' he asked, wringing out a cloth.

'I don't know.'

'Let me see.' Ben knelt down beside me. 'I think you might be okay, but just in case...'

He gently placed the cloth on my bare legs, his hand grazing against my thigh. A shiver of something zipped up and down my body and I jumped.

'Does it hurt? Sorry,' Ben said, completely misinterpreting my reaction.

'Coffee wasn't that hot,' I muttered, very aware that the coffee might not have been hot, but I certainly felt hot with Ben so close to me, touching my legs.

'Are you sure?'

'Sure.'

He finished wiping my legs and feet, while I sat helplessly like a small child being cleaned up after a nasty tumble.

Ben sat down beside me when he'd finished. 'I didn't mean to scare you. I thought you'd be asleep, which is why I came through the other door.'

'I couldn't sleep. Too much on my mind.'

He nodded. 'Tell me about it. Tough day, eh?'

'I'm sorry I didn't listen to you about Sarah. I should've got in touch.'

'I'm sorry I couldn't tell you why but it wasn't my news to share.'

'I know. And I respect you for that. We've had a full confession session. We should have been honest with each other right from the start. In fact, I can look back on pretty much everything in my life and say that I should have told the truth from day one – Daran, the baby, the rape, my past. Elise should have told Sarah about the baby, and Sarah should have told us about what she was going through. Even though the timing was challenging with all those pieces of news, they should have been shared, because the short-term discomfort would have been a lot better than the hurt that's been caused by the secrets. I don't think anyone should have secrets anymore.' I sighed. 'Hindsight's a great thing, so it is. Anyway, everything's sorted now. We're all friends again.'

'I'm pleased to hear it. I know Sarah was pretty devastated that you all pulled apart and I know that, despite the blasé comments, you were hurting too.'

'I'm not blasé about everything, you know.'

Ben looked me in the eye for ages, before he whispered, 'I know.'

It felt as if he could see into my soul. I couldn't hold his gaze any longer and jumped up to get some water. 'Won't Lebony be wondering where you are?' I turned the tap on and let it run for a bit.

'No. She left earlier.'

'Oh.' I couldn't stand there with the tap running forever, so I filled the glass and returned to the table. 'She's lovely, Ben. I can see why you've kept the long-distance thing going for so long.'

Ben didn't say anything.

'Why didn't she stay?' I asked.

'She's going back to France tomorrow... today. She needed to get down to Dover.'

Silence.

'How's Daran?' he asked, after a while. 'Are you looking forward to seeing him next week?'

'Yeah. It'll be grand. I can't wait for him to meet Shannon.'

More silence.

'Do you really think that people shouldn't have secrets?' Ben asked, eventually.

I thought for a moment. 'Well, there are obviously things that you don't want the world to know, but I don't think there should be secrets between friends.'

'Even if revealing the secrets could affect the friendship?'

'If the situation with Sarah and Elise has taught me anything, it's how *not* revealing the secrets can have a massive impact on the friendship, so surely revealing them can't be any worse than that.'

Ben nodded slowly. 'Clare, I—'

'Looks like I'm not the only one who can't sleep,' Chris said, stepping into the kitchen. 'It's quite the party in here.'

'Is Mum okay?' Ben asked.

'She's fine. Thrilled to hear that Kay's alive and not badly injured. I've managed to book some flights to Italy. We're going this afternoon to find out how she is first-hand.'

Ben and Chris exchanged some small talk about flight times and travel arrangements, then Ben filled a glass with water and left the kitchen, followed by his dad.

I sat there for a few more minutes, thinking about the conversation we'd had just before Chris appeared. Had Ben been about to reveal a secret?

54

I needed to get back to Leeds to finish packing, so I got dressed, scribbled a note asking them to keep me posted, then left the house early on Thursday morning.

On Good Friday, Shannon, Callum and Luke caught the train to Whitsborough Bay while I drove across with a packed car. Stevie picked them up at the train station and got them settled into the holiday cottage – a lovely, old, stone detached property with a modern interior, set back from the main street – then helped me unload the car when I arrived twenty minutes later.

'Are you looking forward to exploring tomorrow?' I asked, as we sat down with a fish-and-chip supper that evening. It had taken us what was left of the afternoon to get unpacked and organised, so we hadn't ventured further than the village chippy. The cot was up, though, and it felt like home, albeit a temporary one.

'I can't wait,' Shannon said. 'I've got a good feeling about this place.' She glanced at the two wooden boxes she'd carefully placed on the wooden mantelpiece earlier. 'Hopefully, we've found our forever place and I can finally scatter their ashes.'

'I hope you have too, but shout if it's not what you expected. We can keep looking.' Although an image of Seashell Cottage popped into my head, flooding me with warmth. I really hoped they'd want to stay.

My mobile beeped as I finished my meal.

✉ From Sarah
Mum and Dad have found Kay and Philip. They're
covered in cuts and bruises and she's dislocated
her shoulder and broken her collarbone. Both very
shaken. Two of the people who died were seated
opposite them and they'd been talking to them
when it happened. So awful. Thanks for yesterday.
Sorry I missed you this morning. Hope you're
settled in OK. I'm at work tomorrow but free on
Sunday and would love to meet your family if that
fits in with your plans xx

✉ To Sarah
Such a relief! Send them my best. Cottage is
lovely. Stevie helped us unpack. Sunday would be
great. Will text tomorrow to make arrangements.
Hope you sleep well tonight after a couple of
difficult days xx

✉ From Ben
I'm staying in W'bro Bay for the rest of Easter
weekend. Do you have any time to talk tomorrow?

✉ To Ben
We're going to explore North Bay tomorrow if you
fancy joining us

✉ From Ben
Sounds great, but I was hoping to catch you
alone. Any chance you could meet me early
evening?

✉ To Ben
I'm intrigued. 6pm? 6.30pm? Where do you suggest?

✉ From Ben

6pm. There's a bluebell wood half a mile north of
Little Sandby. Head north out of the village and
you can't miss it on your right. Meet me by the
lake. Sleep well xx

I was early, just in case I got lost, but Ben had been right, as
always – it was really well signposted. Plus, his car was parked in a
lay-by next to the entrance stile, which was a slight giveaway.

Birds chirped their evening song and butterflies fluttered past.
As I clambered over the stile, thankful that I was wearing jeans and
canvas shoes, rather than a dress and heels, butterflies also fluttered
in my stomach. Strange. I hadn't had my dinner yet. It was obviously
hunger pangs, not butterflies.

The woods were quite spectacular. The lowering sun penetrated
through the gaps in the trees, like hundreds of spotlights on the
bluebells. I followed a well-worn path through the flowers, rising
slightly, then dipping back down towards the lake, where I could see
Ben sitting on a bench beneath a giant old oak tree, staring at the
water with his chin resting in his hands. He looked troubled. Hardly
surprising, given the situation with Auntie Kay.

He turned round as I approached him and jumped to his feet.
'You're early!'

'So are you. Are you okay, Ben?'

He nodded. 'Just thinking. It's a good place for it.'

'It's beautiful,' I said, turning in a circle.

'Mum and Dad used to bring us here when we were little. Sarah
and I played hide-and-seek between the trees. She was rubbish at
seeking so I used to let her find me.'

I smiled. That was so Ben, letting someone else win.

'Come and sit down,' he said. He waited for me to take a seat on
the bench before sitting down himself. 'I'm sorry for being all
mysterious and luring you here, but there's something I wanted to
say to you on your own.'

'You're going to tell me I owe you sixteen grand in back rent,
aren't you?'

Ben smiled fleetingly, then frowned and bit his lip. 'Okay. Here goes. You know we were talking in the early hours yesterday about being completely honest with friends, no matter how that might affect the relationship?'

'Yes.'

'Do you still believe that?'

'Definitely.'

'Good. So, I haven't been honest with you about two things. Two pretty big things.'

Butterflies fluttered in my stomach again my heartbeat quicken. 'Go on...'

'The first thing is my relationship with Lebony.'

My stomach churned at the mention of her name.

'We're not together. We split up.'

'Jesus, Ben! When? Was it Thursday night? Was that why she didn't stay over?'

He shook his head. 'No. It wasn't Thursday night. Lebony and I... we... well, we split up about six months ago.'

'What?'

Ben lowered his eyes. 'We're just friends now.'

'But you Skype her and call her all the time. And she rushed to your side on Thursday. That was Lebony, wasn't it? Not some actress?'

He laughed. 'That was definitely Lebony and, yes, we do call and Skype regularly. She's a good friend. She's been giving me some advice recently.'

'I don't get it. Why make out that you're still together when you're not?'

Ben sighed. 'That brings me on to the second big thing I've been lying about. The reason Lebony and I split up was because I'd fallen for someone else. Lebony knew it before I even realised it.' He smiled. 'I was stunned the day she pointed it out but, as soon as she did, it was like the biggest lightbulb moment ever.'

'Do I know her? Or is it a he? After the Elise-and-Gary situation, I don't want to assume.'

'It's a she.'

'Does she know?'

'No, but her sister guessed.'

My walk along The Headland with Aisling popped into my head. 'Oh my God, Ben! Are you talking about me?'

'We used to have such great craic, as you call it, every time you visited. For years, I thought of you as a friend, but it all changed when you moved in with me the first time round. I got to see the *real* you, the person who loves to remove her make-up and put on her PJs as soon as she's home from work; the person who gets all emotional watching a film and pretends she's bored by it so she doesn't cry, and the person who's spent years refusing to be beaten by a challenging past and can proudly declare herself as king of every moment.'

Tears pricked my eyes. I couldn't speak. I could barely breathe.

'I didn't think it was possible to care for you any more than I already did, but when I saw how you were with Luke and Shannon, I fell even deeper. I'd never have said anything while you were living with me. I'd never have risked you feeling awkward and uncomfortable. Lebony gave me a lecture on Thursday. She insisted I tell you how I feel, especially as you were moving out anyway. So, here I am, telling you that, last September, you didn't just become the owner of my spare room, you also became the owner of my heart.'

My heart raced. Oh. My. God! I didn't know what I'd expected Ben to say, but it certainly hadn't been that. So Aisling had been right about him! How did I feel? He was looking at me intently, waiting for me to speak. But what could I say? What could I offer him in return? I'd shut myself off to love for seventeen years. I'd even struggled to let Daran back in and he'd been the person I'd believed I'd love until the end of forever.

Ben reached across and tenderly caught a tear rolling down my cheek with his finger. I hadn't even realised I was crying.

'You don't have to say anything,' he said. 'I'm not expecting some grand declaration of love in return. I just wanted to be honest with you, in case there was the slightest possibility that you may feel something towards me at some point in the future. I just hope that I haven't jeopardised our friendship and you never want to see me again.'

The thought of not spending time with Ben filled me with

panic. I shook my head quickly. 'You haven't jeopardised anything. I'll always want you in my life. It's just that...'

He nodded. 'I know. It's completely out of the blue, it's a lot to take in, and you've got so much going on at the moment.'

'I wish I could say I feel exactly the same,' I whispered.

He lowered his eyes. 'But you don't. And that's fine. It's good. I expected it.'

'It's not that I don't care. It's just that I swore I'd never love anyone ever again. The thing is—'

But I didn't get to tell him what the thing was. Someone called my name. I jumped up, startled. The next moment, Daran had hold of me and was spinning me round, just like he used to in our farmhouse.

55

'I hope you don't mind me coming early,' Daran said. 'The kids were so excited about going on an airplane that I thought, "Why not change the flights?"'

'Oh. So here you are.'

'Here I am. Surprise!'

It certainly was, and not necessarily a good one. He could have warned me. I'd have liked to have been there when he arrived. I'd been looking forward to seeing everyone's reaction and I'd missed it because he'd been impulsive again. I didn't remember him being like that back in Ballykielty. I'd been the impulsive one back then and he'd been the cautious one.

'Where are the kids?' I asked, hoping I'd managed to keep the frustration out of my voice. They'd met and I'd missed it and no amount of sulking was going to change that.

'Shannon and Callum have taken them to the park. Our daughter's gorgeous, Clare, and our grandson is adorable. I'm so proud of you.' He certainly looked it, with a beam from ear to ear and his eyes sparkling. 'Oh my goodness, it's so good to see you.' He grabbed me and kissed me. Startled, I glanced over at Ben. He smiled, but his sad eyes told of his devastation. 'I'll go,' he mouthed.

Awkward. I pulled away from Daran, giggling nervously. 'Emm. We're being rude. This is Ben. He's...' I paused. How could I describe Ben? 'Friend' actually seemed so inadequate for what he really meant to me. My throat felt tight as I said, 'Well, he's just amazing.'

Daran grinned and shook Ben's hand enthusiastically. 'So, you're Ben. It's so great to meet you. I can't thank you enough for everything you've done for this one.' He flung his arm round my shoulder. 'She never stops talking about you. I thought you were her boyfriend at first, but she says you're just a friend.'

Ben nodded. 'That's me. Just a friend.'

'I haven't interrupted anything, have I?' Daran asked. 'Shannon said you were catching up about your auntie. There's been some sort of accident?'

I nodded. Of course. I'd told Shannon that I was meeting Ben to hear the latest on Kay and Philip and I'd told her where. She'd had no reason to believe we couldn't be disturbed, and I could guarantee that Daran would have nagged her to let him surprise me if she'd tried to make him wait.

'I'd better go,' Ben said. 'I'll leave you to it.'

'We'll walk with you,' I suggested.

Daran pulled me closer to him. 'No, you go on, Ben. There's something I want to speak to Clare about.'

Ben shrugged. 'Nice to meet you at last, Daran. You look after her.'

'I intend to.'

Ben looked at me and held my gaze. 'I guess I'll see you around.'

I swallowed hard as I nodded. 'Bye, Saint Ben.'

'Bye, Irish.'

'He seems like a good lad,' Daran said, once Ben had sauntered out of view.

'He is. The very best.'

'I've got something for you.'

'Oh yes?' My eyes were still fixed on the brow of the hill where Ben had disappeared from view. A heaviness settled in my heart.

'Yes, but I need you to sit down.'

I reluctantly peeled my eyes away from the hill and sat down on the bench where Ben had declared his love for me moments earlier.

Daran knelt on one knee on the soft moss in front of me. *Oh no! Oh shit!*

He took my right hand and touched my Claddagh ring. 'I gave you this ring on your sixteenth birthday and told you that I'd love you until the end of forever. I meant it then and I still mean it now. I also told you that, one day, I'd buy you a real one.'

He paused as he reached into his coat pocket and opened up a box. A stunning platinum Claddagh ring, with a heart-shaped sapphire in the middle, gleamed as the last rays of sunlight filtered through the trees and bounced off it. 'I know we've only just got back together, but it feels to me like we've never been apart. If you feel the same way, please will you take this ring and be mine until the end of forever?'

I stared at the ring, my heart thumping uncontrollably. 'Daran. I'm genuinely touched but—'

'I know there are some logistics to sort out. I know I said it wasn't an option but we could move here, the kids and me. They have religious education teachers in England, don't they? I might have to retrain a bit because of the different exams. Or you could move to Ireland. We'd make it work. We would.'

I shook my head. 'It's not just the logistics, Daran.'

He gently stroked my face. 'I know it was difficult for you when I touched you. We don't have to rush the physical side of things. I'll wait for you. We'll get the support you need.'

'It's not that either.'

'Then, what is it?'

'Please will you get up off your knee?'

He slowly stood up and sat beside me on the bench. 'It was too much, too soon, wasn't it? Aoife and Ma warned me that I'd scare you off. Have I?'

I shook my head. 'It probably is too much, too soon, but I understood why you've done it. Your feelings for me have never changed over the years. You said so yourself, but...' I couldn't find a way of saying it without hurting him. There probably wasn't a way.

He twiddled with the open ring box. 'But yours have, haven't they?'

'I'm so sorry. I should have been clearer with you when I was in

Ireland or when we spoke afterwards but I wasn't sure how I really felt until this evening. I genuinely did love you with all of my heart back then and I did mean it when I said it was until the end of forever. But our forever ended when we were separated for so long. It wasn't your fault or my fault, but it happened, and I can't just pick up where we left off. I wish I could, but I can't.'

Daran nodded. He snapped the ring box closed and put it back in his coat pocket. 'If it's time you need, I can give you time...' He smiled ruefully. 'It's not time you need, is it?'

I shook my head.

'You've given your heart to someone else, haven't you?'

A tear trickled down my cheek. 'I'm sorry, Daran. I didn't realise it had happened.'

Daran stood up and gently pulled me to my feet. 'If you're quick, you might just catch him.'

'Who?'

'Who do you think? It's Ben, isn't it? He's your new forever.'

'No. Of course not.'

'You don't need to protect me, Clare. I saw the look on your face when he left earlier. You used to look at me like that when we said goodbye. I hoped I'd imagined it so I stupidly proposed anyway.'

'I didn't know,' I said, tears streaming down my cheeks. 'I'm really sorry. I never meant to hurt you.'

'To be honest, I think I've done this to myself. You didn't promise me anything. I just assumed we could pick up where we left off, which was a bit of a ridiculous fantasy.'

'I'm sorry,' I said, again. It felt so inadequate, but I hadn't led him on. Yes, we'd kissed, but I hadn't told him that I still loved him and I hadn't talked about a future together. That had all come from him. Perhaps I should have set him straight sooner, but I genuinely hadn't known how I felt about him, and I certainly hadn't realised that I'd fallen for Ben.

'Go on! Run!' he said.

'Will you be okay?'

He took a deep breath. 'Actually, I think I will. It's not what I wanted, but it's finally a conclusion to seventeen years of dreaming and wondering and hoping and praying. I can finally lay the past to rest. God's been telling me to do that for years, but I haven't been listening to Him. I'll see you later. Run!'

He didn't need to tell me again. I sprinted up the slope, down the slope and leapt across the stile. Ben's car was still in the lay-by. I charged towards the window but he wasn't there. I gulped in the evening air, trying to catch my breath, but my heartbeat just got quicker and quicker. Where the hell was he? I jogged a little way along the lane, away from the direction of Little Sandby, because there certainly hadn't been anywhere he could have gone closer to the village. A minute later, I came across another stile in the fence, with a wooden sign pointing towards 'Sea View'. It was a long shot, but it was worth a try.

I clambered over the stile and found myself in a wildflower meadow, just like the one surrounding the farmhouse where Daran had first declared his love for me. It seemed fitting that a meadow could be the setting for me letting love in for the second time in my life.

The meadow dipped and I stopped for a moment to catch my breath as I took in the stunning view ahead of me. I was on a clifftop with the sea stretching out below. I scanned the edge of the fence, my eyes adjusting to the approaching twilight, but I couldn't see Ben and my heart sank. I was just about to turn round and go back to the car when something moved along the fence. It was him! I hadn't been able to see him because there was a bush in front of him and he'd blended into it, but his silhouette was clear now that he'd taken a couple of paces to the left.

I sprinted across the field towards him. He must have heard my approach when I got closer because he turned round, and my heart skipped a beat as I saw his tears.

'Clare!' he said, wiping his cheeks roughly with his sleeve and sniffing. 'What are you doing here? Where's Daran?'

'Daran's gone back to the cottage. He asked me to marry him. Turns out I really am irresistible to all men, women and small furry animals.'

'Congratulations.'

'Here's the thing – I said no.'

'Really? But I thought...'

'So did Daran, but you were both wrong. I'm not the same person he fell in love with, and he isn't the same person either. It would never have worked.'

'It might have done. You could have got to know each other again. People do fall in love again after years apart.'

I shrugged. 'True, but it's not going to work for Daran and me. Too much time has passed and too much has happened.'

'I'm sorry,' Ben said. 'I know you might not believe me, in light of my earlier confession, but I really am sorry. I only want you to be happy.'

'I *am* happy. In fact, I'm the happiest I've ever been. I have a new family, the potential for a new home in a town I've grown to love, and potentially a new career. It's all good. And a lot of it is thanks to you.'

'Me? What did I do?'

'You were there for me every step of the way. I've got a little gift to say thank you. Put your hands out and close your eyes.'

'Clare!'

'Quit your nonsense and do as you're told.'

Ben sighed but closed his eyes and held out his hands anyway. I placed the king in his hands, my body fizzing as my hand connected with his. 'Open your eyes.'

'It's the king,' Ben said.

'For everything you've done for me over the past seven or eight months – and especially for putting yourself out there earlier and telling me how you really feel about me – I declare you king of the moment.'

'Clare, I...'

'Shh! I haven't finished. There's another reason why it would never have worked with Daran this time around. Even though I swore I'd never let anyone in ever again, somebody managed to wriggle his way in there without me noticing. Daran had no chance. My heart had already been given to someone else.'

Ben bit his lip. 'Does this person know?'

'Only if he believed what her sister told him.'

His eyes shone. 'What are you saying, Clare?'

'I'm saying that I didn't properly realise it until this evening but, somewhere along the way, my friendship towards you turned into so much more. It's not going to be easy, and I know I have a pile of shite from my past that I still need to address, but if you're prepared to take that rough road, then I'd like you to be king of all my moments from now on. I never thought I'd say this to anyone ever again, but I love you, Ben, more than I ever thought possible.'

Ben took a step closer to me and gently cupped my face in his hands. 'I'm prepared to take that rough road,' he whispered. Then he bent down and kissed me. Despite years of dreaming about Daran, the reality hadn't lived up to the dream when we'd kissed again. Kissing Ben, on the other hand, felt like a dream come true. The best dream ever.

EPILOGUE

New Year's Eve

'I now declare you husband and wife. You can kiss your bride.'

No! Not Ben and me! Philip and Kay, of course. I'm not quite ready for that sort of commitment. Actually, that's a lie because I'd jump at it, but he hasn't asked me. Yet.

I smile as Philip gently kisses Kay, and the guests whoop and cheer very loudly. Ben hands me another glass of Champagne and my heart melts. Wow! That man looks so damn sexy in a tux. He looks pretty sexy out of one too. It took six months and regular counselling before I felt ready to go all the way, but Ben showed the patience of a saint (naturally). We actually did the deed on my thirty-fourth birthday. I had a demon to exorcise from that same evening eighteen years previously. It hurt, physically and emotion-ally, but it was absolutely worth taking that first difficult step. I still have moments where fear grips me, but Ben is so understanding. He knows it will take time.

Speaking of demons, I'm thrilled to say that Nia has exorcised hers too and Jamie Doyle is currently serving time for assault and attempted murder. She'd gone home after our meeting on my last morning in Cork feeling inspired by our conversation. She packed some clothes, intending to seek refuge with Ellen while deciding whether to take me up on my offer to join me in England. As she was walking down the driveway with her case, a taxi pulled up outside and Jamie got out. It was obvious she was leaving him and there was no way he was going to let that happen. He thumped her in the stomach, then pinned her to the garage door by her throat. The taxi driver, an ex-Guard, pulled him off and made sure the book was thrown at him.

Two weeks after we'd settled into the holiday cottage in Little Sandby, Ellen came to stay. Four generations of my family under one roof. Amazing. And that wasn't the only amazing thing. She brought Nia with her. 'I hear there may be a job going for someone with no skills or work experience,' Nia said. 'That sounds like something I might be able to do.'

I have to say that, for someone with no skills or experience, Nia was instrumental in helping me get my business off the ground. Jamie Doyle had stopped her from having ideas, opinions and even thinking for herself, so it took a lot of coaxing, but she tentatively came to me one day with a brilliant suggestion for how I could price my services. I loved it. That one piece of encouragement was like unleashing a party popper because the ideas streamed out of her from that moment. I secured a regular contract with The Ramparts Hotel, Whitsborough Bay's only five-star hotel, to do all their marketing and social media for two days a week. They wouldn't take any credit, but I'm sure I also have Sarah and Nick to thank for that as they're friends with the manager.

I smile at Sarah across the room, looking stunning in her deep-red bridesmaid dress. She's thankfully put some weight back on since losing the baby and no longer has that gaunt, haunted look. She's had some tests and, while there is some scarring on her other fallopian tube, they've been told there's no reason why she shouldn't conceive again. They're not so sure they want children now, though. They've got a new puppy called Twix (with a dog called Hobnob and cats called Kit and Kat, spot the theme!) Sarah told me that they'll give it a couple more years and they might try for a family then but, if it doesn't happen, that's fine.

She must have registered me watching her because she looks over, raises her glass to me with a grin, and continues her conversation with Elise and Stevie. Stevie adjusts his hold on Melody, who is just about the cutest and smallest bridesmaid ever, dressed in a frilly ivory dress with a red sash to match Sarah's dress. Melody was released from the special-care baby unit in late April and she's adorable. Daniel has seen her once. He's finally accepted that she's his but isn't bothered, which suits Elise and Stevie just fine because, let's face it, he'd have been a useless lump of a dad and Melody's better off without him in her life.

I notice Elise place her hand on her stomach. There's no sign of a bump yet, but I know – and Sarah knows – that Elise is eight weeks pregnant. She gathered us both together a couple of weeks ago and said that, although she didn't want to announce it to anyone else until after the twelve-week scan, she wanted to make sure that we both knew at exactly the same time, this time around. Good call.

'What are you grinning at, Mum?' asks Shannon, appearing by my side with a sleeping Luke in her arms.

'This,' I said, sweeping my arm round the room. 'This time last year, I was in such a different place. I hated New Year's Eve with a passion. And now I'm at a wedding surrounded by family I didn't know I had.'

'Are you crying?' she asks.

'No! Okay. Yes, I am! I swear that I've turned into an emotional wreck from the moment I knew you were still alive.'

And it's true. I cry at everything now. I cried when they moved out of the holiday cottage into a rental property with a year-long lease. I cried when Daran and I jointly gave Shannon away to be married to Callum on her seventeenth birthday in June. I cried when I waved them off on their honeymoon in Scotland for a few days, leaving me alone with Luke for the first time since Leeds. I cried when Shannon asked me to meet them at Lighthouse Point for a picnic, then sprinkled the ashes of Paul and Christine into the sea instead, telling me she'd finally found the place she could call her forever home. I cried when she was offered a place at the local sixth-form college and when Callum secured another plumbing apprenticeship. And I cried when Shannon started a part-time job at a school of dance and excitedly told me that the owner had plans to retire in the next five years. She's now grooming Shannon to take over within three years, knowing that Shannon already has the finances in place to buy her out.

'Auntie Nia looks lovely tonight and I reckon Philip's son thinks so too.'

I look across the room to where Nia is chatting animatedly with Michael. Wow! I can practically see the sparks flying off the two of them.

She really does look stunning. Her mousy appearance didn't seem to fit with the confidence she found as she helped the business to grow and discovered her own self-worth so I'd marched her to the hairdressers in early September and ordered a full head of colour and a layered style. We went shopping for clothes, shoes and make-up, and giggled over glasses of wine one evening as she burned her clothes from her former life. Actually, we only burned one item – a cardigan she'd ripped a hole in and spilt paint on – and gave the rest to charity, as we couldn't bear the waste. She stood taller after that, she laughed more, and she even gained the confidence to go out and join a Zumba class and a photography club, where Michael just happened to be a guest speaker in October, having returned from his latest overseas assignment. They've been inseparable since.

I'm going to miss her when she moves out, which I fully expect she'll do within the next few months. We've been living together at Seashell Cottage. Philip's house sold and that gave him and Kay enough funds to buy their new home together. Seashell Cottage had sold too but, luckily for me, the chain broke and the purchase fell through. I asked Kay if she'd be willing to rent it to me with a view to me buying it a few years down the line when my business was more established and I could secure a mortgage. I love it there so much. The moment I walked through the door again, I knew I'd found my true home.

Ben stays over as much as he can but he still has his job in

Leeds. He's been trying to convince them to set up a branch in North Yorkshire, but there've been so many stumbling blocks and funding problems that we don't think it's ever going to happen. We've managed with the commute so far and we'll continue to do so. Somehow.

'Are you looking at Michael and Nia?' Elise asks, joining us. 'That's one seriously smitten pair.'

I nod. 'I think they're perfect for each other.'

'So do I,' she whispers. 'Michael certainly deserves to find love at last, and so does your sister.'

As for the rest of my family, Aisling, Torin and Briyana moved over to Manchester during the summer holidays, and the kids have settled nicely into their new schools. Finn sold his house because, although it was a family home, he wanted their home together to be one they'd all chosen, rather than the one he'd intended to buy with *her*, even though she never actually lived there. Torin and Briyana came to stay with me for a weekend in October while Finn took Aisling away to Venice for her birthday. They came back married!

Éamonn's wife is expecting a baby in March, but it turns out that Ma was actually right about Keenan – he does prefer men. He isn't in a relationship as he's struggling to come to terms with his sexuality, but he's hoping to make this coming year the year he explores a same-sex relationship. I hope he does. I've grown to really like my brothers.

I haven't seen or heard from Ma. The twins tell me she's very bitter and blames everyone except herself for everything that's happened in her life. She's pushed them all away. She'll end up a lonely old woman. Couldn't have happened to a nicer person!

I stayed away from Daran for the rest of the Easter visit, not feeling comfortable about turning down his proposal then getting together with Ben. He also needed time to get to know our daughter. Things were slightly awkward at first when he came over for Shannon and Callum's wedding but I made him sit down and drink a bottle of wine or two with me, and I finally got him to admit that he hadn't really been in love with me for all these years – he'd been in love with the memory of what we'd had together. It had taken a stern talking-to from his mum and sister Aoife after I turned him down to get him to realise this. He's actually met someone else through his church. It's early days and I've made him promise not to rush into anything, but I met her when we all went over to Ireland in November and I think they have a good chance, especially as she's not trying to compete with a ghost of girlfriends past.

Luke wakes up so Shannon excuses herself to feed him, as Sarah makes her way over.

'This time two years ago, things were quite different, weren't they?' she says.

I laugh. 'Christ, yes! I was staying with you at Seashell Cottage, questioning why the hell you weren't chasing after Nick when you knew he was the one for you.'

'I was out with Gary and his work colleagues,' Elise says, 'with no idea that he was gay and that I was heading for a divorce.'

'And you were hiding some pretty big skeletons in your closet,' Sarah says to me.

I glance round the room again. 'Some of whom are in this room right now. What a difference a couple of years make.'

Elise nodded. 'I can't believe how much has changed, how painful it was at the time, but how much better everything is now.'

'To love, friendship and no more secrets,' I say, clinking my glasses with them both.

'To love, friendship and no more secrets,' they repeat.

'What's this about "no more secrets"?' Ben asks, putting his arm round me.

'We're just reflecting on the past couple of years,' I say, 'and how much better life is with everything out in the open.'

'You don't like secrets, do you?' Ben says.

I shake my head. 'You know I don't.'

'Would you be mad at me if I said that I have another little secret? Wait here.'

'Ben!' But he disappears into the crowd. I glance at Sarah and Elise, but they shrug. They know something, though. I can tell by the mischievous twinkles in their eyes.

A spotlight illuminates a microphone on the stage at one end of the function room and Kay steps up to the mike. 'Good evening, ladies and gentlemen. Philip and I have had a wonderful day and would like to thank you all for celebrating New Year's Eve and our wedding with us. We know that many of you might have had other plans, but Philip proposed to me on this night last year, so it seemed fitting that we married on the anniversary of our engagement.' She pauses for applause and cheers. 'The last time I stood in front of a microphone and made a speech, it was at my sixtieth birthday party a year gone June. I'd lured everyone there under false pretences because it was actually an engagement party for my amazing niece, Sarah, and her gorgeous husband, Nick, who I'm delighted to say that I fixed up. I can't take credit for this one but, tonight, I'm hoping I've done the double...'

She moves aside and Ben steps into the spotlight. 'Hi, everyone. For anyone who doesn't know me, I'm Ben, Kay's nephew. I won't take up much of your drinking time but I have an exciting announcement that I want to share with you. As many of you know, I work for a charity that helps find and support missing persons, particularly children. It's based in Leeds and I helped set up a new branch in Birmingham at the start of this year. I've been trying for months to convince them to let me set up a branch in Whitsborough Bay. There've been all sorts of funding problems, and it looked like it might never happen, but at the start of December I got an early Christmas gift when they confirmed the go-ahead. From February, I'll be heading up a new branch right here in The Bay and living here permanently.' Ben pauses for more cheering and I'm aware that I'm grinning from ear to ear. That is the best news ever. We really didn't think it was going to happen. Being able to curl up beside Ben every night will be such a dream come true.

Ben holds his hands up to calm the audience. 'There's something I've wanted to do for a while, but I didn't think it was fair while I was back and forth between here and Leeds. Now that I'm moving here permanently, I think it's time. Clare? Can you join me for a moment?'

Oh. My. God! My legs are shaking so much, I don't know how I manage to put one foot in front of the other. I step onto the stage and smooth down my dress. Ben is kneeling and he's holding the king between his fingers. My heart is beating so fast, I feel quite light-headed, although that could be the Champagne.

'In March, you presented me with this and asked if I would be king of all your moments. I hope I've lived up to your expectation of what being your king would mean.'

I nod, tears swimming in my eyes.

He reaches into the pocket of his tuxedo jacket. I laugh as he pulls out a white king. 'You will make me the happiest man alive if you agree to be the king of all my moments too. And, because you can't exactly wear this, I've got you one of these as well.'

A gasp goes around the audience as he delves into his pocket and holds out a ring. 'Will you marry me, Clare?'

I reach out my left hand towards him, tears streaming down my cheeks. He looks into my eyes, then slips the solitaire diamond onto my finger. 'Yes,' I whisper. 'Yes!'

Ben stands up and kisses me gently, as the audience erupts.

I used to hate New Year's Eve. Not anymore. And I used to dream about Daran all the time but, for the past ten months, all I've done is dream about this day with Ben and us properly setting up home in Seashell Cottage.

At Sarah's wedding just over a year ago, Elise suggested I wasn't as cynical about weddings as I liked to make out and that I simply hadn't met the right person yet. She was right about the cynicism – it had just been an act to protect myself. As for the right person, I'd already met him. I'd met him when I was fourteen. It had been real, it had been passionate, it had been amazing and, if things had been different, it probably would have lasted until the end of forever. But, as Daran's sister Aoife had said: *Sometimes the past is called the past because it's passed.* The time for Daran and me to be together had definitely passed and it was time for us both to build a new life.

After losing Daran and my daughter, I'd built a protective bubble around myself. I hadn't let my friends in, I'd denied my family, and I certainly hadn't let love in. My mission in life had been success in my career and I couldn't imagine anything – or anyone – being more important than that. How wrong I was! I'd discovered the value of friends, I'd found the importance of family and I'd realised that a career gave the financial means to live, but it wasn't what life was all about. I can honestly say that I've never felt as happy and fulfilled as I have since running my own business, based locally, and not working every hour that God sends.

But, more than that, I'd let love in. I hadn't looked for it, yet it had unexpectedly found me, and I was so glad that it had. I'd found my king of every single moment and I knew that, for Ben and me, it really was going to last until the end of forever.

ACKNOWLEDGMENTS

Thank you so very much for reading the fourth and final part of my 'Welcome to Whitsborough Bay' series – *Coming Home to Seashell Cottage.*

This book was originally released under the title: *Dreaming About Daran.* It has been re-vamped and re-packaged with a new title and new cover as part of an amazing publishing deal through Boldwood Books so my first enormous thank you goes to everyone at Boldwood for believing in me, for taking on the series, and for all your invaluable work in giving it a fresh lease of life. I'm so very grateful to my fabulous editor, Nia, for your guidance and suggestions, and to Dushi and Sue for your exceptional copy-editing and proofreading skills.

All my books are uplifting stories of love and friendship. The first book I wrote started off purely as a romance story but, as the story developed, the theme of friendship and how it changes over time and circumstances soon became just as important to me. Friendships fascinate me. How is it that some friends stick around, no matter what different paths their lives take, yet others move on like a changing season?

Susan, to whom I've dedicated this book, is the friend I've known the longest. We can't remember exactly when we met. Maybe age 8-10? We lived in different parts of town, went to different primary schools, were only in one GCSE class together at senior school, attended different colleges, and went to different universities, finally settling in completely different parts of the country. Yet we stayed in touch for all that time which, in the days before social media, included writing long, descriptive letters to each other while at university. Oh, the excitement of going to the pigeonholes and finding a letter had arrived from my best friend!

Susan has been there for me during dodgy haircuts, questionable fashion choices, and boyfriend disasters. We've drunk far too much cider together before going out clubbing, stunk out every shop in Middlesbrough after drenching ourselves in Body Shop Vanilla, Dewberry or White Musk perfume, and spent sleepless nights on Ranger Camp when our supposedly heat-reflective 'moonbags' turned out to be the coldest, flimsiest sleeping bags in the history of the world ever. Good times! She's read all of my books, even though romance isn't the genre she'd normally choose, which I find really touching. She even beta-read the original version of this book for me and provided some really valuable feedback, so it's definitely fitting that I dedicate this book to her and thank her for her support both now and over the past thirty-eight years or so!

I'd like to thank my cousin, Lisa. (Actually, she's my cousin's daughter so I believe that makes her my first cousin once removed, but that sounds ridiculous so let's stick with cousin!) Anyway, Lisa is a nurse and she's given invaluable guidance on everything from how a nurse would introduce themselves to a patient, to medical terminology, to how quickly a patient would be encouraged to walk after an accident. Google is a good friend to a writer, but there's nothing to beat real life knowledge. If there are any mistakes in any of the medical aspects of this book, I can guarantee it's me being a muppet and misinterpreting what Lisa told me rather than her inaccuracies! Thanks, Lisa. Hope there's another family get-together again soon so we can drink wine and have a giggle about sleepy bees! ;-)

As always, thank you to my wonderful beta-reader team – Joyce (my mum), Clare, Liz, Sharon, Jo and, as already mentioned, Susan – for taking the time to read the original version of this book and for giving me honest and helpful feedback to help make him even better. Sorry I kept you up till the early hours reading again, Clare, although that's such a massive compliment that you couldn't put the book down. Every writer dreams of hearing those words!

Thanks go to my husband and daughter for not moaning about the hours I've spent with my fictional friends instead of them, my writing family 'The Write Romantics' for being there through the highs and lows of writing and life in general and to the fabulously talented writer and great friend, Sharon Booth, for always being there.

My final thanks go to everyone who has bought/borrowed/read/reviewed any of my books, promoted my writing, and/or attended the various library talks I've delivered across North Yorkshire. Your support and encouragement is amazing. I hope you enjoy the final chapter of the series and that you're ready to meet a new cast of characters in the next book. Although, never fear, this isn't the last we see of some of the characters you've met already. I love them too much to say a proper goodbye so watch out for the occasional cameo appearance.

Big hugs

Jessica xx

MORE FROM JESSICA REDLAND

We hope you enjoyed reading *Coming Home to Seashell Cottage*. If you did, please leave a review.

If you'd like to gift a copy, this book is also available as an ebook, digital audio download and audiobook CD.

Sign up to Jessica Redland's mailing list for news, competitions and updates on future books.

http://bit.ly/JessicaRedlandNewsletter

ABOUT THE AUTHOR

Jessica Redland is the author of nine novels which are all set around the fictional location of Whitsborough Bay. Inspired by her hometown of Scarborough she writes uplifting women's fiction which has garnered many devoted fans.

Visit Jessica's website: https://www.jessicaredland.com/

Follow Jessica on social media:

facebook.com/JessicaRedlandWriter

twitter.com/JessicaRedland

instagram.com/JessicaRedlandWriter

bookbub.com/authors/jessica-redland

ALSO BY JESSICA REDLAND

ABOUT BOLDWOOD BOOKS

Boldwood Books is a fiction publishing company seeking out the best stories from around the world.

Find out more at www.boldwoodbooks.com

Sign up to the Book and Tonic newsletter for news, offers and competitions from Boldwood Books!

http://www.bit.ly/bookandtonic

We'd love to hear from you, follow us on social media:

facebook.com/BookandTonic

twitter.com/BoldwoodBooks

instagram.com/BookandTonic